"What else do you think of when you think of small towns?"

And then, without planning it, she whispered, "Kissing in pickup trucks."

His smile faded and was replaced by a tension that made her shiver. When he leaned forward, she put up a hand.

With a husky laugh, she said, "I didn't say who was kissing whom."

He froze, then tried to appear casual as he leaned back again.

She unbuckled the seat belt and pulled her legs beneath her to face him on the bench. Slowly she leaned forward, bracing her hands on the leather, watching his eyes dip to her breasts, where her blouse gaped away to reveal the valley between. She was a woman who knew men, who knew how to make them desire her and ensure that they didn't regret it.

Valentine Valley Novels by Emma Cane

THE COWBOY OF VALENTINE VALLEY
TRUE LOVE AT SILVER CREEK RANCH
A TOWN CALLED VALENTINE

Novellas by Emma Cane

A WEDDING IN VALENTINE
THE CHRISTMAS CABIN
(from ALL I WANT FOR CHRISTMAS IS A COWBOY)

EMMA CANE

The Cowboy of VALENTINE VALLEY

A VALENTINE VALLEY NOVEL

AVON

An Imprint of HarperCollinsPublishers

This is a work of fiction. Names, characters, places, and incidents are products of the author's imagination or are used fictitiously and are not to be construed as real. Any resemblance to actual events, locales, organizations, or persons, living or dead, is entirely coincidental.

AVON BOOKS
An Imprint of HarperCollins*Publishers*
10 East 53rd Street
New York, New York 10022-5299

Copyright © 2014 by Gayle Kloecker Callen
Excerpt from *A Promise at Bluebell Hill* copyright © 2014 by Gayle Kloecker Callen
Excerpt from *A Wedding in Valentine* copyright © 2013 by Gayle Kloecker Callen
Excerpt from *True Love at Silver Creek Ranch* copyright © 2013 by Gayle Kloecker Callen
Excerpt from *A Town Called Valentine* copyright © 2012 by Gayle Kloecker Callen
ISBN 978-0-06-224251-8
www.avonromance.com

First Avon Books mass market printing: February 2014

Avon Trademark Reg. U.S. Pat. Off. and in Other Countries, Marca Registrada, Hecho en U.S.A.
HarperCollins® is a registered trademark of HarperCollins Publishers.

Printed in the U.S.A.

10 9 8 7 6 5 4 3 2 1

To my editor, Amanda Bergeron, whose vision and guidance for the Valentine Valley series is always an inspiration. Thanks for everything.

Acknowledgments

My thanks to Jim Callen IV and Melissa Swenton for kindly answering all my research questions. Any mistakes are, as always, mine. And to the Packeteers and the Purples for being available for last-minute plotting sessions.

Chapter One

Whitney Winslow sat on the patio of The Adelaide Bed and Breakfast, trying to get her thoughts in order—trying to avoid the thrill of excitement deep in the pit of her stomach as she awaited the arrival of Josh Thalberg, Colorado cowboy and designer of some of the most exquisite leatherwork she'd ever seen. The August air was scented with columbines, warm without being too hot, as it often was in the mountains surrounding Valentine Valley. The fountain gurgled nearby, a fish jumped in the pond, but none of it relaxed Whitney as she nervously touched her hair and tugged on her pencil skirt. She'd dressed for a business meeting, so Josh would understand their professional relationship, though she'd been the one to make it all personal eight months ago, right in this very B&B.

Then it was too late for regrets. Josh emerged from the garden path, tall and lanky, and she couldn't stop herself from drinking everything in, from his cowboy boots, up his faded jeans, to the Western plaid shirt that covered broad shoulders. He had a worn backpack hanging from one shoulder and held his Stetson against his thigh, leaving his dark brown hair tousled appealingly. The faint shadow of a couple days' growth of beard didn't hide the curved scar on his chin, evidence of the sometimes dangerous work he did on the Silver Creek Ranch. He had a straight, perfect nose, and the cheekbones any male model would envy. But his eyes captured her the most, hazel and changeable as swirling mist but full of warmth and amusement—and, surprisingly, interest, as they swept over her body in return.

A thrill of heat followed wherever his gaze touched. Who'd known she would feel like this? She'd always thought a man was sexiest in an expensive tailored suit, but ever since she'd first arrived in Valentine Valley, worn jeans and broken-in cowboy boots were doing it for her.

Josh arched a dark brow, a hint of the devil in his smile. "Nice to see you again, Whitney."

His deep drawl still gave her the shivers.

She stood up. "You, too, Josh," she said, proud that her voice didn't betray her nerves.

She was never nervous! Why did he make her feel this way?

His eyes grew almost smoky as he studied her. Tension shimmered between them, promising possibilities that she didn't want to face. It had been a long time since her own behavior had embarrassed her, but now it was hard to forget what a fool she'd made of herself.

His expression full of interest and speculation, he said, "You've been gone a long time."

She shrugged. "Business and family. You know how it is."

Well, the family part wasn't really true. Her parents had wanted to spend Christmas in Rio, so Whitney, her brother Chasz, and his wife Courtney had joined them, but only for a week. Then Whitney had gone back to work. She loved her growing stores, her line of lingerie known just by her first name. She was usually so focused on making herself a success—but to her dismay, Josh hadn't been far from her thoughts.

"So I wasn't the one who drove you away?" he asked.

She quickly shook her head. "I wanted to give Valentine Valley time to get used to the idea of my store." She'd been letting things die down after the protests that had split the little mountain town over whether Leather and Lace, her upscale lingerie store, could be classified as pornography and banned from opening. She'd persuaded the town council to her side, but she hadn't done it alone. The Thalbergs and their friends had rallied around her. Josh, beloved local son, had agreed to do some leather tooling for her, which had probably gotten her even more sympathy and maybe carried the day. She'd almost ruined their business relationship before it began. "And as for you driving me away? My own behavior was at fault, not you. I got a little drunk and pushy—"

"You weren't pushy," he interrupted, wearing that easy grin that did things to her insides. "You were sexy as all hell."

"But I was drunk, and you were gracious when you turned me down." The first man to ever refuse her offer of intimacy. "I appreciate it."

"It took all of my restraint," he said in a low voice.

She gave a heavy swallow, followed by a false smile. "Now you're just teasing me. Let's forget about it, okay?"

"Forget? No. Ignore? Okay. For a while, maybe."

"No maybes. Let's concentrate on work."

Work, the story of her life. She thought about the men she'd dated, who, just like her, were interested in nothing but an occasional dinner together, followed by a private evening of fun. No expectations, no commitments. It suited everyone involved. But there was something about Josh and this small town that made her think that kind of anonymous pleasure wasn't possible. Another reason not to like Valentine Valley.

"Have a seat." She sat down, gesturing to the wrought-iron chair across the little table from her. "You said you'd have some sketches of the leather collar necklaces for me when I returned?"

He frowned at her as he sank into the chair. "I thought we were going to discuss what you had in mind for the designs, then I'd draw some up. Did I get that wrong?"

"It doesn't matter now," she said, regretting the miscommunication. "We'll just move forward."

"I did bring some leather samples."

He pulled the backpack off his shoulder and unzipped it. He brought out several strips of leather, different thicknesses, colors, textures, then laid them across the table so she could see them better, all the while talking about vegetable tanning to get the right tooling leather. His explanations were hard to follow when all she could think about was that this leather would be used alongside her lingerie. It was erotic and stimulating, and she began to perspire. He asked something, and she almost jumped.

"Pardon me?"

His smile was far too knowing. "I asked if these samples would be okay."

"Yes, of course. Whatever you think would work best."

"Well, you know your clients and their tastes."

She swallowed heavily. "I do."

"When do you plan to open the store?"

"I'll be consulting with the architects who put in renovation bids in the next week or two before negotiating the contract for the building." As an aside, she added, "You do know the space used to belong to a funeral home? I think I need to make it drastically different, so people forget."

He nodded, one side of his mouth still curled with amusement—at what she was saying? Or how she was behaving? She didn't know.

With mock seriousness, he said, "You know, we country folk don't all believe in ghosts."

"Your grandmother's friend, Mrs. Palmer, reads tarot cards," Whitney pointed out. "Surely *she* does."

"I never asked her."

She must be stoking his amusement, so she cleared her throat and made an effort to slow down her speech. "I don't have a date in mind yet, but a Grand Opening just before the holidays would be ideal. If I approve the designs, can you have stock for me by then?"

"I'm not worried about you approving the designs."

"Confident, aren't you?"

He grinned. "I am. You chose me for a reason."

Now *that* could be taken several ways.

"But as for the amount of goods I can provide, I'll do what I can." For the first time, his expression turned serious. "This isn't my major business, and I never meant it to be. I hope you can be patient while

I figure out how to work everything in, decide what my focus should be."

"Surely your family can help you out on the ranch."

He crossed his arms over his chest and cocked his head. "It's not as if they're sitting around watching me work."

"I remember your telling me you hired Adam Desantis, your sister's boyfriend, to help prepare leather. Is that going well?"

"He learns fast. And yes, he's been a great asset. But the tooling itself takes up the most of my time. Don't worry; I've agreed to do work for you, and I'll make it happen."

Josh had thought things would be awkward between them, and he'd been proven right. She looked ready to bolt, hands on the dainty table to push herself to her feet. She seemed to regret that her advances had altered things between them, as if she thought he didn't want her. Nothing could be further from the truth. He hadn't been able to forget about her as the months had dragged by, dwelling on the confident sexiness of her kiss, the press of her body against his, the way she excited him as no other woman ever had. It was like he'd come alive to the unimagined possibilities of sensuality. She was all understated sophistication and moved with an easy elegance that seemed feminine and bold at the same time if such a thing were possible.

As for turning her down? It had been the right thing to do. He was determined to have her without alcohol clouding their relationship.

But being back at the same B&B where they'd kissed? It both aroused and frustrated him because it was very obvious she was no longer in a romantic mood.

"So did you go home these last few months?" he asked. "And where is home?"

He watched her try to decide how to answer him about her private life, what he deserved to know, and knew he was intruding; but he'd never felt so curious before.

"I spent some of my childhood in San Francisco, some in Manhattan, the main headquarters of my father's company, Winslow Enterprises," she said slowly, as if reluctant. "My parents liked to travel, so we were never in one place for long."

He was surprised how fascinated he was by her background, when her looks were enough to make him tongue-tied. She was on the tall side, with a model's slimness, but with the important curves she'd pressed against his body. He tried to shake off the memory. "That must have been difficult, new schools and all."

"I went to boarding school, so that never changed."

He frowned. "You lived away from your family?"

"Just like Harry Potter but without the magic," she said with a touch of mild sarcasm.

"So your family is wealthy."

She nodded without elaborating. That explained why she chose such classy clothes, which looked like they'd been made just for her, all expensive fabrics and subtle sophistication. He liked her hair, too, shiny black but cut in layers about her face and to her shoulders. Every time she moved, it swung and flowed with her, settling back into place to perfectly frame her delicate features and wide gray eyes. Her mouth spoiled the spare lines of her bone structure with a ripe fullness he'd tasted and hadn't been able to forget.

"So with all that traveling, your parents didn't sell your house," he said, wanting to listen to her talk.

She shook her head. "My parents have several homes."

"Around the world, I take it. Valentine must seem pretty small to you."

"I've been in many small towns, and they always have their own charm."

"Tactful response. So you set your first store in San Francisco because you knew it well." He leaned forward and rested his elbows on his knees. "But why lingerie?"

"Why not?"

She smiled again, and he knew that wasn't the whole story, and she wasn't about to enlighten him.

"I thought maybe you stayed away from Valentine because of your other stores."

"Only partly. I have good managers and a great personal assistant. In fact, I plan to have things so well run someday that I can oversee everything from Europe, where I'd like to work on establishing new stores."

He appreciated her ambition even though a small part of him was . . . disappointed in her traveling plans. "I've never been to Europe, but I hear the snowboarding is incredible. I've explored a lot of famous Western resorts out here. My friends and I take a ski vacation every year. Next February, we might try Tahoe. Sounds like your kind of place. Will I see you there?"

She chuckled. "Now you've warned me off. You don't like to travel besides the snowboarding trips?"

"I'm too busy, and I have everything I need right here." She was relaxing with him, and that was better than the charged awkwardness when he'd first arrived. "So I hear I'll see you tomorrow night at the Widows' Boardinghouse. Grandma says she invited you. You'll come?"

She nodded.

"Then it's a date." He slapped his hands on his knees as he rose to his feet.

"It's not a date," she answered dryly. "But before you go, let's finalize the design ideas for your sketches."

She looked at him with that direct, confident gaze of hers. She thought she had everything under control, but he didn't see it that way. He hadn't been able to forget her these last few months, and by her very resistance, he suspected she felt the same. He could be patient. He sat back down.

After all, if he could be patient after their first kiss, when he'd been so turned on he could think of nothing but her body beneath him, then he could do anything.

They spent another half hour discussing floral designs versus geometric, subtle versus bold, and even whether a hint of animals was suggestive of sexy wildness or simply farm life. She was easy to talk to and definitely had her vision of Leather and Lace well established. He'd sketch her samples of everything they'd discussed and go from there.

"Thanks for the explanations, Josh." She rose to her feet and looked at him expectantly, crossing her arms beneath her breasts, so that the expensive silk clearly outlined the straps of her bra.

After standing up, he smiled at her over his shoulder as he headed for the slate path through the garden. "Do you need a ride tomorrow night?"

"No, thanks, I have a rental car."

"Then I'll see you at the ranch."

Her cell phone rang, and she glanced down at the table, already distancing herself. He inhaled with regret, gave her a nod, and walked away, just like he had last December.

Things were going to be different this time.

Chapter Two

The sun had already dipped behind the Elk Mountains as Josh left the B&B. He rolled down the windows of his pickup and enjoyed the coming coolness of evening. He considered heading home, then remembered Will Sweet's text about meeting up at Tony's Tavern. He should go back to his workshop, but instead, headed across Valentine—all seven blocks of it, then turned down Nellie Street until he came to Tony's near Highway 82.

From the outside it was a nondescript square building with a blinking sign advertising the name, but inside it felt almost as good as home. Tony De Luca, his hockey and softball teammate, stood behind the bar as usual, washing glasses and talking to customers. Neon beer signs decorated any space left over between mounted animal heads. Flat screen TVs let customers at the half dozen tables watch their favorite games, which this time of year meant baseball and the Denver-based Colorado Rockies in particular.

Tony gestured toward the back room with his chin. Josh tipped his Stetson, then raised his hand and took a sip of pretend-beer. Tony grinned and shook his head as if to say, *You're in my bar; of course you want a beer.*

In the back room, a pool table was the main focus beneath lights at the center of the room, scattered small tables surrounding it. Chris and Will Sweet faced off across the pool table, and Josh groaned aloud. They were way too competitive for brothers. They looked alike, with different shades of blond hair, though Will was taller and had a daredevil streak, compared to Chris's shy, serious nature. Their brother Daniel lingered nearby, a newly minted college grad, standing out in Valentine with his multiple tattoos and the stud beneath his lip. Daniel didn't care enough about anything to be competitive for any length of time. He did whatever moved him at the moment. He was darker, like their mom, and the shadows suited him. His teeth flashed in a white grin when he saw Josh.

"Look who tore himself away from the lingerie chick," Will called.

Josh rolled his eyes. At least his brother Nate wasn't here to hear that crack, Josh thought—he'd never hear the end of it.

"Lingerie chick?"

Josh sighed as he heard his brother's voice. Nate was seated at a corner table behind him, playing cards with Adam Desantis and Dom Shaw.

"You didn't have a Robbers' Roost meeting without me, did you?" Josh asked.

"Do we all look like we're playing serious cards?" Adam asked dryly. "We're passing the time—"

"Staying away from your women?" Josh interrupted, then glanced at his brother. "And you a newlywed?"

Nate frowned and looked down at his cards, and Josh couldn't help wondering if he was embarrassed. His dark hair was disheveled from the Stetson he'd tossed on a nearby table, and his ever-present dimples were absent.

"Em's working. She has a cheesecake order for a luncheon at St. John's tomorrow."

His wife owned the Sugar and Spice bakery, and although she had plenty of counter help, with their grandmother and her fellow widows, baking was a talent that she hadn't seemed to trust to anyone else—yet.

"And you don't look happy about her late hours," Josh said, casually heading toward their table. He pulled up a chair, slouched down, and rested one booted foot on another chair.

"He's been whining," Adam agreed.

Adam was an ex-Marine who'd come home late last year to visit his grandma, took a temporary job at the Silver Creek Ranch, and ended up falling for Josh's sister, Brooke. Josh was grateful for his commitment to the ranch, as well as his help with the leather business.

Business. It really was a business now, he mused, not all that certain he was happy about that distinction. Before, it had always been his hobby, what he did to relax. But he'd started to say "yes" to too many requests, starting first with Dom Shaw's sister, Monica. She owned the flower and consignment shop where he'd first placed his work to see if there was any kind of demand at all. And there had been—a lot.

Dom was a tall, broad-shouldered black guy who was as at ease on a horse as the rest of them but had somehow wound up in the world of food, owning his own brokerage catering to high-end grocery stores. He traveled occasionally to search out new products for his clients.

Josh seemed to be meeting a lot of people who traveled, he mused, thinking of Whitney.

"I'm not whining," Nate said, tossing a frown at Adam. "No insults from the guy who hasn't made an honest woman of my sister."

Adam sat back in his chair, eyes wide with pretend affront. "When did this become about me?"

"Never mind." Nate's smile faded. "I just wish I could help Em. I don't suppose you want another part-time job?"

"Only if she wants everything burned," Adam said solemnly.

"You let *Brooke* do the cooking?" Dom asked curiously.

"Hey, my sister has learned a thing or two since she almost burned down your house," Josh said.

"When she was eight," Nate pointed out.

Dom held up both hands as if to placate them, then whipped his hand around when he almost revealed his cards. "It's a great memory, is all. It took weeks to get the smell of smoke out of the curtains. I remember the cookies were little charred lumps—the ones that didn't flame out."

They all looked at each other and grinned.

"Back to the lingerie chick," Nate said, laying down a card and nodding for Adam to deal him another.

"I don't think she'd appreciate that nickname." Josh smiled up at Tony, who brought him a beer. "Can you join us? Let Nicole tend bar a bit."

Tony nodded, then returned a few minutes later with nachos and bowls of mixed nuts. "A healthy dinner," he said.

"How was the lingerie chick?" Nate asked.

"Let it go," Josh said, trying to see his brother's hand.

Nate pulled back.

"There's nothing to say about her. We talked designs, and I'm going to draw some sketches. We'll see."

Will came near, both hands resting on his cue stick propped on the floor. "I checked out her website. I bet your leather will be . . . interesting."

There was grinning and elbowing and even a hoot from Daniel, who saluted him with a shot of tequila, then grimaced as he downed it.

"Naw, I'm not doing anything crazy," Josh said. "I've already told you—necklaces that women like to wear when they want to feel a little kinky, but not really."

"I thought she put leather to other uses . . ." Dom said, giving a leer.

"And you went there today to find out?" Nate asked with interest.

"It wasn't like that," Josh said casually. "We talked business."

"You drove her away for enough months after—whatever you two did," Chris said. He, too, abandoned the pool table.

Josh was starting to feel surrounded, but he kept his voice light. "Hey, I came here to relax, not be interrogated."

"We can't help it," Nate explained. "You don't tend to drive women out of town."

"So you've been telling me." Adam crossed his arms over his chest. "I'm not sure I believe it."

"You two were alone together back before Christmas," Nate pointed out. "*Something* went on. And I know you aren't gonna brag, but you can't blame us for being curious."

Josh dipped a chip in the nacho cheese and savored it. "Look, when there's something to report, I'll say."

"Damn, you really *are* tryin' to get with this chick," Dom said in surprise.

"The *lingerie* chick," Daniel corrected. "Let's use the correct title."

"She's got a name," Josh said with exasperation.

"So if you're not interested," Daniel began, "can I—"

"No." Josh was surprised at the cool firmness of his voice, and he tried to lighten it by adding, "You're a pipsqueak compared to her."

But it was too late. They all exchanged knowing looks, and Josh didn't mind that they all knew where he stood. No one got to put the moves on Whitney but him. "Deal me in."

Will elbowed his little brother in the side. "He put you in your place, *pipsqueak*."

Daniel gave a good-natured scowl, and Josh just grinned at him. That gave him an excuse not to look at his brother, who studied him, smile fading.

An hour later, the others gathered to watch Dom destroy Chris at the pool table while idly discussing what you'd need to survive a zombie apocalypse.

Nate finally got Josh alone, took a swig of his Dales, and said, "So about Whitney . . ."

Josh sighed. "You just can't leave it alone, can you?"

"Well, you spent a lot of last year telling me I was spreading myself too thin, trying to be all things to everyone. I took to heart what you said—"

"Not without a fight."

"—and I changed stuff. I pulled back from some of the day-to-day ranch work and concentrated on the business end."

"Which you're good at."

"Which I'm good at. But now maybe you need a dose of your own medicine. You've been making stuff for Monica's shop, and belts for the feed store. You've signed up to do something for that boutique in Aspen and now Leather and Lace."

"You knew that before she left." Josh pointed at him with the top of his beer bottle. "And you and Brooke both agreed that it would be okay."

"Of course we did. We'll help you any way we can. That's not why I'm bringing this up. I think *you* can't decide where to put most of your time. For me, it was sort of a clear-cut decision once I focused. But you? I think you love every part of your life."

Josh took a sip and squinted as he watched the pool game. "So?"

"And now there's Whitney. I saw you before you went to meet up with her—I haven't seen you this intrigued in . . . maybe never."

"So?" he repeated.

"She's not exactly the small-town girl you're used to."

"Neither was Em before she decided to stay here."

"I just think . . ." Nate hesitated. "I just think you should remember that she had no problem staying away all these months."

"So you're warning me not to fall in love with her?" Josh asked dryly.

Nate blinked at him. "I didn't say—"

"Believe me, I know where I stand with her," Josh interrupted, grinning, "and she knows where she stands with me. If we hang out, then we'll have fun. I'm not expecting more than that." He set down his beer and tossed some bills on the table to cover the food. "I'm heading home."

"Work?" Nate asked.

"Nope, back to my workshop."

"Which has 'work' in the title."

Josh smiled. "So it does. But it doesn't feel like work, you know?"

"Hope it stays that way."

Josh drove his pickup the couple miles home, the lights of Valentine piercing the darkness. As he turned onto First Street, the stone town hall pointed up into the sky, spotlights emphasizing it, the tallest building in Valentine. After he crossed the little bridge over Silver Creek, he was on Thalberg land, the land that had been in his family since the mid nineteenth century. If he took a left, he'd come to the Widows' Boardinghouse, where his grandma and two of her friends, Mrs. Palmer and Mrs. Ludlow, lived, and beyond them was the renovated cabin that Nate and Emily called home. He left the last of the lights behind, and darkness settled in, but for the couple lights at the ranch, like beacons guiding him home. The sky above wheeled with millions of stars, and the mountains rose like black shadows to block some of them out.

Ahead of him was a thousand acres of prime ranchland, small compared to some of the big outfits in other parts of the state. Endless fields of grass stubble were all that was left of the hayfields. In another couple months, the herd would come back down. A lot of other ranches were gone now, sold off as Aspen expanded, or their rich residents wanted a bit more privacy. And the money they offered? Josh couldn't blame many a poor rancher or farmer for selling out. But not the Thalbergs. Things had been tough until the last few years, when their father had turned his small investments over to Nate, the genius college boy, who had a knack for knowing what might pay off. Heck, Nate had even invested in a winery on the Western Slope and organic produce farms for Aspen markets. He'd stabilized their finances, which had allowed them to buy new some equipment.

Their father had sort of retired to spend more time with their mom, who had MS, and Adam had hired on full-time last year after leaving the Marines. With Brooke's new riding school, both she and Josh had part-time jobs that needed to be worked around. Josh couldn't help feeling guilty. Somehow, he had to find a way to make everyone—including himself—happy.

The red-roofed barn and ranch house seemed deserted in the night. His mom and dad had the house to themselves now that Brooke and Adam had their own apartment in town above Sugar and Spice. Adam had lived in the bunkhouse for a while, but now that was just a refuge for the two of them if they worked late.

Last winter, Josh had moved out of the main house, too, although not far. He parked near the barn and got out, and the two cow dogs raced toward him with joyous abandon. Nate's dog Scout lived at the cabin with Nate and Emily, and another of the dogs,

Ranger, had attached himself to Adam. He petted silky heads, rubbed behind ears, and finally made his way into the barn and up the stairs to his recently created loft apartment. He'd been spending so much time in his workshop on the ground floor that it made sense to live just above.

The loft was one big open room, with large windows added on all sides and several skylights above. The space was partitioned into separate areas by the furniture involved—a bed, dresser, and closet in one corner, with a door leading to the bathroom nearby, the kitchen cabinets opposite, with an island separating it from the rest of the space, a table and four chairs between the kitchen and the "living room," another corner of the room with a large flat screen TV, a big overstuffed couch, a coffee table, and a couple chairs grouped in front of it.

Josh found himself standing at the window, where, just over the trees, he could see the faint lights highlighting the pointed towers of town hall and St. John's Church. And past them? The Adelaide B&B, where Whitney had an evening of work planned, no doubt. He understood where she was coming from as he changed into his old jeans and a ripped shirt for some time in his workshop. It was a shame for such a beautiful woman not to enjoy herself. Josh planned to make sure she learned all about the beauty of Valentine Valley—and got to know him at the same time.

Chapter Three

When Whitney drove her compact SUV down the dirt road that ran along Silver Creek at the edge of Thalberg property, she could see several pickups and Brooke's Jeep in a line in front of the white Victorian. Her car felt almost tiny and just for show as she took her place at the end, but she understood the necessity of powerful pickups and four-wheel drive on a Colorado mountain ranch.

For a moment, she sat in her car and wondered what the hell she was doing at this family event. The widows were being kind to her, of course—they'd taken her "under their wing" as the old saying went. Late last year, Mrs. Palmer, Adam's grandma, had contacted her after hearing about some townspeople's determination to oppose her. The widows had supported her by giving interviews to the *Valentine Gazette,* and stood up against their neighbors at several town-council meetings. Mrs. Palmer had invited her to dinner at the True Grits Diner, then shown all her friends the sketches for Leather and Lace's next season. The owner of the diner, Sylvester Galimi, had been the leader of the opposition, and had thrown a fit on seeing Whitney's—very tasteful!—sketches.

That was the evening she'd first met Josh Thalberg. He'd guided her out of the crowded diner, a bulwark against the stares and the anger, then had disappeared without even introducing himself. After she'd seen some of his intricate leatherwork, she'd known that Josh could be the man to help her win over the citizens of Valentine Valley. He'd hesitated, but in the end, her plight had swayed him.

And then they'd celebrated with that kiss.

She winced and almost wished she'd been drunk enough to forget it. As it was, the steaminess had lived on in her dreams, and to her dismay, had made it quite impossible for her to date back in San Francisco. Oh, she'd told herself she was just too busy, but seeing him yesterday had made her realize the truth—she didn't know anyone who attracted her as much as he had.

As he still did.

She took a deep breath to regain some control. They could be friends, employer and subcontractor, coworkers, whatever you wanted to call it. She wouldn't fall all over him and make a fool of herself. This town already mistrusted her.

As she got out of the SUV, she looked down at her heels and sundress. She wasn't certain what she was supposed to wear to a dinner at a boardinghouse. As she carefully negotiated the walk down the dirt road, a bottle of wine cradled in one arm, she noticed there was even a sign that said WIDOWS' BOARDINGHOUSE, which made her chuckle and begin to relax.

And then her phone rang. Frowning, she glanced at it, saw it was her assistant, Ryan, and almost answered it. Then she heard laughter and voices from out back, and the faint melody of country music on a radio. Ignoring her phone with difficulty, she walked around to the back of the house, where picnic tables were scattered beneath the trees, and in the distance, she could see the buildings of the Silver Creek Ranch. She'd known the boardinghouse was part of the same property, but hadn't realized how close. The ranch was where Josh lived and worked.

She saw him at the same moment he saw her. He nodded and continued talking with his parents. She'd met them at the first town-council meeting. Doug Thalberg's brown hair was going gray, along with his mustache. He kept his arm linked with his wife, Sandy, who barely leaned on her cane since her recovery from an MS flare-up last winter. For just a moment, Whitney watched the animated way Sandy spoke to Josh, saw the love and attention the two Thalberg men clearly showed, with their warm expressions and occasional chuckles, and felt a touch of sadness that was deep and old. She pushed it aside like she always did. Maybe she should call her mom. They only talked once or twice a month.

Whitney had hoped this might be a larger party, where she could lose herself, but it was all Thalbergs and their relations. The three widows held court: Mrs. Thalberg, with her dyed red hair and ensemble of sensible jeans and vests; Mrs. Palmer, Adam's grandma, with her big blond wig and her outrageously patterned dresses; and Mrs. Ludlow, the one who fit the classical idea of a grandma, with her white hair, matching pants and blouses, and her walker. The three were part of the Valentine Valley Preservation Fund committee, and they took everything that happened in town quite personally. They wanted Valentine to be the best it could—and thankfully, they thought a romantic town needed a lingerie store and had stood with her to face the town council.

"Whitney!" Brooke called, then squeezed Adam's hand before approaching her.

Brooke had grown up on the ranch and moved like an athlete, tall and lean, her long brown hair swinging free, not in the braid she normally wore when she worked. She was wearing jean shorts and a tank top with her cowboy boots, and Whitney began to realize she herself might have overdressed. Oh well, these were the clothes she felt comfortable in, and knew she looked good in them.

Not that she cared that anyone in particular might think she looked good.

Brook gave her an enthusiastic hug. "It's great to see you again!"

"Thanks. It was kind of your grandmother to invite me."

"Josh first mentioned you were in town but didn't say for how long."

"I don't really know. I guess I'll see how the building goes. I have meetings with architects, and that'll lead to construction companies, as long as I decide to put in a purchase offer. Lots to do."

"I'm not surprised. Come say hi to everyone else—although Nate tells me you already saw Josh." She winked.

Nate told her? Whitney thought with interest. So word got around. But then again, Valentine was a small town, where everyone knew everyone else's business, especially brothers. When she'd been fresh out of college, Whitney had spent a year in the spotlight—she didn't want to go back to that fish-bowl life.

She was welcomed into the gathering with easy smiles and warm hugs. After thanking her for the wine, the widows studied her, with concern lingering behind those smiles.

It was finally Mrs. Thalberg who said, "You look like you've worked too hard this year, my dear. Have you lost weight?"

Brooke winced and shrugged a silent apology, even as Whitney said, "No, at least I don't think I—"

"Really, you should move in with us," Mrs. Palmer said, her Western accent prominent. "We have that extra room and we wouldn't charge you anythin', and we'd make sure you were fed."

"That is so kind of you ladies, but Debbie is taking good care of me at The Adelaide."

"But she only serves breakfast," Mrs. Ludlow pointed out.

"And I'm enjoying discovering all the lovely restaurants on Main Street."

"Let her be, Grandma," Josh said, putting an arm around Mrs. Thalberg. "She needs peace and quiet for all that work she does."

"What would you like to drink?" Doug Thalberg asked.

Soon, she had a glass of red wine in her hand, standing with Brooke and Emily Thalberg, Nate's wife, chatting about Emily's wedding earlier that summer.

"They got married in the gazebo overlooking Silver Creek," Brooke said.

Emily, her blush matching her strawberry blond hair, had a dreamy expression in her eyes. "The day was so lovely. No wonder so many people choose June for weddings! And the best part—I wore my Grandma Riley's dress! The Widows' Boarding-house was originally my grandma's home, and her dress was still in the attic. Mrs. Ludlow did the al-terations. Brooke, Monica, and my little sister Steph were bridesmaids, along with Heather Armstrong, my friend from San Francisco."

"And being that it was a Valentine wedding," Brooke added dryly, "we had to have *double* the romance. Heather fell for Em's brother Chris right there at the wedding!"

"Only in Valentine," Whitney said, shaking her head. "So are Heather and Chris going to have a long-distance relationship?"

"No, she's in the process of moving here, and I'm so excited. I first realized my love of baking when she'd occasionally hire me in a pinch for her catering business. She fell in love with Valentine as well as Chris, and I certainly know how she feels."

Whitney knew that Emily had been born and raised in San Francisco but had to return to Valentine after her mom's death to deal with inherited prop-erty. Falling in love with Nate, and finding the bio-logical dad she'd never known, had all contributed to her wanting to stay in Valentine.

"So did you go on a honeymoon?" Whitney asked.

Emily shot a wince at her husband, who was play-ing horseshoes with his brother. "Not yet. It's hard to find the time."

"Josh tells me ranching is practically a twenty-four-hour-a-day job," Whitney said.

Emily hesitated. "It's not Nate's job but mine that's causing the problem." She gave Brooke a soft smile.

"Everyone was eager to take over for him while we'd be gone, and I was grateful. Sadly, I don't have anyone to take over for me."

"She's at last realizing that her bakery is busier than she'd ever imagined," Brooke said, then gave Emily a mock frown. "Didn't I warn you that this is Valentine, Em, and all this romance demands pastries?"

Whitney chuckled, but Emily could only give a faint smile.

"It's wonderful to be busy," she admitted, "and Whitney, I'll warn you now, you'll be amazed at how eager everyone around here is to celebrate weddings. People come here just for the postage mark on their wedding invitations—did you know that?"

Whitney shook her head, struggling to hide her amusement in the face of Emily's worries.

"The widows have offered to help, but I just can't ask that of them," Emily continued. "They already work the counter, and doing all that baking—no, I won't hear of it. Nate and I can wait until I find the perfect person."

"Surely there are other pastry chefs," Whitney said.

"All the best ones are in Aspen," Emily pointed out. "My little shop doesn't have quite the same draw. But I'll figure it out. And Nate has been more than understanding about having to put off the trip."

Brooke rolled her eyes. "Please. My brother had *better* be understanding."

The three of them glanced at the men, who were now grouped around the horseshoes pit, watching Adam take his turn at a sport he was obviously unfamiliar with.

"It's like throwing a hand grenade!" Doug called.

Adam laughed. "That only proves that you and I weren't in the same branch of the military."

"My dad was in the army in Vietnam," Brooke explained. "Adam served with the Marines in Afghanistan."

Whitney heard the soft pride in her voice, saw the tender way she looked at Adam, as if she knew how much service to his country had cost him. Every man at this picnic was part of a couple except Josh, and Whitney began to wonder if the widows were being more than friendly by inviting her tonight. As she helped herself to salsa and chips, she found herself watching him, playing right into their hands. He wasn't as exuberant or talkative as the rest of his family, but he was right there with a quip or praise (and Adam needed some praise in horseshoes). Surprising herself, she sort of liked that Josh wasn't always perfectly put together. His dark hair was often mussed, and he seemed to shave only when he wanted to. His clothes were casual and worn, as if comfort mattered more than looks. That was a rarity in her world—and she knew from experience, for her feet were already killing her. But the sandals were so cute!

Josh was a man at ease in his own world, much as she'd never understand that world herself. The pace of events in Valentine seemed so . . . slow, as if everyone believed things would work out for the best if you just gave them time. Well, that was crap. She knew from her own experience with her family that you could hope and wish and work toward something all your life, but in the end, other people made the decisions, and you could only pray you could sway opinions, change minds. And in her case, it hadn't worked.

She'd thought herself destined to inherit the majority shares of Winslow Enterprises along with her brother, to work at his side for the rest of her life—until her dad had explained otherwise. She shivered even in the August heat, remembering back in boarding school when she'd been home for a holiday, and mentioned her plans to study business in college, to be ready. Her father had looked at her blankly, then explained that only the men came into the business, that the women of the family stayed in the charitable arm of the company—surely just as worthy, he'd said in a patronizing tone she'd never heard from him before. Not that she'd spent all that much time with her parents, except on the occasional holiday, and even then, the servants had been more involved in her life than her parents were.

She hadn't believed his resolve, of course, being sixteen and confident in herself. Once in college, she'd graduated summa cum laude as a business major, gone on for her MBA, but it hadn't changed his mind.

So Whitney went wild for a year that she'd rather forget.

The Thalbergs and their easy intimacy made her ache for a childhood she'd never known enough to want. She'd had everything money could buy, been treated well—that was enough, wasn't it?

"Give the guy a break," Nate was saying, as Adam lost badly to him in horseshoes. "If this were poker, he'd be doing a lot better."

Brooke groaned. "I can't believe you dragged him into the junior version of Robbers' Roost. He'll take all your money."

"Robbers' Roost?" Whitney echoed, as the men gathered to get the grill going. She followed the ladies into the cow-themed kitchen to help carry out the food.

"It was originally an old barn loft at Deke Hutcheson's Paradise Mountain Ranch," Brooke explained, handing her a bowl of potato salad to carry. "He needed a place to get away from his wife, but not go *too* far. He and his friends, including my dad, gather to play poker, smoke cigars, or spit."

Emily gave a visible shudder as she set a tray of condiments on one of the picnic tables. "So now the younger men have decided they need to band together, too. Rather than an old barn loft, they gather at Tony's Tavern."

"The junior version of Robbers' Roost," Brooke said again. "All the men, they like to batch up."

" 'Batch up'?" Whitney echoed in confusion.

"Sorry, ranching term. The older bulls tend to form bachelor herds. They can be hard to locate in the mountains and bring home. See?"

Whitney laughed. "I see."

Brooke lowered her voice. "And someday they'll be like the widows, scheming nicely to have the town just the way they want it." She gasped and arched forward in surprise, as if someone had—

Adam smiled down at Brooke from behind. "Now, now, no talking about us behind our backs, or you'll be punished, maybe even pleasantly."

She groaned and gave his shoulder a push until he let her pass.

Soon, the smell of grilling steaks scented the evening air. The sun dipped behind the mountains, and Whitney found herself watching the skyline in fascination. The mountains were so tall as to seem unreal, with little visible vegetation above the tree line. There was no snow yet, but she imagined that wouldn't be long in coming. She'd been to many a mountain town, of course, but never lost her appreciation. For some reason, she always found mountain scenery more peaceful than the beach. Not that her parents agreed . . .

Soon, they were seated at three different picnic tables, eating steak, Brussels sprouts, tossed salad, sweet potatoes, and delicious rolls Emily had taken out of the oven. They were mouthwatering—and Whitney could see why she was worried about someone having enough skill to replace her.

Doug lit torches around the yard, and lights strung in the trees winked on. Whitney had a second—and last—glass of wine, knowing she would have to drive. But for some reason, she wasn't in a hurry to leave. The food was delicious, and Mrs. Palmer had baked a blueberry cobbler that Emily should steal for her bakery. And there was nothing like grass-fed beef, fresh from the ranch it had been raised on.

She didn't sit right beside Josh, but they faced each other from two different picnic tables, and more than once she caught him looking at her, because, of course, she was stealing glances at him.

"Whitney," Mrs. Thalberg called, as people pushed their plates away, stuffed. "Are you going to put my grandson's work in your other stores?"

"I'd like to," she said, then gave him an apologetic smile, "after we come to terms with the design and cost, of course."

"We'll manage," he said in his low, slow tones.

He wasn't saying anything naughty, but when he

spoke, she always felt like she could hear other meanings—or maybe it was only her.

"You know, there's a fancy boutique in Aspen that he agreed to work with," Mrs. Thalberg continued.

Whitney paused to keep her frown from showing. "Oh, I didn't realize."

"It was before your request," Josh put in, as if he understood her concerns perfectly.

"He's far too creative just to keep belts at the feed store," Nate added, his voice teasing.

"Items there, too," Whitney said, keeping her smile in place as she glanced at Josh. "I thought your projects were only on display at Monica's Flowers and Gifts."

"I keep different work at different places," Josh said with a shrug. "Key chains, checkbook covers, frames—those are at Monica's."

He seemed indifferent to her concern, but for some reason, she knew it wasn't so. Yet . . . he was only one man, and according to him, that ranch behind the trees needed him. How was he going to do it all? She could hardly advertise his work, then constantly run short of supply.

"And what product will be in Aspen?" Whitney asked.

"Shoulder bags, which are very popular," Brooke said.

"And what will he be doing for you?" Nate asked.

Though Josh didn't lose his lazy smile, he shot his brother a look.

"For your store," Nate corrected himself, even as several chuckles were quickly squelched.

Whitney had no problem answering this question though some might think it loaded. "The fact that you can ask me in front of your grandmother means you've already looked at my website. My customers enjoy tasteful, elegant items, and as I'm sure Josh has told you, his necklaces will make a woman feel beautiful and sexy and little bit naughty. We all need that some days."

Emily clapped her hands, said, "Hear, hear!" then shot her husband her own special narrow-eyed look.

Whitney continued to smile at Nate, and thought maybe he even reddened a bit, but it was hard to tell in the twilight. She'd been in the lingerie business a long time—and before that, she'd worn her share. Nothing could embarrass her.

"This Aspen boutique I mentioned," Mrs. Thalberg continued nonplussed, "this will be the first time Josh does work for folks he doesn't know. I don't think a verbal agreement will do it this time. Do you know about contracts, Whitney?"

"Of course," she answered. "I deal with that all the time with my suppliers."

"That's what lawyers are for, Grandma," Josh said patiently, then took another sip of his beer. "I'll talk everything over with Cal Carpenter before I sign."

"But you could use someone with you, someone to represent you," his mom, Sandy, suddenly insisted. "And Whitney is already in the retail business."

Whitney felt uneasy and wondered if Josh felt the same. But how was she supposed to refuse these women, who'd already led the charge in her defense against all their friends and neighbors?

"I'd be happy to help, Josh," she said, giving him an honest smile. "And I can make sure you're not committing yourself too extensively to another business besides mine."

He studied her for a moment. "All right, thanks."

Talk moved on to other things, discussion of the approaching winter and anticipating when the herd should be brought back in the fall. When the women started to clear the tables—all except for Brooke, who was just as necessary to the ranch discussion as any of the men—Whitney was briefly alone as she stacked the condiments on the tray.

"You don't have to do that," Josh said, coming up behind her. "You're a guest."

She glanced back over her shoulder. "Technically, we're all guests of the widows, right? I can't just sit around and watch everyone work—nor can I contribute anything to the ranch discussion."

"You contributed enough tonight," he said ruefully. "I'm really sorry to put you into something that's plainly not your concern."

"That's where you're wrong," she said, straightening to look up at him. "I didn't know you had agreements with so many other stores. It doesn't make me all that happy."

He arched a dark brow, and in the torchlight, his five o'clock shadow gave him the swarthy look of a pirate. "As long as I meet my quota with you, it's none of your business, right?"

He grinned, and she grinned back, rather enjoying herself. "But think how nervous I'll be, advertising your work, giving it prominent position in my catalogue, then wondering if your cows or your friendship with Monica is keeping you from finishing your delivery."

"My friendship with Monica? Now that's where you don't have to worry. I sell on consignment there, so if I don't have anything for her—"

"She won't care?"

He hesitated.

"Ah, but you're going to become more famous, aren't you, with this Aspen boutique? Maybe she'll feel bad when you don't give her something to lure her own clients—or frankly, with the little bit I know of you, it's more likely *you'll* feel bad."

He chuckled. "You're too perceptive, Ms. Winslow."

"Guilty as charged. That's where I'll come in handy when I accompany you to Aspen."

"We could make a day of it. Have you ever been to..." His words faded even as she smiled. "Of course you've been there," he added, shaking his head.

"Guilty as charged, once again. My parents are beach-resort people, but they certainly have enjoyed the occasional winter week skiing here."

"I bet you ski well," he said. "Lots of lessons?"

"Lots. My parents had to keep me busy, didn't they?"

His smile faded, and his gaze grew sharp, as she realized she'd revealed a bit too much personal detail.

"So you don't have to worry about showing me Aspen."

"We can't make it a date?" he asked.

She chuckled. "I'm flattered, Josh, but I think that would be a mistake. I'm only here a short time, and it's a business trip."

"You don't like to have fun?"

She betrayed the barest hint of hesitation before she shook her head. "Thanks, but that would complicate things. We're all business, Mr. Thalberg."

"Now it sounds like you're talking to my dad," he teased.

"If that's what it takes . . ."

He held up both hands. "You've made your position perfectly clear, but you can't blame a cowboy for tryin'."

"Are you going to keep trying?" she found herself asking. And her voice was *not* businesslike. After all she'd said, was she actually *flirting* with him?

"I just might be doin' that," he said, emphasizing a Western drawl that gave her pleasurable little shivers.

Chapter Four

Josh stared down into her face, the faint lights sparkling in the trees overhead giving her skin a soft glow and shining through her dark hair like little touches of glitter.

Touches of glitter?

He heard his own thoughts and should have laughed at himself, but somehow, he couldn't.

Whitney was lovely in a way that captivated him, full of confidence, yet with a hint of vulnerability beneath, a hint that her life hadn't always gone as she wished.

She had everything, didn't she? A wealthy family, a successful business of her own. But sometimes he thought he saw a shadow when he looked in her mist gray eyes, a hint of something that reached for him, made him want to know more. She was a fascinating contradiction, and not like any other woman he'd ever met.

And damn, did she look good in the bright yellow dress, long legs, toned arms, and her black hair emphasizing her tanned shoulders. And the tops of her breasts—

Whoa, Josh, he told himself. *Rein it in and quit putting the cart ahead of the horse.*

"So when is this Aspen meeting?" she asked.

Did her voice sound a bit breathless? He was watching her mouth and thought for sure her glance had slipped to *his* mouth.

"Monday morning. It's a half-hour drive. How about if I pick you up at nine thirty?"

"Sounds good."

"Then it's settled," Sandy said, beaming, as she slipped her arm through Josh's. "Whitney, have you seen Josh's workshop yet?"

"No, I haven't."

"Then have him bring you over when you get back from Aspen. You should see all the stages he goes through to make each piece perfect."

"Says my mother," Josh said, shaking his head.

Whitney smiled at Sandy. "I'd love to. I can see how organized he is, considering all the promises he's been making lately."

And he could spend more time with her.

"I know how you became a rancher, of course, but how about the leather tooling? It's not something every cowboy can do, I imagine."

"My grandpa Thalberg used to make saddles and boots in his spare time."

"All that spare time you cowboys have?" she teased.

"We have more time in the winter. I used to watch him for hours, and sometimes he let me try. I was twelve when he died and left me his tools. I practiced for several years, then worked on saddles, too, but they take too much time. I didn't want to lose the skill, so I made smaller things with all the extra leather, mirror frames, checkbook covers, watch fobs, and sold them on consignment through Monica's Flowers and Gifts. When that went well, Emily suggested shoulder bags."

"Your sister-in-law knows talent when she sees it."

"She's another San Francisco girl," he said huskily. "Guess my brother and I appreciate the same things."

"No more flirting," she said, smiling.

But she wasn't exactly meeting his eyes.

After she said her good-byes to his family, and he walked her around the house toward her car, the darkness gradually swallowed them both. They could hear birds chirping, and the sound of more laughter as the party broke up. They stopped beside her SUV.

"I could have found it without you," she said dryly, digging into her purse for her keys.

"The porch light isn't very strong out here. And I would have taken a ribbing from my mother about my manners. So if it makes you feel better, I'm humoring her."

She flashed him the smile that still haunted his dreams. Was there a dimple in one corner? And then he was thinking about kissing her there, and he put his hands in his pockets to stop himself from pulling her close.

"Good night," she said, opening the door. "I'll see you Monday morning."

He closed the door behind her, then stepped back onto the grass and out of her way. After negotiating a three-point turn, she flashed her lights once, then sped off toward town. Josh watched her go. It was going to be a long weekend.

He rejoined his family, ready for more teasing, but someone must have put out the word, for the only things he heard were compliments about Whitney. And he agreed with them all.

As he took the wiped-down tablecloth off one of the picnic tables, his mom approached to help him fold it.

"Did you have a nice time with Whitney?" she asked, directly to the point.

As they came together with the folding of the cloth, he grinned. "We all did."

"Hope you didn't mind your grandma asking Whitney to join you in Aspen?"

"I think Grandma wasn't alone in that."

Sandy just smiled up at him, her black hair framing her face. The strain from last year's flare-up had gone away, so slowly that he'd hardly realized it. She looked healthy and happy, tanned from spending hours every day in her gardens. He felt a surge of relief and leaned over to kiss her cheek.

"Not that I minded your interference," he said.

"I didn't think so. It looks like you need some help."

"So that's what the offer to see my workshop was all about?"

She gave him an innocent smile. "She really should see how you work."

"Uh-huh."

"Are you upset with me?"

"Not in the least."

"I didn't think so." She took the folded tablecloth from him and winked.

By Sunday afternoon, Whitney was lonely, a true surprise. She was used to being busy—and she still was—but in between work in San Francisco, there were always friends to have lunch or dinner with, the premiere of a play, an opening at a museum.

Part of her disquiet was that she couldn't yet place a purchase offer that would officially make the building hers. She told herself that she was choosing architects and waiting for a rough idea of what the renovation would cost, but . . . it was mostly feeling not wanted by the citizens of Valentine Valley.

She had made the mistake of having lunch Saturday at the True Grits Diner, and although the waitstaff was friendly, more than once, Sylvester Galimi, the owner and coordinator of the opposition, came out from the back and glared at her, as if wondering why it was taking her so long to eat. What did he think she'd do, drive away customers? People on the streets smiled at her, after all, in the usual small-town way. She used to think it annoying to constantly make eye contact in Valentine, which you didn't do in the city, but lately it was reassuring.

She wasn't used to being disliked. Even in her party-girl days, she'd been popular with her fans, and though tolerated by those who judged her morals, most seemed to *like* her. When had she developed a need to please everyone? Hell, she wouldn't have become involved in the lingerie business if that had been important to her.

By Saturday night, when Debbie Fernandez, the owner of The Adelaide, took pity on her and asked if she wanted to go to a movie at the Royal Theater, Whitney hadn't even hesitated. She'd been so busy admiring the nineteenth-century gilded décor and brothel red walls, she hadn't even realized it was a silent movie festival until someone began playing an organ. She'd enjoyed herself.

But by Sunday, she was restless again and decided she had to get out. She had a temporary membership to the local fitness center, which like everything else in Valentine, was only a short walk—or jog—away, but that wasn't what she wanted. The day was beautiful, brilliant blue skies, the occasional cloud like a solitary cotton ball floating by. She could see the mountains on the far side of the valley and was surprised how desertlike some of it looked, with cacti and low shrubs in reddish earth.

She walked up Main Street, and as usual, never tired of its quaint charm. Clapboard storefronts alternated with nineteenth-century sandstone two- and three-story buildings, built during the silver-boom days, when Valentine Valley was bursting with miners looking to spend their earnings. Before each store was an overflowing planter of flowers, and it might as well have been the Fourth of July with all the American flags hung from the old-fashioned lampposts. At the far end of Main Street, the town hall rose up against the backdrop of the mountains.

She peered in the store windows, and saw that some, like the women's boutique La Belle Femme, would be right at home in San Francisco, while others mostly appealed to tourists, like the Back In Time Portrait Studio, with its clients dressed like sheriffs and saloon girls. Though her mouth watered looking into the Just Desserts, she spent the longest time lingering in front of the Vista Gallery of Art, taking in the Colorado landscapes and thinking she might have to buy one as a memento of her time there.

And then she passed Monica's Flowers and Gifts, and did a double take. Monica had decorated one of her windows with a collection of leather frames hung from or surrounding beautiful vases of flowers. Whitney couldn't help herself—she went inside, drawn by Josh's work, just like she'd been last winter.

Monica Shaw was waiting on another customer at the counter that separated the front of the store from the giant coolers and the door to the back room beyond. But she saw Whitney, smiled and nodded, and continued showing flower samples for the man to choose from. Monica had black, shoulder-length curls and caramel-colored skin, with enviable cheekbones that set off her deep brown eyes. Dressed in an off-the-shoulder top and slim pants, she could have been walking down a runway. But she looked happiest surrounded by the flowers in her shop.

Whitney walked around the scattering of displays, seeing the variety of crafts from knitted layettes to ceramic plates. But of course, as usual, she was drawn to the leather, just like the first time she'd been in the shop. She picked up a journal with its leather cover and ran her fingers over the intricate tracings of vines that had such depth you felt they were swirling together. Josh had created shadows and three dimensions, and it made Whitney want to frame it instead of write inside. Once again, she could imagine this brilliant, one-of-a-kind work around a woman's neck. She wanted to wear it herself, as if she would be marked by him.

She set down the journal and laughed at herself. There was no denying she was in lust.

The tinkling of the bell above the door startled her out of her thoughts, then Monica came out from behind the counter and gave her a hug. "Whitney! It's so good to see you! How long has it been?"

"Eight months. Hard to believe," she added, shaking her head. It felt like she'd never left, like this awareness of Josh had only intensified with the time apart. But she wasn't going to say that.

"So you're back to officially buy the building?" Monica asked. "We'll be neighbors—okay, a block apart, but that's pretty close."

"I'm almost one hundred percent certain I'll be buying it," Whitney hedged.

Monica cocked her head with interest. "Guess you have some thinking to do."

"I'll hear what the architects and contractors say first."

"Cautious and sensible, I guess."

"That's me," Whitney said brightly.

Monica chuckled. "I see you looking over Josh's work." She ran a hand over a checkbook cover that had interlocking diamonds dyed different colors. "Having second thoughts about using our boy?"

"Not a bit. His work is exquisite, and I just know my customers will count themselves lucky to have something so unique."

"Around their necks," Monica said wryly.

Whitney grinned. "Around their necks."

"Whew. I hate to think of his work in . . . other places."

They both laughed.

Someone came through the back door, and Whitney saw a teenage girl setting her purse behind the counter, then using a hairband from her wrist to pull back her light brown hair. Her freckles had darkened with her summer tan.

"Hey, Karista," Monica said. "Right on time as usual." She introduced the girl as one of her sales associates, then narrowed her eyes in thought. "Whitney, do you have lunch plans?"

"I don't, but I would love it if you'd join me."

Monica smiled. "Karista, the place is yours for an hour. I'll have my cell on." She grabbed her purse and followed Whitney out.

"Where shall we go?" Whitney asked when they were back on the street and blinking at the summer sun.

"Have you been to the Silver Creek Café? It's in an old house overlooking the creek, and we can eat on the back deck."

"Sounds perfect."

The walk was only a couple blocks, and soon they were entering another renovated Victorian with a wraparound porch that became a broad deck in the back. The hostess took them through the wood-paneled first-floor cafe, past huge windows and outside, where vine-covered trellises lined the deck, and another across the ceiling shaded them from the sun overhead. The view was spectacular, all lush green parkland with scattered picnic tables, grills, and swing sets. Towering trees bent low over Silver Creek, and she could glimpse the occasional kayak, the red hull peeking through the foliage like a tropical bird.

As she sat down at a table, Whitney asked, "Is that the boardinghouse down the way on the other side?"

"Yep. So the ranch isn't that far off."

Monica seemed to be studying her, so Whitney casually picked up her menu and started scanning it.

"I hear you had dinner there the other night," Monica continued, making no attempt to hide her curiosity.

"It was nice of the widows to invite me."

"You know they never do anything without a reason," she warned, resting her chin on her hand.

"And that reason could be they know I'm a stranger here."

"You tell yourself that." Monica grinned as she picked up her own menu.

"Hi, Monica!"

A teenager approached their table, set down two glasses of ice water, and pulled out a notepad.

"Glad you're our waitress," Monica said. "Whitney, did you ever meet Emily's sister, Steph Sweet?"

Whitney smiled up at her. Wearing a polo shirt and an apron over khaki shorts, Steph was pretty, with her bright blond hair pulled back in a ponytail. Her crystal blue eyes were wide with interest.

"You're Whitney Winslow," the girl said. "I heard all about your store from Em, and of course the bra tree at town hall is already famous. I checked your catalogue out online and ordered a few things."

"Did you now?" Whitney answered, smiling.

Steph made a funny face. "I know, I know, I look young, but I'll be eighteen in a few months, and I have my own money. My mom was cool with it. I saw her looking at the site, too, but I didn't ask any questions."

Monica pressed her lips together as if to hide laughter.

"Well, I appreciate your business," Whitney said.

"Are you both ready to order?" Steph asked. She glanced past them and bit her lip but waited expectantly.

"I'll take the salad with grilled chicken." Whitney looked over her shoulder to see another customer, an older woman, frowning at them over her reading glasses—or more likely at Steph, who gave the woman an apologetic smile.

Monica ordered a turkey sandwich and coleslaw. Then Steph rushed straight to the other woman's table, promising them their drinks in a moment.

"Guess it's a busy day," Monica said, then shook her head. "Eight months might have passed, but everyone still talks about the bra-tree demonstration. It was brilliant."

Whitney put up both hands. "No thanks to me. It was all the widows. I knew nothing about it except that I was told to show up with a bra in hand."

Growing up on the slopes, she'd seen the occasional bra tree beneath a rising ski lift, where skiers dropped strands of beads—or their bras—to land in the branches. The widows had thought to use the same idea to demonstrate on behalf of Leather and Lace. Whitney could still remember seeing Mrs. Ludlow push her walker beneath the tree and hang an old-fashioned white bra on the lowest branch. Others slung their bras up high, to the cheers of the crowd. They carried signs of protest, like I WEAR LEATHER AND LACE and WOMEN NEED PRETTY PANTIES. The widows had succeeded in making the fight against Leather and Lace a fight against women's freedom, a little over the top, but it seemed to turn the tide. It had been a cold winter night, and people sold hot chocolate and hot pretzels like it was a festival. Mayor Galimi—Sylvester's thankfully objective sister—had thought it amusing, and the town council eventually sided with Leather and Lace.

"You left pretty soon after that," Monica said, eyeing her.

"It was almost Christmas, and I had plans with my family."

"Where did you spend it?"

Whitney hesitated. "Rio."

Monica blinked in surprise.

"My parents like beaches."

"I get that. Bet it was fun."

"Of course." Whitney shrugged, knowing that she could hardly say that everyone amused themselves when their family got together at the holidays. Except for one big meal, she'd been on her own. She liked her sister-in-law, and they did some shopping and some beach-lounging, but . . . "What did *you* do for Christmas?"

Monica leaned closer with obvious excitement. "My twin sister Missy came home for an entire week."

"There's another one of you?"

"Fraternal, not identical, but we do look like sisters. She's a reporter for CNN, and she's always in some far-off part of the world. My brother Dom lives in town—oh, you'll probably meet him because he hangs with Josh and their boys' club crowd."

"Brooke said they 'batch up.' "

"Ooh, you're learning the ranching lingo! Yeah, the guys like to hang together, just like we girls do. We talk about them, they talk about us. The way of the world."

They both straightened when Steph brought their iced teas, looking a little more harried this time. She leaned close. "Sorry about the delay. As usual lately, they gave me six tables instead of four, and everyone ends up mad at me."

"Not us," Whitney promised. "You take your time." She took a sip of tea, added a sugar packet, then gave Monica a frank look. "So what do you think of Josh doing work for me, as well as you?"

Monica looked baffled. "He doesn't really work for me. It's all consignment. If he wants to put things in my store, he's welcome to."

"So you won't be offended if his necklaces for me or the shoulder bags for the Aspen boutique get so popular they need more of his attention?"

"Offended? Of course not," she insisted, looking so surprised that Whitney was relieved.

"I'm glad to hear that," Whitney said. "I'm concerned Josh is trying to please too many people."

"Then you could always cancel your order," Monica said, blinking innocently.

Whitney grinned. "Not on your life. His talent is going to take my store's popularity to a new level. I just didn't want to fight over him."

"Fight over him?" Monica echoed, eyes narrowed with interest. "What an interesting way to phrase it."

"Fight over his time—you know what I mean."

Thankfully, Steph brought their food at the right moment, then hurried off to another table, where a guy was actually snapping his fingers at her.

"Jerk," Whitney said under her breath.

"I was going to call him something far less civilized." Monica slanted a glare at him. "Tourists."

"You say that with disdain. Surely they comprise much of your business."

"They do, and most of them are very pleasant. You'll discover that soon enough. But there's a class of tourist who believe themselves better than everyone else because they're *gracious* enough to part with their money in our quaint shops and restaurants. Oh well, no point dwelling on the few rotten apples."

While the breeze teased them with the damp freshness of the creek, they ate and talked, and Whitney enjoyed getting to know Monica better. When they were done, they left Steph a big tip, and she waved them a harried good-bye.

Whitney had been very tempted to ask more about Josh, but restrained herself, knowing how it might look—and knowing that it might be passed along to his sister. Or even Josh himself. She didn't want him to know just yet that she was reconsidering turning down his offer of a night out.

Chapter Five

It was raining when Josh picked her up Monday morning, and Whitney wore a white, belted coat that mostly kept out the rain but looked good while doing it. He'd come into the B&B with an umbrella for her, in case she didn't have her own, but she was a city girl with a big purse and room for everything. Yet she appreciated the gesture and tried to focus on that rather than the way she'd gotten a little breathless when she'd come downstairs and seen him talking with Debbie in the foyer, tapping his wet Stetson against his jeans-clad thigh. Beneath his dark jacket, she'd seen a white, open-necked, buttoned-down shirt that made his skin look so tan. Then his eyes had met hers, and he'd openly let his gaze admire her body.

Breathless had been the least of her reactions.

His pickup was dusty on the outside, the rain beginning to trace paths through the dirt, but as he held the door open for her, keeping the umbrella overhead, she noticed the interior was neat and clean.

"I hope you didn't straighten up just for me," she said, after he slid behind the wheel.

"Nope. I'm not fond of clutter."

"That gives me hope for your workshop."

"Well, that's pretty cluttered to an outsider, but organized the way I like it."

They left Valentine Valley behind, and the rain came down harder on Highway 82 as they headed southeast to Aspen. Their conversation meandered casually, from favorite movies to favorite books. He made her laugh more than once, and though her phone rang several times, she ignored it, then finally put it on vibrate. Her assistant could wait. Almost too quickly, they passed the airport and entered the city. Along Main Street, remodeled Victorian houses were interspersed with newer, elegant homes and the occasional restaurant or hotel.

"So where do you usually stay when you're here?" Josh asked.

"The Little Nell."

"Only the best, and right at the base of Aspen Mountain."

"My parents like to be at the center of all the excitement."

He shot her a curious glance, and she regretted the faintly sarcastic tone of her voice, but he didn't pry, and she appreciated his tact. "So what's the name of this place again?"

"Savi. It's along the Cooper Avenue mall."

They found a place to parallel park, and had to walk a few blocks. She insisted on using her own umbrella, so neither of them would get too wet, which gave her a little bit of breathing room to get control of herself. As they entered the mall, traffic was routed a different way, so only pedestrians could walk along the tree-shaded walkway, with the creek meandering through the center between shrubs and flowers and benches. Shops and restaurants lined the mall.

Savi was in a two-story brownstone with a large window overflowing with women's scarves, shoes, and small, beaded purses. It seemed disorderly, but Whitney understood the pattern and its purpose, to lure the customer with an abundance of items for sale. When they walked up the steps and went inside, they could hear faint jazz music and smell something citrusy. Display tables were scattered about, and Josh randomly picked up a woman's sandal. His eyes widened at the price before he set it back down.

"I better not break anything in here," he said, shaking his head.

Whitney smiled.

A thin woman dressed all in black glided toward them, her blond hair loose, reading glasses on her nose. "May I help you?" she asked, smiling.

Whitney noticed her give Josh a second, longer look, before turning her attention back to her.

"I have an appointment with the owner," Josh said. "Can you tell her Josh Thalberg is here?"

The woman's smile widened, and her eyes openly drank him in. "Mr. Thalberg, I'm Geneva Iacuzzi, the owner. How nice to meet you."

"And this is my agent, Whitney Winslow."

Whitney's eyes widened, but what could she say? In a sense, she'd be acting in that capacity. Maybe she should take 15 percent, she thought with amusement, to give as good as she got. They shook hands, and though the woman's grip was firm and straightforward, she barely spared Whitney a glance, as all her attention was focused on Josh.

"I've seen your work in Valentine," she went on,

"and since you don't have a website, I didn't really picture you. I must admit, you're . . . not what I expected."

He grinned. "Disappointed?"

Did flirting just come naturally to him? Whitney wondered with exasperation.

"Not at all," Geneva almost gushed, then openly looked him up and down. "In fact . . . seeing you reminds me how important 'display' can be. Would you consider allowing me to take your picture and use it to sell your work?"

Josh frowned. "You mean on your website?"

"Yes, but also right here in the store." She turned to the display of shoes beside her. "Imagine your work grouped around your photo, with you looking just like a cowboy."

"He *is* a cowboy," Whitney pointed out, in case that favorably affected the prices they would soon negotiate.

"Oh, I know," Geneva said. "When I first saw your work in Valentine, I questioned the store owner."

"Monica Shaw," Josh said.

"She didn't reveal too much, but I did understand that you work on your family's ranch. You're authentic, and that would be a draw."

Whitney thought it was time to get to the heart of the matter. "We haven't even agreed on price or completion schedule, nor have we seen a contract."

Geneva nodded absently at Whitney. "I'd like some of your work as soon as possible, of course," she said to Josh. "I'll be more than generous with the price." She lowered her voice. "It's amazing what people will pay."

Was she so addled by his handsome face that she didn't care if it raised the price? Whitney wondered in disbelief. This negotiation was going to be a piece of cake.

"So will you let me take a couple photos?" Geneva continued, turning an imploring gaze on Whitney as if for help. "I am quite the amateur photographer, and of course I'd give you approval."

"Allow me to speak with my client in private," Whitney said.

Geneva smiled with relief. "I'll be in my office behind the counter."

When she'd gone, Josh sighed. "Do you really think this is a good idea?"

"What can it hurt? She's obviously excited about selling your work, and if a photo helps . . ."

He looked around. "I don't see other photos."

"Guess the artists aren't handsome cowboys."

He glanced at her, a smile turning up a corner of his mouth. "So I'm handsome."

"You don't need me to tell you that," she said dryly.

"Well, I think I need more than compliments from you."

She eyed him. "Yes . . . ?" she said, drawing out the word.

He propped one hand on a display table and leaned toward her. "If I agree with this, you have to agree to a date."

Whitney hesitated, looking deep into his green-brown eyes, at half-mast like he'd just woken up after a pleasurable night in bed. He hadn't shaved, of course, and she knew with the cowboy hat he'd be even harder to resist.

So why should she bother resisting? It was just a date, and she'd gone so long without a guy as to be baffling. But she didn't want to give in quite so easily.

"You'll only do this great promotion if I agree to being blackmailed?"

"Blackmail?" he countered, all innocence now. "All I asked was a reward for giving in to this silliness. Like I would want to be photographed."

"Oh, all right," she huffed.

He grinned. "That wasn't difficult."

She only rolled her eyes, then walked toward the counter, calling, "Geneva?"

The woman came out immediately, already carrying her camera, as if she had no doubt of their answer. She'd hung something made of black leather over her arm.

Josh arched a brow, but only said mildly, "I'll agree with your plan as long as I like the photo."

Geneva grinned. "I knew you'd see it my way if only because it's harmless promotion. It'll help us both."

"I don't need any help, thanks, but if it helps you sell the bags . . ."

"Speaking of bags," Geneva said, "now that I'm excited about the marketing idea, when do you think I'll have them?"

"Assuming we agree on price," Whitney put in.

"Of course." Geneva waved a hand in easy dismissal.

"Since our first discussion last winter," Josh began, "I've been working on the shoulder bags. I have twenty completed, and another twenty in various stages."

"Wonderful!" Geneva's blue eyes seemed on fire with her eagerness. "Send me one, and I'll make an offer."

"I have one in my truck. Remind me to leave it with you."

"Can we have it for the photo shoot? That would be perfect."

Whitney tried not to smile too broadly. Geneva had definite ideas of what she wanted. Whitney's gaze dropped to the item on her arm, and as Josh fished for his keys in his pocket, she asked, "What's that?"

Geneva held it out. "A leather vest. I thought it would . . . complete the look."

Josh took it and examined it critically, as if making sure there were no beads or sequins. "Seems okay." He removed his jacket, tossed it to Whitney, then slid the vest on over his white, buttoned-down shirt.

"And the hat," Geneva prodded. She glanced at Whitney absently. "Can you get the shoulder bag?"

Josh jingled his car keys. "I'll get it."

"No, let me," Whitney insisted. "You two need to strategize."

"Strategize?" Josh echoed doubtfully. "Don't I just smile, and we're done?"

Geneva glanced up from her camera. "I'd like to take a few different poses. And I think you need to unbutton another button or two."

Smiling, Whitney went out the door, holding it for two well-dressed women who went inside. By the time she returned, there were several other women as well, from teenager to geriatric, all discreetly watching as Geneva moved display tables away from the original brick wall and fireplace mantel.

As she handed the shoulder bag to Geneva, the woman's eyes went wide, and she fingered the soft leather, carved with delicate swirls along all the edges. Understated and elegant, Whitney thought, and it was obvious Geneva wasn't going to argue about Josh's talent. Whitney's negotiating position just kept strengthening.

And then she glanced at Josh, all masculine cowboy, leaning casually against the brick wall like something out of an old Western movie. The black vest brought out the white of the shirt, his tanned skin, and made his eyes luminous. Whitney felt her own pulse take a leap and knew that the other women in the store had shown equal interest.

But none of them were going to go out with him.

So now she was feeling proprietary—and even smug? Good Lord.

But she stayed back and let Geneva bring her vision to life. She hung the shoulder bag from an old-fashioned coat stand to the side, near his midtorso, then snapped a few photos of him lounging against the wall, arms folded across his chest, eyes glimmering with amusement. More than once, he met Whitney's gaze, and she felt the tug of his masculinity. She wasn't immune to the fact that this handsome man was interested in her.

She'd experienced that plenty of times, of course, but Josh was different than the wealthy and educated businessmen she usually favored. He was part of the outdoors, a man of the land and family heritage, who provided food for the whole valley and beyond and took pride in it. He worked with his hands, and none of the men in her past had. The two of them should have nothing in common—but it didn't seem to matter where her libido was concerned.

She heard a click nearby, and turned her head in time to see one of the teenagers snapping another quick photo of Josh with her phone. Whitney wasn't the only one affected by him. It reminded her of those days eight years before, when her fame for her scandalous underwear had caused the original owners of her lingerie store to name an exclusive, expensive line after her. They'd wanted her to model them, and she'd refused. But now, seeing the power Josh had over this small assemblage of women, had she been right?

Geneva soon had him sitting in a chair, and when she suggested he unbutton his shirt all the way, Josh's gaze went straight to Whitney's. She thought for sure he'd refuse, but never breaking their contact, he slowly undid the buttons. When Geneva suggested he lean his elbows back behind him, the shirt gaped several inches, showing the lines of his abdominal muscles, the dark hair scattered across his chest. Whitney couldn't look away, couldn't pretend indifference as her heart thumped heavily in her chest, and the sound of rushing blood filled her ears.

The room had gone silent, but for the jazz music that seemed faintly alien. Even Geneva had stopped talking, placing the shoulder bag on a table near Josh's side. He wasn't smiling now, and she didn't ask him to, only gave quiet commands so that he'd turn his head, or look out from beneath the brim of his cream-colored Stetson.

Geneva suddenly glanced at Whitney, and her distracted gaze focused on her. "That white coat is perfect. Come here."

Bemused, Whitney started to unbutton it, and Geneva shook her head.

"No, keep it on. Wear the shoulder bag, and stand off to the side. Don't worry, we won't see your face."

Was she supposed to be relieved? It was hardly flattering. But as Geneva positioned her, then had Josh glance to the side as if watching her as she wore the bag, Whitney understood the image. She told herself it was only the bag he was staring at, but she was so aware of him, she almost felt as if he'd taken her hips in his hands—as if he had thoughts of what he intended to do. Part of Whitney obeyed commands, while the other part imagined what Josh was thinking.

When at last Geneva said she was done, and Josh hastily stood up, Whitney took her first deep breath in what seemed like hours. He was still watching her, wearing the faint smile of a man who understood what he did to her yet wasn't immune to the charged atmosphere that simmered between them.

The other patrons applauded, and Josh blinked and finally grinned, tipping his hat before buttoning his shirt.

"These will be perfect," Geneva gushed, glancing at her customers with eager curiosity. "See the reaction this will get?" she said for their ears alone.

"They're just curious," Josh said blandly.

"Curious enough to come see your work, we hope. I'll use it on my website, in my promotions, and on social-media platforms."

"That is assuming we come to an agreement," Whitney said cheerfully, glad to focus on something practical as her racing heart slowed back to normal.

"Then come into my office." Geneva smiled. "We can look at the photos together."

Josh found it hard to listen as Geneva and Whitney negotiated. He was still thinking of the photo shoot, which had started out so awkwardly and ended up being the best persuasion he could have imagined for his cause where Whitney was concerned. She certainly wasn't unaffected by him and couldn't hide it. He'd felt like he was . . . performing just for her, then when she'd been part of the shoot itself, he'd barely noticed the camera or the curious customers.

Geneva now passed the camera to them to look at the photos, and although he didn't see what the fuss was about, none were objectionable.

He smiled as Whitney focused all her attention on the paperwork Geneva offered, made changes until Geneva reluctantly reprinted the contract again and again, until at last they were satisfied.

A thousand dollars a shoulder bag. He'd have been happy for five hundred, so it was a good thing Whitney had come along. This was Aspen, of course, and the women here knew how to spend money—and so did their husbands, Whitney had pointed out.

When they were back outside, Josh glanced at Whitney. "That was impressive."

She waved a hand dismissively. "Your work is impressive. That's what did the trick."

"My leather tooling or my modeling skills?"

She shot him a grin. "Both, I guess. I thought Geneva and all those ladies would have their tongues dragging on the floor."

He resisted the urge to ask if she'd been affected. Her color was high, and she wasn't quite meeting his eyes. That was all right because he felt the same way—he'd been glad to sit down for the rest of the shoot so he could disguise his erection. There'd been something powerful about watching Whitney watch him.

And he didn't want these feelings to end. "You must be starving," he said. "How about a late lunch?"

They settled on Ajax Tavern at the foot of the mountain, where just outside, a gondola took summer tourists up for the view. Sadly, the rain wouldn't let them use the patio. The inside was wood-paneled, with red booths along the outer walls, tables in between, and a large bar taking up a corner.

After they'd ordered their food and were already sipping drinks, Josh cleared his throat. "I want to thank you for your help today."

She smiled at him over her white wine, dipping her head forward a bit as if using her hair to shield her face. "Believe me, it was nice to use my negotiating muscles again."

"You certainly used them last winter in dealing with the town council. And I bet you've been driving a hard bargain with the owner of the old funeral home."

She shrugged, which made him glance down at her top, a sheer, green-patterned fabric that draped in folds across her breasts and rippled when she moved.

"Your gratitude is nice," she said, "but you know you probably didn't need me. Geneva was pretty straightforward, and she wanted your bags regardless of the price—and wanted the exclusivity at Savi, of course. I just think you enjoyed letting me do all the work even though this might interfere with the necklaces you're making me."

"I won't let it, I promise." He took a sip of his beer, then leaned his forearms on the table. "One thing that would have changed without you here—I probably wouldn't have done all that posing."

"I didn't twist your arm behind your back."

"You didn't have to. You agreed to a date, and that was enough for me."

She glanced at the large windows that framed the grass-covered lower mountain stretching up above them. "You didn't have to work so hard to get me here."

He straightened. "Oh, this isn't our date. This is a business lunch."

"I see." She smiled and took another sip of her wine.

"I can be much more creative than this. I'm an artist."

"Any hints?"

"Nope. It'll be a surprise."

They both sat back as the waiter brought over their appetizer, pâté.

"If you want to thank anyone for my presence," she continued, "it should be your mother."

He grinned, spread the pâté on a hard, round crostini, then closed his eyes as the taste coated his mouth. "I'm not exactly thinking about my mother at this moment."

"Well, think about her. She looks a lot better than she did last winter."

"She is, thanks. She's had flare-ups before, but I'm always worried there'll be a day she won't be able to leave the wheelchair."

"When was she diagnosed?"

"In her midtwenties, when Nate was just three years old."

Her gray eyes seemed to melt with concern. "So young! I'm sure your dad helped her."

"They weren't married then."

"Excuse me?" she said, blinking her surprise.

"She was married to Nate's dad, who, when he found out her diagnosis, wiped out their bank accounts and took off."

She covered her mouth with one hand, eyes wide. "I had no idea! Oh, Josh, your mom is even more courageous than I thought."

"She is pretty amazing. She just carried on, supporting Nate as best she could as a teacher. Then she met my dad, and they fell in love. He adopted Nate, and soon Brooke and I came along."

"To complete the family. Perfect."

"You have a brother, right?"

She nodded, but he thought she withdrew a bit inside herself.

"Yeah, his name is Chasz, well, Charles, after our father."

"Does he work for your father?"

"Yes."

There was a tension in the way she carried herself that hadn't been there before. She didn't like talking about her family, but he could hardly drop the subject so abruptly.

"Married?"

She nodded. "Her name is Courtney. She and I went to college together, which is how they met. No kids yet."

She barely withheld an expression of relief when their double cheeseburgers and truffle fries arrived, so he didn't press her further. But his curiosity was hardly appeased, and he hoped someday she'd feel able to speak more freely with him.

Someday?

What was that about?

Chapter Six

It was still raining when they arrived back in Valentine Valley late that afternoon. The windshield wipers seemed to have lulled Whitney into some kind of trance, for she found herself listening to the soft country music rather than doing much talking. She kept glancing at Josh, only to find him glancing at her. They were like teenagers on a first date.

But it was not a date—it was a business lunch.

Yet she'd agreed to a date and found she couldn't regret it. Josh was right—why shouldn't she have fun while she was in Valentine? Maybe there was a bowling alley; she'd never bowled in her life!

"Your smile is wicked," Josh said.

He pulled up in front of the Queen-Anne-style B&B with its single tower and steep, pointed roof. Trees shaded the road and surrounded the house, hiding the intricate gardens Debbie took such pride in.

He turned off the pickup, unbuckled, and twisted to face her, knee up on the bench. She leaned back against the door and studied him, while rain drummed softly on the roof, and the fog began a slow climb up the windshield.

"I was wondering if, on our big date, you were going to take me bowling," she said.

"Bowling? What made you think about that?"

She shrugged. "I think I've always linked bowling and small towns."

"No bowling lanes in San Francisco?"

"There must be—somewhere."

His smile was sexy as he studied her. "What else do you think of when you think of small towns?"

And then, without planning it, she whispered, "Kissing in pickup trucks."

His smile faded and was replaced by a tension that made her shiver. When he leaned forward, she put up a hand.

With a husky laugh, she said, "I didn't say who was kissing whom."

He froze, then tried to appear casual as he leaned back again.

She unbuckled the seat belt and pulled her legs beneath her to face him on the bench. Slowly she leaned forward, bracing her hands on the leather, watching his eyes dip to her breasts, where her blouse gaped away to reveal the valley between. She was a woman who knew men, who knew how to make them desire her and ensure that they didn't regret it.

After crawling toward him, she braced her hands on his hard thighs and felt them tense. His narrowed gaze moved back to her face, and she saw the way his jaw clenched beneath his lean cheeks. Slowly, oh so slowly, she leaned closer and closer, until she could smell the faint scent of his aftershave, hear the way his breath came quickly, matching her own.

She touched his lips with her own, gentle kisses that lured with promise. She took his broad shoulders in her hands, let her torso slide up against his until he groaned against her mouth.

But he played by her rules and didn't take over.

Most men liked being under the control of a strong woman who knew her own sexiness, knew what she wanted. Wasn't it their fantasy, a dominant woman in the bedroom?

She deepened the kiss, flicking her tongue against his, feeling the languidness of heat and desire steal over her.

"Hold me," she whispered against his lips.

His hands slid up her back, pulling her even more firmly against his chest. She felt his heart thump against her ribs, knew hers answered. The windows steamed from the heat of their kiss. He slanted his mouth over hers, then held her head in his big hands to keep her there.

When she sensed he wanted to turn her in his arms, she realized the steering wheel was in the way. She broke the kiss and smiled up into his eyes, trying to catch her breath.

"Wow," she said softly, then groaned as he leaned forward to nip at her lower lip.

He kept going, arching her back so that he could bury his face against her neck and inhale.

"You smell fine," he murmured, taking little nips with his teeth.

She shuddered, then at last pressed herself upright. As she slowly pulled away, his hands only very reluctantly released her. They faced each other across the bench, still breathing heavily.

"You were going to take me to your studio," she reminded him, "but I think it's too late today. What about tomorrow morning?"

"Sure, stop by whenever you'd like."

"No one will mind?"

"We're pretty casual out on the ranch," he said, those hazel eyes twinkling. "I know the boss." He paused. "Wait, I *am* one of the bosses. My dad's been sort of retired since winter, and it's still strange."

"Why?" She made herself more comfortable, reluctant to leave the cozy cab.

"Because he's still around, of course, and helps at the big events, like branding or calving. He wanted to spend more time with Mom, but since she's recovered, she's gotten herself elected to the school board and still tackles the rest of her commitments. I was hoping they'd travel, but so far, they've stayed put."

"Then they must love it there. I'm looking forward to visiting." She reached for her purse, but before she could open the door, he touched her arm.

"Thanks, Whitney. I really appreciated your help today." His voice suddenly grew huskier. "And you were my inspiration during that photo shoot."

She smiled. "You sure it wasn't all those women taking surreptitious pictures?"

He blinked at her. "Other people were taking pictures?"

"You're easy to look at, Josh, and their interest only proves that those photos will be a success. You mark my words."

She opened the door, climbed down, and gave him another smile before slamming it shut. She entered the iron gate and walked up the path, knowing he watched her, and barely resisting the urge to exaggerate the swing of her hips.

At ten the next morning, Whitney drove onto the dirt roads of the Silver Creek Ranch beneath a bright blue sky. The Elk Mountains formed the backdrop as the pastures and fields stretched away. To her surprise, she didn't see any cows, just endless grass as far as the eye could see—or was that hay?—and fences separating fields.

The newest building was Brooke's indoor riding arena, a square metal structure with windows along the sides and huge double doors open at each end. She glimpsed dirt floors inside, but no one was riding there—who would, in this beautiful weather? She bet it had proved useful the day before during all that rain.

The main house, two stories tall, was made of logs, with wraparound porches on both floors. The red roof matched the one on the barn just across the yard. Pickup trucks and Brooke's Jeep were parked nearby. Across another field was the old log cabin, now a bunkhouse that Adam and Brooke occasionally used as their own. A half dozen horses grazed in a pasture beyond the barn.

Whitney parked her SUV and stepped out of it onto wet earth, regretting wearing her favorite sandals. She'd been so focused on how to appear her best, she hadn't considered where she was actually going. This was a working ranch, with equipment that muddied up meadows. Sighing, she walked gingerly, looking for patches of grass to hop between.

Both doors of the big barn were open wide, and Whitney stepped inside, smelling hay and manure, calling, "Josh?"

There was no answer, not even a horse looking over its stall door. But then she'd seen them out in the pasture. She heard the sound of barking coming closer, and before she knew it, two dogs rounded the corner of the barn and came at her, barking furiously. But their tails were wagging, and she let them sniff her hands. Soon they were taking turns leaning against her legs while she petted them. One tossed up her skirt with his nose to walk between her legs, and with a little gasp, she rubbed his hips as he passed on through.

She heard the sound of a gasoline-powered engine from somewhere behind the barn. Walking back outside, she circled it and found Josh. He didn't notice her, and she stayed in the shade of the building and ogled him.

He was wearing a gray, sleeveless t-shirt, smudged with dirt, and worn jeans that hid most of his broken-in cowboy boots. He was maneuvering a two-foot circumference of tree trunk into what must be a gasoline-powered wood splitter, using all his strength to hold the wood in place, while gripping the handle to bring the splitter down. Then he worked to turn the log a fraction, and split another line down, then tossed out the triangular piece.

The sun shone on his damp arms, and more than once, he took off his hat and swiped the back of his glove across his forehead.

Whitney didn't think she'd made a sound, but suddenly he turned his head and saw her. That moment of connection was so powerful, it was a little unnerving. He waved, then turned off the machine. She almost regretted that his manly display was finished. And though she was already warm, she felt another surge of heat watching him stroll toward her, so tall and long-limbed. She flashed back to their kiss and enjoyed the moment.

"Whew, glad to have a reason to rest," he said, picking up a can of soda and guzzling.

She couldn't stop staring as his Adam's apple bobbed, and perspiration slid down the cords of his neck toward his collar.

"Can I get you something to drink?" he asked.

She swallowed and tried to get ahold of herself. "Not now, thanks. I haven't been working as hard as you."

He glanced down her body. "I can see that. You look so fancy, I'll have to work hard to keep you clean."

"Fancy?" She looked down at her short skirt and sleeveless, v-neck top. "This is dressing down for me." She'd always been very conscious of her clothes, of course, and presenting a professional appearance. She'd had to separate herself from her party-girl days.

"Then I'd like to see what you'd wear if you were working outdoors. No wading in the creek for you."

"And was that on the agenda? No one told me."

He smiled and finished his soda. "Anything's on the agenda."

"But aren't you busy, cutting wood and . . . whatever cowboy stuff you have to do?"

He shrugged. "Brooke and Adam have gone up to our grazing allotment in the mountains to check out the herd. Nate's down valley talking bull genetics, and my parents are in town. Who's going to know what I do? I promised you a tour, and the logs'll wait. Don't need 'em until winter anyway."

As they circled the barn again, Whitney noticed

that several of the horses came closer, and she said, "Quarter horses?"

He gave her a surprised glance. "You know horse-flesh?"

"Boarding school, remember? Riding is considered a gym class."

"Nice. Same out here, I guess. I'll have to get you up on a horse one of these days."

"Will that be our date?"

"Naw, too predictable that a cowboy would want to ride."

She grinned. "It's been a while for me. I might fall off."

He looked down her body again, making her feel that little flush of pleasure. "That skirt might prove interesting up on a horse."

Laughing, she pushed at his bare arm. "Like I'd wear this if we were riding."

They walked into the cool shade of the barn, where at the far end, he opened a door. The room was dim, with only a single window surrounded by several stands of floor-to-ceiling shelves.

"My workshop used to be one of the tack rooms until I converted it," he explained, turning on the light switch.

Whitney walked in behind him, looking at several benches with leather goods in various stages, movable lamps clamped nearby. His tools were neatly stored in trays. The shelves bore supplies.

She moved closer to the first bench, where he'd set down some kind of chisel. She peered at the small piece of leather, and he turned on the light of a magnifier so she could see it better. The letter D was prominent, the leather depressed all around it.

"I'm making a wallet for my dad," he explained.

She smiled up at him. "Not shoulder bags?"

"Christmas is only four months away. I have to work on gifts when I can."

She strolled through the shelves, swept up by the beauty of his work, excited at the possibilities for his future. She saw leather being glued together to form an even thicker surface that he could cut shapes out of and not go all the way through.

"You're so talented, Josh," she said quietly, starting to touch a piece of darkened leather.

"That was just stained yesterday. Should be dry . . ."

She quickly pulled back her hand. "I know you enjoy ranch work, but when I see what you can create—and only you can do it—I'm surprised you don't hire someone to do things like split wood."

He studied her, his expression unreadable. "I'm sure it seems menial to you, but this is my home, and I'm glad to help provide for it. We all do our fair share of the basic chores, along with the more challenging work of dealing with the herd. My family has been here for five generations, since the late nineteenth century. There's history and expectations and pride. When it looked like we might lose it all ten or so years ago? Watching my father almost shrink with the realization that the economy and ranching had changed so much, we might not be able to survive in it? I never want to experience that again."

She hadn't imagined him so serious and saw a new depth to him. "I hope you don't think I meant any disrespect."

"No, but you haven't been around this sort of business before. I know your family has an international company. Did you ever want to be a part of that?"

She hesitated. "I . . . I don't talk much about it." And she wasn't going to start now. She barely knew Josh. "Suffice it to say, I couldn't be a part of the business, so I was determined to make my own way, my own success. I never even used my trust fund for Leather and Lace. Every dime I earned, it was by myself."

"Your family must be really proud of you," he said gently.

Were her eyes actually stinging? How did he see through to the heart of her problems, the fact that she was pretty certain they *weren't* proud of her, that they didn't care at all? She had to get past this. "Regardless, I do understand the generational thing. Winslow Enterprises started out in manufacturing late in the nineteenth century. Sewing machines, of all things."

He grinned.

"Those did so well, my great-grandfather was able to expand, getting into shipping his products, then eventually importing materials other manufacturers needed. Now . . . now we own so many varied businesses, from diapers to airplane parts. And it's important to me, it always has been. So I understand you."

He took her hand then, rubbing her knuckles under his thumb, giving her a little shiver.

"See, we have stuff in common," he said. "You know what else we have in common? Hard work. When you were here last winter, and now here again, your cell phone was ringing all the time, or you closet yourself at The Adelaide immersed in your work. That's why you need to have fun—why both of us need that escape."

She deliberately fluttered her lashes up at him. "You haven't told me about our date."

"I prefer to remain mysterious, so that you can't help but be drawn to me."

She laughed. "You are one of the least mysterious men I know, Josh Thalberg."

"Some men wouldn't think that a compliment; I do." His smile faded. "I'm not pretending to be someone I'm not, Whitney. I'm just a cowboy who has a hobby, and I'm trying to figure out how to make it all work."

Was it all really that simple? she wondered. Everybody had a part of themselves they hid, a past they wanted to forget.

"I guess I am thirsty after all," she said, looking around.

"Then come with me."

She followed him out of his workshop, and, to her surprise, he opened the next door to reveal a set of stairs, which looked far more recent than the rest of the barn. At the top, he opened another door and stepped aside so she could walk ahead of him into a beautifully renovated loft, air-conditioned, with windows looking out on the ranch from all sides. On the walls, Colorado landscapes were mounted in the most beautiful leather frames, different shades of brown to emphasize the painting. There were no walls separating any part of his life, and it sort of made sense—it seemed there was nothing separating her from the real Josh.

But she couldn't believe that.

"So this is your place?" she asked, moving past the gleaming silver-and-black kitchen. "Wow! When did you have this done?"

"Last winter. I did most of it myself, and occasionally Nate and Brooke helped me."

"*Yourself?*" she echoed, eyes widening as she stared at him. "Is there nothing you can't do, Josh Thalberg?"

His gaze dropped as if he were embarrassed, an "aw shucks" cowboy move that would seem fake on anyone else.

"I'm sure there's lots I can't do. But when you work on a ranch, you have to fix all kinds of things, so I picked up the skills along the way. And plus, I was tired of worrying about waking up my parents at all hours. When I have an inspiration, I tend to work the leather until I can't see straight."

She shook her head, smiling. "I thought you were going to say you snuck home late from dates."

"Well, that, too," he said blandly. "But I thought that dedication to my craft sounded more impressive."

"Of course you need your space with women," she said. "And was a drink really the motivation to get me up here?"

"During an unusually hot August day? You bet it was." He looked so totally innocent, but she still didn't know if she believed him.

"All right, so serve me a drink."

To her surprise, after pouring them each a soda, he led her onto a tiny balcony that looked over their land where it stretched all the way to the mountains.

"See that?" he pointed to the west.

"A mountain?" she said hesitantly.

"No, at the base of it. It's the Valentine Valley cemetery, on our side of the Silver Creek. All of my ancestors are buried there. Most of the time I think they watch over us with pride. But on a bad day, I'm thinking not so much."

"That's ridiculous, of course they're proud of you. Your ranch is a success, and your family is happy."

"Some people have started to point out that both Nate and Brooke have found their partners, that it's my turn to make myself perfectly happy."

She frowned. "I don't believe people have to find 'true love'"—she air-quoted the last two words—"to consider their lives successful. Everyone has a different path to happiness. Right now, yours is making your leatherwork a success. Speaking of which, when are you going to ship those bags to Geneva?"

"Already did, first thing this morning."

"You're an easy man to represent," she said with satisfaction. "That'll be a nice check."

"Wonder how I'll spend it?" he mused.

"You could take a trip."

"This winter, maybe. I don't have time to travel more than that."

She blinked at him, unable to imagine not traveling as she wanted to. But, of course, she'd had a wealthy childhood, and it made her different than most people. But she was beginning to realize she'd spent much of the last ten years among people who'd been raised just like herself. Friends from boarding school, then college. It was an insular world. Being in Valentine Valley had reminded her of how special her upbringing was.

She thought of Josh, and his devotion to his family, and had to consider that maybe she wasn't the lucky one after all.

But no one would believe that.

Chapter Seven

Josh did his best to persuade Whitney to stay longer, but she insisted she had work to do, and he was left standing at the barn, watching her drive away, the two cowdogs trying to offer their sympathy. He noticed that his dad's going-to-town pickup was back, which meant his parents had come home without his even hearing it. It was far too easy to focus on Whitney. He ended up playing fetch with a tennis ball for a few minutes until he got his mom's text that lunch was ready.

In the kitchen, the sun came streaming in through a row of windows lining the long kitchen table. Sandy stood behind the breakfast counter, assembling tacos as Doug put together the big salad. Lou Webster, their old part-timer, was already seated at the table, his bald head bent over a ranching magazine so that the tufts of white hair at the back seemed to stick straight up in the air.

Lou glanced up as Josh passed by, blue eyes twinkling with curiosity. "Saw a shiny SUV parked out front. Here I was, workin' in the storage trailer, and no one came to introduce me to guests."

Josh grinned as he washed his hands at the sink. "Sorry, Lou. Whitney came to see my workshop, and I just forgot."

"I'm gettin' the feelin' he forgets everythin' when he's with Whitney," Doug said, grinning.

Sandy almost giggled.

Josh rolled his eyes. "You'll be happy to know we're gonna go out. Tease all you like—doesn't bother me."

"Of course you're going out," Sandy said, sliding the platter of beef-filled tacos across the counter to Josh.

He set the platter on the table, where there were already lots of bowls with taco fixings. Doug carried around the salad, as Josh grabbed a soda out of the fridge. When they'd all sat down, Sandy said a prayer, and they dug in.

"So Whitney's the Leather and Lace lady?" Lou asked, eyeing Josh. "You're makin' leather stuff for her, right?"

Josh nodded, mouth full of taco, swallowed, then said, "Necklaces. Sort of like collars, but not really."

"Delicate work," Lou said, nodding, as he helped himself to a big bowl of salad.

"Are you officially making shoulder bags for that place in Aspen?" Doug asked.

"Yep. Signed the papers yesterday." He saw his mom's concerned look. "I already have twenty bags made, and plenty more already started. I'll manage it all just fine."

"Was Whitney helpful at the boutique?"

"Sure. She knows those clauses inside and out. Changed a few things I wouldn't have thought to. But the owner, Geneva Iacuzzi, was pretty eager for the bags, so she was willing to negotiate."

"Geneva?" Sandy said, frowning. "I've heard of her."

"Gotta ask, son," began Doug. "How much are the bags worth?"

Josh poured dressing on his salad, and tried to be casual. "A thousand each."

Lou coughed, and Josh hit him on the back.

"You okay, old man?" Josh looked around and saw that even his parents stared at him with shocked eyes. "It's just Aspen. You know how the prices are."

"But Josh, that's . . ." His mom's voice weakened for a moment. "That's just incredible. I knew you were talented, and Monica always swore your things flew off the shelves, but . . . I had no idea."

"We're very proud of you, son," Doug said.

"Thanks." Josh smiled at them all.

"Wait until Nate and Brooke hear," Doug continued.

"At least they can see that all the problems I've caused them over the years paid off some."

"*Now* I remember Geneva," Sandy exclaimed. "And you haven't caused your family problems, Joshua James," she added sternly.

"Thanks, but what about Geneva?"

"She entered her photographs into last year's fall craft festival. She has quite the eye for detail. I think she won several ribbons."

Josh began to sprinkle cheese and lettuce on his next taco. "Yeah, she pulled out the camera and snapped some photos of me. Wanted them for her display of my bags, something about the 'cowboy artist.' I don't know."

"Maybe she knows what she's talking about," Sandy said.

Doug looked doubtful, and Josh couldn't help grinning at him. "She had me put on a vest, so I'd look a little more Western." He left out the part about his unbuttoned shirt—he'd only done that to get Whitney's attention, and it had worked.

"Well, whatever sells your bags," Doug said, sounding baffled.

Josh's smile faded. "You know, Dad, that I won't let this interfere with my ranch work. Make sure Nate knows that since he would never express any doubts to me. I want him to know that he can count on me the moment he's ready to take his honeymoon."

"That'll be a while yet," Sandy said with a sigh, fork toying absently with her lettuce. "Emily interviewed a pastry chef from Denver, and it went badly."

"How can anyone not cotton to that pretty little girl?" Lou scoffed.

"Apparently, he felt himself quite her superior, and let her know it." Sandy's brown eyes flashed. "She's no fool—she knows she's self-taught and would enjoy learning even more, but not from a man like that."

"That's too bad," Josh said, pushing back his plate and reaching for a homemade chocolate chip cookie piled on another platter. "I still think she should take Grandma Thalberg up on her offer to do some baking."

"Emily's dead set against it," Sandy said, "and I don't blame her. Those widows do too much as it is. We don't want their health affected."

"Maybe it'll keep them from more mischief," Josh teased.

"They have been pretty quiet lately," Doug said with a distracted frown.

Josh's amusement faded. "Do you think something's wrong? They all seemed just fine when we were there for dinner."

"They may be healthy for their ages," Sandy said, "but I know for a fact they each went to bed early that night. Emily's right about their not baking for the store. She'll solve the problem eventually, with patience."

"Something Brooke doesn't have," Josh said, pouring himself a glass of milk from the pitcher to go with the cookies. "We were shoveling out stalls early this morning, and she's still talking about itching to be engaged."

Doug rolled his eyes. "That girl. She needs to settle in to her new business. That arena's not going to rent itself."

"She's having professional posters made for advertisements, Dad," Josh said. "She showed me the design."

"Oh. Well, then."

Sandy narrowed her eyes at her husband. "*Who* needs to practice patience in this family?"

Doug cleared his throat and bit into a cookie.

"And who knows, maybe Adam's proposing right now," Josh offered. "They took camping supplies and are making a night of it up there."

"How romantic," Sandy said. "I'm surprised she didn't mention a camping trip."

"I was supposed to tell you." Josh rose to his feet. "And so I did."

His mom tossed a napkin at him as he started clearing the table.

Late Friday morning, four days after her trip to Silver Creek Ranch, Whitney was once again trying to do her work in the B&B's garden. She could see Debbie on her hands and knees, weeding her vegetable patch farther in the backyard, but that was the most distracting that Debbie ever was. She was very good at giving her guests space, even within her own home.

The Adelaide had become Whitney's home away from home, and to her surprise, she'd found a rare peace there. She worked when she wanted, ate meals at the different restaurants in Valentine, experimenting. And for a woman who'd eaten at the most exclusive restaurants all over the world, she was surprised by how much she'd enjoyed them all. Brooke had even driven her to Glenwood Springs for an afternoon, once a major train stop in the nineteenth and early twentieth centuries. Presidents had given speeches in the old hotel there, and the natural hot springs drew tourists even in the winter. Brooke had mentioned her camping trip, and *that* was something Whitney just didn't understand. Tents? Bugs? The closest she'd come to camping was her own exclusive bungalow on safari in South Africa. The personal chefs there didn't exactly make it feel like a camping trip . . .

Suddenly, she heard the doorbell ring and saw Debbie turn her head.

"I'll get it!" Whitney called, heading around to the front of the B&B.

A man in his fifties stood on the porch, wearing a suit, something that already seemed strange to her. Even the lawyers around Valentine wore polo shirts and jeans. Then she saw the thin gray ponytail hanging down his back. Not quite the same as everyone else after all.

"May I help you?" she called.

He turned and came back to the top of the steps, smiling. He was slightly overweight, the kind that was easily disguised by the right suit. The double chin, not so much, but he looked like a pleasant guy, peering at her through glasses that winked in the sun. "I'm looking for Ms. Winslow."

"You've found her."

He came down the stairs, extending a hand. "Henry Birdsong. I'm a real-estate developer in Aspen. Do you have some time to talk? I promise I won't take up too much of your time."

"I can talk," she said. "Come on inside. Debbie always has a pot of coffee going."

"Sounds good."

He followed her inside the house, and both of them stepped aside as a young couple trailed their children out the front door. They were such good kids, Whitney barely knew they were sharing the same B&B. In the dining room, billowy lace curtains swayed in the breeze of the open windows. The table was covered by an immaculate tablecloth, ready for the sumptuous breakfasts Debbie put on. On the old-fashioned buffet, she'd left several carafes of coffee and hot water for tea, along with a platter of brownies with what looked like peanut butter chips inside.

"Help yourself," Whitney said, already coveting the brownie.

They carried everything into the glassed-in sunroom, surrounded on three sides by Debbie's gardens, like a tropical forest. She sank onto a wicker couch and set her cup on the coffee table. Henry sat across from her.

"What can I do for you?" Whitney asked.

He took a sip of coffee, then set it down. "I like to keep an eye on my competition, so I tend to browse the stores in Aspen. I saw the Josh Thalberg display at Savi and on their website."

"Geneva works fast," Whitney said in surprise.

"His leatherwork is quite impressive, but that's not what I'm here to talk about. She mentioned that you were representing him, and your name was so familiar to me."

She chewed her brownie with slow deliberation, wondering at the implication. Did he remember her from eight years ago? She hadn't been in the gossip rags in so long.

"So I asked Geneva, and she mentioned that she knew you were considering opening an upscale lingerie store in Valentine Valley, Leather and Lace."

Whitney relaxed a bit. "That Geneva, you can't put anything over on her."

He smiled. "I'm no slouch either, because I did some more research and discovered you hadn't officially bought a building here yet. I was wondering if you would consider a proposal from me."

"I'll be honest, Mr. Birdsong, I did my research on Aspen. I'd considered it for my third store, but the rent was prohibitive. I would actually like to make a profit."

After a brief smile, he leaned forward over his coffee, eyes earnest. "I have a building that I've developed into a wedding center that I call Simply Weddings. Bridal boutique, formal wear, florist. I think Leather and Lace would complete the quartet, and I'm prepared to negotiate a generous lease."

"I don't know, Mr. Birdsong—"

"Henry, please."

"Henry. Since coming to Valentine, I've really liked the romance vibe here. It has a totally different feel than in Aspen."

"But where will you find the clientele I can offer

you? And I can guide you in business matters far better than a cowboy artist—"

He broke off and frowned past her. Whitney turned and saw Josh leaning in the doorway, eating a brownie. He lifted it to her as a toast and smiled, and the pleasure of seeing him made her almost blush. Not good for a businesswoman.

But she couldn't help returning his smile before she turned back to Henry. "I know Josh because he is also doing work for Leather and Lace."

"I see," Henry said, setting down his half-eaten brownie. He rose to his feet, reached into his breast pocket for a business card, and handed it to her. "I won't keep you any longer. Consider my offer, and please get in touch. I'd like to go over some numbers with you." Then he looked to Josh. "I was very impressed with your work at Savi, Mr. Thalberg. You have quite the career ahead of you."

Josh reached out and shook his hand. "Thank you, Mr. . . ."

"Birdsong. Henry Birdsong. I'm a real-estate developer in Aspen." He smiled and nodded at Whitney, then went back through the house.

After hearing the front door shut, Josh said, "Damn, these brownies are good."

Whitney laughed and relished another bite of hers.

Josh took Henry's chair. "So he tracked you down about Leather and Lace?"

"He did, and it's thanks to your work that he and Geneva struck up a conversation. He wants Leather and Lace to open in Aspen, in his bridal center."

"An interesting idea. Are you going to consider it?"

She hesitated. "I think I will. It might make good business sense if he can meet my price on the lease."

He cocked his head and studied her. "I thought you liked it here."

"Oh, I do, trust me. But it seems half of Valentine does not like me," she said ruefully.

"That's not true. Sylvester Galimi was just doing his best to sway some of them. Now that you've been 'officially' granted the right of a permit, I'm sure things will die down."

"But will I sell enough goods to survive? I don't know, Josh. I can't just rely on tourists."

"I guess you have to make your own decision then. Are you in a rush?"

"I should probably decide in the next week or so."

"It sounds like a lot of business, and that's what you're doing every time I see you."

"Oh, but not you?"

"I find some time for poker and pool and base-ball."

She winced. "Don't strain yourself."

"I have to spend time with my buddies, don't I? What do you normally do for fun?"

She leaned toward him and grinned. "I *do* have fun, you know. Museums, the theater, charity events, dinners out."

"We have a museum here."

She put a hand to her chest, eyes widening. "You do?"

"Dedicated to the history of our town. Fascinating subject. I had to go in elementary school."

" 'Had to' being the operative words."

"I'm sure I'd enjoy it more with you."

"Is that our big date?" she teased.

"Nope." He took a big bite of the brownie and finished it up.

She did the same, then said, "Henry mentioned that Geneva has your display up already, including on her website. Shall we take a look?"

He grimaced. "Pictures of myself? I don't know . . ."

"Pictures representing you and your art. As your pseudoagent, I need to make sure she did you justice."

"Well, if you put it that way."

"Hold on, I'll go get my iPad." She got to her feet.

"If it's in your room, I'll be more than happy to accompany you."

Grinning at him over her shoulder, she said, "No, it's in the garden. I'll be right back."

When she returned, Josh had helped himself to another brownie and set one near her coffee.

"I don't want you to get too skinny with all this work."

She practically snorted. "No worries about that."

She set her iPad on the coffee table, and Josh came around to sit down beside her on the wicker sofa— quite gingerly.

"Will this thing hold me?" he murmured, frowning.

It didn't even creak with his weight. They both hunched over the tablet and brought up the boutique, only to find Josh's work and photo the main focus of the home page.

"Wow," Whitney breathed, knowing she hadn't been wrong about Josh's magnetism. In the photo, he was leaning back, elbows on the table, all languid repose, his torso in shadow as if hinting at the rest of his body. His changeable eyes stared out from beneath the brim of his cowboy hat, all smoldering and intense, and she remembered he'd been staring right at her.

Josh suddenly stood up as if restless, then asked with doubt, "Do you think I look ridiculous?"

She glanced at him in disbelief. "Ridiculous? Are you kidding? Women are going to love this. Check it out, Geneva has a page devoted just to your work."

He came around behind the couch and looked over her shoulder. Several of the shoulder bags were featured on the page, some that looked masculine enough for a man's computer case, some with short straps as well as the long one. And there was another photo of Josh, looking to the side at his bag that was perched right against her hip. Thank God she regularly had her nails painted, for her hand held the strap against her side. The white coat was the perfect frame. And the photographic Josh was staring at her as if he wouldn't let her leave him behind.

Yikes.

She glanced up and over her shoulder and thought she detected a reddening of his skin.

"Are you embarrassed?" she demanded with disbelief.

"Well, it's just . . . I don't know. I don't look like myself."

"Yes, you do! Are you trying to make me think you're shy?"

"Naw, of course not, and don't get me wrong—I don't regret it. That photo shoot did make you kiss me."

"*Make* me kiss you? Like I don't know my own mind?"

He cupped her head between his hands and tilted her back until she was staring up at him leaning over her.

"Good, I'm glad it wasn't just my seductive wiles," he said huskily.

And then he kissed her again, and it was so strange to be arching backward for the taste of his lips, feeling his nose brush her chin, and the feather-soft caress of his fingers along her collarbone, even as his other hand rested against her neck. She opened her mouth for him, met his tongue with her own, groaned as he flattened his hand across her collarbone, his fingers touching the upper slope of her breast.

Not in Debbie's sunroom, she suddenly thought, breaking the kiss.

"Okay, that was nice," she said breathlessly. "But Debbie could come in . . ."

"Then let's go somewhere else," he said in a strained voice, even as he brushed aside her hair and bent down to kiss her neck.

Unspoken were the words: *your room.*

She could barely think, so distracted and aroused and trembling was she. But there was something she couldn't let herself forget. "Wait, wait, we can't do this. I have a conference call with my store managers in a half hour. And then more work on what the call was about."

He straightened up, letting his hands briefly glide through her hair before stepping around the couch. "I hate when you're logical."

She rose to her feet, surprised to feel shaky, to know that Josh could do that to her.

"You know," he continued, "you push me away a lot, considering you're the one who propositioned me."

"And you turned me down," she reminded him. "You were the sane one. Now go back to work!"

He heaved a sigh. "All right, all right. I was distracted by the thought of you, and I just had to see you."

She felt a flush of warmth at his flattery. "That's very sweet."

He took her face in his hands, and said in low voice, "I don't want to be sweet."

He kissed her once more, hard and deep, leaving her reeling and confused as he let her go.

Chapter Eight

After dinner, Josh took a break from work and met up with the guys for Robbers' Roost at Tony's Tavern. That night, it was only Nate, Adam, Chris and Will Sweet.

"Where are Dom and Daniel?" Josh asked, as he pulled up a chair at the table in Tony's back room, where poker chips were piled in the center. He took a sip of beer and reached for a handful of nuts.

Adam said, "I saw Dom at the grocery store. He was heading down to Denver for a sales meeting."

"Daniel is . . ." Chris began. He exchanged a look with his brother. "I'm not sure what he's doing. He said he was busy, and I didn't press."

Will chewed and swallowed a mouthful of nuts. "Since he graduated college, he seems . . . I don't know, different."

"Isn't college supposed to help you figure things out?" Chris asked doubtfully.

"Maybe he's considering changing his mind about a career," Adam said. "I did."

Nate rolled his eyes. "You left the Marines feeling aimless. It was Brooke who changed your career."

Adam shook his head even as he smiled. "I could have done something else. Happens that I like working with muddy cows."

"Speaking of careers," Will said, eyes narrowed as they focused on Josh, "Nate told us about the website."

Josh gave his brother a look.

Nate's eyes widened with innocence. "It's out there for all the public to see. Why shouldn't your closest friends see you flashing your abs for customers?"

Josh smiled at them all as the hooting and teasing made its way around the table. "I'm not making excuses. Sometimes you have to sacrifice for your art."

"Sacrifice?" Chris echoed, sounding doubtful. "You looked like you were focused on someone in particular."

"Whitney's now his agent," Nate said, leaning back in his chair and eyeing his brother with amusement. "I can guess who he was focused on."

Josh started shuffling the cards. "A man needs inspiration." He paused, then met Nate's gaze. "Did you show Mom and Dad the website?"

"Nope. Thought you might want to do the honors."

"I do. I told them about it already, but—"

"Seeing it might be a different thing," Nate said with a grin.

Tony came in, wiping his hands on a towel he tossed on a nearby table. "Let's get this game going, men. I've got to pick up my kid from his mom's in a couple hours."

On her way to dinner, Whitney decided to walk past the building she'd been hemming and hawing about.

The sun was already behind the mountains, making her glad she'd worn a cardigan.

Why couldn't she make up her mind and just set a closing date? She'd thought about Henry Birdsong's offer, and he'd even called back and given her some lease information. It had been reasonable although still pricier than buying her own building in Valentine.

Was she putting too much emphasis on the personal, this concern about being "liked"? Or was her attachment to Valentine already more than that?

She rounded the corner from Bessie Street onto Fourth and walked past the Rose Garden, with its arched stone bridge over a pond, where lovers often had their picture taken. She reached the Victorian she was considering buying, turned up the walkway— and came to a stop.

Someone had written crudely on the sidewalk in chalk: "Go back to SF, Whitney Wild."

She hugged herself as if a cold breeze had blown by. That hadn't been there earlier in the day.

A person had to search through a lot of articles online to reach that old tabloid nickname. But someone had despised her enough to do it.

With the keys the real estate agent let her borrow, she went inside and found a bucket, filled it with soap and water, and using a brush, scrubbed away any evidence of disdain. A weary sadness settled over her. Whitney Wild was gone and never coming back, but apparently, her old persona had become ammunition in someone's stupid vendetta.

She put the supplies away, locked up, and walked along Fourth until she reached Main. She headed toward town hall and the view of the mountains, no longer even certain she was hungry but not ready to return to The Adelaide.

When she passed Sugar and Spice, she couldn't help but look in the cheery plate-glass windows, with displays that day of various cookies all tumbled against one another and down several steps like a delicious waterfall. She heard her name called, muffled, and looked up to see Emily waving as she rushed to the door.

Opening it, Emily grinned, and said, "Did you hear us talking about you and magically show up?"

Whitney stiffened. Had word of the graffiti spread around town? She didn't even have to answer, as Emily dragged her inside, where the store was divided into glass display cases on the left, little tables and chairs in a "coffee corner" to the right, and a cooler in the back that lured cheesecake lovers. There was a small vase of fresh wildflowers at every table—probably courtesy of Monica—and the woman herself was sitting at one table beside Brooke, both grinning at Whitney. They looked too happy for it to be about the graffiti, she realized with relief.

Without another word, they pushed a newspaper across the table at her, and she slowly sank down onto a chair. On the second page of the *Valentine Gazette,* the photo of Josh smoldering all his sex appeal out toward the viewer was front and center, along with an article.

Emily pulled up a chair but said nothing as Whitney scanned the article. It was about Josh's dual careers as cowboy and leather craftsman, and how his work was now being featured in an exclusive Aspen boutique. There were no actual quotes from Josh, so he probably hadn't been interviewed. So who took the initiative and went to the paper?

At last, Whitney sat back and, feeling better about the world, said, "Damn, I'm a good agent."

Brooke groaned. "You mean my brother takes good photos."

"He wouldn't even have done it if I hadn't persuaded him."

"And how did you persuade him?" Monica asked, leaning toward her. "Our Josh isn't a guy who does things he doesn't want to do."

"I agreed to go out on a date if he'd pose."

"Oh well, was that all?" Brooke said, shaking her head.

"I think it's sweet." Emily brought over a coffee-pot and held it up inquiringly.

Whitney nodded for a cup. "Thanks."

"Cookie, brownie?"

"Haven't had dinner yet, so I'll hold off."

"My motto is: Life is short—eat dessert first," Brooke said, pointing to her pastry.

Whitney smiled. "So will your brother mind being famous?"

"If you call the *Valentine Gazette* famous," Brooke said, chuckling.

"Famous around here then. He's probably going to get teased."

"He's pretty laid-back about that kind of stuff. Comes from being mercilessly teased by an older brother and sister."

Whitney thought of her older brother, so remote and cool toward her, even when they were children. Not that they'd had better examples from their parents. She was an afterthought to her brother, and since they went to different boarding schools, they only saw each other on holiday. Five years' difference in age had seemed insurmountable. She remembered one Christmas where she'd gotten a board game as a present, and hounded him the entire time to play. He never had, though at last she'd gotten a tournament going with the staff. Josh and Nate were around the same age difference, with Brooke in between, and she'd never seen siblings so close.

"Well, it'll all be worth it," Whitney said, "if it sells more shoulder bags."

"And you notice, my store was mentioned, too," Monica said happily. "I had an upsurge in purchases this afternoon, before I had any idea about the article. The big seller? Frames. People love those."

"Your window display captures the customer and doesn't let go," Emily said.

Monica grinned at her.

"Whoever was behind this thought of everything." Whitney frowned as she took another sip of coffee. Why was she mildly uneasy about this? Perhaps Josh knew all about it—or had gone along with Geneva's new request for promotion. But even Geneva wasn't quoted in the article. "You know, that boutique did some promotion for me, albeit accidentally."

"What do you mean?" Brooke asked.

All three women looked at her expectantly, and Whitney found herself telling them about Henry Birdsong's offer.

"You're not considering it!" Brooke said with disbelief. "People really fought to bring Leather and Lace here."

Emily put a hand on Brooke's arm. "And others fought against it. I can understand why Whitney might not feel exactly welcome."

Whitney smiled her thanks at Emily. "I'm only considering it to be objective, and trust me, I felt very important that a bra-tree protest could break out in support of me."

The mood eased as they all chuckled.

"I'm going over the construction bids right now and negotiating."

"Is Sweet Construction bidding?" Emily asked. "My uncles are great guys, very conscientious."

"You don't have to persuade me. They're in the lead right now."

Whitney had been feeling hemmed in by Valentine and some people's narrow-mindedness, their high-school cliques, but sitting there with Emily, Brooke, and Monica was nice. They made her feel at ease in a way her party-girlfriends never had. And she hadn't had time to make many truly close friends these last few years of hard work.

"You know, Whitney," Brooke began contemplatively, "you could change people's minds about your store. Consider putting up a display poster at the community center, like I'm about to do for my riding school. I want to expand beyond word of mouth. I've got a copy here—would you take a look at it?"

They all bent their heads over the poster, and Whitney gave some suggestions for how to make it pop in the eyes of someone browsing lots of displays.

As they talked, several customers came in, and Emily waited on them, adorable in her ASK US WHY WE'RE SUGAR AND SPICE apron. She brought out several cardboard boxes from the kitchen and one from the cheesecake cooler.

When at last she sat back down, Whitney gave her an amazed look. "How do you do all this by yourself?"

"Normally, my part-time help is here, but Mrs. Ludlow has a cold, so I sent her home."

"I mean the baking. No luck interviewing chefs?"

Emily told them all about an arrogant pastry chef who thought himself so much better than her. "I'll find someone," she insisted, trying to be cheerful. And then she truly did relax as she said, "I'm learning some really neat recipes, spending time with my new grandma. After I was a toddler, I never had grandparents."

"That's Mrs. Sweet, the owner of Sweetheart Inn?" Whitney asked.

Emily nodded. "She has incredible recipes, and she's so gracious about sharing them."

Brooke winced. "I'm glad she's sharing with you because I grew up hearing a lot of gossip otherwise."

Emily frowned. "What do you mean?"

"It's nothing," Monica reassured her. "You just don't know the history. Mrs. Thalberg—frankly all the widows—never did get along with Mrs. Sweet."

"Surely everyone's mellowed after all these years," Whitney said.

"Then you don't know the widows," Brooke answered ruefully. "Sorry, Emily, but apparently Mrs. Sweet used to come off as if she thought she was better than others, owning the hotel, her mom a silent-film star."

"She doesn't come across that way at all," Emily insisted.

Whitney widened her eyes. "How did a silent-film star get to Valentine Valley?"

Emily put up her hand like an eager schoolgirl. "I know this! Grandma told me the story, and I thought it was so romantic. Her mom was staying in the beautiful old hotel in Glenwood Springs, on her way from LA to New York. My great-grandfather was in town selling cattle at auction, and since he'd just gotten paid, he was treating his ranch hands to a drink at the hotel bar. She walked past, their eyes met, and they fell instantly in love. She gave up everything for him."

"The days of silent films were pretty much over by then," Brooke pointed out.

Whitney and Monica frowned at her.

"But it's a great story!" Brooke hastened to say.

"They built themselves a beautiful house in town," Emily continued, "and that became the inn you see today."

"The family didn't want to stay in it themselves?" Whitney asked.

"Times got tough before ski resorts brought people here after World War II," Monica said. "It was hard to keep both a ranch house and one in town going. Trust me, they're doing fine now, with a beautiful new home on the ranch. You should check out our museum for more of the history."

"Josh mentioned it to me," Whitney said, "since I like museums. But he said it won't be our blackmail date."

"I should hope not," Brooke said indignantly.

"What's wrong with a museum?" Emily demanded.

Whitney smiled, knowing both she and Emily had

grown up in San Francisco. Well, compared to Emily, Whitney *hadn't* grown up there after she started boarding school, but still . . .

"So Mrs. Sweet and the widows just rub each other the wrong way?" Whitney asked. "Hard to believe those sweet little old ladies have a problem with anyone."

"Oh, there's never been open warfare," Brooke said.

"That you know of," Monica interjected.

Brooke shrugged. "But they never played bridge together or anything. The ladies tended to be on opposite sides of school-board issues, according to my mom. And my grandma and Mrs. Palmer aren't exactly the garden-party types. I do hear that Mrs. Ludlow occasionally crosses to the dark side, but no one could be upset with her about anything."

Emily folded her arms beneath her chest and frowned at Brooke. "The dark side? So you consider me part of that, too?"

Brooke put up both hands. "It was a joke!" She glanced down at the table, focusing on the newspaper as if to distract Emily. "Anyone know if Josh has seen this?"

"He didn't call me about it," Whitney said.

"My brother reads most of his news online. But *this* news he should get in person. And I happen to know just where he and the other guys are. And you can eat dinner, Whitney."

"I'm in."

Emily looked at her watch. "And it's seven, perfect timing. Let me put up the CLOSED sign, and I'll join you."

Chapter Nine

By the time Josh grew bored with poker—Nate said it was only because he was losing—Tony's back room was beginning to fill up. It was a Friday night, of course, but to his surprise, there seemed to be a lot more women than normal.

Not that he, or any of his buddies, were complaining. He knew some of the women, of course, like Julie Jacoby, the redheaded summer hostess at the Halftime Sports Bar, and Shannon Russell, a paralegal who could really dance. Of the rest, some were strangers, a rarity at Tony's, which was too close to the highway to attract tourists. He managed to grab the pool table before any of the newcomers did, and was chalking his cue when Adam, his opponent, came up to him, and said, "Are we getting some unusual stares here?"

Surprised, Josh glanced around. Whenever he met someone's gaze, they smiled and waved, not all that unusual. "I don't think so. It's a Friday night, and we're single guys."

"Speak for yourself."

"Well, how would anyone know, where you're concerned?"

Adam rolled his eyes, said, "Everyone knows," and walked away to put money in the coin slot.

Josh grinned. "True, my sister can't exactly keep that sort of thing secret."

They racked the balls, and when Josh bent over to line up his shot, he heard this resounding cheer. Straightening, he glanced at Adam, who looked both disbelieving and amused at the same time, then behind him, to his "audience." The women, instead of looking embarrassed or laughing over their joke, were all openly displaying . . . interest. Toying with their hair, for God's sake, batting their eyelashes like Southern belles. Some of them were women he'd spent his life talking to in the grocery store, ordering a drink from at a bar—and was that his dentist, older than him by ten or fifteen years, displaying her slow, naughty grin?

Josh faced his buddies and spread his arms in confusion. Nate spread his hands back with a shrug.

All right, he was being paranoid—or something. People must have just started drinking early. He leaned back over the table. An even louder cheer erupted, followed by a hoot or two. Before he could decide what to do, even more women crowded into the back room, but only one of them did he wish would cheer at his butt.

Whitney, Monica, Emily, and Brooke paused as they came through the doorway. Josh's eyes were drawn to Whitney's tight white jeans and the bright pink sleeveless top with ruffles spilling down between her breasts, a blue sweater draped over one arm. She looked as delicious as a pastry. Monica, who stared around the room in surprise, checked her watch like she'd gotten the time wrong.

"Is there a party we don't know about?" Brooke called, as Adam approached her.

He swung her into his arms for a quick kiss, then, keeping his arm around her, turned so that Josh could hear him. "We're clueless. All we know is that Josh is popular tonight."

Josh looked over his shoulder, and someone actually called, "Oh, Josh, let me buy you a drink!"

"Now Mrs. Chong, aren't you still on the school board with my mom?" he asked patiently.

Many of the women laughed, but Mrs. Chong put her hands on her wide hips. "Don't go spoiling my Girls' Night Out, Josh Thalberg."

He shot Whitney a bemused look, and to his surprise, she laid the newspaper on the pool table, open to the second page. And there he was, sitting around like he had nothing better to do than keep his shirt unbuttoned while he ogled a camera. He *did* look pretty damned ridiculous—except Whitney liked it, he reminded himself.

"Geneva put an ad in the paper?" he asked.

"Nope, it's a whole article about the 'cowboy artist.'" She looked past him at the women, biting her lip.

He knew she was trying not to laugh, and he didn't blame her.

"Guess your fans read the article and hunted you down." Her last few words wavered, and she broke into a laugh at the end.

The Sweet brothers were right behind her, and even his own brother joined in. Will grabbed the newspaper, and all his buddies crowded around to read, but Josh found himself watching Whitney in appreciation, the way her gray eyes shone with happiness, the deep dimple to the right of her mouth that made her look young and carefree—when he was beginning to suspect she had more on her mind than Leather and Lace.

"I think I can get some action from this," Will said, looking inspired even as he eyed the array of women.

Brooke rolled her eyes at Josh. "So now you're a celebrity?"

"What do you think, big sister? Should I unbutton a few buttons?"

He didn't think he was talking loudly, but a few more whoops of excitement erupted from behind him, and he started to chuckle himself.

"Ew." Brooke turned to Adam. "Hey, Marine, buy me a drink."

They walked off together, arm in arm. Nate pulled Emily onto his lap and whispered something in her ear that made her blush and giggle. Monica faced down Will and challenged him to a game of pool, as if Josh wouldn't dare bend over the table again.

Maybe that wasn't such a good idea, anyway.

"You can buy me a drink," Whitney said. "Might quiet some of your fans."

"But this isn't our big date," Josh warned her.

"No? Hanging out with you and your"—she dropped her voice—"*groupies* might be the thrill of a lifetime."

Over the next hour, he ignored his "groupies" and watched cool, elegant Whitney begin to unwind amidst all of his friends. She laughed at Chris's dry sense of humor, let Will tease her about being the object of Josh's lust in the newspaper photo, discussed the progress of the latest home Adam was renovating for a vet, and was even persuaded to dance with Brooke and the other girls before Josh could get around to asking her.

But he didn't mind, leaning back in his chair and watching as she moved her hips and swayed to the music, occasionally catching the beat with a bump that set his heart thumping. Those white jeans practically glowed in the low light. He politely turned down several offers to dance because he couldn't stop looking at Whitney. How would that be fair to another woman?

Her dark hair swayed about her shoulders, and the layers brushed her cheeks and chin. He was uncomfortably aroused but could hardly adjust himself in front of everybody. She glanced at him once, paused, then returned her gaze to him again and again. He was starting to feel like they were the only two people in the room, focused on each other, feeling the heat and power of passion.

Had he ever fallen for someone so hard and so fast?

When he couldn't take it anymore, he got up and approached her just as a slower dance started, and as if she'd been waiting, she turned into his arms. He saw the knowing looks as his friends stepped away, but he didn't care. He and Whitney swayed against each other, his one hand low on her back, the other holding hers. She wasn't shy about letting her breasts brush his chest. He responded by occasionally sliding his thigh between hers, saw her intake of breath, and the needy way she met his eyes.

"Why, cowboy," she murmured in a husky voice, "you seem pretty eager. Are you trying to wrangle an invitation to my bed?"

"Nope." He rested the side of his jaw against her hair so she couldn't see in his eyes how desperately he wished the opposite. "I think courtin' a woman is half the fun."

"So I'm being courted," she mused. They moved in a slow circle for a minute before she continued. "You know that's not necessary. I'm a big girl from the big city. I've always been very casual with the men I dated."

He didn't like being equated with such "casual" men, but he understood she'd been raised differently than he had. "What does that mean?" he asked, not bothering to hide his curiosity.

Her shoulders lifted in a little shrug. "I've never had someone long term. The men I've been with are just like me—we know it's temporary, dinner after work, the occasional movie or play, then sex. No big deal."

He lifted his head to look down at her. "No big deal?"

"Not at all. We're adults who know what we want, and a little fun is always good for everyone—as long as we know the score."

She was saying things he should be glad to hear—but he wasn't. He didn't plan on being "no big deal" to Whitney Winslow. Not that he looked down on the type of relationship she was talking about; he'd had plenty of those himself, just two people having fun. But this time, he wanted more than fun.

"Have you ever had a long-term girlfriend?" she asked, a smile turning up her lips as she gazed up at him.

He moved her easily through the crowded little dance floor. "In high school. Jill and I lasted two

years. I used to sneak out to meet her, and we'd ride
for hours."

She arched an eyebrow.

"Our horses," he insisted.

She grinned. "Thanks for the explanation."

"We did other things, too. Then she went off to
college, and swore she'd still be my girlfriend, but I
wasn't surprised that we drifted apart."

"Were you hurt? Were you planning marriage?"

"She was honest with me." The music transitioned
into another slow song, and Josh ignored the many
women who looked as if they were considering cutting in.

"But there's something more," Whitney said.

"I'm told I'm not all that transparent," he answered, mildly surprised.

"So tell me. I've just told you I've had more than a
few partners. That's pretty revealing. You can't hold
back."

"It's nothing that mattered in the end. We had
a scare our senior year when Jill suspected she was
pregnant." He heard her inhalation, but she said
nothing. "She lost the baby before we even had to
confess the truth to anyone."

"I'm sorry," she murmured.

"Sorry? Most people would say we were lucky. We
learned a lesson and were far more vigilant after that."

"I guess I'm sorry because I know how you feel
about family, and I know you probably planned to
marry her, and probably would *still* have married
her, pregnancy or not, if she hadn't found someone
else in college."

The memory was momentarily painful, in the way
of old wounds long since healed, but still surprisingly

able to affect you. Whitney read him too well, and he didn't take that as a bad sign. He dipped her a little, making her clutch his arms with a gasp. "I don't want you thinking you always know what's coming. You're way too sure of yourself."

"Any women since then?" she continued.

It was his turn to shrug. "I haven't lacked for dates, but no one special. What about you?"

"The same. I don't think men thought of me as the marriage type."

"You mean you didn't give them that impression?"

She tipped her head back to meet his gaze. "I've made no secret of how focused I've been on work."

"No secret with me, either. But I must be more stubborn than most."

"You have me at a disadvantage. I'm not in my element and, therefore, in a weakened state."

He chuckled. "Not possible. But I do agree you're not in your element. I could have sworn I saw chalk on the sleeve of your sweater."

He saw the happiness leach right out of her expression, and he found himself pulling her a little closer.

"What happened?" he asked.

Her hesitation spoke volumes, as if she debated revealing whatever secret was hurting her. He touched his lips to her forehead.

"I don't like to see you unhappy," he murmured.

She sighed. "It was not very important, and after last winter, I guess I'm used to it."

"Used to what? Don't make me pull every detail from you."

Her smile was as faint as a ghost, and just as sad. "Someone wrote in chalk in front of the building, telling me to go back home."

"Graffiti?" he asked in disbelief? "Someone hiding in anonymity?"

"You can't be surprised."

He frowned. "But I am. You know Sylvester and his friends—right up front about their disagreement with your store."

"Disagreement?" she echoed, but her amusement seemed forced.

"Opposition, whatever you want to call it. But childishly scrawling angry words on your sidewalk? That just doesn't make sense."

"I'm not denying that. But it happened. I cleaned it up, but it's making me wonder whether even the town council's support can change the feelings of some people in Valentine. I'm just not sure I'll have enough customers if I stay here."

"But in Aspen, you think it might be different," he finished for her, knowing she had even more reason to consider Birdsong's offer.

She gave him a brief hug as the dance ended, and stepped back. "Thanks for listening. I didn't tell anyone else about the graffiti, and I'd appreciate it if you wouldn't either."

"You know I won't."

"Thanks." She paused, regarding all their friends with a faintly pained look. "I should get going."

"It's still early—and a Friday night."

She looked at him speculatively. "Why don't you drive me home?"

As she sat quietly in the dark pickup, Whitney considered all she'd confided in Josh—not just the graffiti incident, but her history with men. And he'd told her about his one meaningful relationship, too. Communication between them was far too easy, leading her to think how good they could be together in more physical ways. Even their dance at Tony's Tavern had felt as erotic as one could be when fully dressed.

And for a man whose private life was about to be invaded—in a way she understood far too well—he was surprisingly nonchalant, as if nothing fazed him. That kind of demeanor was far too appealing to someone like her, used to Type A men who had trouble relaxing, except in bed. And it was there, she realized, that she'd been able to control them.

Was that what she'd been trying to do with Josh from the moment they'd realized their chemistry? She'd made a pass at him, and he turned it back on her, dictating the terms of their relationship. And since then, she'd felt nothing but out of control around him, aroused and needy and frustrated.

By hoping to get him in bed, was she trying to prove something to herself? What did that say about her? His offer of a courtship was sounding more and more appealing.

He pulled up in front of the B&B and studied her by the faint glow of the dashboard lights. "Why are you smiling? I haven't done much to ease your mood."

"A good dance with a cowboy will do that to a woman."

They stared at each other, an electric silence sizzling around them. Whitney wasn't used to waiting when she wanted a man; it was strangely arousing.

"I guess I better go," she murmured, reaching for the door handle.

He opened up his door. "I'll walk you in."

"That's not necessary . . ." But she didn't sound very convincing.

After slamming his door shut, he was already rounding the hood of the pickup; she wouldn't crush his male pride by opening her own door. Instead, she smiled and took his hand as if she were too delicate to alight to the curb unassisted.

He continued to hold her hand even as he opened the gate in front of The Adelaide, then remained at her side up the path. The foliage rose higher than their heads, and the scent of roses was intoxicating and romantic.

At the porch, he came to a stop, and since she was already up a few steps, she met him eye to eye. "I thought you were escorting me in."

He shook his head, and said huskily, "I don't trust myself."

With a moan, she draped her arms around his neck and kissed him, long and openmouthed, until they were both breathing hard. "Are you sure you don't want to come in?" she whispered against his mouth.

Taking her waist in his hands, he held her for a moment, then set her away. "Nope. Work in the morning. Animals never take a day off, so we can't either. Good night."

Aching, she watched him walk away, then silently cursed whatever morals were rising between them.

But at least he'd taken her mind off her troubles for a little while . . .

Chapter Ten

Josh hit the steering wheel hard with his hand when he got back in the pickup, but he didn't go to Whitney. The invitation to join her had been far too appealing, and he was going to regret it in the depths of the night when he couldn't sleep.

But there was no chance to be alone when he got back to his loft. As he pulled into the yard next to the barn, his Grandma's old station wagon was prominently displayed, angled haphazardly to take up two parking spots. It was late for the widows to be out, wasn't it? He glanced at the house, only to see the front door open and his dad step out.

"Josh, come on in, we've been waitin' for you."

Curious, he waved and sauntered up the stairs.

Inside the spacious living room, all three widows were sitting in the furniture grouped in front of the big stone fireplace. His mom was just bringing out a platter of cheese and crackers, and Josh made a beeline for her.

"Uh-uh-uh," she said, holding back the food. "You've been a bad boy."

"I can't believe I had to hear about it at Wine Country!" Grandma Thalberg complained.

"Hear about what?" Josh asked.

And then he saw the *Valentine Gazette* spread over the coffee table and his picture staring out at him.

He winced. "I just found out about the article myself."

"And the website?" Mrs. Palmer reminded him, shaking her head. "That came up when I Googled your name."

"I told you about the photos," Josh said with exasperation, reaching past his mom's shoulder for the cheese platter.

Sandy held it out to him. "That's true enough."

He took it from her and set it down on the coffee table, pushing aside the newspaper.

"If I'd have known," Grandma Thalberg began, gesturing to the newspaper, "I could have told my poker club!"

Josh folded it up and put it out of the way. "It's no big deal. No idea how it got in the paper, though."

"I'm not surprised," Mrs. Ludlow said quietly. "A photo like that will cause talk."

He blinked at her. "Excuse me, ma'am?"

"You're quite handsome, and you know it," she said, almost looking down her nose at him.

"You're gonna make me blush, Mrs. Ludlow."

She rolled her eyes and helped herself to a slice of cheddar. "My oldest granddaughter always said, if she weren't married—"

"She's ten years older!" Mrs. Palmer said with exasperation.

Josh thought of Kim Ludlow—now Avicolli—in surprise. He'd had a crush on her when he was a kid, and she was a hot, high-school cheerleader.

"The article will probably sell those shoulder bags of yours," Doug said, sitting down on the raised stone hearth so he could be near the food.

"Hope so. No choice but to put up with all the fuss."

"Fuss?" Sandy echoed, watching him closely.

He shrugged and stuffed a cracker in his mouth. No one said anything until he was done, so he was forced to explain. "Some of the ladies in town came out to watch me play pool. Bored, I guess."

Grandma Thalberg and Mrs. Palmer glanced at each other and started to chuckle.

"It'll die down," he insisted.

They only laughed harder.

Josh worked hard all weekend. When he wasn't dealing with ranch chores, he closeted himself in his workshop and focused on the many projects he'd promised to three—no four different stores, if you counted Leather and Lace. At last he was able to put to paper all the designs that had been running around his head for the collars Whitney wanted. He called her up and told he'd bring them to her when he was done, and she told him to take his time.

As if she didn't want to see him, he thought, amused.

His amusement didn't last through the beginning of the workweek, when the ranch started getting phone calls for him from a couple national reporters. His dad took messages, and Josh swore he'd get around to calling back . . . one of these days. It must have been a slow news week because he couldn't figure out why anybody would be interested in a story about a leather craftsman in a small Colorado mountain town.

By Tuesday lunch, his mom had a newspaper spread across the table when he arrived.

"That article again?" Josh said, barely pausing to glance as he went to the sink to wash up.

"But it's not the *Valentine Gazette*." Sandy trailed him across the kitchen, limping with her cane. "I had to buy it at the Open Book, where they get several national papers. Now we know why reporters have been calling you. The article was picked up in LA."

He frowned at her. "How?"

"It went to the *Aspen Times* first, and now it's spreading." She smiled. "Josh, you're becoming quite famous."

He rolled his eyes as he washed his hands. "It's no big deal. It'll die down soon."

"You keep saying that," Doug said, setting a stack of paper in front of him. "More messages for you."

"I don't have time to call all of them back," Josh said in disbelief. "I mean, it was a one-time thing. No one'll care in a day or two."

"But it could be great for your work," Sandy pointed out.

Josh stared at the messages and felt the first clench of pressure in his gut. He already had far too much to do, and now he was imposing on his family even more.

His mom touched his arm and lowered her voice, as Nate, Adam, and Brooke came through the back door. "Let things happen as they will, Josh. Nothing is so important you should feel stress over it."

"I wasn't—until now. But you're right. Everyone knows I work at my own pace."

"And no one's asking more of you," she insisted.

Josh looked around at his family and friends, and wondered if perhaps they should.

"There's someone here to see you, Josh," Brooke said, smirking. "And don't look too excited—it's not Whitney. I left him in the office."

He found a rangy, young man carrying a camera bag and his press credentials from the *Post*.

"I'm Brandon Vogt. You didn't call me back," he said, reaching to shake Josh's hand, "so I thought I'd come on over."

"From Denver?" Josh said wryly.

Brandon shrugged. "It's my job. Seems our readers are sending e-mails and calling, wanting more information about you. I'm sure a reporter will call for more background stuff."

"There's really nothing more to tell," Josh said, baffled.

"Then let's start with some more pictures. You don't have anything to hide, right, if you're just a regular old cowboy?"

Josh remembered his mother's calm words about ignoring the stress. What would it matter, after all? "I'll be working in the barn. If you want to take some pictures, it's up to you. As long as you promise to leave after that."

Brandon grinned. "It's a deal."

Josh soon found himself having his picture taken as he cleaned out the hoofs of his sorrel, Bandit, and at last he was persuaded to ride around the corral.

When the photographer had gone, Josh decided it was time to have a talk with his "agent" about this newfound fame. He stopped in his workshop to pick up the folder of sketches he'd prepared and headed into Valentine.

He found Whitney at the building she was considering, architectural drawings spread out on a folding six-foot table. She looked up from her perusal when he knocked on the front door, and her wide smile did things to the inside of him that he better not think about during the workday.

She opened the door, gesturing for him to come inside, and he couldn't help the second look he took at her, in her skinny black pants and sandals, and the sleeveless print blouse.

"Damn, you look good," he said. "Is this corporate wear in the big city?"

"Hardly," she said, smiling. "But I can get away with it in Valentine Valley."

He walked to the table and looked at the drawings. "Still making decisions?"

"Decision's made. I just talked to Howie Deering, and he's getting the lawyers together for a closing in the next few days."

He grinned his approval but had to ask, "What changed your mind? I thought Henry Birdsong had almost persuaded you, helped along by the graffiti."

She shrugged as she came to stand beside him and looked down at the drawings herself. "I like Valentine, including most of the people I've met—not just you," she pointed out dryly.

"I'm very likable."

With a roll of her eyes, she continued, "It's a nice place to come visit a few times a year. Aspen's wonderful, too, of course, but it's . . . different. I think Leather and Lace will be more appreciated here, where it'll stand out."

"For the good reasons, of course."

"Of course. Women here would like to feel just as pretty as they already do in Aspen."

"No lack of confidence there."

"And I decided I'm not going to let some coward with a piece of chalk drive me away." She gestured to the folder. "What's that in your hand?"

"The sketches you've been wanting."

"Wonderful!" She reached for them eagerly.

He held them out of her reach. "But first, I need to talk to my agent."

"About what?" she asked, studying him with surprise.

"Reporters. I'm getting phone calls at the ranch, and a photographer even showed up today. I let him take a couple photos, but this can't keep happening."

"*National* reporters?" she clarified.

"The article's been picked up by several papers, and now I seem to be famous."

She covered her mouth and looked away.

"I don't blame you for laughing," he said, shaking his head. "I still think it's ridiculous, but apparently, it's not going away. Can you stop it?"

"I don't think so. And I know from experience, the more reclusive you try to be, the worse it will get. Letting that guy take a couple photos was probably a good idea."

"Unless more photographers show up."

"Well there is that . . ."

"And my brother took another message for me from a *modeling* agency." Josh grinned. "I'm never going to hear the end of *that* one."

Her gaze roamed down his chest. "I can't say I blame them . . . Are you interested?"

He snorted a laugh and enjoyed her relaxed, easy expression. Something had changed for her in the night—he liked to see her all fiery and optimistic again.

"You know I can't really put a stop to this," she said. "Enjoy your brief moment of fame and concentrate on how it'll highlight your work. You can even tell your grandchildren about it someday."

Rolling his eyes, he said, "I think it's highlighting me rather than my work. We'd better go on our date soon, so people don't think I'm a free agent."

"Hey, we danced a long time at Tony's. That was a date."

"No, you barged in on a guys' night out."

"Barged in?" she echoed, hand innocently pressed to her chest. "We just thought you'd want to know about the article. It was your sister who tracked you down."

"Can't be surprised." He opened the folder and spread out his drawings. "So what do you think about these?"

They spent a half hour going over his work, and she only had a few suggestions and no complaints. He liked seeing how excited she was at his designs, and knew she'd find the best way to sell the collar necklaces. In fact, he kept getting distracted picturing something of his around her neck, and he felt positively possessive.

As he was putting away the drawings, Whitney said, "Remember, every time a reporter bothers you, it could lead to even more sales."

"And more work for me?" he said wryly.

"Or more value to your work because it's rare and exclusive. You're an artist. No one says you have to 'churn' things out. As for being in the spotlight, trust me, people will forget about you soon enough, so don't worry about it."

"You sound like you've had some experience."

She shrugged. "When you grow up wealthy, there are always people fascinated with how you live because it might be so different than their own lives. Or it takes them away. I don't know."

He wanted to ask more, but just then, someone knocked at the door. Whitney opened it for Gary and Allen Sweet, owners of Sweet Construction. They were Emily's uncles, a little younger than her dad, Joe, and both had variations on the family's fair hair, now fading toward white.

After exchanging hearty handshakes, Josh excused himself and left them to their business. He caught Whitney's eye as he started to close the door, and they exchanged slow, knowing smiles.

Damn, she made him feel good.

And curious, he realized. How much had she really been in the national spotlight?

When he got back to the ranch, he took two stairs at a time up to his loft and sat down at his laptop. Feeling a bit like he was invading her privacy—but how private was any information he could find online?—he searched her name, and after a few recent, business-oriented or philanthropic photos, he clicked on the "next" button, and his jaw dropped.

She was so young in the earlier photos, yet so aware of her appeal, with her sly smiles at the camera. He saw shots of her wearing a tiny bikini on Mediterranean beaches, and even a grainy one of her sunbathing topless on the deck of a luxurious yacht. Damn, the zoom button only made the photo quality worse.

She was wrapped in fur during an Aspen winter, laden with shopping bags on New York's Park Avenue. And then there were the evening shots entering exclusive clubs and parties, where her dresses clung to her, or revealed a thigh with a long, enticing slit in the fabric. He saw her "casual" men, some older, all handsome and privileged. The photos of her leaving clubs weren't always so pretty—glazed eyes, an occasional strap off her shoulder, and once someone carrying her to a waiting car. She'd been young and foolish—hell, who *hadn't* gotten drunk in college? But for most of the world, their shame didn't live on the Internet forever.

And then he saw the photo of her getting out of a limousine, long legs parted—and the flash of lacy underwear. He almost stopped breathing at the sheer sexiness of that unguarded moment. He skimmed the articles associated with that photo, then the underwear line named after her because of it. Was that the beginning of Leather and Lace? Had she taken her notoriety and turned it into something positive, even as she straightened out her life?

He couldn't help but admire her ambition and achievements, even as he saw another photo of her, early in her teenage years, accompanying her parents through an airport. She could barely keep up, and her parents didn't even look over their shoulders to see where she was. Her unhappiness was palpable, and he experienced a moment of gratitude for all the good things in his life. Their childhoods couldn't have been more different.

But money certainly didn't buy happiness. And neither did fame. But it had made her the woman she was.

And now it was his turn to find out what fame did to him.

Not that he was all that worried.

After spending Wednesday at the new Leather and Lace, watching the Sweet brothers begin to work and asking questions, Whitney knew it was time to give the men their space. They hoped they'd have the first floor remodeled within a month, but there was lots of special work involved preserving the historic touches. The funeral home had put a stained-glass window above regular windows in the dining room, and an artist had to be hired to repair the deteriorating lead. Only then would the construction company start on the second floor, which would have offices and a small apartment for when she visited Valentine.

On Thursday morning, she called Josh and asked if he'd like to go to the museum with her.

"This isn't our big date," he'd insisted.

She'd just laughed.

They met for lunch at the Halftime Sports Bar, then walked up to the museum across First Street from the town hall. For two hours, they explored the silver-mining history of the Colorado Rockies, and Valentine Valley's part in keeping the miners entertained and fed. The old photographs were fascinating, and Josh was eager to show her one of his great-great-grandfather, who'd bought the family ranch in the 1880s and begun their little empire.

"Now that wasn't so bad," Whitney said, as they emerged back into the sunlight at midafternoon. "You seem pretty proud of your heritage."

"I'm sure you can't compare it to San Francisco museums," he said, taking her hand.

"No need to compare, is there? We can enjoy all kinds."

He smiled down at her, and she smiled back, caught up once again in the magic of his charisma, in the way he made her feel like no other woman mattered.

"Yoo-hoo, Josh!"

Surprised, they both turned around at the sound of a woman's voice. Their hands slipped apart, and at the sight of a woman rushing across the street, arm raised in greeting, Whitney almost clasped his hand again. Was she actually feeling territorial, something no other man had ever made her feel?

"Hey, Sally," Josh said, in that easy way he had of making a woman feel like he "got" you. He turned to Whitney. "Whitney Winslow, this is Sally Gillroy, a clerk at the town hall."

Sally was a broad-shouldered woman with short hair who wore pressed pants and a no-nonsense vest over a button-down shirt. She smiled absently at Whitney, even as her gaze focused on Josh.

"Hey, Josh," she said.

Whitney wasn't certain if her jog across the street had made the fortysomething woman breathless, but she suspected not, what with the light in her eyes when she looked at Josh.

"What can I do for you?" he asked.

"I saw all the photos of you in the paper," Sally said, even as her cheeks reddened. "I'm so proud that a resident of Valentine Valley is having such international success."

"I don't know about international . . ." Josh said with doubt, giving Whitney a glance.

She just blinked at him, certain he didn't need any help where women were concerned.

"My—my mom collects autographs," Sally said, "and she'd love it if I gave her yours, right on the newspaper article. Would you mind?"

"Uh . . . not at all," Josh said.

Grinning, Sally held out the newspaper she'd kept folded under her arm, and a pen as well. He signed his name and handed it back.

"Thanks a lot," Sally said. "I know my mom will be thrilled. Nice meeting you, Whitney." And she started to jog back across the street.

Both Whitney and Josh saw the oncoming car and called her name, but she'd already stopped short at the last moment rather than run right into traffic. She disappeared up the steps to the town hall.

Whitney turned to stare at Josh and tried to keep a straight face. "Well, that was interesting. An autograph for her . . . mom?"

Josh grimaced, although it was good-natured. "Let's just forget that happened."

"I don't think we can," she said, trying to hide her amusement with earnestness. "Your fame is growing, Josh, and we have to take advantage of it. I'll have to come up with a promotional flyer, and next time this happens, you can hand it out and tell them all about the lingerie at Leather and Lace."

He groaned and shook his head.

"No, no, really, you can talk about the leather necklaces you're designing, and say how lovely they'd look around the throats of the Sally Gillroys of Valentine—"

He put his arm around her neck and pulled her close, then covered her mouth with his other hand.

"You're making me a little queasy. I think I'd rather run and hide than tell my mom's friends about lingerie."

She giggled and ducked out from beneath his arm, walking backward in front of him, both hands raised. "But seriously, Josh, no running and hiding. You know making yourself scarce will only make things worse. Just accept your fleeting popularity and use it to our advantage—says your agent."

He caught up with her, and they resumed their walk side by side down Main Street, where US flags fluttered, and the occasional shopkeeper weeded window boxes filled with flowers.

Josh sighed. "I guess I could mention that I have some of my crafts in Monica's already."

"*Now* you're catching on."

They didn't have long to wait before it happened again, when a dark-haired woman came out of the lobby of the Hotel Colorado. "Hey, Josh!"

Once again, he made the introductions, this time to Carmen Suarez, a manager at the hotel, whose dark eyes were played up with lots of eyeliner.

"Nice to meet you, Whitney," Carmen said, her accent faint. "Josh, you'll never believe this. I just had a woman check in, all the way from Las Vegas, who told me she came deliberately to meet you! Should I put her off?"

"Uh . . ." Josh began, looking bemused.

"Of course not," Whitney interrupted. "Josh, you don't want to make your fans angry. Let's go meet her."

Carmen grinned and started back up the stone stairs into the hotel, while Josh gave Whitney an incredulous look.

"I can't believe you surrendered me like that."

"Hey, I have a store in Las Vegas, remember? Let's tell her all about it."

Twenty minutes later, Whitney was showing her catalogue on her cell phone to four women before the stone fireplace in the lobby, only one of whom was the out-of-town visitor. It had been a long time since she'd been able to represent her own company directly to customers, and she'd forgotten how excited she could get helping average women feel beautiful and sexy. Until now, she'd been used to big cities, or exclusive, wealthy towns like Aspen. Valentine Valley was a different clientele, one she needed to learn to understand if she was to market her products correctly. Understanding these women meant understanding the town itself.

And there was Josh, quiet and calm and smiling, the kind of guy any woman would want to feel sexy for. He didn't put the women down, or act like he had somewhere else to be, even though she knew he was busy.

She tried to tell herself that discovering Valentine's joys and eccentricities wasn't really about Josh. But understanding the town he loved would help her understand him even better.

When they parted at the B&B, she kissed him good-bye and watched him walk down the path through the gardens, broad-shouldered, slim-hipped, so sexy ducking beneath an arbor vine. She was determined to be comfortable in Valentine—comfortable in Josh's world—and who better to help her understand the town than the ladies of the Widows' Boardinghouse?

Chapter Eleven

Every Friday, Debbie Fernandez hosted a formal Afternoon Tea at The Adelaide. After clearing it with the widows Thursday night, Whitney made reservations.

Friday at three, the old station wagon pulled up to the B&B, and Whitney walked down the garden path to accompany the ladies.

"Don't you look lovely!" Mrs. Palmer gushed.

"Thanks." Whitney glanced down at her billowy lavender sundress. "I wasn't sure what to wear—formal or not? I'm glad we all look good together." She didn't make any comment about Mrs. Palmer's rather vivid use of purple-and-orange patterns in her belted dress. The woman had her own style, and it was part of her charm.

"Debbie would make you feel at ease whatever you wore." Mrs. Ludlow used her walker to rise from the car, gently turning down Whitney's gesture of help.

They slowly made their way up the garden path, and when the ladies would have gone inside, Whitney said, "It's such a beautiful day, Debbie is hosting the tea in her garden. Will that be all right?"

They all spoke their agreement at once in chirping voices, so Whitney led the way along the slate stone path until she reached the patio.

Mrs. Thalberg gasped when they all saw the formal table Debbie had laid out. Debbie had included beautiful linens and china that didn't perfectly match but echoed each other in various colorful flower designs. Different tiers of platters showed off finger sandwiches and scones. Whitney didn't think she'd seen anything finer in London, and told Debbie so, making her blush.

"Go ahead and make yourselves comfortable," Debbie said. "We have three more guests, and they should be arriving anytime."

While they waited, Mrs. Thalberg discussed gardening with Debbie, and Mrs. Ludlow showed Whitney pictures of her granddaughters on her iPhone.

Whitney heard Debbie call another "Hello," and saw Mrs. Ludlow's expression both lighten and grow tense in rapid succession.

Frowning, Whitney said, "What's—"

And then she saw Emily, her sister Steph, and another older woman about the widows' ages.

"Oh dear," Mrs. Ludlow said softly.

"Let me guess—Mrs. Sweet," Whitney said, intrigued.

"Eileen Sweet, the matriarch of the family," Mrs. Ludlow murmured. "A dear woman—but rather used to being in charge."

So this was the woman who didn't get along with Mrs. Thalberg and Mrs. Palmer—who Whitney had a hard time imagining could dislike anyone. Mrs. Sweet was thin and elegant in a floral chiffon dress, wearing a perfect little straw hat atop her chignon-styled white hair.

"She's a strong woman," Mrs. Ludlow continued. "Took it upon herself to open the Sweetheart Inn to help support her family at a time when most women didn't do such things. It meant she had to move back to the old family homestead, a log cabin. This was before they were able to build the new ranch house, of course."

Emily finished greeting Debbie, and then her blue-eyed gaze met Whitney's—and widened. She gave the faintest, helpless shrug, and Whitney returned the gesture. After all, there was nothing to do but continue on with the afternoon. Steph was already pointing to the table in surprise, looking adorable in a tank top, short skirt, and flip-flops.

"It's my fault," Mrs. Ludlow said, shaking her head. "I mentioned Debbie's tea to Emily, but never explained that we were actually attending today."

Whitney touched her arm. "Oh, please, there's nothing to apologize for. I've been wanting to meet Emily's grandmother, and what a beautiful day to do so."

Mrs. Ludlow looked beyond her to the other two widows. "If you say so, dear."

Mrs. Thalberg and Mrs. Palmer stood stiffly together for a moment, and then Mrs. Thalberg approached the new arrivals, hand held out to clasp Emily's, Steph's, and then Mrs. Sweet's.

"Emily, dear, how thoughtful of you and your sister to escort Eileen today."

Mrs. Sweet turned to her granddaughters, and said in a too-pleasant voice, "I had no idea this would turn into a garden party."

"Me neither," Emily fairly chirped. "Hi, Whitney!"

"Hi, Emily!" Whitney responded just as cheerfully.

Steph hid a smirk, as if she knew exactly what was going on.

Debbie displayed a moment of uncertainty, looking from one widow to another. "Give me a moment, ladies, I'm sure the hot water must be boiling by now. Please take your seats."

When Debbie had gone inside through the sunroom, Emily brought her grandmother over and introduced her.

Whitney shook the woman's dry, thin hand, knowing its fragility must be deceptive. "Mrs. Sweet, it's wonderful to meet you. Emily has told me the romantic history of your parents, and I found it inspiring."

Behind Mrs. Sweet's back, Mrs. Palmer rolled her eyes, and her eyebrows almost climbed into her blond wig.

"Thank you," Mrs. Sweet said. "My parents were very much in love and set such a fine example of happiness. Their love built my inn, of course."

"It's great you can share it with guests," Whitney said.

"I'm surprised you didn't choose a suite there for your stays in Valentine." Mrs. Sweet took a seat near the head of the table.

"Now don't let Debbie hear you say that, Eileen," Mrs. Thalberg said. "You'll hurt her feelings."

Patiently, Mrs. Sweet answered, "Which is why I chose *now* to mention it, Rosemary."

"Oh, Grandma," Steph said, plopping down in the next seat. "Some people like a cozier place to stay. I really think B&Bs are adorable."

"And this one is very well run," Mrs. Ludlow said,

sitting down across from Mrs. Sweet. "This tea table is so meticulous in detail. I won't want to eat, for fear of disturbing the lovely setting."

Whitney admired Mrs. Ludlow's attempt to steer the conversation, even as she took her own seat in the center, beside Emily. The other two widows sat at the opposite end.

Debbie came out carrying a large china teapot, a creamer, and a sugar bowl on a matching platter.

The women all complimented the set in overlapping voices, and Whitney, exchanging a relieved glance with Emily, was just thinking this might go better than she'd feared.

Debbie handed down a carved box filled with an assortment of tea, and everyone chose their flavors. She poured steaming cups of water and passed those along, too.

Mrs. Sweet took it upon herself to educate Steph in the proper tea etiquette. "My dear, you should never use the cream itself. Save that for the scones. Cream masks the taste of the tea. Instead, use milk."

Whitney saw Mrs. Thalberg and Mrs. Palmer exchange a silent, aggrieved look.

Mrs. Sweet smiled at Debbie. "And you remembered lemon slices rather than wedges."

Debbie blushed. "I've done my research."

When Steph went to lift her teacup with both hands, Mrs. Sweet said, "No, no, you must always grip the handle, but not loop your fingers through. And your pinkie finger isn't an affectation—it's for balance."

"Oh, knock it off, Eileen," Mrs. Palmer grumbled. "Can't we just enjoy the afternoon without lessons?"

Mrs. Sweet frowned at her over the top of her

reading glasses. "How will the girl ever learn if she's not taught properly? For instance, Stephanie, did you know you should never wrap the string around your teabag? Just set it on your saucer."

Mrs. Thalberg, in the process of wrapping her string, paused, then continued, her jaw twitching as if she gritted her teeth.

As they devoured finger sandwiches of salmon and cucumber, and watercress egg salad, Whitney knew it was time to change the subject.

"Ladies, I thought you all could help me with a project. I'm used to clientele from San Francisco or Vegas. I want to learn about the women of Valentine Valley, get to know the town itself, to help me market my store the best way possible. Are there any public events I can attend that would help?"

Mrs. Thalberg opened her mouth, but before she could speak, Mrs. Sweet said, "Oh, I know the perfect event. The Royal Theater is hosting a fund-raiser to bring opera back. It was so popular in the nineteenth century—"

"When people had little choice if they wanted to be entertained," Mrs. Palmer pointed out.

"—and I know we can make it popular again," Mrs. Sweet continued, as if Mrs. Palmer hadn't spoken. "You'll meet all kinds of people, some even from Basalt and Carbondale and Aspen itself."

"God forbid we not socialize with the wonderful people of Aspen," Mrs. Thalberg said.

Mrs. Ludlow wiped her lips with her linen napkin. "I'm attending."

Her two roommates stared at her.

"I was going to invite you both, but if you'd rather not attend, I'd understand."

"That's not what this is about," Mrs. Thalberg said patiently. "If Whitney wants to get to know Valentine, I think she should attend an event that is more casual, fun, and relaxing."

"I know just what you're goin' to suggest," Mrs. Palmer gushed.

Then together, the two women said, "The St. John's Parish Festival."

Mrs. Sweet frowned as if she smelled something bad.

"Oh, is it this weekend?" Steph demanded, clapping her hands together. "I used to love the rides when I was a kid."

"They take over the whole parking lot and still bring in all the rides," Mrs. Thalberg said. "But now you're old enough that your boyfriend can play the games and win you a prize."

"Steph could actually win her own prize," Emily said with amusement.

"Boyfriend?" Mrs. Sweet said coolly. "Are you still dating that wild young man?"

Steph rolled her eyes. "Grandma, Tyler's a nice guy. We're researching colleges together. He's not going to end up in jail like his brother did."

Mrs. Sweet winced. Debbie looked around her in bewilderment, as if her Afternoon Tea was getting away from her.

"I could attend both events," Whitney said. To Mrs. Sweet, she added, "I do love to dress up for a good cause."

"There will be auctions, of course," Mrs. Sweet began.

"Bachelor auctions?" Steph interjected with glee.

"Nonsense," her grandmother said firmly. "That is crass. No one needs to *buy* men."

"I don't know, Eileen," Mrs. Ludlow said on a sigh. "We've all been widowed a long time."

Whitney barely withheld a snort of laughter at the image that invoked.

Mrs. Sweet's eyes narrowed. "It would seem that your grandson would enjoy being part of a bachelor auction, Rosemary. He is putting himself on display lately, is he not?"

Steph's eyes went round and she looked from one old woman to the next with anticipation.

Mrs. Thalberg inhaled deeply. "My grandson is incredibly talented. Geneva Iacuzzi wanted photos for her website. It is not his fault that his appeal is spreading."

"It's mostly my fault," Whitney said, trying to re-direct the tension. "He hesitated, but I told him it was a good idea for marketing purposes."

"And he's so talented, Grandma," Emily said, leaning forward eagerly. "Monica says that since the first article mentioning her store, she has so many more customers, and they're not just buying Josh's work."

"That is wonderful, of course," Mrs. Sweet said.

"Maybe it'll help sell your work, too, Grandma," Steph said, gingerly lifting a scone off the tray, then pausing at the sudden lengthy silence. "What?"

"You have somethin' on consignment at Monica's store, Eileen?" Mrs. Palmer asked, her expression gleeful. "I had no idea you dabbled in crafts."

"You act as if I've been hiding something, Renee."

"Not at all," Mrs. Palmer said, drawing out the last word in her Western drawl. "So what do you make? Doilies?"

"I like doilies," Emily said in a small voice.

"I paint vases," Mrs. Sweet informed them.

Mrs. Thalberg and Mrs. Palmer looked disappointed.

"Now if I've satisfied your curiosity," Mrs. Sweet turned to Steph, "let me show you the proper way to eat a scone. You break it, not cut it. Try it with clotted cream."

"It looks kind of gross," Steph said, "but I'll try it."

"Eileen and I once took a painting class together," Mrs. Ludlow said. "She has quite the talent."

"I've seen the vases," Mrs. Thalberg said. "They're lovely."

Mrs. Sweet's faint smile was her only acknowledgment of the praise.

"So the parish festival is this weekend," Whitney said to no one in particular as she broke her own scone.

Emily smiled. "We're all going. I'm sure Josh would love to bring you."

"What do I wear?"

Emily frowned. "I haven't even seen you in shorts."

"I didn't bring any except to work out in. But I do have short, casual skirts."

"Perfect. What about cowboy boots?"

"Uh . . . no. My riding boots are at home."

"Then you and I need to head into Aspen for a quick shopping trip tomorrow morning. My dad took me to this great store when I first moved here."

Mrs. Sweet looked up. "Joseph is so thoughtful."

Emily's smile was all soft and tender. "He is," she said quietly. "I'm very lucky that you raised such a wonderful son."

Whitney knew that Emily hadn't known she had a biological father different than the dad who'd died

when she was a little girl. Emily was now being exposed to the wonders of a thoughtful dad. Much as
Whitney still had her own father, she felt a little . . .
jealous. Her dad's idea of taking her shopping meant
handing her a credit card as the limousine dropped
her off at Bloomingdale's. He had continued with his
phone conversation without even a wave good-bye.

"So how's the job going at the cafe?" Emily asked
Steph, as they both worked on a second scone.

Steph made a face. "I don't know what's going on
there. I've tried to be as patient as I can, but I can't
keep covering so many tables, nor picking up extra
shifts, now that school is about to start. They could
hire more people, but they won't." She hesitated.
"I'm thinking of quitting, but I'm worried I won't be
able to find another job easily. And I need to save for
college."

Whitney watched Mrs. Sweet open her mouth,
then close it, and found herself impressed by the
woman's restraint. It would obviously be easy for her
to solve all her granddaughter's problems and offer
her a job at the inn.

Emily gave Steph an encouraging nod as she
chewed her scone.

"So I was wondering . . ." Steph began slowly,
" . . . if maybe you have an opening at the bakery?"

Emily's smile burst from her like a sunrise. "Yes,
I do! I would *love* it if you'd come work with me!"

She slung her arms around her sister's neck, and
the two shared a brief hug that made all the other
women smile with tenderness, their tension forgotten. Mrs. Sweet even dabbed at the corner of her eye,
and Mrs. Palmer slipped her a tissue. Everyone knew
how rocky Emily and Steph's relationship had been at

first, when Steph had discovered she wasn't Daddy's only little girl. Now, to see how close they were becoming, well, it made Whitney hope for a better relationship with her own family.

So before calling Josh that evening, she called her mom, filling her in on the news that she'd just bought the building, and would be staying a while to oversee the renovations—and to keep seeing Josh, but she didn't mention that. To her surprise, her mom was actually in Manhattan, instead of off in Europe as she often was that time of year. And instead of sounding vaguely distracted, she seemed . . . distractedly worried, but Whitney couldn't get anything more out of her.

When their phones disconnected, she stared at hers a moment, wondering what was going on.

That night, as Josh was working late over a piece of leather, looking through a magnifying glass, his cell phone rang. He gave it an irritated glance until he saw it was from Whitney.

Answering it quickly, he said, "Hey, Whitney."

"Hey, Josh."

Just the sound of her voice made him close his eyes and imagine her with him.

"Am I interrupting you?" she continued.

"Not a bit."

She seemed to blow out a breath. "Did you hear about the Afternoon Tea your grandmother and friends attended with me?"

"Nope, I haven't seen her today."

"Well, let's just say . . . Mrs. Sweet was there, too."

"The elder Mrs. Sweet?"

"The same."

"Fireworks?" he asked, grinning.

"Not too bad. But they did mention a parish festival this weekend, and how I just wouldn't get to know Valentine without attending."

"Are you asking me out?"

"Nope. This cannot possibly be our big date. *I* asked *you* to the museum, and *I* barged in on your Robbers' Roost night at Tony's to claim a dance. I do believe I'm doing most of the work in this relationship."

He chuckled and turned about on the stool so he could lean back against his workbench. "So it's a relationship now?"

"A courtship—those were your words. I'm not feeling very courted right about now."

"Then let me make up for my terrible neglect—"

"And your use of me in a business capacity as your *agent,*" she pointed out.

"I will make up for that, too. There's a church festival this weekend."

"Really? How fascinating!"

He smiled. "Would you like to attend with me?"

"A group date again?"

"Some of my friends might be there."

"Those weren't the groupies I was talking about. No more women chasing you down the street?"

"I haven't left the ranch. Too busy working for various slave drivers. I'll pick you up around three. Most of the fun begins in the evening, but you can't miss the Married Women Race."

"The what?"

"It's a holdover from the early 1900s. They used to actually have a race called that. St. John's brought it back. Emily entered."

"Oh, she forgot to mention that! Someone to cheer for. See you then, Josh."

"Wait, you can't hang up. What about phone sex?"

Her laugh was throaty and wicked. "No phone sex during courtship. Good night, Josh."

Chapter Twelve

When Josh arrived at the B&B the next afternoon, he gave Whitney a smoldering once-over and a whistle. She did a little spin in the foyer, thinking that might be the first whistle to make her feel giddy rather than annoyed. She wore a short skirt and a bead-embellished white tank top. "Like the cowboy boots?"

"Heck with the boots, I like the legs they show off. And that little green skirt does things for your—"

She put a finger to his lips, and gestured with her head toward the dining room, where they could hear murmuring voices. He caught her fingers between his teeth for a brief, gentle bite, then put his hand on her ass and pulled her against him in a proprietary way that made her shiver.

Breathless and weak with pleasure, she said, "Come on into the parlor. I have something to show you."

"God, that sounds inviting," he whispered in a husky voice.

"Now, now, we're going to a *church* festival. Keep your thoughts clean." It was difficult to remain levelheaded at all, seeing him in snug jeans and cowboy boots, and a faded tractor-store t-shirt that hugged his pecs and biceps. When had a man in an old t-shirt turned her on? "It was hard for me to keep *my* thoughts clean when I saw the paper."

He grinned. "The *Gazette* again?"

"Nope. The *Denver Post*. You mentioned letting a photographer take pictures a couple days ago. Here they are. My, you do look . . . delicious."

He shot a glance at her, then propped one hand on the table as he bent over the photos. There were a few photos under the heading of "Our new Colorado celebrity," him working on his horse—

"My backside is way too much of the focus," he said, bemused.

—and then riding around the corral, sweating in the sunshine.

"Seems pretty harmless," he finished. "He captured Bandit's good side."

She smiled. "When I saw this layout, I felt like I'll be the queen of the festival today, attended by the newest Colorado celebrity."

He rolled his eyes, then looked at something past her. She glanced over her shoulder to see two of the other female guests boldly staring at him from the dining room.

Josh waved, and they waved back. "Time to go," he murmured, keeping his smile in place.

She laughed but let him take her arm and firmly escort her out the front door. They walked the couple blocks to St. John's Church, even meandering through the paths in the Rose Garden that filled the central block between the Four Sisters B&Bs.

Holding her hand, Josh said, "When we talked last night, I never thought to thank you for taking my grandma and her friends out to that tea ceremony. She called me early this morning, gushing over what a good time she had."

"Even with Mrs. Sweet there?"

"Even then."

"There was an interesting vibe between them all. Any idea what started the problem?"

"Nope. Grandma won't talk about it, and my parents are either sworn to secrecy or just as clueless and trying to hide it."

She laughed and leaned her head casually against his shoulder as they walked. He was so easy to be with.

As they got closer to the festival, she could see the rides rising up above the one- and two-story buildings, and cars and pickups lining both sides of every street. Carnival music blared from speakers, competing with the sounds of hundreds of people mingling and laughing. Then, at last, they took the corner, and the church parking lot spread out before them, the stone church and its tall spire rising up behind it. Banners and streamers hung from poles high overhead, looping over streets blocked off to make way for dozens of booths. The lot was crowded with carnival rides, spinning and turning for the delight of children and teenagers—and a few adults. Mixed in were more food and game booths. Whitney caught sight of a cotton-candy sign, and her mouth began to water.

"I haven't been to a carnival in . . . I have no idea how many years," she said. "It wasn't something my parents regularly took us to, you know? Although once, when we were spending time in Manhattan, my dad insisted Chasz and I had to attend the New York State Fair with our nanny because of some businessman he had to meet."

"It can't be in Manhattan," Josh said with doubt.

She laughed. "Nope, it's a five-hour drive up to the state fairgrounds in Syracuse. We flew, of course," she added wryly.

"Of course."

"And Dad's assistant didn't realize how hard it would be to get a hotel at the last minute. You can't believe how many hotels were booked with state cops there to work the fair. The farmers themselves stay right on the fairgrounds, sleeping on cots and hay bales next to animal stalls."

Josh gave her an amused look. "And this surprises you? I did the same thing growing up, when I wanted to enter my favorite calf."

She gave him a considering look. "I can't believe it was all that comfortable. In Syracuse, the farmers brought along fans for the heat."

"For their cows, too, I bet."

She laughed. "Them, too. All I can say is that I had so much fun. The people were so varied, and the food! Please tell me they'll have fried dough here."

"It wouldn't be a festival without it."

She grinned with excitement, then they strolled up Mabel Street, past the first booths.

"Speaking of my grandma . . ." Josh said.

The widows were manning a craft booth, where signs advertised that half of every purchase benefited the church, and the other half went to the Valentine Valley Preservation Fund.

"Do you have any of your work here?" Whitney asked.

"I've run out of the smaller items. Other bosses are keeping me too busy."

She gave him an innocent smile.

Before they reached the booth, several men with cameras jumped out in front of them for a quick series of shots. Whitney turned her back but wasn't sure she escaped the photo.

"Josh!" his grandmother called from her booth.

Josh took Whitney's hand and pulled, ducking beneath the tent and circling behind the display so he could kiss the cheeks of each woman. This didn't seem to be the sort of photograph the men wanted, so they soon disappeared.

"There's our famous cowboy artist," Mrs. Palmer said with satisfaction, pinching both his cheeks.

Today, she was wearing the bright red billowy pants of a clown, complete with white shirt, bow tie—and clown feet. Instead of elaborate makeup, she'd painted a red circle on each wrinkled cheek. Whitney couldn't stop smiling as she took in the sight. She could still be surprised with every newly revealed eccentricity of the widows.

"So I take it you saw the latest photo spread." Josh crossed his arms as he leaned back against a table.

"Oh, we did," Mrs. Ludlow said, nodding. "And your grandmother made certain everyone we know heard about it."

He winced. "The whole town's probably sick of me by now. Who wants to get jumped at by photographers?"

"Not at all," Mrs. Ludlow said with grave patience.

Whitney bit her lip to keep from laughing at the crestfallen look on Josh's face. To change the subject and relieve his embarrassment, she said, "What time is the Married Women Race?"

"I have a schedule right here," Mrs. Thalberg said,

picking up a flyer, even as Mrs. Palmer went to help a customer. She murmured to herself, "Let's see, there's a Dog Agility show—"

"We have to see that!" Whitney interrupted.

Josh nodded.

"—and the Chain Saw Carving demonstration."

Whitney's eyes widened. "Really?"

"Wait until you see his wildlife sculptures," Josh said. "Incredible. Maybe you'll want one for your store."

Well, she probably wouldn't go that far . . .

"—ah, there it is," Mrs. Thalberg said with satisfaction. "Married Women Race is at five o'clock, starting in the field up above Second Street." To Whitney she said, "That's across from the entrance to the Sweetheart Inn. They race out toward the Sweet Ranch, and then back to finish where they started. It says 5K." She frowned. "Is that far? I never remember how to convert."

"Around three miles," Whitney explained. She turned to Josh. "Then we have some time before it starts. Let's get some cotton candy."

"Not fried dough?" he asked, smiling.

"We have all evening."

As they wandered from booth to booth, Whitney inhaled the scents and tried not to moan. More than once, people called out a tease to Josh about his newfound fame. They ran into all three Sweet brothers, and Chris told Josh he should have set up an autograph booth for charity. With a sly smile, Will amended that to a kissing booth, and Whitney firmly dragged Josh away before the guys got any more bright ideas.

She brought her Walk-Away Sundae to the race

field, and when they were still a hundred yards or so away, she found herself squinting over the top of her chocolate-coated ice cream cone. "Uh . . . what is everyone wearing?"

Josh grinned down at her. "I didn't tell you because I wanted to see your reaction. I did say the race was originally from the early 1900s."

She slowly smiled. "And so you did."

The race participants were easy to spot by the number pinned to their clothes—and the very nature of those clothes. She saw women wearing Nikes beneath prairie gowns and bonnets, others with bloomers beneath shorter skirts—and then there was Emily waving at them from near the starting line as she returned from a warm-up jog, wearing a 1920s flapper dress with beads and sequins.

"Whalebone corset optional," Josh said, rocking back on his heels, wearing his "aw shucks" expression.

"I think Em has the best idea," Whitney said, licking at her almost-forgotten ice cream.

To her surprise, Josh caught her cone-holding hand, and capturing her gaze with his, slowly licked the long trail of ice cream that had traced down over her knuckle. Whitney stared at him, her smile dying, feeling that spark of urgency and longing and incredible heat he always made her feel.

Distantly, she heard Emily say with amusement, "Oh, go get a room—after my race."

Whitney blinked her way back to reality, then turned away from Josh. "Oh, sorry. Em, I have to say—what a gorgeous outfit to run in. Please don't fall in the mud."

Emily wore a sequined headband across her forehead though her blond hair was still caught back in a ponytail. "I seem to be in the wrong era—but they said early 1900s, and didn't specify frontier."

The other Thalberg and Sweet family members strolled up, Sandy grinning as she looked Emily up and down.

Josh looked around at the forty or fifty women of all shapes and sizes. "So, Em, do you have any competition?"

She straightened up from a hamstring stretch. "Of course I do."

"But she's gonna win," Nate said with confidence. "That's the reason we got married—so she could enter."

Emily ignored him, while his mom gave him an elbow to the side.

"So what do you think of our festival?" Sandy asked Whitney.

Whitney held up her ice cream. "I'm loving it, especially the food."

Nate gave a whistle. "You sure look good in cowboy boots."

"Thank you," she said. "But you are not the first man to whistle at me today."

"I hope not," he said, glancing meaningfully at his brother.

Josh just gave an enigmatic smile.

"Good luck, Emily!" Steph called.

Emily gave her a quick hug, then turned to the young man at her side, "Hi, Tyler, thanks for coming."

Steph's boyfriend was a lanky young man with longish, curly black hair, a lean, bony face, and sparse stubble on his chin. Whitney remembered that the first time she'd been in town, Tyler had gotten into some trouble just as his brother got out of jail. But Steph had had a good effect on him, and he seemed to be doing better.

Soon a man with a bullhorn announced the start of the race, and Whitney laughed aloud at the sight of all the women in costume—and running shoes. A starter pistol sent the pack off across the field toward the Sweet Ranch.

Each entrant had had to make a poster with a picture of herself in costume, and a historical description, so Whitney strolled among them with Josh.

"Wow, you people go crazy," she said, popping the pointy end of her cone into her mouth and chewing with satisfaction.

Josh spread his hands. "Hey, you can't win the costume competition without a poster."

"So there's two ways to win? Exciting."

About twenty-two minutes after the start of the race, the first woman could be seen running toward the finish line—and it wasn't Emily. But Emily came in second, pumping knees making her skirt lift and the sequins sparkle.

She didn't win the Costume portion either, and confided to Whitney, "How could I compete with a woman who tied herself into a corset and *still* ran?"

Whitney and Josh strolled back to the festival, and she found herself gaping as a man drove by in a golf cart that had cutout wooden horses on each side.

"We're not exactly sophisticated," Josh said ruefully.

She linked her arm through his. "That's what I like about Valentine, though. You guys don't take each other too seriously. Sometimes . . ." She paused, not knowing how to make her feelings clear. "Sometimes it's easy to forget that there's more to life than the pressures and ambitions of work."

"Remember who you're talking to," he said, covering her hand with his. "I haven't exactly been lazing around."

"No, but you occasionally make time for relaxation. You know what's important."

"I don't know about that. I don't seem to be good at saying no."

She came to a stop and ended up tugging on his arm. "If you regret our deal, just tell me now."

"No, that's not what I meant. I *want* to do the necklaces. I probably shouldn't have agreed to the shoulder bags . . ."

"Because of the fame?" she asked.

People streamed by them, maybe even his family, but no one disturbed them, and she almost felt alone with him, even though from the fringes of the crowd, eyes still followed them.

"No, just the demands on my time. Those people in Aspen don't mean anything to me, unlike you or Monica."

"But the *work* means something to you."

"Yeah, it does," he said after a moment.

"And that's what's driven me to expand Leather and Lace. The work is way too important to me. I'm a prime example of a driven businessperson." She decided to lighten the mood. "I can think of another way you're good at saying no—to me." She gave him a saucy grin.

He tried to kiss her, and she ducked away from him. "I haven't had a gyro yet. And you haven't taken me on that little Ferris wheel."

"If they say it'll hold us, I'm game."

"Then come on!"

Josh watched her dart ahead of him, that short skirt barely covering her ass, her legs long and tan above cowboy boots, and thought he might follow her wherever she led. The elegant, businesslike Whitney Winslow had disappeared tonight, leaving in her place a woman who kissed him with lips sticky from cotton candy, who ended up carrying around a stuffed gorilla he won for her at one of the shooting games, and eventually snuggled with him atop the Ferris wheel, with the night stars blazing above them and the colorful festival lights below. The music and voices almost faded up there, as did the laughter from her eyes when their gazes met and held. Though restrained by a safety bar, she leaned into him breasts first, and her kiss was hot and knowing and demanding. They made fireworks of their own in the dark, and the ones that started erupting in the sky faded in comparison.

When their lips parted, he looked into her eyes as the wind picked up, then gently slid a curl back behind her ear. His parents had always told him he'd know the right woman when he met her, and now he knew. Whitney was the only woman for him, but he suspected she'd take some convincing. How could they possibly merge their very different lives together? Could she live in Valentine, when she had homes all over the world? Or could he find a purpose and place for himself at her side, even if it was on another continent? He wanted kids, and didn't know if a woman whose parents dumped her off at the state fair with a nanny would ever want to be a parent herself.

Or was he prepared to change everything about himself for her?

Chapter Thirteen

On Wednesday night, Whitney agreed to go bowling with Josh. She'd never bowled a day in her life, but she was game to try anything new—as long as it involved Josh. Especially sex, but he was still in the courtship phase—or so he'd told her after the festival Saturday night, when they'd been making out in his pickup, and she would have gladly lifted her short skirt for him right on the bench.

God, he was frustrating—and she'd never wanted a man more. He'd wooed her with carnival food, then cruelly ignored her true desires, even when she worked her best kissing techniques on him.

No man had ever said no to her before Josh, and she was starting to feel the tiniest crack of insecurity—which she immediately pushed aside.

At the bowling alley on Sixth and Clara, she was rather shocked to find out you still had to rent shoes.

"I'll go buy my own," she told him, wincing.

Josh just laughed. "They spray 'em, don't worry."

She grimaced and held the shoes gingerly while she followed him toward their lane. While she was putting them on, she heard the first feminine, "Yoo-hoo,

Josh!" and sighed, thinking that this fame had better sell a lot of necklaces and shoulder bags. It was even starting to get on *her* nerves.

Or maybe she was just jealous and wanted Josh all to herself.

"Josh, you naughty boy," the woman said, her voice sounding titillated and amused.

Curious in spite of herself, Whitney straightened to see a middle-aged black woman, her motherly smile directed at Josh. She wore a bowling shirt touting the Halftime Sports Bar, and there were several women in the next lane that matched her, including identical expressions of glee.

Josh looked bemused as he turned to Whitney. "Whitney Winslow, this is Gloria Valik, Monica's aunt and Nate's secretary. She's going to tell me how I've become naughty and not just famous."

Gloria put her hands on her hips. "Fame brings out the worst in reporters, that's true. So you haven't seen the *National Intruder* today?"

"Not my usual paper," he said dryly.

"You're featured, but you might not like it."

She went to her lane, leaving Whitney and Josh to exchange uneasy glances. Gloria returned and laid out the paper on their table. Whitney couldn't help her intake of breath. The picture was a night scene, very grainy and almost out of focus, but she could see the naked backside of a dark-haired man jumping out of a hotel fountain. The headline read: COWBOY ARTIST HAS RACY PAST.

"They can't get away with lying about you like this," Whitney said briskly. "I'll talk to my lawyer."

"No point, because it's not a lie."

She almost gaped at Josh, and he gave her a shrug,

his expression amused and resigned at the same time.

"It was on a snowboarding trip in Sun Valley. We got a little drunk and dared each other to run through the snow from the hot tub to the fountain and back. Some of the girls we were with took photos. Guess one of them needed a little cash."

"Are there more to be sold—speaking as your agent?" Whitney asked with exasperation.

"Only more of those. I can't remember another trip where things got so out of hand."

Gloria glanced at Whitney. "The operative words being that he can't remember."

Whitney sighed. "Okay, you were young and stupid. Guess there's no harm done. There's far worse you could have done to harm your reputation."

He put his arm around her shoulders. "Now that's an understanding girlfriend."

"Girlfriend?" she echoed, feeling the faintest bit uneasy but dismissing it. "I wouldn't call me that since you keep telling me we haven't had our big date yet. And now you've proven you can't keep your clothes on."

Gloria gave Josh's shoulder a little push. "Not sure you're boyfriend material after that, Josh Thalberg. You better watch yourself." And she sauntered off to join the rest of her team, who all had a good laugh at whatever she said.

Whitney shrugged out from under his arm, then looked up at the electronic scoreboard. "Do you know how to set this thing?"

He studied her almost warily, and Whitney was satisfied. No point in being predictable. He was just explaining the way to score in bowling, when they heard a man's voice say, "I bet you think that photo is funny."

They turned around, and Whitney's cheerfulness took a hit. Frowning at them was Sylvester Galimi, owner of the True Grits Diner and last winter's leader of the opposition to Leather and Lace on the grounds of "pornography." The man was in his sixties, with curly gray hair, and glasses perched on a prominent nose. Instead of his usual tasteful suit, he, too, was wearing a bowling shirt, this one advertising his diner.

Josh smiled. "Hi, Sylvester. Is your team winning?"

Sylvester's sister, the mayor of Valentine Valley, in her matching bowling shirt with her white hair styled short, gave them an apologetic and pained smile. "Really, Sylvester, is this necessary?"

He shrugged her off. "I told you she and her store would be a bad influence."

"I haven't even opened it yet," Whitney pointed out.

"And yet already people associated with you have appeared nude—nude!—in a national newspaper."

"Not sure you can call the *Intruder* a newspaper, Sylvester," Josh said, "but let me point out that this photo is five years old. I was reckless and drunk without Whitney's help."

"Your disgraceful foolishness would have stayed hidden if she hadn't talked you into posing for that Aspen boutique."

Whitney opened her mouth, but when Josh touched her arm, she stayed silent.

"No one had to talk me into anything," Josh said with patience. "And if I'd had any idea how far this would spread, I probably wouldn't have done it. But it's done now, and hopefully this"—he jabbed a finger at the paper—"is the last of it."

Sylvester gave an exaggerated roll of his eyes, and

his voice became pleading. "Josh, don't you see she's trying to get you to make a name for yourself the same way she did?"

Whitney gave an involuntary flinch, but she couldn't be surprised that he'd finally Googled her name. She bet he was kicking himself over not discovering her Whitney Wild persona when they faced off in front of the town council. And now Josh would know, but she didn't regret that either. He should know everything about her if they were going to keep seeing each other.

"Make his name the same way I did?" Whitney said. "Sylvester, even you have to agree that jumping into a fountain is a pretty tame stunt. I certainly have him beat."

Sylvester briefly put a hand to his eyes. "It's not a competition. I just want what's best for Valentine. Leather and Lace is just encouraging the wrong element."

"You mean women?" Whitney said coolly. "Uppity women who should only wear what their men tell them to?"

"Okay," Mayor Galimi said heartily. "You're up, Sylvester, and if you cause me to lose this match, you'll regret it."

"Go on, Sylvester," Josh said, still smiling, though he spoke between clenched teeth. "Try to remember that everyone has stuff in their past they regret— you're just lucky to be too old to be Googled. But I bet my grandma might know a thing or two."

His face reddening, Sylvester marched to the next lane, where he hefted his bowling ball and tossed it down the lane without lining it up. His entire team groaned, some flinging up their hands.

Mayor Galimi, still by their lane, shook her head, then gave Whitney a conspiratorial smile. "Love your new fall line."

Whitney's tension eased. "Thanks." When they were alone, she said to Josh, "I should probably explain Sylvester's reference to my past."

Josh sat on the edge of the table and took both her hands. "You don't need to. I hope you don't mind, but after you talked so much about the price of fame, I searched for you myself."

She squeezed his hands. "Of course I don't mind. I'm surprised no one dug deeply last winter." But part of her wished he'd brought it up right away. She was surprised by the touch of hurt, especially about her past. She'd thought herself beyond that—why was he able to make her feel things she'd thought herself beyond feeling?

"You were very young," he began.

"Stop, Josh, I wasn't sixteen. My bad behavior started at twenty-two, when I graduated summa cum laude from college and my father still wouldn't allow me to work for the company."

He winced. "We shouldn't have this conversation here. Let's go talk privately."

She looked around the bowling alley, at the people all having fun cheering for or against each other. "No, really, it's okay. I've long since come to terms with it. The Winslow women always go into the charity arm of W.E. Of course I didn't know that until my father told me point-blank when I was a teenager."

"It's a hard thing to hear that your work isn't wanted," he murmured, pulling her closer to rub her arms gently.

"That's how my father is, no-nonsense, when

he isn't detached. Of course, I should have had no problem understanding how things were. I thought I could be so gifted and brilliant that he'd have to change his mind, but I was wrong. So . . . I went a little wild. Whitney Wild, if you didn't catch that cute nickname."

He gave a faint smile. "I caught it."

"That's what someone wrote in front of my building last week, 'Go Back to SF, Whitney Wild.' A command and a jab at my past all in one."

"You didn't tell me they'd mentioned your past."

She shrugged. "I'm sure all the photos online showed you my entire year of partying and men and spending sprees."

"What was your parents' reaction?"

"You're far too perceptive," she said ruefully. "I not only thought 'I'll show them,' but I wanted their attention. I wanted them to know they couldn't take me for granted anymore. Attention was something my parents weren't good at giving."

"Which is why you went to boarding school."

"Bingo," she said, pointing at him. "But to my surprise, they really didn't care about how I acted out, like . . . they'd expected it or something. After all, the kids of their rich friends did the same thing. All right, I didn't get into drugs or commit crimes, but still . . ."

"You could have gotten into serious trouble. Or one of the men you dated—"

"No, don't go there. I was very careful with men, and only chose the ones I could control. And I made them glad I chose them."

She heard the faint bitterness in her voice, and this time, Josh said nothing. She was relieved because she didn't want to explain about her men or her motives.

"And then came the underwear shot—I'm sure you saw it," she added with amusement.

"Well, yes . . ."

She thought he looked a little embarrassed, but she didn't call him on it. She could have kissed him then, even though all around them, people shouted or groaned as they sent their balls down the lane, and pins smacked each other as they scattered.

Josh controlled himself because he was experiencing the rare feeling of wanting to punch someone. He hated that Whitney had been neglected and ignored by her oblivious parents, that she'd wanted desperately to be a part of the family business—a part of the *family*—and no one had cared. He couldn't imagine his family not supporting him in anything he wanted to do.

Of course, maybe now his family was being too polite, now that his fame in leather tooling was threatening to take over his life.

"The papparazzi called me Whitney Wild, and the name just stuck. And when I stupidly got out of the limousine and exposed too much, well, it made me famous—but I bet not to hardworking cowboys like you."

"I don't exactly make time to read that gossip stuff," he admitted.

"You have your own life, and don't need to know every salacious detail of others'. But I can't regret the publicity. That's when the company contacted me about naming an exclusive underwear line 'Whitney.' I almost didn't do it—and I certainly refused to model for it—but I couldn't help being intrigued since I'd been a business major. And, of course, I was still trying to get my family's attention," she added, smiling. "So I said yes. As long as I received stock in the company itself. It went well, and eventually I was managing the small company for the owner. I bought him out and changed the name to Leather and Lace."

"And you succeeded."

"I became the businesswoman I'd always meant to be. My parents treated my store as if it were just another rebellion I'd grow out of. Although it may have started as a rebellion, it became anything but, to me. Now I'm dedicated to watching it grow in the US, and to expand it into international markets."

She'd said that the first night she'd returned, but now it made even more of an impact. She had the world to conquer—why would she care about a small-time cowboy? *Cowboy artist,* he amended to himself with faint sarcasm.

"You must be proud of yourself," he said, cupping her cheek briefly.

She smiled at him. "I am. And I'm proud of the journey, too. Yeah, sometimes I wish Whitney Wild would fade away, but how can I regret what she led to?"

He thought of "Whitney Wild," remembered how uncomfortably aroused he'd been by every picture, the sly, sexy way she had of playing up to the cameras, the way the men on her arm had worshipped her with their eyes, showed their possession of her. Their brief possession. None of them had held the wild young woman, and from everything she'd told him, no man had held her affection since.

But he didn't want to be one of the men she eventually left behind. Somehow, he would find a way to make her see that she could change her life once again, and it could be better than she'd ever imagined.

"Hey, you two haven't even set up the scoreboard,"

Will Sweet called as he approached them, followed by Dom Shaw.

Whitney whispered, "Do you and your friends do *everything* together?"

Smiling, Josh turned his head but didn't let go of Whitney's hand as he spoke to Will. "Some things are more important than bowling."

"Like that new article," Dom said. He picked the paper up from the table.

Will grinned. "Man, I think I'm famous."

Whitney leaned over Will's arm to scrutinize the tabloid again. "You? All I see is Josh's moon over the fountain."

"I'm still *in* the fountain. See that light-haired guy? That's me."

He spoke a little louder than was necessary, and Josh saw more than one woman turn his way.

"Are you actually bragging about being publicly nude in a freezing hotel fountain?" called Carmen Suarez from the lane on their other side.

"I got nothin' to hide," Will said, genially spreading his arms wide.

"I gotta see this."

Carmen and her other girlfriend came over to see the paper, and Will and Dom met them halfway.

"I've met her before, haven't I?" Whitney asked in a low voice.

"She's a manager at the Hotel Colorado. Remember, I was meeting a fan in the lobby?"

"Right."

Josh couldn't quite hear what Will and Carmen said over the sound of the balls rolling and striking the pins, but he could see Will pointing to his hair, then to the picture.

Whitney leaned on the table next to Josh. "Was that really him in the fountain with you?"

"It was," Josh answered, smiling.

"Who led who into trouble?"

Josh put his arm around her waist. "Which answer would get me your attention?"

"The truth, of course."

"Then sadly, it was me who drank too much and dared him. When he did it, I had to do it, too . . ."

"All for the amusement of your various girlfriends?"

"Our apparently greedy girlfriends," he said, glancing at Will and the paper again.

She turned serious. "Will this hurt you somehow?"

"Naw, why should it?"

"I'd hate to think this all came out because I dared you to pose for Geneva Iacuzzi."

"I'll never regret giving us something in common."

She laughed and kissed him lightly. "So back to bowling. What do I need to know?"

For the next couple hours, he taught her how to bowl, putting up with Will and his outrageous play for women. Chris, Nate, and Adam eventually showed up, and at one point, someone went to take a picture of the whole group. Josh couldn't help noticing that Whitney ducked out of the photo, but he didn't say anything about it. He couldn't decide if she didn't want any more publicity—or didn't want to be seen having small-town fun.

Chapter Fourteen

Two days later, Josh, Brooke, and Adam decided to take a ride across their pastures, gathering up the tarps and poles, the temporary dams they'd used to manipulate the flooding of the fields as the hay had ripened back in May and June. The equipment had been left behind in the rush to harvest the hay, but now they had to make time for all the chores needing to be finished up before winter came to the Rockies in October.

But Brooke had gotten stuck in a muddy creek bed, and Adam had gone to help her. Both had ended up falling in, then made sure, at the next bend, that Josh had had to wade through mud for the tarps until he fell in as well.

So as they rode back to the barn, Adam in the pickup with all the dams, Josh was a muddy mess.

"You should see yourself," Brooke said, riding Sugar at his side as they approached the barn.

He glanced at her. "Unless you're wearing new makeup, that's a lot of mud on your face."

She wiped at her cheeks, only making matters worse. When he laughed, she leaned across and tried to smear some on the one clean part of his arm, but his horse danced away with a whinny.

Josh dismounted, feeling his mud-caked clothing crack, but he knew he had to take care of Bandit first. He pulled off his shirt, tossing it in a heap by the door, when suddenly the dogs shot past him and through the barn doors, growling.

Josh exchanged a concerned look with his sister.

Then they heard the sound of feminine shrieking, and two young women came rushing out of the barn, hay in their hair as if they'd been hiding, herded by the cowdogs. One started to snap pictures, and Josh heaved a sigh.

"Really?" he said wearily, hands on his hips. "You want pictures of me like this?"

One of the girls pushed her blond hair out of her eyes and gazed down his chest as if she'd never seen a man before. "Josh Thalberg, you could be wrestling steers in the mud, and I wouldn't care."

"Nothing so glamorous as that," he said.

"Doesn't matter. Now I'll have something to post."

"But you do know you're trespassing, and I could call the sheriff."

The other girl, chubby beneath her stylish clothes, stiffened at his threat. "Go ahead. My dad won't let anything happen."

Brooke and Adam stood to the side and talked in low voices.

"I don't know who your dad is, and I don't care," Josh practically growled. He was about to say more, when he saw Brooke wince and shake her head. He hesitated, then realized the girls hadn't caused any harm except to his temper. "Go on, get out of here before I call the sheriff."

They blew him kisses as they ran toward their expensive car, the one he'd originally figured belonged to friends of his parents. They roared away, tires spinning in the dirt, the dogs chasing them down the road.

Brooke looked him over. "All this fame is finally getting to you."

He sighed and walked into the cool shadows of the barn, knowing she trailed behind. "It's harmless, I know, but I'm starting to feel . . . hunted."

"Or already mounted on display?"

He turned and gave her a look even as she grinned at him.

Their old ranch hand, Lou, limped into the barn and picked up as if he'd heard the whole conversation. "I'll be your bodyguard, Josh. I'll frighten all them scary women away."

Lou snorted a laugh even as Josh winced. And then he got to "enjoy" some more ribbing at lunch about the *National Intruder* photos. His family hadn't let that go since they'd seen them. Luckily, he could look forward to Whitney, whom his parents had invited to dinner, before he and Whitney went to the opera fund-raiser at the Royal Theater that night.

Throughout dinner, he watched her relate to his family, easily teasing Nate (who needed it), discussing girly stuff like clothes with Brooke and their mom, and even some of the places she'd visited in the world with his dad, who admitted he used to collect international postcards when he was a kid. How had Whitney gotten him to confess that? Josh wondered with amusement.

She seemed to fit in easily, but now that he'd gotten to know her better, he could see the touch of eagerness she couldn't quite hide when sitting at his family dinner table.

She insisted on helping clean up the kitchen, then he was able to drag her outside, ostensibly to look over some of his preliminary work. But he was hoping to get her up to his loft sooner rather than later. They had time for a little fun before dressing for the fund-raiser at nine.

As she stood at his workbench, touching the various pieces of dyed and trimmed leather strips, she gave him a curious look.

"What?" Josh asked. "I thought these were what you wanted. I can have Adam—"

"No, no, it's not that. These are perfect so far." She glanced at another workbench strewn with larger pieces. "Shoulder bags, too, I see. But no, that's not what's on my mind. Your family couldn't wait to tell me about your trespassers today."

Josh winced. "As if that will heighten your interest in me or something?"

"Oh, trust me, I don't need anything more for *that*." She hesitated. "Brooke mentioned that one of the girls wanted photos to 'post.'"

"What about it?"

"Post where? I'm assuming online. Have you checked it out?"

"Isn't that your job as my agent? Let me escort you to my computer."

"I was waiting for that excuse," she teased.

But although he wanted nothing more than to drag her to his bed, very noticeable in the corner of the big room, he put his laptop on the coffee table and gestured to the couch.

She gave him a glance but sat down, lifted the lid, and when the desktop appeared, she clicked on the browser and began to type. He sat down beside her, making sure to let their thighs touch, enjoying himself far too much. It wasn't as if he really cared about any search online—

"Got something," she suddenly said.

He leaned in, letting his face brush along her hair, nuzzling her neck just behind her ear. "Hmm?" he murmured.

"Jesus, Josh, you have a Facebook Fan page."

That took a moment to sink in, as he was inhaling the scent of her. At last something pierced his brain. "What did you say?"

"Facebook. You've heard of it, right?"

"Yeah, I've heard of it, but I'm not a member. No time." He faced the screen, and right there on a Facebook page, he saw that ridiculous photo of him at the Aspen boutique, gazing out at the camera as if the weight of the sexual world was on his shoulders. "That photo is everywhere, right? Surely—"

"No, you don't get it. You have over thirty thousand likes, Josh."

She seemed shocked, even fascinated, as he studied her expression.

"So . . . thirty thousand people like the photo?"

"Not just that. They're posting about you, where they've seen you—and here you go. Those girls today? They uploaded a photo of you all muddy and bare-chested."

He frowned and finally gave his full attention to the screen. "You told me to let people take my picture, that it'd die down."

"I assumed it would. Wait a sec."

She called up another browser window, even as he sank back on the couch.

"Josh, you are actually trending on Twitter. Worldwide."

She gave him the wide-eyed look of someone in awe.

"Don't you start looking at me like that," he said wearily.

"It means people are talking about you on Twitter. And they're sending people to Facebook, which of course has all the information about where you're from. No wonder people have found you so easily."

"They put that info in the first article. It's been no secret." And for the first time, he honestly felt exposed, as if he could never have a private life again. How much longer could people stay interested in him if he never left Valentine, if he didn't promote himself? Of course, his own work promoted him all the time . . .

"Is that one of my journal covers?" he asked, squinting to see a tiny thumbnail of a photo.

"Yes, it is. This girl is bragging that she was able to buy some of your work."

"So if this keeps up, I will have women and photographers trailing me all the time." He'd tried to make light of it, but the reality was beginning to sink in. "What are you going to do about it?"

She straightened from her bemused stare at the computer screen. "You're going to make this agent stuff hard work, aren't you?"

"I probably wouldn't have posed for Geneva but for you."

She lifted up a hand. "I know, I know. Believe me,

most people would kill for this kind of publicity, and it just seemed to happen to you."

"Lucky me," he said, trying not to sound strained.

"All right, let me see who the Facebook admin for your site is."

He watched her type a few keys and frown.

"All I see is an e-mail address, JoshFan@yippee.com."

"JoshFan?" he echoed, rolling his eyes. "Hardly original."

"I'll send an e-mail and try to see who's doing this." Another minute went by. "There. I'll let you know what this person has to say for herself, see if we can get her to take down the page. Although a new one would probably pop up. Of course, I'm just assuming it's a her . . ."

He pulled her away from her hunched-up posture over the laptop and back onto the couch, where he could keep his arm around her.

She linked her hand with his. "You know, this can really help your career. We'll have to contact Geneva and see how your shoulder bags are selling. Fame helped me—why wouldn't it help you?"

"But I don't need fame—I'm not certain I can produce enough work right now, let alone if the demand rises."

"And that's when you charge higher prices. And you hire more help." She held up a hand when he was about to protest. "I know you've been training Adam to prepare the leather, but here's another thought. You could just do the design work."

He blinked at her. "You do know that my skill carving leather is what people are paying me for, right?"

"But not everyone has your eye for design."

"Bull. Sorry, Whitney, but that's just bull. I enjoy every phase of what I do. It's been something I do for fun, a hobby, and I don't want to lose that."

"Josh, you're fooling yourself. When you get paid—and paid well—it's no longer just a hobby but a job. What about hiring someone to take over your work on the ranch?"

He took her hand between his. "That's not just a job, either. This ranch has been in my family for over a hundred years. It's important to me to be a part of nurturing it. Surely you felt the same way, when you wanted to go into *your* family business."

He saw her flinch, felt it in her fingers, but he didn't let her go.

"What your grandfathers built meant something to you," he continued, "and it wasn't fair of your family to deny you. And I won't deny myself."

"I saw that picture of you today, Josh. You were a muddy mess. Manual labor—you could cut back to the important stuff."

He shook his head. "It's all part of it, along with doing it all with my family. You didn't see Adam and Brooke—they were just as muddy."

She shrugged. "I had to try."

"So if people want to pay over a thousand dollars for a purse, then they'll just have to wait. My time is important, and so are the necklaces I've promised to you. I've always wanted to live life on my own terms, and I won't let that be taken away from me. Perhaps you need to see some of what I do that's so important to me—and I don't mean looking over my shoulder as I carve leather. Spend a day on the ranch with me."

"Is this the big date you keep promising me?" she teased.

He leaned forward and gave her a swift kiss. "Nope. You'll know when I take you on our big date."

"I'm getting impatient."

"Then take out your impatience on that computer. Did the Facebook person respond?"

"The admin. I'll check." After a few minutes she looked up. "Nope, but that's not surprising. Some people don't check their e-mail regularly. I seem to remember you being guilty of that."

He grinned. "I got better things to do than hang out online. So you'll spend the day with me?"

"The next nice day," she amended. "I think you still have mud behind your ears from this afternoon."

"Then I better wash it before we hit the theater tonight. Can't wait to see what you wear."

Whitney was at the Silver Creek Ranch the next morning, just after dawn, because she didn't sleep all that well. And it was all Josh's fault. He'd looked incredible in a charcoal suit at the opera fund-raiser, and had been patient for everyone who wanted his picture. She managed to keep out of the way whenever anyone pulled out a camera. They'd eaten scrumptious appetizers and drank excellent wine, and even bid on a few of the auction items—a vacation package to Hawaii for her, snowboards and apparel for him. Then he'd dropped her off after 1:00 A.M. and gone home. She'd lain awake thinking about him and sex and unfulfilled desires, and kept imagining putting him in the shower that afternoon to wipe all the mud off him.

Josh knew how she felt—and she wasn't about to

make another pass at him. But oh, how she wanted to . . .

He came out of the barn just as she parked her SUV. He waved, then continued to his pickup truck with a horse trailer hitched behind.

"Is someone going somewhere?" she asked, glancing into the empty trailer.

"We are."

After opening the back door to the trailer, he studied her thoroughly, and she was once again reminded of feeling overheated and lustful in the night.

"Nice outfit," he said. "Haven't seen you in regular jeans. They fit real good. And is that a Western shirt?"

"Complete with pearl snaps," she said, looking down at the pink-and-green checks. "I might have bought more than cowboy boots when Em and I shopped in Aspen. Just needed an excuse to wear it."

"Fancy," he said, giving her that grin that melted the hearts of all his fans. "Did you hear back from that Facebook person?"

"The admin? No, not yet. But again, we haven't given her much time yet. So where are we going?"

"Up to the White River National Forest to move some of the cattle to a different pasture. You up for some horseback riding?"

"It's been a while, but you never forget. So introduce me to my horse."

Montana was a black-and-white paint mare with just enough years on her to be mellow with each new rider. Whitney approached from the side, not meeting Montana's eyes at first, then let her sniff her shoulder, all the while talking to her softly about the day ahead.

"Brooke uses Montana a lot for her students," Josh said.

"So in case I lied about my experience with horses, Montana will take good care of me."

Josh sent her a sexy grin. "I'd never accuse you of lying. But if you'd like to prove yourself, go ahead and saddle her up."

Whitney took her time, brushing Montana and checking her hooves before centering a saddle pad. She shooed Josh away when he would have lifted the saddle for her.

"Would you do that for Brooke?" she demanded, huffing as she swung the saddle up high.

"Nope, but she's my sister. You're the woman I'd like to stay on the good side of."

"Any particular reason?" she asked, as she cinched the saddle tight.

"A few," he murmured, coming up behind her and resting his hands on her waist.

"Hey, now, let's not get Montana too excited." She pushed his hands away when she really wanted to bring them up to cup her breasts.

"Who's excited?" he whispered in her ear, then pressed his hips into her backside.

She shivered and pushed back against him, feeling his erection. "Are you going to be able to ride like that?"

He laughed. "I've been riding like that a lot since you came to town."

She turned around, and soon they were kissing, wrapped in each other's arms.

"How much longer are you going to make me wait, Josh?" she asked, panting and overheated.

"I don't think I can make *me* wait any longer,"

he said, then groaned as he lowered his head to kiss her again. At last he took her upper arms and held her away from him. "But right now, we have work to do."

She felt almost helpless and weak with longing as he slipped a halter on Montana and led the mare to the trailer. He put his own horse beside her and made sure they could both reach the hay.

At last, they were in the pickup, two cowdogs on the bench behind them, headed away from the Silver Creek Ranch and toward the Elk Mountains.

Whitney sighed and leaned her head back. "Hard to believe when the sky is this blue, that soon the snow will start falling."

"Heck, you were here last winter. We have a lot of blue skies. But then there are the winters where the snow piles so high, people used to have to put bandanas on their car radio antennae so they could see each other at intersections. Or so I'm told. You can't have missed how cold it's already getting at night. A couple mornings this August, I had to break the ice on the dogs' water bowls."

She spent the rest of the trip quizzing Josh about cattle grazing up in the mountains, and how ranchers had a permit that covered several pastures as their allotment. She, Josh, and the dogs were moving a herd of cows to fresh pasture. He made even that topic interesting, and she found herself relaxing and just watching him talk.

The road grew steeper, and eventually became more of a dirt track, and they finally parked near a gated fence. After unloading the horses and slipping on bridles, they led them inside the enclosure and mounted up.

The sky was still so blue, and behind them, the world dropped sharply away, through stands of trees, aspen and evergreen, and fields full of wildflowers sloping and twisting between streambeds and rock outcroppings.

"You may be used to the altitude in Valentine," Josh warned her, "but take it easy up here. Drink water regularly."

"Yes, sir," she said, pointing to the water bottles she'd stowed in a saddlebag. "So what do we do now?"

"We round up the cattle."

For the next several hours, they gathered fifty head. Whitney watched in amazement as the dogs took their cues from Josh and forced the much bigger cows and calves to do their bidding, barking and prancing, then running full speed until the cows veered in the direction Josh wanted. When they were at last all together, they herded them farther uphill, following a path Whitney couldn't see but Josh seemed to recognize. When they came to another gate, he opened it wide without dismounting—"Showoff!" she called— and the cows grudgingly followed him through, with Whitney and the dogs urging them from behind.

When the gate was closed, Josh reined in as he rode up beside her. "Good work."

"Thanks."

"And you're impressive on a horse."

"Isn't that a prerequisite for dating you?"

"Well, no," he said, smiling that slow, easy grin. "A woman can have other talents I admire."

They stared into each other's eyes, smiles dying.

At last he cleared his throat. "Come on, I know of a good picnic spot. I brought some lunch."

He eventually spread a blanket across soft moss beside a gurgling stream, while Whitney finished un-saddling the horses. When she turned around, he was stretched out on his side, propped up on his elbow as he reached into a saddlebag and began to pull out small containers. His hat was set carefully on a nearby rock, and the wind ruffled his wavy, dark hair. He looked up and smiled at her, and she almost lost her breath at the beauty of the picture before her. This was a picture that would make Facebook ex-plode.

She sat down cross-legged beside him, grateful for the fried chicken that gave her something to do other than stare at him. But that could only distract her for so long.

Her lips parted, and before she knew it, she was leaning over to kiss him, tasting the sweetness of soda mixed with fried chicken. She explored his mouth slowly, rasping her tongue along his, until an urgency began to take over, and she came up on her knees. When he rolled onto his back, she slid her torso, her sensitive breasts, along his chest until once again they were kissing, breath mingling, the sun warm on her back.

He rolled again until she was beneath him, his body blocking out the blue sky. Parting her legs, she moaned as his thigh rode between.

"Oh, Josh," she whispered.

He kissed his way down her cheek and neck, and she arched to give him even more access. He didn't stop there, tracing his way down the front of her shirt, unsnapping as he went. She pressed her hips against his thigh, a long, slow movement that also brought her intimately against his erection.

The dappled sunlight through the trees was warm on her skin as he parted her shirt, then lifted his head so he could watch his fingers slide along the lacy edge of her black bra. She watched, too, her anticipation climbing and climbing, until at last he brushed her nipple through the silk, and she gave a shuddering jerk.

"Poor thing is starving for attention," he murmured, then lowered his head to take her nipple in his mouth right through her bra.

She flung her head back as she held Josh to her. He played with her, teased her for long minutes until she thought she'd come apart if they didn't start removing clothes.

As if she were a doll, he lifted her up to straddle his lap. Her hair fell forward, brushing his face as they kissed, slow, deep kisses that mimicked what they were about to do. She felt her shirt being tugged down her arms, then the loosening of her bra as he unclasped it. She just wanted to feel his skin against hers and reveled in being able to pull his shirt wide as all the snaps came apart. They stroked and caressed each other, and she bent to lick his nipple, even as he cupped her breasts and played with them.

"We have to get out of these jeans," she finally said. "Let me help you."

When she pulled his belt loose, he set his hands on hers. "No."

"No?" she almost squeaked.

"Not *no,* just—let me undress you first."

He helped her to her feet, although he stayed low, so he had a prime view as he unsnapped her jeans and slowly pulled down the zipper. She knew just a touch of lace appeared, and she saw him swallow heavily and pause, as if he were frozen in anticipation. It made her feel so sexy.

At last she couldn't wait anymore and started to push them down her hips. Again, he stopped her, then did it himself, in slow, maddening degrees.

"Josh . . ." she began, not even knowing how to form the next words.

"So impatient," he murmured, then leaned forward to press his mouth just beneath her navel.

She shivered, and her legs threatened to buckle as he watched the slow progress of her jeans from up close, until at last he was tugging them down her thighs. She kicked them aside along with her cowboy boots and stood there in her black thong. He licked his lips and leaned toward it, but she moved back.

"My turn." Pressing hard on his shoulders, she made him lie back, then she took just as much time examining his belt buckle and the tightness of his zipper over his erection, playing, teasing, tormenting.

At last he groaned and reached for her, but she still eluded him, bringing down his zipper and spreading his jeans wide.

"Boxer briefs," she murmured. "Black. We match."

"Whitney!" He said her name on a groan.

"Lift your hips."

He did, and she pulled everything off at once although he had to help a bit with his tight boots. She admired his nudity, feeling almost faint with dark anticipation. On her hands and knees, she crawled up his body, then hovered over a very eager part of his anatomy.

He suddenly rolled, and she couldn't stop him from putting her on her back.

"Hey! I was going to—"

He put a finger to her lips, holding his body just off of hers although she could feel the heat of him all along her skin.

"I know you want to please me," he said hoarsely, "and I'm grateful. But right now, what would please me is pleasing you. Let me look at you, Whitney, let me touch. And don't worry, I've had a condom in my wallet like a teenager since the day we met."

And how could she say no to that, even though a part of her felt . . . strange just lying there? She never did that. But then Josh started to touch her, using his fingers and his lips, exploring every part of her body until she actually heard herself whimper, so close to the edge of exploding that even his slow removal of her thong made her writhe beneath his touch.

Eyes closed, she heard the sound of plastic being torn and whispered, "Oh, thank God."

And then he was kissing her, sliding on top of her body, and she was greedily opening her thighs to him, wrapping her legs about him, moaning her pleasure when he settled between.

And yet still he teased her with his erection, sliding up and down her wetness but not quite entering. Her only lucid thought—and that was fast leaving her—was: *How much stamina does this guy have?*

Chapter Fifteen

Josh held himself still, staring down at her, entranced by the passion that seemed to make her face glow. Her eyes were half-closed, but she still watched him with urgency and need and even satisfaction, as if she knew what she did to him.

How could she not? He was trembling on top of her, and at last he thrust inside. Swallowing her cry with a kiss, he stayed still, enjoying the heaven of her slick, tight warmth, and used his tongue in her mouth the way he was using his body.

She was undulating against him, and he joined her in that age-old rhythm that swept them both away. Holding back took everything in him, but he tried to read every quiver of her body, and only when she was swept away in an orgasm that made her shudder over and over, did he let himself go, thrusting repeatedly until, with a groan, he stopped moving and lay forehead to forehead with her. Their bodies were slick with perspiration, and just seeing the faint sheen on her breasts made him want to start all over again.

Instead, he slid to the side and pulled her tight against him. She was staring at him wide-eyed.

"What?" he asked, cupping one beautiful breast with his hand and teasing the nipple.

"For a while there, I thought you were superhuman," she said, smiling even as she shook her head.

"And I proved you wrong by how quickly I finished," he answered ruefully.

"Oh, no, believe me, I couldn't have taken much more. You waited just the right amount of time. And practice makes perfect."

He smiled down at her, then rested his head in the crook of his arm and just relaxed. The breeze was slightly cool on the mountain, but the sun playing peekaboo with the leaves gave them enough warmth. Her nudity was just as elegant as her clothes, and he couldn't stop looking at her, couldn't stop thinking how lucky he was.

He thought about the men she'd dated so casually and knew he could never be that content, that easily sated.

"I thought once we'd made love," he began, "that a part of me would relax."

"I think a part of you is doing that right now," she teased.

But he didn't smile. "You've been like a fire that burned inside me from the moment we met."

Her smile faded, and she watched him with wary intensity. "Josh . . . ?"

"And now that we've made love, that fire only feels hotter."

She gave a shaky laugh. "I didn't know your creativity extended to poetry."

"I'm serious, Whitney. I won't be content with bits of you doled out here and there. I want it all with you."

She sat up, and he knew he'd scared her off when she reached for her bra.

"Josh, We've been dating yes, and it's been fun—you were the one who told me that's all dating was."

He gently caught her arm and tried to ignore the wariness in her eyes, which saddened him. "I'm not going to pressure you, and I won't bring it up again, but I wanted you to know where I stood. But as you *know*, I'm very good at being patient, and I'm going to keep courtin' you"—he drawled the word lightly and felt some of the tension leave her—"for as long as it takes."

She put her bra on, still watching him with faint confusion, but at least the wariness was gone. "For as long as it takes until *what*?"

He shrugged. "I guess I'll know when it happens."

She shook her head and donned the thong next, and he watched it slide up her thighs and barely withheld a groan as it covered the part of her he'd just had but not tasted.

He sat up and leaned toward that perfect juncture, but she held him back.

"Josh, we can't stay out here all day," she said, not quite meeting his eyes.

"Why not?"

"Because we both have work to do."

"I thought I had you for the day."

"True, but . . ."

She slipped her cute shirt on, and he knew that he'd lost her. For today, anyway.

He searched beneath the rumpled blanket until he found his jeans. "Okay, guess we've taken enough chances on being seen."

She froze, both feet tucked into her jeans to the ankles. "Seen? Up here in the wilderness?"

"Well, other ranchers have allotments nearby. You never know . . ." He expected her to berate him or hurry into her clothes.

Instead, she gave him a seductive glance, and said, "Why didn't you tell me? The fear of being caught might have made everything even better."

"Not possible. And you're a she-devil."

"I try."

They picked up their picnic, saddled their horses, and made their way slowly back down the mountain. Conversation was easy again, but Josh couldn't forget that she wasn't at all pleased he wanted something deeper with her. But he wasn't dissuaded, especially after they returned to the ranch. They were seen by a group of middle-aged women whom Brooke was giving riding lessons to, and Josh saw them do a double take when he appeared. Ignoring the imminent dispersal of the women, Whitney put him against the wall in a dark corner of the barn and kissed him until he saw stars.

"Worried those ladies'll lead me astray?" he asked huskily.

"You go ahead and think that, Josh Thalberg," she answered, then kissed him again.

He was barely coherent when his sister began to return the first of the horses to the pasture beyond the barn. Only a few of them were kept in stalls during the winter—otherwise, they enjoyed the outdoors all year long. And then Steph arrived for a barrel-racing lesson with Brooke, and he found himself leaning against the fence at Whitney's side, explaining the competition to her.

She could have left anytime, but she didn't, and that gave him hope.

That night, Whitney went dancing at Outlaws with the girls, who wanted to show her country dancing at its finest. It was the perfect way to take her mind off Josh, who probably wouldn't dare show up for fear of being mobbed—not that she'd invited him.

The next morning, she was groggy and tired. She should have been able to sleep after a day of riding, dancing—and sex. But instead, she'd lain restlessly in bed because every time she closed her eyes, she'd relived the memory of Josh's hands practicing magic on her, the faintest whisper of his kisses.

He'd had control of every part of her body, and it unsettled her. He'd stopped her from working her own magic on him, and when he'd gotten her all hot and bothered, she'd simply forgotten. And she *never* forgot to make a man feel special. She usually enjoyed making sex a lavish production, being every man's desire. After all, she had to live up to that underwear photo and the fantasies it seemed to inspire.

But Josh had slowed it down and made it all about her, the first guy who ever did. She didn't like the feeling of vulnerability, of tenderness.

She couldn't get back to sleep, of course, so she decided to go check out the renovations on the building. It was Sunday, the crew wouldn't be working, so she could take her time examining the changes.

Sunday morning in Valentine, bells announced the start of church services, something her parents had never considered important. As a kid, she'd been glad not to wake up early; now, as an adult, she sometimes wondered what she was missing. As she walked to Leather and Lace, she passed lots of people heading toward St. John's, the closest church.

She turned down her street, picking up her speed in her excitement to see the changes . . . and came to a stop in growing dismay. One of the plate-glass windows was partially shattered. Clenching her jaw, she hurried up the stairs, then gingerly walked across the porch, only to see that most of the glass had blown inward.

She unlocked the door, staring at the mess, knowing there hadn't been a storm to blow something through. And then she saw a large rock where it had rolled to a stop against a toolbox.

Inhaling at the stab of pain that lanced her chest, she pulled out her cell and dialed 911. Fifteen minutes later, she was sitting on the front stairs when the sheriff arrived. He was an older gentleman in his sixties, a slight belly above his belt, but with shoulders stiff from lifelong military bearing. His white hair was styled in a crew cut, and his piercing green eyes focused on her as he held out a hand.

"Ms. Winslow? Sheriff Buchanan."

She rose to her feet as they shook hands. "Sheriff, thanks so much for coming so promptly for a non-emergency. I did make that part clear, didn't I?"

"You did, ma'am. But there's no sense putting off something important. Vandalism hurts more than the building if you ask me."

For a moment, she felt the sting of tears as she realized the truth of his statement. It wasn't just about some punk with a rock, she knew that. It was just another sign that she and her store weren't welcome in Valentine Valley.

A pickup pulled up to the curb, and she recognized Josh immediately. She wondered if it was the sheriff or one of his staff who'd felt the need to tell Josh what had happened. It made her almost angry, then she reminded herself that it wasn't Josh she was angry with. He got out and approached, holding out a hand to the sheriff. He was wearing jeans and a light blue buttoned-down shirt, opened at his tan neck.

"Good to see you, Josh," Sheriff Buchanan said. "I thought I heard you knew this young lady. She'll need your support."

Whitney tried to smile. "It's not all that tragic, honestly. Just a rock. Probably a kid."

Josh frowned as he stared at the damaged window. "Considering the opposition to Leather and Lace last winter, you can't assume this was a random act."

Sheriff Buchanan glanced from Josh to Whitney. "I heard something about that."

"Who didn't?" she asked with more sarcasm than humor.

"Was there someone particularly vocal against you?"

She hesitated and met Josh's eyes. "I can't believe . . ."

"Ma'am, just by saying a name, you're not accusing anyone. I should know everyone who'd have a motive for these damages."

"The leader of the opposition was Sylvester Galimi," she said in a wooden voice, then briefly covered her eyes. "Oh, this is foolish. He speaks openly—he wouldn't hide behind such a cowardly act."

The sheriff wrote something in a notebook. "Anyone else?"

Whitney glanced at Josh. "I can't think of anyone else who was as vocal. The rest just followed his lead. Once they lost their complaint to the town council—"

"Complaint?" the sheriff interrupted.

Josh said, "They tried to get her lingerie store classified as pornography, so that it would be denied a permit to open."

"It didn't work," Whitney said, mildly annoyed that Josh had spoken for her. "The town council saw the silliness of it all, and I received my permit."

"That was last winter, I believe?" Sheriff Buchanan said. "What took you so long to return and start up again?"

She sighed. "I was busy with my other two stores, and frankly, I was hoping some of the anger would die down."

He glanced again at the broken window. "So who would have been here last?"

"Sweet Construction, and that was yesterday."

"And Sheriff," Josh added, "it's not all that destructive, but someone wrote in chalk on her front sidewalk a week or so ago for her to go back to San Francisco."

"How could I have forgotten?" Whitney asked dryly.

He closed his notebook. "All right, I'll see what I can do. Maybe people saw someone lingering here last night. Sorry to meet you under such poor circumstances, Ms. Winslow." He nodded to them both and left.

Realizing that she was hugging herself as she stared at the broken glass, Whitney dropped her hands to her side.

Josh put his arm around her waist. "You could have called me," he said in a low voice.

She stared up at him, sensing a hint of anger, which quickened her own. "My first thought was the police.

I would have told you when I saw you. Just because we slept together doesn't mean you're involved in the more personal aspects of my life."

He arched a dark brow. "Sex isn't personal? Oh, sorry, you did tell me it's that way in San Francisco. But those men weren't me."

"Don't get possessive, Josh."

"Possessive? All I'm saying is that I care about you, every part of you, and not just your body. I'd like to be of help, not take over."

She exhaled slowly. "I'm sorry. I understand what you're saying. It's just that—when you showed up, I felt like I couldn't be trusted to handle my own problems." Her biggest worry with her parents.

"We both know that's not true. Sheriff Buchanan's clerk called the ranch, since she knew we were close to you. It didn't occur to me that my arrival would bother you."

"I know, I know." She put a hand on his arm and squeezed. "Can you forgive me?"

He gave her a gentle hug. "Nothing to forgive."

She felt strangely safe in his arms and let herself relax and absorb his strength. Gradually, their bodies both seemed to remember what they'd done yesterday, and the intimacy went from comforting to arousing.

She stepped back.

Josh didn't seem offended. "How about if I go pick up a sheet of plywood while you sweep up the glass?"

"Thanks. I'm sure the Sweet brothers can put in a new pane tomorrow."

As she watched him measure the window opening, she couldn't help wondering if someone might just break it again. It was such a troubling feeling.

It didn't take all that long to dump the glass in the garbage, and Josh returned from Hal's Hardware. He ignored the girls on their way home from church who snapped his picture and giggled.

When Whitney approached the pickup, she murmured, "I think the women of Valentine Valley have memorized the make and license plate of your pickup."

He rolled his eyes. "I'm ignoring them, remember? I'm not hiding or creating any kind of scene that would be even more fun to photograph. Eventually, they'll get tired of me."

She helped him carry the large piece of wood up the porch stairs and held it in place while he nailed it secure.

She stepped back and frowned. "It makes the store look like crap."

"Luckily, it's not open. In twenty-four hours, it'll look like new. Now why don't you show me around inside?"

And using that easygoing manner of his, he succeeded in calming her down much faster than she would have on her own. He took her out for Sunday brunch at the Silver Creek Café, where they held hands, looked into each other's eyes, and even shared a conversation. Whitney told herself that things would be more normal between them now. The aftermath of sex was something she understood.

He dropped her off at The Adelaide, and apologized that he couldn't come in. Sex would have taken her mind off her troubles, she grumbled to herself as she climbed the stairs to her room. So instead, she decided to concentrate on *his* troubles. When she still hadn't received a response from the Facebook admin, she logged back in and decided to explore his fan page.

She discovered a fan-club tab she hadn't noticed the other day, and, to her surprise, they were selling Josh's autographed photo. Autographed? Now someone was trying to make money off him! It was only seven bucks, and she imagined at least half of that covered the photo and shipping, but still, with thirty thousand "likes," a lot of fans might be desperate for something he'd supposedly touched. She used to get requests for her autograph, too, back in her Whitney Wild days, and she'd never understood it. There were just some people who liked mementoes.

The directions were easy: send seven dollars cash or money order to Josh's Fan Club, at a Denver post office box. So who owned the PO box? Whitney knew it was pointless to call the postal service. The names of box owners were private by law. Maybe if she had one of the photos, she'd be able to discover something from it.

But send for it as herself? No way. If this person was truly a fan, he or she would know Josh was dating her. More likely it was someone out to make a quick buck, but Whitney didn't want to take any chances.

So she called up her assistant to order a photo to his own address, then asked him to forward it on to her.

"Josh's Fan Club?" Ryan teased. "Isn't Josh the hot cowboy who's doing that leatherwork for you?"

Whitney smiled. "So you've seen his picture?"

"Who didn't? You sure you don't need me up there?"

She laughed aloud. "Trust me, you'd be looking on from afar."

"Pretty straight and macho, is he?"

"Very straight."

"And it sounds like you'd know."

"Ryan!" But she was smiling.

"Sorry, sorry, okay, fan-club photo. I'm on it. So when are you going to be back in town?"

"I honestly don't know. But my managers are doing a great job, as are you. You can do without my actual presence for a while longer."

But how long? she wondered as she hung up.

Until the renovations were done. And she'd need to hire a manager, of course, and several sales associates. It was time to get on with that. She opened the browser on her phone and started looking up local sign companies. She'd order a sign that would jut out from the building, so that people on Main Street couldn't miss it when they glanced down Fourth Street. No one was going to stop her from opening the newest Leather and Lace.

Chapter Sixteen

Josh called Monday evening, and Tuesday, too, and she found it easy to lie on her bed and have a teasing conversation with him. When she asked him how the necklaces were going, he said he'd been working hard, but it was time for recreation. He invited her to his rec-league softball game Wednesday evening at the Silver Creek Park.

"This is our big date?"

"No, it most certainly is not. Just be ready."

He called when he pulled up.

"I feel so special that you invited me and all your Facebook girlfriends," she teased.

The phone was silent for a moment, then he briskly said, "I'll be right up."

When he knocked on her door, she called for him to come in, then posed provocatively in front of her closet, wearing some of her best lingerie, white and lacy, sheer and—short.

When he saw her, he froze, then slowly shut the door behind him and leaned against it.

"I just can't decide what to wear," she said in a helpless voice.

He walked deliberately to her side, and she held her breath, waiting for his touch. Instead, he looked in her closet.

"You've got to have something that costs less than a thousand dollars in here. This is just a softball game."

Whitney didn't answer, only batted her eyelashes at him and shrugged one strap off her shoulder.

She was on her back on the bed before she could take another breath, giddy with delight, and this time, she rose up on top, straddling his hips as she looked him over.

"I don't know about *your* clothes," she said, shaking her head, looking critically at his white team shirt with the Tony's Tavern logo and blue baseball pants. "You should take them off right now. You have a few minutes, don't you?"

"Someone has to sit out the first inning," he said hoarsely.

She helped him undress, then showed him how truly powerless he could be as she used every secret to bring him to the point of ecstasy before riding him to their mutual pleasure. He collapsed in exhaustion, head lolling off the bed.

"Oh, my, we really will be late," she said, slowly removing her bustier.

He flung an arm over his eyes and groaned. "But it was worth it."

At the baseball game, the stands were full, and Josh, carrying her lawn chair, pulled up short, tipping back his ball cap as if he needed to see better.

"I told you someone had posted it on Facebook," she said.

"And then you made sure to distract me so I forgot

all about it," he said. "Oh, well, I'm sure both teams will enjoy having an audience for a change."

As they walked toward his team, Will Sweet, stretching out his hamstrings, straightened and glanced over his shoulder at the crowd. "Impressive, huh?"

"Sorry about this," Josh said.

"Nothing to be sorry for," Will answered, then grinned. "I posted the game time and place on your Facebook page. You're no longer available, but the boys and I can console your disappointed fans."

"Thanks for the sacrifice," Josh said dryly.

Whitney sat in her chair near the dugout, away from the piercing screams of girls in the stands. Brooke was on the team, along with several men Whitney knew: the rest of the Sweet brothers; Matthew, a Sweet cousin; Monica's brother Dom; Nate; Adam; Tony; and others she hadn't met yet.

All these men just took it for granted that she and Josh were an item. She hadn't been in this kind of relationship since college. There hadn't been a single man she trusted enough to be that special in her life—but she'd gone right along with it where Josh was concerned. What made him so different?

She watched him jog onto the baseball diamond and play shortstop, an athlete who knew how to use his body. And she'd already been the lucky recipient.

He was kind and funny, loyal to his family and friends, deeply creative in a way that went beyond what she understood. She saw patterns and fabric and knew how to combine them in a way that would look good on a woman. He saw images in leather that weren't even there and could create them so realistically. He worked so hard at both his jobs and never complained, even putting up with an occasionally intrusive grandma. Now he'd come under the kind of stress he would never have been able to imagine, and he put up with it—the fame, the lack of privacy, the obsessive behavior. A lot of other people would blow a fuse, but not him.

He was focused, and right now, that focus was all on her. She knew it would fade; it always did. No one could stand up to such intensive scrutiny. And she'd be leaving, too, so surely, in the back of his mind, he wouldn't let himself get attached.

She wouldn't, and had lots of practice keeping men at arm's length, emotionally anyway. She was all about the physical and was glad he'd finally come along for the ride. They could date for a few weeks, anyway.

If his fans let him, of course. She had to smile when he made a play getting an opponent out on second base, and the crowd went as wild as if he'd hit a home run.

"What did we miss?" cried Mrs. Thalberg as she approached, carrying two lawn chairs.

She was followed by Mrs. Ludlow, leaning over her walker, and Mrs. Palmer, wearing a tiny baseball cap perched on her blond wig and a Tony's Tavern baseball shirt, ready to cheer on her grandson, Adam. No sooner had she set down her chair, than she pulled a pair of pompoms from her oversized purse and started waving them.

Mrs. Ludlow sank slowly into her chair, a white sweater draped over her shoulders, and gave Mrs. Palmer a long-suffering glance. "Renee, you hit me with one of those at the last game. Please do be careful this time."

"Don't be a killjoy, Connie." Grinning, Mrs. Palmer shook both pompoms and yelled, "Go Tony's Tavern!"

As Josh's team filed back into the dugout, Mrs. Thalberg put her own chair right beside Whitney, then gave a pointed glance at the full bleachers. "Guess we're not the only ones who follow Josh's Facebook page."

Whitney widened her eyes. "You're on Facebook?"

"Of course I am! How else would I see any pictures from my grandkids? I kept telling them to attach pictures to me—I do have e-mail, you know!—but they kept grumbling that they'd just loaded them or uploaded them, whatever, to Facebook. So I joined. It wasn't very difficult after all. So when I was Googling Josh's name to see all these articles, his Facebook page came up. Now, I was shocked, because he's my one grandchild who's just not with the times where all this computer stuff is concerned."

Whitney bit her lip to keep from laughing. She'd seen Josh's extensive computerized business records, but she didn't mention it.

"He doesn't even have a website!" the old woman continued, shaking her head. "Think how he could display his work."

"I think he doesn't want that, Mrs. Thalberg. And you know he didn't set up that Facebook page."

"Well, I sorta guessed that."

"He's already got more work than he needs. I've felt very honored he agreed to do those necklaces for me when it's surely difficult to find the time."

"Well, that's easy—he's sweet on you."

Whitney actually found herself blushing at the old-fashioned term.

"And you can't deny you're sweet on him."

"No, no denying," she said, nodding ruefully.

Mrs. Thalberg narrowed her eyes and studied her. "You don't sound all that happy about it."

"I—it's not that. Josh is wonderful. But . . . to be honest, I've never been in this kind of relationship before."

"A grown woman like you? You've gotta be near thirty."

"You have a good eye. I just turned thirty."

"Ah, he's a younger man of twenty-seven."

"And in some ways, at least where relationships go, he's far more mature than I am."

"You've just been scared off by all that stuff in your past."

Whitney sighed but couldn't be surprised that a computer-savvy grandma would know those things about her. She'd probably thought she was protecting her grandson by discovering all she could about Whitney.

"Just take your time and enjoy his courtin'. He's enjoying it, too."

Well, there was no doubt about that . . .

"Thanks, Mrs. Thalberg, I'll remember that."

"Be quiet, you two," Mrs. Palmer shouted. "Josh is up at bat!"

Mrs. Thalberg winced and wiggled her finger in the ear nearest Mrs. Palmer, but the other woman didn't get the hint, only kept on cheering.

Whitney smiled, then rose to her feet to shout as Josh hit a line drive between first and second base. The screams from the stands were deafening, and the setting sun reflected off dozens of cameras and phones aimed at Josh. When he pulled up on first base, he just tipped his baseball cap.

Whitney glanced back to the dugout, where she could see the backs of Brooke's and Adam's heads as they leaned toward each other. They were doing exactly what Mrs. Thalberg said, taking time and enjoying the courting. When she thought of all the things Adam had to overcome since his discharge from the Marines, she reminded herself that although her past could hardly compare, she could learn from his example. He was moving forward with his life, back in Valentine Valley with a steady girlfriend, a steady job, and a way to help other veterans find homes. But if it was taking him a while to propose, who could blame him? Marriage was a serious commitment, and when things from the past could rise up and hurt your relationship, a person needed to take time. Just like Mrs. Thalberg said.

But Whitney wouldn't tell that to Brooke.

In the fourth inning, when Josh was sitting on the bench in the dugout waiting for his turn at bat, he found himself glancing often at Whitney. Emily and Monica had shown up, and the three of them sat with the widows, casually chatting while watching the game.

The sun had faded behind the mountains, but there was no need yet for field lights. It was simply a lazy, late-summer evening at one of America's favorite pastimes.

Tony's son Ethan was playing catch with another teammate's son, and Josh found himself thinking about Tony. He'd married a driven woman whose job eventually became the focus of her life. Tony had thought he could change her, especially after Ethan had been born, but you can't change anyone who doesn't want to be changed.

Josh knew he couldn't really equate Whitney with Tony's ex, except for the career part. And most women had those nowadays. As for kids, he didn't even know if Whitney wanted any after the crazy way she'd grown up. But all these things were running through his head, bringing up his own past, and Jill, who he'd almost been married to.

And then he let it all go, watching Whitney laugh, her dark hair swinging against her shoulders and neck. He'd always been a positive sort of guy—he wasn't going to stop that now. Things would work out for the best.

Will sat beside him, looking at his phone. Glancing up, he said, "So where shall I post we'll be tonight?"

Josh tossed his glove at him.

Early the next afternoon, Whitney was cleaning the front windows and preparing space for the autumn window displays that Ryan was overnighting. Now that her sign was up, she was drawing a tourist or two from Main Street, and they should have something tempting to look at, so they'd want to return. She glanced out at the rainy street and saw Emily, Monica, and Brooke all huddled together under one big umbrella, laughing as they ran up her front steps.

She was surprised by the warm feeling of joy that rose within her. She had friends, of course, ones she had dinner or went shopping with, but they all seemed to serve that kind of (shallow?) purpose in each other's lives. They didn't discuss their deepest problems, didn't share anything more intimate than . . . Whitney's lingerie. And it wasn't as if she and her sister-in-law Courtney were close, living on opposite coasts.

But these women of Valentine shared a closeness that went beyond friendship to sisterhood, and for some unfathomable reason, they'd included Whitney.

She went to the door and opened it. "Come on in!"

Emily peered in cautiously. "We're all wet. Will we ruin your wood floor?"

"They haven't even started refinishing it yet, so no worries there."

After leaving the umbrella on the front porch, they all trooped in, wearing a rainbow of raincoats and carrying several brown bags. A waft of cinnamon made her stomach growl loudly.

Monica laughed. "We brought lunch."

"And dessert from me," Emily put in, grinning.

"Care to join us?" Brooke asked.

"Great idea, thanks. There's a table in the kitchen the workers have been using."

As they filed through the rooms, they oohed and aahed at the newly open space since the workers had torn down the walls between the large living room, the dining room, and the pantry. French doors led from the dining room to the back porch and a large, fenced-in yard.

"It's good that you're keeping the character of the house," Brooke said, nodding her approval.

"That's what's taking so long, of course," Whitney replied. "The wood trim is exquisite. You can't get that kind anymore, so they have to work slowly and with care, especially since much of it had been painted over. It's a lot of work removing layers of paint. The carved banister heading up to the second floor might as well be a work of art. And the backyard?" She paused at the French doors. "I'm going to have it landscaped, of course, and I'll make it look like a peaceful retreat."

"From our hectic city life?" Emily said, chuckling.

Whitney smiled and led them through an arched doorway into a plainer hall, then the kitchen. "I'm told that back in the old days, guests in the dining room should never have to see into the kitchen; hence this little hall."

In the kitchen, a long row of plain cabinets indicated storage and not much decoration. "Only the servants were in this room, so they didn't decorate like our modern kitchens. I'm going to use this as an office slash employee break room. Someday, I'd like to replace the cupboards. I considered moving them upstairs but changed my mind. Not pretty enough."

"Upstairs?" Monica echoed, placing her bags on the table.

"After Emily's uncles are finished down here in the next few weeks, they're going to remodel upstairs for storage and a small apartment I can use whenever I'm in town."

"Thinking ahead," Brooke said, nodding. She pulled a folded newspaper out of one of the bags even as Emily began to lay out plastic containers on the kitchen table near the big bay window. "Did you see the recent *Gazette*?"

"Ah, I wanted to see if they had my ad in the Classifieds for a manager and sales associates. I know it's on their website, too."

"I didn't check the Classifieds, but I did see another article on my brother. There are more photos, of course."

"Of course," Whitney said. "The man is very photogenic."

Brooke frowned. "You sure he shouldn't be hiding from these guys?"

"That'll just lead to chases and even more obsessive interest. And he doesn't want that."

Monica opened up a large container of salad and brought out a couple different bottled dressings. Next came sandwiches, and a little cooler with an assortment of sodas.

"My mom made the sandwiches," Brooke said. "She says hi."

And then Emily opened up her box, revealing an apple pie, and they all groaned.

"Wait, wait, don't distract me," Brooke said. "You should read the article, Whitney. It focuses on his connection to Leather and Lace."

She took the newspaper and scanned it while the women set out paper plates, napkins, and plasticware. She felt the tension leave her spine when there was no mention of her Whitney Wild past. She didn't want Josh tarnished by the scandals she'd gotten herself involved in. None of it had hurt her stores in San Francisco and Las Vegas, but then again, she was selling daring lingerie.

"Well, this isn't too bad. I'm not sure they're saying anything all that new since Josh isn't giving interviews. But someone is pushing to keep this in the papers, even feeding them information. Do you guys have any ideas? Does Josh have enemies?"

"Josh?" Brooke said, blinking in surprise. "Even when he brands cows, they don't seem to hate him for it."

"Gross," Monica said, making a face.

"You might work with dirt," Brooke said glibly, "but I get to castrate bull nuts."

Unconcerned, Emily heaped salad on her plate. "Once, this would have disgusted me, but now I'm married to a cowboy."

"You know, I couldn't help my curiosity," Brooke said, sitting down at the table and reaching for a sandwich. "I went to the newspaper myself and asked questions about the article."

Whitney sat down and leaned toward her. "Really? What did you find out?"

"They wouldn't say anything about their 'source'"—she gave sarcastic air quotes—"but a secretary accidentally revealed that it was a woman. And that's all I got."

"A woman?" Whitney sank back in her chair in confusion. "That could be . . . anyone. Josh's groupies come in all shapes and sizes and ages." She wished she could discuss the photo and the fan club, but since she hadn't spelled everything out to Josh yet, she wasn't about to tell anyone else. "Guess it'll have to remain a mystery."

"I'm sure it'll all die down eventually," Monica said, "but until then, I'm enjoying Josh's success as if it were my own."

"It kind of is your own," Brooke pointed out.

"I *am* profiting handsomely." Monica wiggled her eyebrows. "So, Whitney, tell us what's next for the store."

They spent a lively hour talking about her coming search for employees and ideas for Christmas displays across all three stores. But always in the back of her mind, Whitney wondered about this strange woman, if she was the one behind Josh's fan club.

Monday morning, after spending an hour setting up appointments with the people with the best résumés, Whitney was kneeling in the window arranging displays on the uneven shelves, when she saw Sylvester Galimi march up the stairs. She looked over her shoulder at the four men working on the trim, and a saw whined.

Sighing, she went out the front door before Sylvester could even knock.

He glanced past her at the tasteful lingerie she'd begun to drape over the partial torsos of mannequins, and she waited for a response.

His wince was minor as he lifted his chin and spoke coolly. "Sheriff Buchanan talked to me a few days ago. It's taken me until now to decide what to say to you."

She gave her own wince. "I didn't tell him you'd thrown the rock. I don't think you did."

He flung his arms wide. "Then why give him my name at all?"

"Come sit down, Sylvester," she said, motioning to the new wicker furniture she'd recently purchased for the porch.

"I don't want to sit. I just want some answers."

Whitney sighed. "I had to tell the sheriff the name of the person who led the opposition against Leather and Lace."

"But rock-throwing?" he said with exasperation. "I went the legal route with the town council and lost."

"But you're still not happy."

"Of course not, but I can urge people not to patronize your store and its indecent clothing. There are other *legal* ways to fight back." He rubbed a hand through his curly hair and sank down on a cushioned chair in bewilderment. "This was Saturday night—I even have an alibi, and believe me, my sister wouldn't lie for me. But this was so embarrassing. I've known Sheriff Buchanan for so many years . . ."

He looked . . . hurt and confused at the thought of any criminal conduct. Whitney felt a stab of sympathy for him. For the first time, instead of the enemy, she saw him as a person who was obviously uneasy with overt displays of sexuality. Or maybe he was just a deeply religious man, trying to do what he thought was right and moral. Small towns had all kinds of people, after all.

Of course, he was projecting his own morals on others . . .

"Sylvester, I'm sorry Sheriff Buchanan had to question you. I'm glad it led nowhere. I hope we can put this behind us."

He stood up and glanced again at her window displays, then at her new sign advertising the business.

"I don't know, Miss Winslow. I'm never going to agree with what you're doing."

"I know."

He nodded and walked back down the stairs, and this time he didn't march so heavily. She watched him turn back toward Main Street and his diner. Still her enemy, but not a vindictive one. She could live with that.

That night, as she talked on the phone with Josh, she told him about Sylvester's visit.

"You sound . . . pensive," he said in a quiet voice.

She lay back on her bed beneath the open window, and listened to the sound of the evening birds chirping a good night. "I don't know. It was kind of sad. *He* was kind of sad."

"It's not your fault, Whitney. Maybe I can come over there and cheer you up."

She smiled. "Only if you want to traipse through Debbie's book club. I was invited to attend, but not having read the book . . ."

"Oh. Guess I'll skip it then."

She laughed.

"What about tomorrow afternoon?" he continued. "I'm having lunch with your real-estate agent and his family. They take turns inviting us pathetic bachelors over. You could help me defer their pointed interest."

"This better not be our big date since it sounds like you want to use me."

"Well . . . I think we could both come up with better ways to use each other."

His voice had dropped into that low, rumbling range that gave her goose bumps.

It wasn't until they'd said their good-nights that she realized she still hadn't told him about the woman who'd been the source for the latest article on him. She'd wait until she had something more concrete than that. Surely Ryan would soon receive the fan-club photo of Josh. She prayed that there was some sort of clue . . .

Chapter Seventeen

Howie Deering and his wife Tara lived in a little bungalow a few streets off Main. Though only in their late twenties, they already had the settled, married look of two people too busy to exercise much. They had two toddlers and a house overrun with toys. Oh, they were all on shelves or in baskets, but Whitney thought that might have been a hasty cleanup job just before she and Josh arrived.

The two little boys had the carrot hair of their mom and both parents' freckles. They stared up at her with surprising indifference—something she could relate to.

She didn't remember the last time she'd been around kids. Only a few of her friends were even married though she was about to turn thirty, and none had started families. It seemed that she naturally gravitated toward career women like herself, who were still working their way up the ladder. Children weren't even on their radar—or hers. Her brother Chasz and his wife Courtney had been married for seven years with no kids, and Whitney sometimes wondered if they planned to have them at all. Not that she'd ever ask, of course. She frowned, realizing she hadn't spoken to either of them in weeks. She and Courtney had a love of shopping in common, and Courtney usually sent her a quick photo of her newest purchase at least once or twice a week. But not lately.

And then Josh hunkered right down beside Howie III and asked about the puzzle he was working at on a child-sized table. Did it bother him to be around children? She wondered if he sometimes thought of the child his high-school girlfriend had miscarried, the path that had altered with that one tragedy.

Tara said, "Whitney, can I get you a drink?"

She followed her into the kitchen, but Josh remained behind. Howie was stirring something on the stove and looked up to give her a smile.

"Is white wine all right?" Tara asked.

Whitney nodded, even as she found herself glancing back into the living room.

"He'll be okay," Tara said, smiling. "I've taken my oldest boy out for riding lessons with Brooke, and more than once, Josh was happy to do some cowboy stuff with little Howie. He has a man crush on Josh."

Smiling, feeling surprisingly relieved, Whitney accepted the wineglass.

Howie turned a frown on her. "I heard about the window at your store. Have they found out who did it?"

She shook her head. "And they probably won't although the sheriff tells me there are a few people who might have seen something. We'll see."

"Still . . . I can't imagine it feels good."

"No, it doesn't."

While Tara and Howie finished lunch prep, Whitney eventually wandered back to the living room and sat down on the floor beside their youngest, Kyle. He was banging two blocks together, then froze, staring up at her with wide chocolate brown eyes.

"Don't start crying, kid," she murmured, smiling as wide as she could as she began to stack the blocks. "Wanna knock it down?"

Kyle continued to stare, and his bottom lip quivered.

"See, this is fun!" she said cheerfully, then knocked down her little tower of blocks.

Kyle blinked, and Whitney held her breath while quickly setting up another tower. Then Kyle knocked it over and gave her a cautious smile.

Thank God.

She glanced up to find Josh watching her, grinning.

She stuck out her tongue. "You have the easy kid," she whispered.

"I'm easy?" Howie said loudly.

She winced, even as Josh chuckled.

"Whitney just means you're good at puzzles," Josh said. "Now she'd like to come help you. She loves puzzles. Do you mind?" he asked the kid.

Howie seemed to shrug with indifference, his gaze focused on the big puzzle pieces.

Sighing, Whitney exchanged places with Josh, where she knew she was about to prove Howie wasn't easy at all. Sure enough, Howie kept insisting he knew where each piece went, and tried to force it into place if she so much as voiced a different opinion. It worked best if she chose her own piece and pretended that it was taking her a long time to find the right spot. The pieces *were* two inches wide, after all. She couldn't blame the kid—she didn't like anyone's telling her what to do either.

At the sound of a baby giggle, she turned her head and saw Josh on his back, holding Kyle high in the

air above him, before bringing him down and blow-
ing raspberry kisses into his neck. He lifted the baby
back into the air, and a drop of spit landed right on
Josh's forehead, and he didn't care at all.

And something in her went all soft and gooey at
the sight. Damn, this wasn't good, she thought, hastily turning back to Howie's puzzle. But she continued to cast quick glances at Josh and thought how
genuine he was, how little he hid any part of himself.
Surely, he was just too good to be true.

Lunch was not exactly relaxing, with two little
boys in attendance, but it was certainly lively. Josh
answered cowboy questions from Howie, and little
Kyle kept tossing his spoon at Whitney, to his parents' mortification.

It wasn't until she was back at the B&B that she remembered her brother's long silence. She called both
him and Courtney, and their phones went to voice
mail. She left cheerful messages but didn't hear back.

Josh drove home from the Deerings and couldn't
keep from smiling at the memories of Whitney with
the little boys. It wasn't hard to tell she was unused
to kids, but he admired her willingness to learn. And
the shocked look on her face when Kyle spit a pea
and it landed right on her cheek . . . Josh was still
laughing.

At the ranch, there was an unfamiliar car parked
by the barn, but he thought nothing of it, what with
Brooke's riding-school students coming and going.

He went into the office and found her sitting across
from two men, who gave him interested smiles when
they shook hands.

"Rich and Brian have come to interview me about the riding school," Brooke said. "It's going to be great publicity."

He was about to leave them in peace, when Rich called, "Josh, we'd love to get your take on having another business here at a busy ranch, especially since you have a side business, too."

And soon the interview questions were mostly about him, and he kept giving Brooke apologetic glances. The photographer took a photo of Brooke, then several of them together.

When at last they'd left, Josh and Brooke didn't have time to speak before their parents came in, Sandy a little breathless as she leaned on the cane.

"So how was it?" Sandy asked, smiling eagerly.

Brooke gave her a rueful smile. "You should probably ask Josh. I think he was the true reason for their visit."

Josh grimaced. "I'm sorry, Brooke. That was nasty subterfuge, and I would have kicked them out of here, but I didn't want to risk harming your new business."

"It's okay," she said with a sigh. "I'm still enjoying watching you squirm under all this attention. And if they mention me—and they better—it *will* truly help my business."

That made him feel relieved.

Doug frowned. "I didn't think this nonsense would go on so long."

"Are you calling our son nonsense?" Sandy teased.

"Of course not." Doug turned on Josh. "You know I'm proud of you, right?"

Josh grinned. "I've never doubted it."

"But it seems to me that this fame is only growin', rather than fadin' away, what with the photographers and the trespassers and the people followin' you around or accostin' you on the streets."

Giving a shrug, Josh said, "Whitney thinks if I show I'm upset, they'll know they can get a rise out of me and draw all of this out."

Sandy limped toward him. He started to get up to give her his chair, but she waved him back down and put a hand on his shoulder. "But we can see what it's truly costing you. I haven't missed how late your workshop light stays on, and yet you're up at dawn working on your chores."

"You make it sound like this is new," Josh said. "I've always worked late when inspiration strikes me."

"But this isn't inspiration," Doug pointed out. "You have deadlines now and people's expectations to meet. You're stretchin' yourself too thin."

Josh rubbed a hand down his whiskered chin. "Seems to me I was telling Nate this same thing last year."

"It runs in the family," Brooke said. "Seems none of us are content with just one direction in our lives."

Josh spread his hands. "We hired Adam—that's been a big help. And I'm sorry I overslept last Tuesday. It won't happen again."

Sandy rolled her eyes. "Oh, please, that's not what this is about. I just wanted you to know that your father's restlessness is getting on my nerves."

Josh and Brooke exchanged a confused glance.

Doug smiled at his wife. "So I'm comin' out of retirement and back to semiretirement. I miss my ranch work."

Josh felt a cold moment of unease. "Wait a minute, you're not doing this for me."

"Nope, I'm doin' this for me."

"And me," Sandy affirmed. "I'm not used to all this togetherness. I'm not helpless yet," she added, lifting up her cane. "And I don't want to be treated that way."

"But Dad—" Josh began.

"Are you goin' to talk me out of this, you who loves the ranch so much you don't see that your artistic callin' is probably more important?"

"The ranch will *always* be important," Josh insisted.

"I know. So you understand why I miss it," his dad said softly.

Brooke was smiling at him, nodding.

Josh had no choice but to exhale, and say, "All right, I'll try not to feel guilty about this."

His dad patted his shoulder. "Good, you shouldn't."

"But I've made a decision. I'm going to stop making belts for the feed store." He held up a hand. "It's no sacrifice. I'd rather be making the shoulder bags—"

"For a thousand a pop," Brooke muttered, shaking her head.

"—or the collars for Whitney."

Brooke grinned. "It's fun to see you making a fool of yourself over a woman."

"He's not making a fool of himself," Sandy scolded.

"We're just dating," Josh insisted.

Sandy did a double take. "Well, I don't know about that . . ."

Laughter broke things up, and soon Josh was back outside, escaping his sister's supposed humor by riding fence. The hours stretched on as he covered several of the empty pastures, where the fence had to be examined and repaired before the cattle came down from summer pasture.

But he couldn't escape the uneasy feeling that his father had had to come out of retirement for him. Oh, he knew there was truth to his father's restlessness, but maybe if all three kids weren't so busy, his dad's "restlessness" could have been solved by a long vacation.

Was Josh being too selfish, trying to have it all?

Josh called Whitney that night—which was starting to become a ritual—and told her all about his dad coming out of retirement.

"Your dad is hardly old," she pointed out, standing next to her window and looking out at the twinkling lights of Valentine.

"He's sixty, and when you've done hard work outside for your whole life, your body starts letting you know. Heck, I have mornings when I ache getting out of bed."

"But it's still his decision."

"I think they should travel."

"Oh, I love to travel," she said eagerly. "To just drop everything and go is so exciting."

"It does sound fun."

She thought about how tied to his various jobs he was and how much she enjoyed her freedom. Was she thinking of them as a couple now?

When they said their good-nights, she once again stretched out on the bed as her thoughts ran wild. How would it feel to live here permanently, to know she could only leave once or twice a year? It would be like settling for an ordinary life instead of pursuing all her dreams. It almost made her pick up the phone and book a plane for a long weekend in San Francisco.

But . . . even that wouldn't be as refreshing as it could be. She began to realize she'd miss Josh even for those few days—what would it feel like when she left permanently? She'd never been in love with a man, had no idea how it was supposed to make you feel, but this didn't make her feel good.

So she rolled off the bed and went to her desk, where the day's mail had brought her a manila envelope from Ryan. She'd glanced briefly at the photo of Josh before going out to dinner, but now she really studied it.

The signature in bold black marker was close to his, but not perfect. She studied the glossy paper, wondering if she should hire a lab to analyze it. And what was she supposed to find, that a rare photo paper was used? Hardly. Exasperated, she flipped it over—and then grinned with satisfaction.

There, in the bottom corner, was the photo company's mark: Back in Time Portrait Studio, right in Valentine Valley.

She went there first thing the next morning, but the owner refused to tell her who'd ordered it, citing customer's privacy and never quite meeting her gaze. That could be considered another dead end, but Whitney refused to look at it that way. Josh's fan club was based right in Valentine, and *someone* had to know about it.

She wasn't going to discuss it with Josh until she knew more. How could she tell him that someone he might know was illegally profiting from his fame?

She didn't hear from Josh all day, which was probably good, because she conducted several interviews in The Adelaide's library. Just before six o'clock, he showed up with flowers, dressed in a navy suit with the faintest pinstripes. A suit and tie! She backed up a couple steps so she could take it all in, her gaze roaming his body with appreciation and outright lust. She settled on his face, looking as unshaven as if he hadn't bothered that morning.

Now that was more like Josh.

She grinned. "So what's the occasion?"

"Tonight is our big date." He held out the flowers, already settled in a beautifully etched glass vase that Monica had surely picked out.

She took them, inhaling the scent of roses. "So . . . what would you have done if I had plans?"

He eyed her with amusement. "You only know the people I know. I would have convinced them they didn't need you tonight."

"You're so confident in yourself, aren't you?"

"And you think that's sexy."

He had her there. "I have to get changed."

"We have a reservation in forty-five minutes."

"All right, wait in the parlor, and I'll be down."

He looked disappointed. "I can't watch?"

"Nope."

"Listen to that, with one word, you sound like a Western gal."

"I *am* from the west. The Far West." She pointed to the door. "Out! Forty-five minutes is barely enough time."

He closed the door behind him, and she practically ran to her closet. Thank goodness she knew how to pack for any occasion.

Forty minutes later, she came downstairs slowly in a red silk dress with a high neckline in front, a little peekaboo hole to display the tops of her breasts, and a back that plunged just below her waistline. Her heels were high, her hair caught in a French chignon at the back of her head. She was all set to knock Josh on his ass, except he wasn't in the parlor.

"Josh?" she called hesitantly.

She followed a low murmur of voices to the back of the house, and there was Josh, sitting with several of Debbie's female guests, who were smiling broadly at everything he said.

"Josh?" she called again.

He stood up so hastily that she suddenly knew he was waiting to be rescued. And then she got her re-action. He stilled, and his lids lowered as he studied her. When he met her gaze again, a shot of heat seemed to flare between them, as if they were alone.

Several women tittered their amusement, and the spell was broken.

"So where are you two going?" Debbie asked. "The Sweetheart Inn?"

"Nope," Josh said. "It's a surprise. Have a nice evening, ladies."

He offered her his arm, then escorted her through the foyer and outside. This time, instead of his beat-up old pickup, he drove a shiny, brand new pickup.

"You bought a truck just for our date?"

He chuckled as he opened her door. "Nope, it's my dad's going-to-town pickup."

She slid onto the seat, and watched Josh take in the slit of her skirt that revealed her to midthigh.

"I'm in, Josh," she said, smiling serenely. "You can close the door."

He seemed to shake himself before slamming it shut.

He didn't have far to drive, pulling into an open spot near Sugar and Spice.

"We're going to Em's bakery?" she asked with amusement.

He didn't say anything, just came around to open her door, then looked both ways before guiding her across the street to the Hotel Colorado, a massive old three-story stone hotel with arched columns running almost the entire length of the block.

"Main Street Steakhouse is inside," Josh explained. "We supply their beef. Wait until you taste it."

Excited, she only clutched his arm tighter as they reached the stone steps. Suddenly, two men and a woman, off to the side, started snapping photos with professional cameras, making sure to get the name of the hotel in the background.

One of the men grinned as he lowered his camera. "Is Whitney Wild back? You guys off to get a room for the night?"

When she might have said something, Josh tugged on her arm and they went into the lobby, with its nineteenth-century floral wallpaper, a circular red ottoman in the center, with a huge vase of flowers rising through the middle.

Josh took her upper arms in his hands, and said quietly, "I'm so sorry for that. I made a dinner reservation, and I guess somehow they got word. My supposed fame is getting worse and worse."

She smiled although she wasn't quite feeling it. "Don't apologize, Josh. And this is hardly bad. When you're surrounded by papparazzi following your car, not allowing you to walk down the street—now *that's* bad. But I'm really sorry about that Whitney Wild comment. You don't need to be linked to my past."

She'd thought she was at peace with that part of her life since she'd used it to begin her business and make her the person she was. But now the thought of censure and disapproval surprised her. She'd become used to being taken seriously.

Was it because she was in Valentine, a small town that could be very narrow-minded—as she'd seen last winter in the opposition to Leather and Lace? She wasn't used to people caring so intimately, perhaps so disapprovingly, of her behavior because it wasn't the same thing as being hounded by reporters. They were just doing their jobs, even if some did take a little too much glee from it.

"Do you want to go home?" Josh asked, taking both her hands in his.

She squeezed his hands in return. "Not at all. You can't tease me with the mention of steak and not follow through."

The Main Street Steakhouse was just off the lobby, with darkly paneled walls, low lighting, and the occasional touch of antique furniture. Their table was near another stone fireplace, where, in place of an actual fire, wildflowers overflowed several vases mingled with different size candles.

"Very romantic," she murmured to Josh, then smiled as the hostess handed them menus before departing.

The steak was everything he'd claimed, and she took his advice about the dessert, a chocolate lattice tower filled with berries. They didn't talk about the papparazzi again, and she found herself praying that she could discover and stop this fan club perpetuating his fame. Josh was a quiet cowboy, not a man who needed any outside influence to know his own self-worth.

As they were passing through the lobby again, he leaned down to speak near her hair, his mouth brushing her until she shivered.

"I'd take you to The Adelaide, but there are too many people around. We'll go to my loft, where I plan to make you scream with pleasure."

Suddenly weak in the knees, she hugged his arm close, letting her breast brush against him. "I won't scare the horses?"

"To hell with the horses."

They were silent on the drive to the Silver Creek Ranch, and she caught him occasionally glancing at her with serious regard that smoldered underneath.

At the barn, he again opened her door, and this time he swept her into his arms.

"Can't have those pretty shoes tracking through a dirty barn," he said.

She looped her arms around his neck, then dropped her head back and laughed when he took the stairs up to his loft two at a time.

"Show-off," she whispered in his ear.

"No, just desperate to have you."

He turned on only one small light near the kitchen, leaving the rest of the open loft in shadowy darkness. Very gently, he placed her on the end of the bed, then slowly began to pull off his tie. She watched him, leaning back on her hands to see the whole length of him. He shrugged out of the suit coat and shirt next, and as he drew her to her feet, she pressed her hands to his warm chest and gave a moan of pleasure.

He found the hook at the back of her neck and slowly peeled the dress forward so that it revealed her breasts, covered in the adhesive bra. He stared.

"You just pull them off," she said, smiling, and he

did so, as slow and reverent as if she were a piece of delicate china.

Next she showed him the hidden side zipper, and soon she was only wearing her thong and heels. And then he walked away.

"Josh?"

He switched off the only light, and they were in almost total blackness. And still he didn't come to her although she could hear the rustling of clothes being removed.

"Let me help," she called.

"I don't want your help. Just lie there and think about what I'm going to do to you."

She shivered, then was reduced to a moan when suddenly his mouth brushed a kiss near her ankle. He proceeded to tease and caress every bare inch of her skin, and with the darkness, she had no idea where he would touch her next. The restless aching of pleasure rose higher and higher as he very skillfully drew out their lovemaking until she'd never felt so desperate for him. At last, her orgasm crested over her, almost bringing tears to her eyes as she shuddered in his arms.

She'd never let any other man have such control over her. And to her surprise, she wasn't bothered by it. She only took him into her arms, guided him into her body, and held him and stroked him and showed him without words all the things he made her feel.

Chapter Eighteen

Afterward, as they lay entwined, Josh thought he sensed a pensiveness about Whitney's mood. He didn't know whether to question her or wait until she was ready to speak. He just continued to stroke her and kiss her hair and think to himself that he could do this for the rest of his life.

"You know," she said quietly, "it can sometimes be hard to live up to being the Leather and Lace lady."

He leaned his head against hers as both looked up through the skylight at the stars overhead. "Why?"

"Men expect certain things of me—and I expect certain things of myself," she amended with faint amusement. "With my Whitney Wild past, it just seemed . . . natural to be the one in charge during sex, to make my partner *very* happy."

"It sounds like sex could easily become a competition between you," he murmured against her hair.

She shrugged. "It was fun. But it was never tender." She paused. "Before you."

His occasional concern about how he might compare to the men in her past faded completely away.

And then he realized that she almost sounded troubled, not exactly happy with the revelation.

He wanted her to be happy, to share in his feelings. In that moment, he realized that he'd fallen in love with her, her confidence and brains, her ability to get through her family's indifference and come out stronger. But whatever she felt for him didn't give her the same feeling of peace it did him.

But part of that peace was patience. He would hold back the words, knowing she wasn't ready. If he told her the truth of his love, asked her to marry him, he might hear an answer he didn't want, even face her pity. Not that that would stop him. He would find a way to win her love.

After lunch the next afternoon, Whitney stopped at Sugar and Spice for a box of cookies to bring to the renovation crew. Steph waited on her, wearing a bright smile.

"So how's the job going?" Whitney asked. "Any problems between sisters?"

Steph shook her head. "Not really. Em knows what she's doing, after all. I know most of the people I wait on, and everyone's patient. And it's really fascinating to watch her subtly change a recipe and have it taste so different. I'm learning a lot."

The swinging door to the kitchen slowly opened to reveal Mrs. Ludlow pushing her walker while also carrying a stack of mail and her sweater. Before Whitney could reach her, she gave another push, the door rebounded on her walker, and she lost control of the envelopes.

As they poured around her feet, she said a crisp, "That was unfortunate."

"Let me help," Whitney said, kneeling.

Mrs. Ludlow's brief look of panic was so fleeting that Whitney almost missed it.

"Oh, no, dear, I can—"

But it was too late. As Whitney straightened with the stack of twenty or so envelopes, she caught sight of a familiar PO Box number in Denver, and the forwarding address to a Valentine box. She raised her surprised gaze to Mrs. Ludlow, who gave a sigh.

"You weren't supposed to see that," the old woman said in a low voice.

"See what?" Steph called from behind the counter. "Are you okay, Mrs. L?"

"Fine, dear."

The widows were behind Josh's fan club? They'd been egging on his fans, risking mail fraud? Whitney felt laughter tickling her insides but held back.

"All set here," she said, holding on to the letters, although the widow tried to take them from her. "I'll drive Mrs. Ludlow home."

"I always call Rosemary—" Mrs. Ludlow began.

"Then isn't it a good thing you don't have to disturb her?" she interrupted sweetly. "I was running errands, so my SUV is right here."

Mrs. Ludlow studied her. "Why are you acting so peculiar?"

Whitney lifted the envelopes, leaned closer, and whispered, "Why do you have letters meant for Josh's Fan Club?"

Mrs. Ludlow blinked. "Oh dear."

When Whitney turned around, Steph's customer

was her boyfriend, Tyler Brissette, and they leaned over the counter and spoke in low voices.

"Perhaps you shouldn't leave them alone," Mrs. Ludlow said quietly. "Not until Emily returns."

"Em trusts Steph, so I trust Steph. Now don't be a coward, ma'am."

"Name-calling isn't necessary. But I imagine it's too late to hush this up."

"I imagine it is. Shall we go?"

After Whitney ran the box of cookies in to her construction crew, she and Mrs. Ludlow were silent on the short drive to the Widows' Boardinghouse. All the while, Whitney stifled the amusement that was threatening to bubble into laughter. She held the widow's arm and the walker as Mrs. Ludlow made her slow way up the back stairs to the porch off the kitchen.

Mrs. Palmer opened the door, her bright dress more neon than pink, and looked with confusion from Mrs. Ludlow to Whitney. "Connie, why didn't you call us for a ride? Is everythin' okay?"

"The jig is up, Renee," Mrs. Ludlow said. "I told you it was only a matter of time."

They crossed the threshold into the sunny, cow-themed kitchen.

"You tell me that all the time," Mrs. Palmer said patiently. "Which jig are we discussin'?"

Whitney fanned the letters in her hand, displaying the PO Box address prominently.

Mrs. Palmer put a hand to her chest. "Oh my."

"Is Mrs. Thalberg here?" Whitney asked. "We might as well discuss this all together since I'm certain none of you did this alone."

Biting her lip as if hiding a smile, Mrs. Palmer

marched down the hall toward the front stairs, and yelled, "Rosemary!"

When she returned, she was no longer even trying to hide her amusement.

As Mrs. Thalberg arrived, dressed in comfortable jeans and a crocheted vest over her blouse, she gave Whitney a big smile. "So wonderful to see you!"

"I hope you still think so after you see this." Smiling, Whitney held up the letters. "I know the truth."

"Sit down, dear, sit down," Mrs. Thalberg said. "Would you like some coffee?"

"Thanks, I take it black. But please, can one of you explain why you did this?"

"We aren't hurtin' anybody," Mrs. Palmer protested, setting a coffee mug on the table in the breakfast nook and pointing to a chair.

Amazed, Whitney sank into her seat and spread both hands. "Let's just try it from the beginning. Whose idea was this?"

Mrs. Ludlow slowly lowered herself into a chair across the table. "It doesn't matter whose idea it was. We always work together on our projects. We've been trying to come up with a new source of income for the Valentine Valley Preservation Fund."

"Really?" Whitney said in amazement. "You did something illegal for your nonprofit committee?"

Mrs. Thalberg didn't take coffee and didn't sit down, only crossed her arms over her chest and studied them all.

"Illegal?" Mrs. Palmer echoed, acting as shocked as a priest hearing his first confession. "Josh's amazin' stroke of good luck enabled us to help our community, not do something illegal." She stirred sugar into her coffee.

"I hate to break it to you, but it's illegal to charge people for an autograph when you know it's not the real thing. And you don't own the rights to the photo."

"Hollywood assistants sign autographs all the time," Mrs. Ludlow said with certainty.

"But their clients *pay* them to do that."

Mrs. Ludlow ignored that. "As for the photo, Miss Iacuzzi gave us permission in writing to use it. The publicity has been wonderful for her, too."

Whitney took a sip of her coffee and eyed the three women. "The Fan Club, the Facebook page—it was the three of you?"

Mrs. Palmer's grin was proud. "I *am* good with the computer. We always knew Josh would find out eventually, and he'd never press charges, so how is that illegal?"

Biting her lip to keep from laughing, Whitney briefly closed her eyes. "People are following him, even trespassing, all in an attempt to get his picture or even just his notice. Did you consider you might be making him miserable?"

"Miserable?" Mrs. Thalberg spoke for the first time. "I admit, I was reluctant about this idea, but I haven't seen any evidence of that."

"All right, 'miserable' is too harsh. How about exasperated? And this Facebook page is contributing."

Primly, Mrs. Ludlow said, "We do not post his whereabouts on the page although his own friends do. That William Sweet, so naughty," she added, shaking her head.

"But you can't be surprised."

Mrs. Thalberg took her own seat, then spoke to Whitney across a potted violet. "Well, we were a little surprised."

"I taught William in second grade," Mrs. Ludlow said, "and the things he tried to get away with even then—"

"Connie, it doesn't matter," Mrs. Thalberg interrupted. "Whitney, we were all as taken aback as anyone by Josh's photo going viral."

"You sound like a jubilant marketing firm," Whitney said with bemusement.

Mrs. Thalberg ignored the interruption. "He's bringing more attention to Valentine Valley, and that's a good thing. We want to keep our town strong yet faithful to its beginnings. And we want to encourage and assist unique businesses to open here, like Leather and Lace, rather than chain stores. That's what the preservation fund is all about. We help keep historical buildings as they were, encourage, with assistance, the people who might need help doing that. We even offered Leather and Lace a grant."

"Which I appreciated, but I don't need."

"We have another way to help the fund," Mrs. Palmer said eagerly.

Whitney winced. "Do I want to know?"

"It's great fun," Mrs. Palmer continued. "A calendar of the young men of Valentine Valley."

Whitney almost choked on a laugh as she took a sip of coffee.

"Of course, Josh would be prominent," insisted Mrs. Palmer. "Our Facebook page will really come in handy then."

"After all this attention, I don't know if Josh would want more."

"But it's for a good cause," Mrs. Thalberg said firmly. "Josh always believed in that." She paused. "Are you going to tell him?"

That must be the question they were all dying to know as they leaned toward her. Whitney stared at each of them one by one, then a chuckle escaped her. Their relief and answering smiles only made her laugh harder.

"Oh, man, this is too much," Whitney said, pressing fingertips to the corners of her eyes to staunch tears without smearing her mascara. "If you could have seen your faces, all worried I'd turn you in to the police."

"Not the police, but Josh," Mrs. Thalberg pointed out.

"I know." Whitney's amusement gradually faded. "And this is a dilemma for me since I promised him I'd look into the Facebook thing. I won't lie to him, but if he doesn't ask, I won't volunteer the truth unless I think he needs to know." Mrs. Thalberg was his own grandma, after all.

Mrs. Ludlow patted her shoulder. "What a dear you are."

"I don't know—I'm feeling like a bad girlfriend. Even though this is all very funny, he's not laughing right now. I don't think this can go on much longer. If you're going to keep sending photos, make sure you track the money, so that it's obvious it's a donation."

"We're very meticulous," Mrs. Ludlow insisted.

Whitney started to rise.

"No, no, you have to stay," Mrs. Palmer said. "Let us show you the photo album for the Preservation Fund, all our good works."

"You don't need to convince me, ladies."

"But we want to—we're proud of our little town and how it's kept the spirit of romance, as well as the historical links to our past."

Whitney ended up spending an hour looking at photos of their many escapades, from their bra-burning in support of the Equal Rights Amendment in the 1970s, to the time they stole an abused horse and backed up traffic for miles, just to stop the governor's car and plead for more awareness of animal cruelty. Whitney laughed and was amazed at their daring, and learned even more about the town that had a hold on Josh.

Feeling uneasy about her sister-in-law's continued silence, Whitney placed a call to her mom before dinner and left a message when she didn't answer. She began to wonder if everyone in her family would ignore her, but as she was getting ready for bed, her phone rang, and this time, it wasn't Josh.

She saw the caller ID and answered, "Hi, Mom."

"Darling, I'm sorry I couldn't take your call earlier."

Vanessa Winslow spoke in her usual measured tones, and Whitney pictured her dark-haired mother lying languidly on a lounge on the balcony of their Manhattan penthouse, the lights of the city spread out below, a martini at her side. It might have been two hours later on the East Coast, but her mom was a night owl.

"I don't mind, Mom. As I said in my message, have you heard from Courtney or Chasz? My brother doesn't always reply to my messages, but she usually does."

Vanessa didn't answer right away, letting the silence lengthen into awkwardness.

"Mom?"

Vanessa sighed heavily. "The news isn't good, darling."

Whitney slowly sank onto the bed and stared unseeing into the dark garden behind the B&B. "Are they okay?" she whispered, picturing an accident that landed them both in the hospital. Chasz was a terrible driver in the city, so convinced he could out-maneuver every cab. Fear was suddenly a stimulant in her veins, and she had to jump back up and pace.

"It depends what you mean by okay . . ."

"Not lying in a hospital bed somewhere or . . ." She couldn't go on.

"Oh, no, no, nothing like that."

Whitney found she could finally swallow past the lump in her throat. "Good. Then please just tell me what's wrong."

"Your brother has gotten into some minor trouble."

For a moment, Whitney was tempted to stare at the phone. *Legal* trouble? That hadn't happened since Chasz was a teenager and caught smoking pot. Underage, and with a great lawyer provided by their dad, he'd done some community service more than once, but it was all expunged from his record. Now, drinking and driving . . . that wouldn't surprise her. Chasz always overestimated his sobriety. Courtney was usually on top of that whenever they went out together.

"Mom, just say it. What has Chasz done?"

"Courtney is leaving him."

"What? Because of his trouble with the law? I don't get it."

"No, not trouble with the law—oh, let me tell you a different way. She caught him cheating on her."

Whitney groaned. Her brother used to be a player,

but he'd seemed mostly content with the beautiful Courtney during their marriage. And Whitney thought "mostly" because she'd seen him eyeing a gorgeous woman on more than one occasion. But looking and touching were two different things.

"So he's stupid, and might have lost Courtney because of it," Whitney said. "How is this 'minor trouble'? It seems pretty major to me. Is he trying to wreck his life?"

"It turns out that the other woman was an employee of a rival corporation."

"Did he know?" she exclaimed.

"Of course not! She took advantage of him and passed on anything he thought he was saying in private."

Whitney fell back on the bed with a groan. Well, at least she didn't have to picture her brother in a jail cell somewhere. "He was telling her company business?" she demanded, aghast. "Is he developing a drinking problem? I can't imagine him spilling secrets otherwise."

"It's nothing like that. He . . . your brother trusted her. And she betrayed him."

"Courtney must know just how he feels," Whitney said bitterly. When her mother blew her nose, Whitney softened her tone. "I imagine Dad and the shareholders are up in arms."

Her mom sighed. "Yes. Reporters will probably be calling you. Please don't comment."

"Like you have to tell me that, Mom?"

"Now don't be like that, Whitney. Your father just wanted to be certain you understood."

Whitney often wondered if her dad didn't think she could even be loyal. Logically, she knew his failings were about women in general, but it still felt very personal each time it happened.

"Mom?"

To her surprise, she heard a stifled sob.

"Oh, Mom," she whispered. "I'm sorry Chasz did this."

"I am, too, Whitney. I—I'll call when I know more."

"Good night."

The phone clicked, and Whitney was alone again in the darkness. She understood why the reporters would be bad—Chasz was already a senior vice president at Winslow Enterprises, heir apparent. Now he'd had an affair with a business competitor, and who knew how bad the damage was. Her father had to be scrambling to shield the company.

And then there was Courtney, betrayed by her husband, and Whitney felt sick with sorrow. She placed another call, but Courtney didn't answer, and Whitney had to wonder if she'd ever want to talk to a Winslow again. She left a "Call me if you need to talk" message on her brother's phone. She'd never felt so distant, three-quarters of a continent away from her family.

She almost called Josh to share everything and receive his comfort—but she couldn't do it. She had to stand on her own, like she'd always done before she met him.

The phone rang, and she saw that it was Josh, but she didn't answer it.

It had been a while since she'd felt so alone.

Chapter Nineteen

The next morning, Josh awoke before dawn to do some chores before heading over to The Adelaide. Whitney hadn't answered his call last night, and hadn't returned it either. It just felt . . . wrong. Hell, spending nights without her now felt wrong, too, but still . . .

When he arrived at the B&B, the aroma of bacon and eggs through the open windows reached him the moment he stepped out of his truck, and he inhaled with appreciation. Debbie Fernandez always took the "and Breakfast" portion of her business just as seriously as the rest.

He rapped on the front door and stepped inside, following the scent through the foyer as he removed his hat. He paused in the doorway of the dining room and saw six people seated at the long table, a buffet alongside with china platters overflowing with pastries and croissants, and covered dishes on warmers.

All eyes turned toward him, but none were Whitney's gray.

"Josh Thalberg!" squealed a high-pitched voice.

Two young women shook each other's arms, as if

making sure they'd each seen him. The one flushed red, even as she lifted her chin in defiance. And then he recognized her as the expensively dressed girl who'd hidden in his barn to take photos.

The other four people looked him over, as if they, too, had seen some of the publicity. One couple was young and mostly had eyes for each other, hands so entwined it must be hard to eat. Newlyweds. Valentine Valley attracted a lot of them. The other couple was older, maybe retired, both gray-haired but looking fit, as if all their vacations involved hiking and skiing.

"Hi, Josh," Debbie called as she came in from the kitchen bearing more food. "Whitney hasn't come down to breakfast yet."

"Then I'll head on up." He started to back up and almost ran Whitney down.

She smiled at him but not from the eyes. He'd been right—something had happened. He gave her hand a squeeze, then she looked past him.

"May I invite a guest for breakfast?" she asked.

More than one woman agreed right along with Debbie, and Josh felt himself redden as the older man looked him over with a hint of disapproval. He ended up seated at one end of the table, with Whitney to his left, and his lawbreaking, unapologetic groupie on his right.

"I'm Andrea," she boldly said.

"Nice to meet you, Andrea. I'm Josh."

She smirked and eyed him with unabashed invitation. "I know." Then she looked across the table at Whitney, and the air seemed to chill, as she said sarcastically, "Nice picture of you two in the paper."

He saw Whitney's face pale, and he wished he

could ask her what was going on. Passing by, Debbie lifted a newspaper off a low table and handed it to Josh with a wink.

It was the *Denver Post* again, and the picture of the two of them outside the Hotel Colorado was in blazing color, Whitney's red dress making her stand out like a movie star. Now she looked over his shoulder, her lips pressed together in a thin line. The headline read WHITNEY WILD LANDS COWBOY ARTIST, and he scanned the article, which highlighted some of her scandalous boyfriends, all-night parties, and of course, the underwear shot heard round the world.

Very carefully, Whitney folded her napkin and sent Debbie a faint smile. "I'm sorry, I'm not hungry."

Josh met Debbie's worried look with one of his own, and he followed Whitney up the stairs to her room. When she was about to close her door, he caught it from behind, and she actually looked startled, as if she'd forgotten he was there.

She gave a tired smile and released the knob. "Sorry. Come on in."

He braced a hand on the doorjamb. "Are you sure? I thought you might need someone to talk to, but I'd understand if—"

"Stop being so noble and just come in," she said, with a wan attempt at her usual enthusiasm.

He shut the door behind him and, without saying anything, drew her into his arms. She didn't resist at all, instead melted right against him and released a heavy sigh.

"What is it?" he whispered against her hair. "You were upset before you even saw the newspaper."

"That article was the icing on the cake, just what my family needs."

"I don't understand. I thought you said they didn't care all that much about your wild ways, even back then."

She leaned back so she could look up into his face. "Everything's changed. My brother has stupidly had an affair with a business rival—and apparently she got some secrets out of him."

He frowned. "He *knew* she was a business rival?"

"I don't know," she said ruefully. "His wife has left him regardless. Apparently the press are getting wind of this, and my father—through my mother, may I point out—has told me to keep quiet. So I don't imagine being reminded that I had my own rebellions—and am apparently back to my old self—will sit well with them just now."

"You didn't do anything illegal," Josh reminded her, "then or now. We were going out on a date. Your parents will certainly understand that the press can say anything they'd like."

"True. But I bet they're not clearheaded just now."

She sat down on the edge of the bed, and he sat beside her, still holding her hand.

"Josh, my brother is a senior vice president of Winslow Enterprises. How will this look to the board and the rest of the shareholders?"

"I don't know, Whitney. All I can suggest is that you not dwell on it until you know one way or the other."

She gave a sideways glance and a faint smile. "Good advice, but oh so difficult to follow."

"Then I think we need a distraction. What do you say we go out tonight?"

"The Cowboy Artist and Whitney Wild? They'll say I'm corrupting you. Two dates in two days!"

He leaned in to nuzzle behind her ear, inhaling the exotic scent of her. "A man likes a little corruption from his woman." Then he kissed her cheek and rose. "Wear a little skirt and those cowboy boots. We might need to do some dancin'."

The next day, after nervously scanning the news online and seeing no mention of her brother, Whitney made herself relax, just like Josh advised her to do. She spent the morning at Leather and Lace, conducting several more interviews for the position of general manager. She had narrowed it down to three women, and had some references to begin calling. It was all a good distraction from the turmoil of her family situation.

She was sitting at the kitchen table, the door separating her from the sound of hammering and sawing. But just as she picked up her phone, it began to ring. The caller ID showed her father. Had he seen the Return of Whitney Wild?

She answered carefully. "Hi, Dad."

"Good morning, Whitney. Your mother filled you in?"

She thought of Charles Winslow sitting behind his desk in his glass-walled Manhattan office, the Statue of Liberty presiding over the harbor below him like it was part of his landscaping.

"She did, Dad. This is terrible for everyone, especially Courtney. How's Chasz? He never called me back."

"I imagine he's far too busy packing up his office. He'll have to step down."

She withheld a gasp only through great effort. Her

dad wasn't big on emotion. "Step down? It's not like he's committed a crime . . . has he?"

"Of course not. He didn't know where that woman worked."

Would others think that a lie? Whitney wasn't about to ask.

"The scandal is about to break, and we can't have him upsetting the board. We have to project confidence and stability. That's why we need you."

For a moment, she simply blinked at her phone, wondering if there'd been a disruption, if she'd actually heard those words. "I don't understand, Dad."

"I need you to come to New York and step into the company. Of course you can't just become a vice president overnight, but your arrival will signal that the family is stable and responsive. You have the necessary degrees to appear competent."

Appear competent? The degrees she'd tried desperately to prove herself with, she thought bitterly.

"Uh, Dad, it's not so easy for me to abandon my work."

"Work? You're not even in San Francisco."

"I'm opening a store near Aspen, remember?"

"That will wait. The fate of Winslow Enterprises lies in the balance right now."

"I—Can I call you back, Dad? I have to give this some thought."

"Thought?" he echoed coolly. "I didn't think supporting your family required thought."

She winced, then stiffened. "Uprooting my life requires thought. I'll call you tomorrow, Dad."

"Tomorrow?" he barked. "I need an answer today."

"I can't do that. I'll talk to you later." She hung up, then stared at the phone, waiting to see if he'd call back. She was relieved and only a bit disappointed when he didn't.

All around her, a new Leather and Lace was coming to life. Her third store, the next step in her plan to take over the lingerie world. It was so close to being finished, and now her father had called her to come back to the family business, as if she'd been the one to abandon it instead of the other way around.

In the beginning Leather and Lace had been a way to show her parents she could succeed on her wits and not their money. It had been a fallback because she couldn't have what she really wanted. And now? Now the stores were her pride and joy, her success story. Though she'd waited several years in the beginning to hear her parents applaud her business acumen, their silence had long since stopped mattering.

And now they were asking her to give all that up and return to the "family fold" because her brother had disappointed them. It wasn't about needing her—it was all about them. Once she would have gladly accepted their offer and flown away without looking back.

But now . . . now there was Josh. And this store she hadn't yet opened though it needed to happen before the holiday shopping crush.

And Josh. They were dating, and she couldn't kid herself that it was "just for fun." She'd gotten to know him, to know his close-knit family, to even like this insular small-town life.

But she'd open the store in a couple weeks, and she was supposed to head back to San Francisco, right?

What was she contemplating? Did she like it so much she was considering moving here—seriously considering a life with Josh? Would things be different if she knew Josh might move wherever she needed to be?

Where was this coming from? They'd never even discussed such a thing. Josh would probably laugh at her musings, and he damn well would never leave the Silver Creek Ranch.

And they *were* musings, not based in reality at all.

She moved through the rest of the day in a state of numbness. Though she answered one of her mom's calls, promising to give Dad's request a lot of thought, she disconnected politely when the wheedling began. Her dad's word was law, of course, always had been. She was certain her mother was shocked that Whitney wouldn't *jump* at the chance to be a part of Winslow Enterprises, the company she'd embarrassed herself over by rushing sobbing from the dinner table as a teenager when Charles had first told her she couldn't work there. The company she'd focused on throughout college and business school, so certain her father would change his mind when he saw how accomplished she was. It had been hard to ignore the fact that her brother had coasted through a lower-tier school, but she had never wanted negativity to affect her laserlike focus on her education. Chasz always did what was easiest and most convenient—including some woman who'd probably thrown herself at him. And now Whitney was making excuses for him, just like her mother. But he was her brother. Why didn't he call her to explain?

That night, she didn't tell Josh about her dad's request, not wanting to embarrass herself with whatever emotion might leak out. She had to make a decision all on her own. And shouldn't she be used to keeping secrets, now that she knew the truth about Josh's fan club?

But first, she needed to escape. She insisted Josh take her to Wild Thing, even though it eerily echoed her nickname. She danced like she hadn't danced in years, swaying her hips seductively in her short, short skirt, Whitney Wild to the tips of her red fingernails and the tight cropped shirt that showed off her abs. Every time Josh put his hand on her bare waist, she felt alive in a way that only pride in her body induced.

Afterward, in the dark cab of his pickup, she seduced him—without much protest on his part, of course. They steamed up the windows, and some of the wildness in her blood at last began to recede along with her orgasm. She let him take her home to his loft, and almost set fire to his bed with her eager domination.

At last they were sprawled naked, bodies perspiring, chests heaving. And if he looked a little puzzled and concerned, she ignored it, sinking blissfully into the exhausted sleep she craved.

Josh's cell phone ringing in the darkness woke her up. She was disoriented, still sluggish, and as he reached for his phone, she glanced at the alarm clock. It was only 3:00 A.M., too early for anyone to be claiming he'd overslept.

"Josh? What's wrong?" she asked.

She came up on her elbows at his tense silence, then reached over and turned on the bedside light.

He was already throwing back the covers. "I'll be right down." He tossed the phone on the bed and reached for his jeans on a nearby chair.

"What is it?" she demanded.

"A brush fire."

His voice was more sober and tense than she'd ever heard from him, and it gave her a chill of foreboding.

"We've had a dry summer," he continued. "If the fire gets too big . . ."

He didn't have to finish his sentence. He'd already told her that they had hundreds and hundreds of acres of grass in their pastures, waiting for the herd to come down from summer pasture. And if all that went up—and the buildings along with it . . . she shuddered and got out of bed.

"Did someone call the fire department?"

"Nate did, but they protect the buildings more than anything else. We'll handle the rest."

Wide-eyed, she swallowed and tried to tell herself he'd done this before. He was dressed before she was, of course, and he hesitated as he glanced at her.

"Don't worry about me," she said. "Can I go keep your mother company?"

His look of relief and gratitude was moving, and she felt tears actually sting her eyes.

"Sure, thanks," he said, then cleared his throat. "Josh?"

With his hand on the doorknob, he turned. She hugged him quickly and let him go.

"Be careful," she whispered.

He nodded and left. She knew his mind had already been on the problems ahead, but that hug had probably helped her more than him.

Ranching could be a dangerous way of life—she only had to look at the curved scar on his chin to remember that.

After throwing on one of Josh's flannel shirts over her nightclub clothes, she descended into the barn. She thought for sure they'd be saddling horses or something, but she was at least a half century behind. The taillights of several pickups dwindled down the road. Brooke and Josh were tossing shovels and other tools into the bed of his pickup. Brooke spared her a nod as Whitney stood there hugging herself, feeling useless. And then they were gone, the tires spewing rocks behind as they accelerated.

As Whitney reached the porch, more lights appeared from the direction of town, and pickups streamed past the ranch house as if they'd called in reinforcements. Neighbors risked their own lives to help each other. It wasn't as if that didn't go on in other cities, of course. She'd read incredible stories of what people sacrificed for each other during the last major San Francisco earthquake in 1989, when she was just a little girl. Neighbors had rescued people from the collapsed freeway. It never failed to amaze and humble her.

When she knocked on the front door, it opened almost immediately, as if Sandy Thalberg had been staring out the window. A shaft of light bathed Whitney, and she was embarrassed by her bare legs beneath her short skirt, but Sandy only gave her a relieved smile.

"Want some company?" Whitney asked, rubbing her hands up and down her arms.

"Come in, come in, it's too chilly to be outside."

"Dressed in my dancing clothes," Whitney said awkwardly, as if it wasn't already apparent that she'd been with Josh in the middle of the night.

"Come on into the kitchen. There's a lot of work to be done. They'll all be starving when they get back."

"Can I help?" Whitney asked, trailing behind.

"I'd love it, thanks."

The big wall of windows looked black in the middle of the night, and there was a strange sound that Whitney soon realized was the crackle of a two-way radio. For a moment, she stood transfixed, listening to various voices discuss the direction of the wind and where to dig the fire line. Then she caught sight of the revolving lights of a fire truck headed their way. It went past the house, probably stationing itself between the buildings and the fire, the last line of defense.

"So many people have come to help," Whitney heard herself say.

"That's how it is around here," Sandy said matter-of-factly. "Can you start breaking eggs into a bowl?"

Whitney jerked out of her strange reverie. "Oh, of course!"

Emily arrived soon after, her cheerfulness stretched tight as if it might soon break. Over the next hour, Whitney broke eggs, stirred together batch after batch of cornbread under Emily's direction, and cut up all the fruit she could find in the refrigerator. Bacon and sausage sizzled, coffee percolated; and the aromas made her stomach growl.

Through it all, the radio crackled like the sound track to their lives. No one screamed for help or sounded out of control, and Whitney used that to keep herself calm.

She kept sneaking glances at Sandy, who worked methodically at her stove or made pitcher after pitcher of orange juice. Her expression was calm, and she'd probably experienced all this before. Like her son, would she hold off worrying because there was no reason to until you knew the worst? Well, of course, she'd probably taught her son those practical qualities, Whitney reminded herself.

But those were her children out there fighting a fire, and her sixty-year-old husband.

Whitney shuddered and accidentally sliced her thumb with the knife as she was cutting canteloupe. Hissing, she watched in disbelief as the blood welled.

"Come on over here and wash that out," Sandy said. "I'll get a bandage."

"No, please, don't worry about me. It's just a small cut." After she wrapped a paper towel around it hard to stop bleeding, blood began to seep through, so she used another. She washed it, trying not to wince as it stung, then applied more pressure. Surely it would stop bleeding. She couldn't believe she was distracting Sandy at a time like this.

Suddenly, she heard an approaching roll of thunder, except . . . not. It made a whump-whump sound that crested, then faded. She turned to Sandy in surprise.

"The Sweets have a helicopter," the woman explained. "For fires, they attach a giant bucket and pull up water from our ponds."

"Impressive," Whitney murmured, taking the first-aid kit from Sandy without showing her her thumb. She used several bandages, and tried to ignore the telltale seepage of blood slowly spreading beneath.

People were speaking on the radio again, and Sandy, closest to it, had her head bowed, listening. Then her shoulders seemed to lower, as if tension had been holding them stiff, and Whitney just hadn't noticed.

Sandy beamed. "The fire's out. They're coming home, and no one's injured."

Relief swept over Whitney with a rush of gratitude that made her eyes swim with tears. She put her hand on the counter to steady herself, and watched with surprise as her fingers trembled. How did Sandy bear this worry over and over again? Then Emily gave a whoop of delight and hugged them both.

Within twenty minutes, a parade of pickups began to fill the yard, and men and women entered the kitchen by twos and threes. Though they all removed their boots, they smelled of smoke and were spattered with soot. No one would dirty a seat by sitting in it, so after washing and lining up for food, they milled around and ate standing up, talking about the fire. She recognized the younger generation of Sweet brothers, their fair hair filthy. They introduced her to their dad, Emily's father, Joe Sweet. Whitney hadn't even realized that Emily had to worry about more than her husband that night.

The Thalbergs were the last to arrive, as the sky was lightening with the approach of dawn. Although Whitney knew no one had been injured, she studied Josh's tired face closely. Above the nose his skin was mottled black, but below he'd obviously been wearing his bandana to breathe through. It hung wet and limp around his neck. After giving her a tired but triumphant smile, he moved slowly to the sink to wash.

She started to follow him but couldn't help pausing as she overheard raised voices in the mudroom. Brooke and Adam were standing close together, talking intently.

"Look, everything turned out okay, right?" Brooke said to Adam with exasperation. "You can't do that to me again."

"Worry about you? It was a fire, dammit!"

"And I work on this ranch. Get used to it, Adam, I won't back down just because you think something's dangerous. Please promise you won't second-guess

what I do. I've spent my whole life proving I'm as
good as a man on this ranch, and I won't let you interfere with that."

Brooke turned her back, arms crossed over her
chest, and Whitney caught a glimpse of Adam's
stony expression before it melted into tenderness. He
hugged her from behind, whispered something into
her ear, and she turned into his embrace. Whitney
couldn't help feeling for them both, working side by
side in a job many might think too dangerous for a
woman. It must be difficult for a trained Marine to
turn off his protective instincts. But they loved each
other, and obviously they would work it out.

Whitney went to Josh. "How'd it go?" She had to
raise her voice amidst the chorus of excited conversation.

As he dried his hands, he leaned back against the
wall. "The blaze was a hundred yards long, and we
all fanned out, chopping at anything the fire could
use for fuel."

"He grunted and swore a lot," Brooke said, approaching them. She glanced down at Whitney's
skimpy skirt. "Nice outfit."

Whitney actually blushed, then said breezily,
"Can't dance in anything else."

Adam followed behind Brooke, as if he didn't
want to let her out of his sight.

Josh gave a tired smile. "Every time a new burn
started, the helicopter was able to put it out. We did
a lot of shoveling and resoaking some hot spots, but
we got it all. We'll take a ride back out there soon and
make sure."

"After you get some sleep," Sandy called from her
position near the stove.

Whitney listened as people recounted little incidents, and was amazed at how easily they could all laugh about it. She kept watching Josh, thinking about how he risked his life for his family. All hers asked was that she take a position they originally wouldn't offer her but that she'd wanted her whole life. Was she being self-centered, that she wished they thought she deserved it on her own merit, and not grudgingly out of desperation? There was even an ugly part of her that was glad that they finally needed her though the situation was hurting so many people. She didn't know what to do.

Then Josh lifted up her hand and studied the blood-soaked bandage on her thumb.

"Whoops," she said, smiling.

"Let me shower, and we'll take you to get this stitched up," he said.

"Josh, no," she said, feeling ridiculous. "It's already stopped bleeding."

But he wouldn't take no for an answer. He dragged her to his loft, where he made her wait while he showered. She tried to get in with him, but he refused, saying she'd start bleeding again. At the medical clinic off Main Street, they waited for Doc Ericson to arrive, alone in the waiting room because of the early hour. Josh's head sank back against the wall behind his chair, and he fell asleep.

Whitney couldn't stop watching him. She saw soot behind his ear that he'd missed because he'd been in a rush to take care of her. He took care of everybody. She brushed a lock of hair back from his forehead, feeling both strangely tender and strangely frightened at how he made her feel.

Chapter Twenty

Josh spent the day thinking about Whitney's distracted air. He had other things to do, of course, like answering a *Gazette* reporter's questions about the fire that just happened to morph into a discussion of his "heated" romance with Whitney Wild. And when was he going to jet off to decadent European capitals?

"I'm not leaving Valentine," he scoffed, slamming down the office phone at the ranch.

Nate looked up from his computer. "Was that Whitney?"

Josh frowned at him. "What are you talking about? You heard me talking about the fire with a reporter."

"Oh, right." Nate eyed him, then looked back down at his work.

"You think I'd leave Valentine?" Josh asked in surprise.

Nate shrugged. "You're getting pretty close to her if last night was any evidence. She doesn't live here. I just thought you might be considering . . . things, a long-distance relationship or something."

He *was* considering "things," but leaving Valentine? It seemed utterly foreign to him. This was where his family and their history coexisted. He'd never wanted anything else.

But what would he do to have Whitney? Wouldn't leaving Valentine mean he was giving up everything else that was important to him?

He thought about Whitney's behavior since she'd found out about her brother's problems. Of course she'd been distracted and upset, but she was also . . . distant, as if she'd put up a see-through barrier to keep him at arm's length—emotionally, anyway, certainly not physically. Things were always great between them physically. Of course, she worked hard to make it that way, he thought with a touch of confusion.

Or maybe she was considering leaving altogether, to join her family. He knew *he* would if his family were in trouble. But if she left Valentine so soon, she might never have the chance to fall in love with it again—to fall in love with him.

He imagined that the fire hadn't helped. Being a rancher's wife sometimes meant sleepless nights of worry. That would sober anyone, make her reconsider any further involvement with him.

Josh ran his hand through his hair. "Nate?"

Nate looked up expectantly, and Josh realized he didn't even know what to ask.

"Never mind."

Nate studied him for a moment. "Are you sure?"

"I'm sure. I've got to work this out on my own."

"Won't be easy." Nate leaned back in his office chair and linked his hands behind his head.

"*What* won't be easy?" Josh asked.

"Whitney."

"I'll figure it out."

"You can't push things, you know. She has to figure out for herself what she wants."

"And that's the lesson learned once too often by my big brother."

"And learned the hard way. I was desperate to make Em see she could be happy here, but she had to come to it on her own."

Josh hesitated, then sighed. "I never knew how hard just stepping back could be. Nothing ever mattered this much before."

"My little brother is all grown-up," Nate said melodramatically.

Josh tossed a pen at him. "And you're still having to wait around, aren't you? But this time it's for a honeymoon."

Nate shrugged. "I don't mind. I have Em to myself every night. What would it matter if we were in some exotic resort? She wouldn't enjoy it a bit if she wasn't happy about how things stood with the bakery."

"Since when did you turn into the patient one in this family?" Josh asked.

Nate just grinned.

But Josh did have second thoughts about a way to help Whitney fall in love with Valentine. Why not use what she was used to—the high society of Aspen? When he invited her on another date that night, she seemed glad for the opportunity to get away from her worries about her brother. Josh didn't bring it up, and neither did she.

More than once she checked her phone, as if she was waiting for a certain message. From her family, he assumed.

She apologized the third time. "I know it's foolish, but I keep searching the headlines, waiting for the news about my brother to break."

They kept getting glances from strangers, and the old Whitney, the one who'd said "Ignore it!" was gone. Aspen had been a bad idea.

The next day, Whitney had breakfast at the Widows' Boardinghouse. They wanted to talk about the fire, and, of course, their fan-club adventure. But their request for her help designing a newsletter didn't sit well with Whitney, who ducked out as soon as she could, using changing the bandage on her couple stitches as an excuse. She was withholding too much from Josh, and it was weighing on her conscience.

Midafternoon, in the middle of reviewing references, she received another phone call from her mom and braced herself to resist the pressure to make a decision. But it was worse than she'd thought.

"Hi, darling, wonderful news."

Whitney stared at the phone, shocked by her mother's forced cheerfulness. "Uh, what is it?"

"We've just taken a suite at The Little Nell right in Aspen! Isn't that marvelous?"

Whitney's mouth dropped open. They'd been trying to persuade her, but this was pulling out the big guns.

"Wow, Mom. Who's 'we'?"

"Your father, brother, and I."

"*Chasz* is with you?"

"He is."

"And they both left New York in the middle of this—" She broke off, about to say "disaster."

"You're important to us, Whitney, darling, and we haven't seen you in a while."

She grimaced. "You mean my falling into line is important to you."

"No," Vanessa said patiently, "your understanding of the complexities of our situation is important, yes, but so are you. I didn't like forcing all this on you so quickly. Your father saw that I was right. So will you come see us? How far away is Valentine Valley? And isn't that the cutest name? A perfect place for Leather and Lace."

Whitney shook her head. Her mother was trying very, very hard to pretend that all was normal when it wasn't. Whitney could no longer duck phone calls, not when they were so close.

Sighing, she said, "I'm about a half hour away, Mom. I'll be there soon."

Whitney didn't take any special care with her clothes—unless you counted in the reverse. Wearing jeans, cowboy boots, and her pink-and-green-checked Western blouse, she strode into the understated elegance of The Little Nell lobby as if she was wearing a fur coat and Jimmy Choos.

When her mother opened the door to the suite, her pleased smile faded only slightly, to her credit. And then she hugged Whitney hard.

"Darling, it's so good to see you. And being here in Colorado has agreed with you! Such color in your face."

"Thanks, Mom." Whitney stepped back. Vanessa was still tanned and fit, her dark hair impeccably styled, her face subtly assisted where any new wrinkles were concerned. Behind her, the suite was a rich backdrop of paneled walls, hardwood floors, and art from The Little Nell's private collection. Columns supported the ceiling, separating the living room from the dining room and sunroom. The panorama of Aspen Mountain filled every window.

Past her mom, Whitney could see her dad, just rising from the leather couch near the gas-log fireplace with his iPad in one hand. He wore perfectly pressed pants and a buttoned-down shirt open at the collar, as if he hadn't just flown across the country. But then again, the Winslow Enterprises jet hardly crammed them together into too-small seats. The gray above his sideburns was a little more pronounced, but otherwise he looked successful and rich and aware of it.

He blinked at her cowgirl outfit but gave her a faint smile anyway. "Hello, Whitney."

"Nice to see you, Dad." She crossed to him and he leaned over for the perfunctory kiss on the cheek. She looked around. "Where's Chasz?"

"Playing tennis," Vanessa said. "It was . . . a long flight. He should be back any—"

The door opened, and Chasz breezed in, dressed completely in white, including the towel around his neck. He had dark, wavy hair, bright blue eyes, and a grin that had gotten him too much in life.

"There you are, Whitney," he said. "I can see why you've stayed here during this summer."

Whitney arched a brow and said dryly, "You mean my work?"

"The weather! Not humid at all. I don't think I've ever been here this time of year before."

"Are we really going to talk about the weather? Or maybe how you screwed up?"

She heard Vanessa inhale; her father said nothing, but Chasz's eyes narrowed. He was still cheerful as he said, "My problems will blow over just like yours did."

She laughed without humor. "My problems didn't include aiding corporate theft, now did they?"

"Just drop the act, Charles," their father said.

Chasz winced at his formal name, which only their father used.

"We're here for an important reason, one caused by you," Charles Sr. continued. "I suggest you not begin to bicker with the one person who can help you."

Whitney rounded on her father. "*I'm* the one person who can help? Not his lawyer? Not a therapist? Please don't assume I am so easily manipulated."

Charles frowned. "I don't think manipulation is involved. I asked for your help, and I've been waiting for an answer. I can't wait much longer."

"What's the plan if I say no? I have important work that has to be finished before the holidays, and people waiting to hear if I've hired them."

"There's no other plan, Whitney," Vanessa suddenly said, her hands clenched together. "You're our only hope."

Whitney groaned and walked to the window, looking out on the ski slope, which was now green and dotted with wildflowers. Her brother was the one at fault, but they were acting like the fate of the company—of their family—rested firmly on her shoulders.

"I haven't made a decision yet."

"That's all right," Vanessa said brightly. "You take the time you need. Let's go have dinner together."

Chasz left the room to shower, walking at stiff, wounded attention.

"Did you bring something to change into?" Vanessa asked hesitantly.

"Nope, so let's go hit the barbecue place on Main Street where I'll fit right in."

Throughout dinner, Whitney tried to pretend this was just any other family reunion. She asked about her mother's charity work, and her father's golf game. Chasz seemed . . . glum, but what was she going to ask him: *So is your wife planning to take half of everything? How's your mistress? Was she worth throwing away your marriage, your respect, and company secrets?*

Whitney had never been all that close to him, but the chasm between them just seemed to keep widening.

And then she remembered Josh, Nate, and Brooke, fighting a fire together or riding beneath a blue sky, so at ease with each other. It just seemed so far from her reality. And it made her sad.

Her father downed another gin and tonic, then looked at her. "So why did you choose this Valentine place over Aspen for your next store?"

She'd told him, but even if he'd forgotten, at least he was asking. "Valentine Valley is all about romance, as you can guess from the name. I like the vibe there, the old-fashioned Main Street—and frankly, the building prices."

"And the men?" Chasz interrupted. " 'Whitney Wild Lands Cowboy Artist'?"

"We said we weren't going to bring that up," Vanessa said tightly.

Even her father shot Chasz a disapproving look. It

was a little strange to see the golden boy out of favor. Chasz picked up a rib and went back to eating.

"It's all right," Whitney said. "As Chasz knows, sometimes you can't control the reporters. I've been in town for a few weeks, and yes, the man I've been seeing is the artist who's doing some work for my stores. He's incredibly talented, and a nice guy. He's introduced me to his family and friends, so I'm not so alone here."

"You've been here over a month?" her dad asked. She nodded.

"And your other stores are under good management, to be doing well without you."

"They are, but I'm in the process of hiring for this third store, and the renovations are almost done." *So I can't easily jet off to Manhattan with you.*

But she hadn't quite said no. When had she ever been so wishy-washy? She was angry that her stores mattered so little, and angry that they thought she could save them—and deep down, ambivalent about Winslow Enterprises itself. When had *that* happened?

Her father only nodded, and she was rather surprised. No insistence that these "little stores" didn't need her? Or maybe he was just planting some seeds of doubt he hoped would flourish.

The rest of the meal was strained but cordial, and they walked back to The Little Nell in the darkness.

"Stay with us tonight," Vanessa said when they entered the lobby. "It's too late to drive back."

It *was* a dark, winding drive, though a four-lane highway. Before she could answer, her phone rang, and she saw the ID. "I have to take this call."

"This late?" her mother said. "Oh, but of course

it's not business. If that's Mr. Thalberg, invite him to have breakfast with us. I'd like to meet him."

Whitney could only nod and turn away as she answered the call. "Hi, Josh."

"Hey, Whitney. I dropped by the B&B, but you weren't there. Sorry, I should have called."

"Trust me, I didn't have any idea what was going to happen." She looked over her shoulder and found her parents and brother talking close together near the columned half wall separating the lobby from the more casual gathering area. They didn't leave, as if they thought she'd head back to Valentine Valley if out of their sight. She took a deep breath. "I'm in Aspen. My parents surprised me by arriving today."

"Wow. Well of course you had to go."

"We just had dinner, and it's late enough that they want me to spend the night."

"You should."

"And . . . they'd like to meet you. Want to come for breakfast tomorrow—if you can spare the time, of course?"

"I'd like that."

She could hear the pleasure in his voice, and knowing how important he viewed family, understood him. She felt a little awkward, unused to bringing a man to meet her family. Had she ever done that before?

"One problem," he continued. "I have to work in the morning. Is lunch okay?"

"Sure." She closed her eyes, imagining her mom taking her shopping since she hadn't brought a change of clothes. That would at least seem a normal way to pass the morning. "Why don't you meet us at noon in The Little Nell lobby?"

"They travel in style. I'll be there. Have a good night."

There was a pause, and she found she didn't want to hang up, as if he were the only normal thing in her life.

"Josh—" She broke off, hearing how wistful she sounded.

"I miss you, too. Sleep well."

She stared at the phone and shook off his spell.

Chapter Twenty-One

When Josh walked into the lobby of The Little Nell, he saw Whitney right away, dressed upscale casual in a light pink sweater, lace tank top, and pleated skirt. She was sitting in a chair, long, tanned legs crossed, frowning intently as she scanned her phone. Though it had only been a day, just the sight of her made his heart beat faster.

"Whitney?"

She looked up, and the welcoming smile that broke over her face felt like the warmth of the sun emerging through the clouds. She rose and came easily into his arms. He held her for a moment, before taking her face in his hands for a quick kiss.

"My, you clean up nice," she said, stepping back to admire his khakis and polo shirt.

He felt stupid because he'd even shaved, something he usually only did every couple days.

"I don't have to wear this all the time, do I?"

She laughed. "Not for me. And not even for my parents. I think you're fine the way you are." She leaned closer conspiratorially. "You should have seen my mom's eyes widen when I arrived yesterday in jeans and a Western shirt. It was fun."

He reached for her hand and held it loosely as they faced each other. "How did it go?"

She shrugged. "My brother is an idiot. He seems to think his troubles will just go away. Maybe he's had some reason to believe that," she added with faint sarcasm. "But not this time. Somewhere inside, he's probably regretting destroying his marriage because I think he and Courtney suited each other."

"So they're here to get away from it all?"

She shrugged again, but her gaze didn't quite meet his. "Partially, yeah."

He suspected there was more family drama than she was discussing, but he wouldn't grill her. He didn't think it was about trust. Embarrassment, maybe? He just didn't know and could only hope she'd eventually confide in him.

"Whitney!"

They both turned around to see her family approaching. Josh could see her resemblance to her elegant mom, who barely looked old enough to have had her. Mr. Winslow was a commanding man, not tall, but radiating power and confidence. There was some of that presence in her brother Chasz, but it was dimmed, as if his problems had chipped away at his feeling of invincibility. But he was still putting on a good show, the first to reach out a hand.

Josh shook it, smiling.

"Josh Thalberg," Whitney began, "meet my brother, Chasz."

"So this is the 'Cowboy Artist,'" Chasz said. "You don't look too much like a cowboy right now."

"I left my Stetson and boots in my pickup truck," Josh said.

Whitney rolled her eyes at her brother. "Josh, this is my dad, Charles Winslow."

As they shook hands, Josh said, "Good to meet you, Mr. Winslow."

He was not invited to call him by his first name, but the man smiled at him.

"Josh, you have a beautiful valley here," Mr. Winslow said. "I always enjoy visiting. Do you ski?"

"Snowboard, mostly. But I've done some skiing, too."

"I can remember in my youth, when snowboards weren't even permitted at some resorts. Things have really changed."

"For the better, I hope," Josh said. "Luckily, there's room for all of us."

He turned to Mrs. Winslow, and she gave him the warmest regard.

"I'm Vanessa, Josh," she said, leaving her hand in his a moment too long. "It's so wonderful to meet a special friend of Whitney's."

Special friend? He'd accept that.

Outside, they walked around the corner to a little restaurant for lunch, and after they'd ordered, Josh found himself the object of lots of questions, as expected.

"So how large is your father's ranch?" Mr. Winslow asked.

"A thousand acres, sir. My brother Nate oversees our diversification and investments into other businesses, like organic produce, rodeo stock, even a winery."

Mr. Winslow nodded. "A sound strategy for a small ranch. How many employees work on a ranch that size?"

"Dad," Whitney said in a warning voice.

Josh smiled at her. "It's no secret. It's mostly family, my dad, mom, Nate, Brooke, Brooke's probably future husband Adam, our secretary, and an old part-timer. Neighbors help out certain times of the year, like branding, and we, of course, do the same. If you're here a while, you'll have to come visit."

Vanessa smiled. "What a nice invitation."

"Lately, they've been having much-less-welcome visitors," Whitney said. "It's my fault, of course. I talked Josh into the photo that went viral."

"Talked me into it?" Josh said, leaning back as the waitress brought their drinks. He took a swig from his beer bottle and eyed Whitney. "You bet me."

She blushed. "I didn't see any other way. I knew it would be great marketing, and it has been."

"Whitney showed me your shoulder bags this morning," Vanessa said. "Exquisite detail work. I bought one for a friend for Christmas."

"That was kind of you, ma'am." Josh didn't know how he felt about it—embarrassed at the ridiculous price? Grateful, even though it might be a perfunctory purchase to appease her daughter? Vanessa hadn't *had* to buy one. Unless she felt compelled for some reason, he mused, eyeing the way Vanessa cast eager glances at her daughter.

"What did you bet?" Chasz asked idly.

Josh could tell he hadn't been all that interested in Josh's mundane life, but at last he'd mildly intrigued him. "That if I did the photo, she had to go on a date with me."

Vanessa chuckled, and to Josh's surprise, Mr. Winslow's tight mouth showed the faint shadow of a smile.

"Little did he know, I'd have probably given in without the bet," Whitney admitted.

"*Now* you tell me," Josh said, smiling at her.

"Mom showed me the bag," Chasz said. "You do the whole thing?"

"Most of it. Recently I've hired one of our hands, Adam Desantis, to work with the leather. That's a process in and of itself, what with the dying or gluing thin sheets together."

"So have you made my sister a bag?"

"She's kept me slaving away in my workshop to meet all my requirements."

"Hey!" Whitney said.

"I do have something in mind just for her," Josh admitted.

"I bet you do," Chasz said.

Josh frowned at his tone of voice but said nothing. Whitney looked furious, her mother worried, but her dad had begun to scan his phone.

To forestall a problem, Josh said, "Not sure what Whitney told you, but that photo has led to all kinds of complications. I don't know how people do it regularly, being recognized on the street by strangers. This morning, I caught a photographer sneaking across a pasture. Seems he thought a 'cow' wouldn't bother him, not realizing it was bull we've been doctoring. Barely got him out of there before he got gored."

"So you saved his life?" Vanessa asked, wide-eyed.

Josh shrugged. "Couldn't let him die of stupidity. Couldn't exactly get angry with him either, when he was near collapse with relief."

Josh felt like he was working hard to keep everything light and amusing. He sensed the tension moving between Whitney's family, like a shark under a calm surface. And he didn't think it was all about him, either. He knew some of Whitney's problems with her family, but why couldn't they see what she'd accomplished, how hard she'd worked?

Whitney steered the conversation back to his ranch and his family in a proud way, and he had the first inkling that maybe her pride in him masked a deeper emotion—even love. But he didn't want to get his hopes up. He listened to the family arrange to come to Valentine the next day for lunch and a tour of Leather and Lace, but everyone seemed . . . false, filled with hidden agendas. What a tiring way to live.

Whitney drove back to the B&B after lunch, and to her surprise, Josh's pickup followed her rather than heading to the Silver Creek Ranch. She looked in her mirror and felt all soft, remembering his handsome charisma and cowboy charm on display for her parents. Josh hadn't exactly cracked her dad's shell, but her mom had definitely warmed to him. And Josh's presence had allowed her to put off a private talk with her family, who would keep pushing her on a decision about joining Winslow Enterprises.

And she just . . . couldn't make a decision. It was what she'd always wanted, but somehow, it felt wrong, like she was "cheating" on everything she'd worked toward. Yes, her two shops were operating without her day-to-day involvement, but she was never going to be able to expand without giving it her undivided attention.

And her parents' request felt far too desperate, what with Chasz's ethical—and maybe legal—troubles.

She raised her hand to wave, assuming Josh would drive on by now that he knew she was home safe (on a beautiful, cloudless day), but he pulled in behind her and got out.

"Long time no see," she said wryly, leaning against her SUV.

"Got a message from the sheriff that he was looking for you," Josh said. "He should be here any minute."

She tensed. "Is it about the rock-thrower?"

"I don't know. You having other legal issues I don't know about?"

To her surprise, he seemed only half in jest, and she studied him for a moment. Before she could speak, the sheriff's car cruised around the corner and parked.

Sheriff Buchanan got out of his SUV and took a moment to place his cowboy hat perfectly on his head. Then he walked toward them with his military gait.

"Mornin', ma'am," he said to her with a nod, then shook hands with Josh. He glanced back at her. "I mentioned I'd be interviewing neighbors for witnesses to the rock-throwing incident, and I finally found a couple."

"I'm stunned," Whitney said, trying to keep her eagerness at bay. "Since there hasn't been a repeat performance, I sort of thought we were just going to let it go as a one-time prank." She thought of Sylvester Galimi and hoped he hadn't lied to her.

The sheriff arched a brow. "I don't do that, ma'am."

"Sorry, I just thought . . . you know, there must be more important crimes to occupy your time."

"You mean like an escaping pig?" he deadpanned.

She opened her mouth but couldn't think of a thing to say. Then she saw Josh's shoulders shake and realized he was barely containing laughter. Sheriff Buchanan watched him almost idly, but she detected some humor there as well.

"Okay, okay, I get it," she said. "Were the witnesses of any help?"

"They identified a stranger, a young woman not from around here."

Not Sylvester, she thought with relief. But then—it also wasn't a person upset with Leather and Lace "corrupting" Valentine Valley. What the heck was going on?

"That's unusual for a rock-thrower, isn't it?" Josh asked.

"It is, especially since she was expensively dressed. I checked out the hotels and B&Bs, and I found her."

Whitney stared at him. "You're kidding. Did she claim she was drunk?"

"No, ma'am. It took a while to get the story out of her, but it seems she's a big fan of Josh here."

Josh, who'd been leaning against Whitney's car, now straightened. "What? This is connected to me?"

"Wait, wait, is her name Andrea, the girl who's staying at The Adelaide with me?" Whitney asked, thinking of the smug young woman who'd been giving her snide looks the last couple weeks and refusing any kind of conversation over the breakfast table.

Sheriff Buchanan nodded.

"I remember her," Josh said slowly. "I found her trespassing to get a photo, then met her again here."

"She's one of your biggest fans," the sheriff said impassively. "And very jealous, it seems."

Whitney momentarily felt relief and elation that people in Valentine weren't trying to drive her away. Then she watched Josh's face darken. "Now, Josh . . ."

"So this is my fault?" he said. "That damn picture started all of this?"

And your grandmother's fan club fanned the flames, she thought, but didn't say so aloud. "You can't blame yourself because some foolish girl had nothing better to do than imagine herself infatuated with a guy in a photo. And as you so recently pointed out, I made you do it."

The sheriff looked back and forth between them with interest, then mildly said, "Guess you're just too good-lookin', Josh."

Whitney's suppressed laugh came out as a snort, then she held up both hands to placate Josh. "This'll die down, I swear. You're not doing anything new and interesting to encourage it."

He glanced at Sheriff Buchanan. "I'm still seeing Whitney. You think she's in any kind of danger from this?"

Whitney snorted in earnest, but the sheriff took Josh's question seriously.

"I don't believe so. I've fined the girl and told her in no uncertain terms it's time for her vacation in Valentine to be over. She moved out of the B&B while you two were gone."

"It was that easy?" Whitney asked.

"Well, I did tell her I would make sure this didn't appear on her record as long as she went peaceably. She seemed to appreciate that. And she left a check with Debbie for your damages."

"Good," Whitney said, feeling relief lighten her shoulders. Josh was still glowering, so she said, "Thanks so much for solving this, Sheriff. I feel much better."

They shook hands all around, Sheriff Buchanan got in his SUV, and Whitney turned to Josh. "Now *you* have to let this go."

He blew out a breath. "I'll try. I just can't believe my stupid fame affected you. What if it had been something worse?"

She put her hands on his chest. "It wasn't. Just a silly girl with a crush and no impulse control. It wasn't the citizens of Valentine Valley trying to drive me out of town."

His gaze sharpened on her, and he seemed to relax. "I'm sorry you had to worry about that."

She shrugged. "It was hard to think otherwise, after my less-than-warm welcome last winter. Of course, Sylvester and his gang might have given up trying to dissuade me, but now there's my family."

He cupped her cheek with one hand. "You don't have to be some kind of symbol to their success, only of your own happiness. Surely they'll care about that. They seemed nice."

"They were on their best behavior," she said darkly.

"For me? Should I be impressed?"

With a sigh, she put her arms around him. "I'm impressed, and that's all that matters."

"You mean because they like this small-town cowboy?"

"Yep."

She pulled his head down for a kiss, and only broke apart several minutes later, when someone beeped at them as they drove by.

"Invite your family out to the ranch for dinner tonight," Josh said.

Whitney blinked up at him. "Really? You want that kind of stress?"

"It won't be stressful. *Real* stress will be my mom's reaction if I *don't* invite them."

"I don't want you to suffer that. Thanks, we'll accept."

After Josh left, Whitney dropped off shopping bags in her room before heading to Leather and Lace. Her silence about the real reason her family had come was beginning to weigh more heavily on her, but how could she tell Josh when she didn't even know what decision she was going to make? And she didn't want to be persuaded by anyone other than herself.

Her family arrived a couple hours later in a limousine. Her mother hugged her again, as if she hadn't seen her in months instead of hours, and Whitney felt uneasy. It was far more affection than she was used to, and she couldn't trust the motivation. She'd spent much of her life away from her mom, after all.

On the sidewalk, her father stared up at the new, prominent Leather and Lace sign, which could be seen on Main Street, up the block.

"I see why this large sign is necessary," Charles said, glancing toward the busier street. "You might have done better to locate there." He pointed toward Main.

"No suitable buildings, Dad. As it is, this one used to be a funeral home."

Chasz rolled his eyes even as their father frowned.

"Will you have enough customers to make this work?" Charles continued.

"Did you see the tourists on Main Street? And the

summer season is over. Imagine the holidays—or ski season. I've already had lots of people stopping by and asking about our Grand Opening. But come on in and see what they've done to the place. They're almost ready to start putting together all my display tables."

She chatted on, describing the antique theme she was going for, to match the house itself. In winter, she'd have a fire going, the gas kind, because she wouldn't want her lingerie to smell like smoke. When she mentioned that the Sweet brothers would next be working on an apartment upstairs, her mother frowned.

"An apartment?" Vanessa echoed. "You don't plan to live here permanently."

Whitney hesitated. "I don't know what I'm planning, Mom. But I need a place to stay when I'm in town."

"Speaking of a place to stay," Vanessa said, "we saw that beautiful old inn at the base of the mountains."

"The Sweetheart Inn. I've met the owner. She's a nice old lady. But it's not something I'd—"

"I didn't mean you," Vanessa said brightly, "but us. We'd like to be closer to you while we're here. We already brought our luggage."

"Oh." Whitney tried to sound upbeat. How long did they plan to stay? Until they wore her down, and she decided to give in to their demands? It must be taking everything in them not to constantly bring it up.

But Chasz himself was enough of a reminder. Already he gave his wandering eye free rein and looked at every pretty woman they passed on the street. She wanted to shake him and say, *You don't care about Courtney?*

She didn't know what to think. He'd always boasted with pride of his work for the company. And now . . . what was next for him? Was he trying to forget that he'd screwed up everything in his life?

Or was he going to happily drag her in as well, until she was just as dirtied by his deeds?

Chapter Twenty-Two

She saw her parents settled in to the Sweetheart Inn, introducing them to Mrs. Sweet, the owner, who promised Whitney she'd take good care of them. After giving directions to the chauffeur, Whitney left early for the ranch, saying she'd promised to help. Sort of a lie, but she just couldn't hang out with her family any longer, their expectations a weight around her neck.

As she drove onto the ranch, she saw Brooke finishing up Steph Sweet's barrel-racing lesson in the corral beside the indoor arena. Whitney pulled over and watched Steph race the clover-leaf pattern, the smooth way her horse leaned into the turns, accelerated in between each barrel, then whinnied in triumph when she pulled up at the end. Whitney found herself shaking her head in wonder at the way Steph moved with the animal. Oh, Whitney could ride well, but that kind of synchronicity took thousands of repetitions, and Steph and her horse had put in the work.

When Steph had gone, Brooke rode along the corral fence until she reached Whitney, then dismounted and let her horse Sugar start nibbling grass.

"Pretty impressive," Whitney said, a foot on the lower rail, leaning her arms on the upper.

"Thanks. Steph is really good." Brooke hesitated and eyed her. "How are things with you? I hear your family's in town and coming for dinner."

Whitney shrugged. "I can hardly say 'you know how family is,' because you won't understand my sentiments at all. Your family is generous and forgiving, open-minded and loyal. Mine can be . . . trying."

"Our relationships come from years of working and living together," Brooke said, leaning her back against the fence, elbows resting on it, as they both watched Sugar. "And from what I've heard, you didn't have much of that. Boarding school, huh?"

Whitney shrugged. "It's how my parents grew up, so it's all they know."

"Sounds like you've been understanding."

"I try. I wish they would. Sometimes I think they believe the Leather and Lace stores are my little Legos, and someday I'll get tired of playing with them."

Brooke chuckled, tipping her hat back on her head so she could glance sideways at Whitney. "And Josh? Where does he fit in?"

Whitney rested her chin on her fist and watched Sugar toss her head. "I don't really know. He was great about meeting my strange family, and he impressed them."

"For a cowboy," Brooke said dryly.

Whitney smiled. "So you've met my family."

"Not yet, but I can't wait. So . . . do you need your family to be impressed by Josh?"

Whitney frowned. "What do you mean?"

"Is it important they like him for any . . . particular reason?"

"I'm dating him," Whitney hedged. "It would make things easier if everybody liked each other."

"But your store will open in a couple weeks. How does dating go then?"

"Are you actually pressuring me on behalf of your brother?" Whitney asked with amused disbelief.

"No, on behalf of myself. Guess I'm worried about him. Never quite seen him like this over a woman."

"More pressure. Nice."

"Now don't get all prickly. I'm observing, not pressuring."

Whitney was quiet for some time, listening to the cries of birds flying overhead and the faint chewing sounds of Sugar enjoying her grass. "I don't know what's going to happen, Brooke. My family . . . wants something in particular from me, and I don't know how to deal with it. Josh wants something from me, too, I think, and I'm being torn in several directions."

"But what do *you* want?" Brooke asked, turning to look at her directly, soberly.

Whitney felt tears fill her eyes, to her mortification. "I don't know."

"Geez, Whitney, I didn't mean to make you cry," Brooke said, trying to give her a hug over the top of the fence.

Whitney found herself laughing as she awkwardly patted Brooke's shoulders and released her. "That's okay. I'm making myself cry lately. I just keep telling myself to be patient, that it'll all work out."

"Sounds like good advice."

"If only I had time," Whitney added.

Brooke shot her a curious glance, but Whitney decided to change the subject. "Are you and Adam okay?"

"What made you ask that?" Brooke asked, sounding so baffled that Whitney found her worry dissipating.

"Only that I overheard you the morning after the fire, having a disagreement."

Brooke grinned. "No need to worry. I guess it's hard for a man, especially a soldier, to watch 'his woman'"—she used air quotes—"in danger, but he knows how important the ranch and my work are to me. We've talked it out."

"I'm glad. And I hope I didn't step on your toes by bringing it up."

"I think we're beyond that. In fact, when he *finally* gets around to popping the question, you'll be one of the first to know."

Whitney blushed with a sense of warmth and family she'd only begun to know in Valentine Valley. "You're a woman in a man's world; you don't think you could ask *him* to marry you?"

"He knows I want to marry him, and I'm going to be a girl about it."

"I don't blame you." Whitney turned back to her car, raised a hand, and said, "See you at the house."

"Race ya!"

Brooke flung herself into the saddle, and Whitney into her car, fumbling with her keys even as Brooke and Sugar took off at a gallop. They beat her the couple hundred yards to the house.

Whitney flung open the car door, and yelled, "Not fair! The road twisted and turned, and you could ride straight."

"Whiner!" Brooke called, dismounting and leading Sugar toward the barn. "You just don't know how to drive on gravel. Go on, get in the house and tell Mom I'll be in as soon as I rub down Sugar."

Whitney glanced into the barn's interior, where there was a light on in Josh's workshop, but she didn't go in. She didn't quite trust herself to be alone with him. She was afraid she'd abuse his comfort and the distraction of his embrace. That's all she would need, to forget about her parents' arrival.

Inside, she found Sandy Thalberg in the kitchen, wrapping baked potatoes in foil. She put an arm around Whitney's shoulders and squeezed. "Whitney, I'm so excited to meet your family!"

Whitney smiled and began to tear off squares of foil. "Thanks for the invitation. I really wanted them to meet all of you, so they know just why I've fallen in love—with Valentine Valley." She'd made a horrible pause in the wrong place, but she didn't meet Sandy's eyes.

Fifteen minutes later, Brooke came in, freshly showered, her long hair pulled back in a wet ponytail. They both started chopping vegetables for a salad. As the men took turns showering, they trooped in and out, gathering extra chairs, lengthening the dining-room table, setting up another table, and firing up the grill for steaks. The widows arrived next, bearing asparagus to roast and a bowl of coleslaw.

Emily trooped in last, huffing and puffing as she put a cheesecake in the fridge. "Had to wait for Steph to get to work. Thanks for keeping her so late, Brooke," she said with faint sarcasm.

"No problem," Brooke answered mildly.

Josh slowed to a stop behind Whitney and put both hands on her shoulders for a brief squeeze. She found herself leaning back against him, and he murmured into her ear, "Heard your family moved into town."

"Word spreads," she said quietly. "Have the employees at the inn already revolted?"

He chuckled. "Not so's I've heard. How'd the tour of Leather and Lace go?"

She shrugged, then found herself briefly pressing her cheek against the back of his hand, and it seemed the most natural thing in the world, even with his family all around them. "They were polite and even sort of interested."

"It's a beautiful old building, and you're using its character perfectly."

She glanced up and back at him. "Why thank you, Mr. Thalberg."

He squeezed her shoulders again and released her, and she watched the easy way he moved in the intricate dance of a crowded kitchen, as people opened the refrigerator or drawers or cabinets. Adam and Nate went by, carrying a cooler full of beer because the fridge was too crowded with food. The kitchen hummed with activity, and Whitney found herself watching more than participating in the teasing and the stories of the day.

Adam called to Josh, "So, have any other women committed crimes to win your favor?"

A general groan went up, and Whitney couldn't help laughing. Even though he'd been embarrassed and upset, he'd shared the news with his family, just like he shared everything.

Josh put up both hands. "Now that's just not fair."

"Give some women pretty lingerie," Nate called, "and they turn into cavewomen."

"Hey!" Whitney said, grinning, hands on her hips. She was about to protest that the rock-thrower had nothing to do with her store when she heard someone clear his throat, then saw Josh wince before shooting the others a warning look.

Already knowing what she'd find, Whitney slowly turned around and saw her parents and brother standing beside Doug Thalberg in the kitchen doorway. He must have intercepted them before they'd even rung the doorbell. The Thalbergs were dressed in jeans and t-shirts or polo shirts, while her brother and dad wore sport coats and open-necked dress shirts. She wanted to say, "It's a ranch!" but held back her comment. At least her mom's skirt and blouse were a bit more casual though elegantly out of place. Maybe that was Whitney's fault, for not having made the informality of the place clear.

"So this is Whitney's family," the elder Mrs. Thalberg said, bustling right to them with an outstretched hand.

Whitney thought with amusement that Mrs. Thalberg had pressed her jeans for the occasion, and her bright red hair could match the setting sun. She shook Vanessa's hand so hard, her mom lurched to avoid falling forward.

"I'm Rosemary Thalberg, Josh's grandma."

"Vanessa Winslow," her mom said, looking a bit dazed as she glanced around. "My husband Charles, and my son Chasz."

"What's this about a crime mixed up with Leather and Lace?" Chasz asked.

Whitney thought he was working hard to keep his glee to himself. And not succeeding, as far as she was concerned, she thought sourly.

"Shouldn't I introduce everyone first?" Whitney asked.

"Nice attempt at a distraction," Brooke whispered behind her.

Whitney shot her a narrow-eyed look. She made

the introductions all around, getting Brooke back by pointedly introducing Adam as her "friend," when she knew Brooke wanted a ring, and bad.

"The crime?" Charles reminded her, when he had a glass of red wine in his hand, and they were more spread out in the living room among the overstuffed leather furniture.

"Oh, that," Whitney said. "It was nothing, really."

"All my fault," Josh said after swallowing his cracker loaded with artichoke and spinach dip. "Ever since that photo for Savi, there are some people who're getting a little fixated. This young woman came to town, trespassed on the ranch to get photos of me, then threw a rock through the window of Leather and Lace. I tell you, we're finally tempted to lock the gates of the ranch, which we've never done in a hundred years."

"I'm not tempted," Doug said, taking a sip of his beer as he rested an elbow on the mantel.

"But why target Whitney's store?" Charles asked, frowning.

"Simple jealousy," Mrs. Ludlow said, shaking her white-haired head. "The young are so susceptible to it."

Vanessa looked confused. "The girl was angry you're dating Josh?"

"That's our fault," Mrs. Thalberg said.

Everyone turned to stare at her. The widows exchanged several glances and nods, and Whitney found herself relieved that their guilt threshold had finally been reached.

"Grandma, what are you talking about?" Josh said, dripping cracker forgotten in his hand. "I'm the one whose ridiculous photo is splashed all over every gossip rag in the country."

"Inspiring lust everywhere he goes," Adam said in an undertone to Nate that everyone heard.

Josh frowned his exasperation at him.

"When we saw how popular you are," said Mrs. Palmer, "we thought you wouldn't mind if we . . . used you for a good cause."

"I don't get it," Josh said.

"Mom, what did you do?" Doug asked.

"We have a page on the computer," Mrs. Ludlow said. "Oh, dear, what is that site again?"

"Facebook," said the younger people in the room.

"You ladies are part of that fan club?" Josh said, eyebrows raised.

"We . . . started it." His grandmother implored him with a smile.

Whitney was too busy watching the drama unfold to even pay attention to how her parents might be taking all this.

With sudden laughter, Josh choked on his cracker, and Whitney hit him hard in the back. He eyed her, and she strove for innocence. He rounded back on the widows, who looked unapologetic in the face of his humor.

Josh put on a serious expression that fooled no one. "Why would you do that, Grandma, making everything worse? Women are following me around."

"And cheering at his ass every time he bends over," Nate pointed out to nobody in particular.

Whitney winced, and this time she did glance at her family. Chasz had shed his sport coat, rolled up his sleeves, and was picking and choosing among the appetizers. Vanessa looked far too curious, and Charles hadn't taken a sip of wine in a while. He wouldn't dare to judge after what his own son had done—hell, after the scandals Whitney had *knowingly* created in her early twenties. It was a very freeing thought. She took another piece of shrimp and listened with interest as the widows explained themselves.

"We had a good purpose," Mrs. Thalberg insisted. "All the money we raised benefited the Valentine Valley Preservation Fund."

"Mom, how did you raise money?" Doug demanded.

Sandy glanced at him in surprise. "You didn't know you could order an autographed photo of our son for seven dollars?"

Josh threw his arms wide. "Mom, *you* knew?"

"I knew about the page, not who was behind it."

Doug stared at his own mother, who looked matter-of-fact and unashamed.

"Wait a minute," Chasz said. "That's illegal."

Whitney glared at him; their mother whirled and frowned at him. He blinked, then shut his mouth.

"What's so important about the Valentine Valley Preservation Fund?" Charles asked with actual interest.

Whitney watched her father as the widows expounded on the virtues of keeping Valentine the small, unique town it had always been and preserving their heritage.

"We don't like chain stores, either," Mrs. Palmer said with distaste. "Nothin' original there."

"So Leather and Lace isn't a chain?" Vanessa asked.

"A young woman, the sole owner, branching out with her stores?" Mrs. Ludlow asked. "We think it sets a wonderful precedent. We even offered Whitney a grant to help renovate the building, but she was too kind to accept it."

Mrs. Palmer grinned. "Your daughter is so creative. My favorite lingerie is—"

Adam put a hand over his grandmother's mouth from behind. "None of that personal stuff, Grandma."

"We did have something else in mind," Mrs. Thalberg began.

Whitney knew what was coming, and turned her fixed attention on Josh. He shot her a curious look, then returned his gaze to his grandma.

"Now that you're famous, we thought you should do one of those calendars, you know, with you working hard on the ranch. We could sell it to raise money. Think how many people we'll help."

"And how many fantasies he'll inspire," Nate said to Adam, who snorted.

"Well, you two would be part of it, too," Mrs. Palmer pointed out. "And some of your nice young friends."

Adam's snort turned into a cough, and Brooke sweetly patted him on the back.

"Grandma," Josh said, "we're not discussing this now."

"He didn't say no," Mrs. Thalberg said to her two best friends.

"But I am saying no to the autographed photo and Facebook. Take them both down, please."

The widows exchanged looks and sighs, but all at last nodded.

"Let me go get the steaks on the grill," Doug said, heading through the kitchen.

Whitney expected Josh to join his dad, but he bravely stayed by her side and listened to her mother start a new conversation by gushing about her educational accomplishments—as if she was *proud* of her. Whitney wished she could believe that was the only purpose.

Josh put an arm around her shoulders. "I've always liked a smart woman."

Whitney bit her lip to keep from laughing.

"Where did you go to school, Josh?" Charles asked.

"Just high school, sir. I went to work on the ranch right afterward."

"Oh."

Whitney understood that everyone her parents knew sent their kids to college—even if they ended up dropping out.

"My brother has a degree from Colorado State," Josh continued, "and he enjoys handling the business aspect. Whitney tells me you took a suite at the Sweetheart Inn?"

Whitney was glad he changed the subject.

"You'll want to walk the paths behind the hotel and find the hot springs," he continued. "Nothing like sitting outdoors in nature, getting the worst of the stress out of you."

"The hot springs are outdoors?" Vanessa asked in surprise. "They didn't build something around them?"

"Nope. We kind of like nature around here."

Her mom's smile looked pained. Could this conversation get any more awkward?

After a pause, Charles said, "Josh, I took a look at the bag you made. Very impressive."

"Thank you, sir."

"Have you ever thought about expanding your operation, hiring more employees to reach more markets?"

Josh smiled at her. "Whitney suggested that, and explained how it would work, but it just wouldn't work for me. I get the most satisfaction out of doing the creative part myself. But I thank all of you Winslows for trying to help."

When dinner was announced, Whitney found herself relieved to have something to do rather than talk. The two tables fit well enough, since the dining room was an extension of the living room, without walls separating it.

Whitney ended up sitting beside her mom, and as they ate salad, Vanessa said, "I really enjoyed the tour of your store today."

Whitney blinked in surprise. "Thanks, Mom."

"You've given a lot of thought to the character of the neighborhood and the buildings wherever you've opened a store. It makes each seem very unique, rather than just another one of a chain, as the older ladies pointed out."

"Uh . . . thanks again, Mom."

"It makes me so happy to see your success, all by yourself." Vanessa lowered her voice. "And it's nice that you've proven your business sense to your dad."

Whitney almost gaped at her. "You've never told me any of this before."

"But . . . of course I did, maybe not in so many words. I congratulated you on each store."

Had Whitney just read into that whatever she wanted? Or was Vanessa just now saying what she wanted Whitney to hear? It was pretty confusing.

But Whitney wanted the sentiment to be real, wanted to experience at least some of the closeness that the Thalbergs had. But she didn't know how she could have that if she chose not to help her family.

Throughout the meal, Josh found himself watching Whitney from across the table. He was seated near her family, so he couldn't miss the tension that only seemed to be increasing the more he saw of them. And her brother Chasz kept sending her these unreadable looks, and she wouldn't meet his eyes. Josh didn't know how much longer he could wait to hear an explanation.

When at last her family's limousine pulled up as the sun was setting, he stood on the porch at Whitney's side to say good-bye. He didn't ask how long they'd be staying, and they didn't volunteer it. But once they'd gone, he drew Whitney over to the porch swing and made her sit down.

"Josh, there are so many dishes in there. I have to—"

"There are plenty of people for that. We can help in a minute. Shouldn't they be allowed to finish gossiping about your family?" he teased.

Her smile was halfhearted. He pulled her against his side and started the swing slowly gliding front to back.

"So I'm not very funny tonight," he said, kissing her temple. "And I'm real sorry if we came off as a bunch of rednecks, with my grandma practically pimping me on Facebook."

That got a laugh out of her.

"And you knew about it, didn't you?"

She met his gaze. "I'm sorry. I knew a couple days ago. Remember all that detective work I was doing on your behalf? I found out the photo was from the Back In Time Portrait Studio, but they wouldn't give me a name. At least I knew whoever was behind it was from Valentine. It took an accident to discover the rest. I helped Mrs. Ludlow pick up her dropped mail and saw the fan-club envelopes."

"And you didn't tell me because . . . ?"

"Because your own grandmother was involved, and she asked me not to. It was killing me, Josh, I swear."

He cupped her face and kissed her. "I've no doubt it was. But I don't mind. Those widows are a force of nature."

She relaxed and snuggled back against his side, and for a moment, they listened to the sound of the wind stirring the grass and the faint laughter from inside.

"So . . ." Whitney began tentatively, "I should be apologizing to you for my own family. They may not be redneck, but they're snobs."

"It's all right. They're not used to how we live, and we're not used to them either. And you're stuck right in the middle. Do you mind bridging two worlds?"

"That's what they're calling it nowadays?" she said wryly. "And no, I don't mind. It makes life interesting."

And it was the perfect opening. "Whitney, there's something—"

She jumped up fast, and said brightly, "We'll have to talk later. I couldn't live with myself if I didn't clean up. Thanks for being so nice to my family."

And then she was gone without waiting for him, and he followed at a slower pace. He wasn't exactly going to propose, but he was going to have a more serious conversation than she obviously wanted. He sighed. Women were complicated wherever they came from. But that wouldn't stop him.

Chapter Twenty-Three

The next morning, Josh was behind the barn, carrying sacks of mineral pellets from his pickup to the single-wide trailer they used for storage, when he thought he heard the sound of an unfamiliar engine. He shrugged, figuring whoever it was would go to the office. Just as he loaded up his shoulders with two more sacks, a stranger peered around the side of the barn, then walked toward him.

Josh sighed. He didn't see a camera, but he'd been fooled before. And then he recognized Chasz Winslow and paused.

"Hey, Josh."

Chasz approached, wearing jeans, the first time Josh had seen him so casual.

Chasz glanced at the sacks. "Heavy?"

Josh smiled. "Yeah. I'll be right back." He came out of the trailer and wiped his dusty hands together. "What can I do for you?"

Chasz looked into the bed of the pickup. "I'd like to talk, but I can help you unload the rest of those first."

Josh eyed him curiously. "Okay, thanks."

Chasz tried the two-sacks-at-once method, but it was more unwieldy than it looked, and he settled for one. In ten minutes they were done.

"What did we just unload?" he asked.

"Mineral pellets to help keep the cattle healthy through the coming winter."

Chasz looked past him into the pastures. "I haven't seen a cow yet."

"They graze up in the mountains. We'll be bringing them down in another month or two."

"Oh. Interesting."

"Want something to drink?"

"No, thanks. I imagine you'd just like to hear what I have to say."

Josh put his hands in his jeans' pockets and cocked his head. "Okay."

"Did Whitney tell you the trouble I've gotten into?"

Josh nodded. "She did."

Chasz didn't bother to explain himself, which Josh sort of respected.

"Did she tell you that our father asked her to come work for the company in my place?"

"Nope." *So that's what's been going on,* Josh thought, the uneasiness rising inside him like a slow spill of oil.

"Well, since you've only just begun dating, we didn't think she'd told you, but we thought perhaps you deserved to know."

Or maybe her family thought she wouldn't be so easily swayed if left to her own devices. It saddened him that Whitney couldn't tell him something so important. He knew how she'd felt about being shut out of the family business.

Or maybe their relationship just wasn't serious enough for her to confide such major decisions in him.

"After dinner last night, I could tell how essential family is to all of you," Chasz continued.

Josh eyed him, not liking his tone—serious, but with hint of condescension. Or was that desperation? Whitney obviously hadn't jumped at the opportunity to bail her family out. And that's what it would be, a way to stabilize the company after Chasz's indiscretions were revealed.

"Family is important to us, too," Chasz went on. "But it's obvious Whitney doesn't want to hurt you."

"Or leave her business? That's what you're asking her to do, right?"

"That's not true. She might not be able to concentrate on the stores at first, but that would come with a little time."

Yeah, right. "So why are you trying to convince me?"

"Look, it's obvious a woman of the world like Whitney has been with more sophisticated guys than you. You can't be fooling yourself to think she could be happy in a place like this, right?" Chasz narrowed his eyes. "I don't know what you think you want from this relationship, but to me, it's obvious—you're holding her back."

"Excuse me?" Josh said in a low voice, feeling his muscles stiffen.

"She's always wanted to be a part of our family company. I think she's hesitating not because of Leather and Lace but because of you."

"Then you don't know her very well," Josh shot back, but part of him worried that Chasz was right.

He knew how crushed she'd been when her family rejected her. Now she had the opportunity she'd always wanted. Was she really hesitating because of him? How could he be the one to stand in the way of her family reuniting when he of all people knew how wonderful it could be to work together?

"Look," Chasz said patiently, "I don't want to argue about who knows her better. I just want to know what it would take to make you back off."

"You're offering me a *bribe*?" Josh asked in disbelief.

"That's kind of a harsh way to put it. How about an incentive?"

"How about you take off now, and I'll pretend this didn't happen?"

Chasz sighed. "I can see you want to play for bigger stakes."

"That's not what I'm—"

"I know you're no stranger to scandal yourself," he interrupted. "The whole country saw that shot of you naked in a fountain."

Josh rolled his eyes. "Really? Are you going to compare my drunken prank to the way you slept with the enemy?"

Chasz acted like he hadn't heard. "All I'm saying is that a lot worse can come out about you if you won't back down."

"Worse? I haven't done anything that could be worse than what you're doing right now."

"Rumors are insidious things, Josh." Chasz's gaze darted away even as his forehead started to shine with sweat. "What if there was a rumor that your photographer girlfriend at that ski resort also filmed you having sex?"

For a moment, the thought of how that would hurt his family made Josh a little crazy. He found himself standing menacingly over Chasz. "Knock it off before I deck you."

Chasz raised both hands. "I don't need to resort to that, of course. Just thought it gave us a little bargaining room. I'm offering a hundred thousand for you to back off."

"I don't want to hear it. See yourself out."

Josh walked past him and into the barn, feeling like his skin was afire, and he needed to burst out of it. A few minutes later, the limousine glided away, and he stood still, hands fisted at his sides at the audacity of that asshole.

And then he thought about Whitney, fighting this all alone. She'd done everything alone because of that self-absorbed family of hers. Of course she hadn't confided in him—she'd never had anyone to confide in.

He wanted desperately to talk to her, to help her, but didn't know if he would be welcome. And how could he tell her that her family had tried to bribe and blackmail him?

Whitney looked up when someone knocked on Leather and Lace's front door. She saw the silhouette of a slim woman, and although it could be many people, she just somehow knew it was her mother.

With a sigh, she unlocked the door and met Vanessa's worried gaze.

"Come on in, Mom," Whitney said, stepping aside. "Can I get you something? Coffee? A soda?"

Vanessa winced and tossed her purse on the table

Whitney was using. "You're treating me like a guest rather than your mother."

Whitney could only shrug. Vanessa had become that all by herself.

"Is anyone else here?" Vanessa asked.

"I gave everyone the day off. They're going to start the upstairs soon, and that won't take as long, but . . . I don't know, I just didn't feel like listening to the pounding. It's pretty peaceful right now. I'm considering the suggestions of the interior designer I've used for the other stores and . . ." She trailed off when Vanessa didn't even look down at the sketches. "Okay, Mom, what's going on?"

"I—I have to tell you something, and you're not going to like it," Vanessa said, not quite meeting her gaze. "I didn't know anything about it until it was over. I'm not even sure your father knew, but—"

"Mom, just spit it out," Whitney said, feeling tense.

"Chasz went to Josh this morning to talk about your coming into the company."

Whitney inhaled and gritted her teeth. "I hadn't even told him yet, Mom. I've told you all along I haven't made up my mind."

"Well, Chasz didn't know Josh was clueless, but maybe somehow this is all for the best?"

"Even you don't sound convinced of that. What happened?"

"I just . . . I just don't think you mean as much to Josh as you think you do."

"Mom, tell me what happened!" Whitney said in a sharp voice.

Vanessa twisted her fingers together. "After Josh told him that Winslow Enterprises needs you, he offered Josh money to step aside."

Whitney felt her mouth drop open. "He *what*?"

"Oh, Whitney, I knew you were going to take this badly, especially since Chasz told him you couldn't possibly want to live in this small town, living such a . . . small . . . normal kind of life."

Now Whitney's face flushed. "I can't believe this," she hissed, then covered her mouth with both hands.

"I know, I know, it was a terrible thing to assume, but maybe it worked out for the best. Because Josh seems to want to bargain for more money."

"What? That can't be possible. Tell me *exactly* what happened."

"Just that Chasz offered money, and Josh made him leave. Chasz fully intends to counter with a higher offer, he was that confident that he could persuade Josh to let go of this whole thing."

"*This whole thing?*" Whitney echoed icily. "You mean *me*. Let go of *me*."

Vanessa winced. "You've only been dating a few weeks, darling."

Absolutely nothing about this whole conversation was making sense. Her family actually thought Josh wanted a higher offer?

It should chill her, but for the first time in a while, she felt . . . hope. They saw Josh's behavior from their own skewed point of view. She saw it in another light. He didn't laugh in Chasz's face; he threw her brother out. Had Josh been angry? Maybe even angry because he felt something for her, and was offended?

But was this a good thing? Or would it make her decision even more difficult?

"I just thought you should know all this," her mother finished in a lame voice, "and that your father is deciding our next response."

"No, Mom, no response, no bribes, nothing. Just leave us alone and let me make my own decision!" Her voice rose so loud by the end that the final word seemed to thunder in her ears.

With a shaking hand, Vanessa picked up her purse. "I didn't want this, Whitney, any of it. But somehow it's all happened, and we have to make the best of it."

Whitney felt her anger deflate into tired sadness. "Chasz made it all happen, Mom. There was no 'somehow.' I'm sorry he disappointed you and Dad so much. But you have to promise me you'll make Dad and Chasz leave Josh alone."

Vanessa nodded. "I'll do my best."

"Thank you." She opened the door and waited for her mom to go through.

Vanessa hesitated, looking back at Whitney over her shoulder, then lowered her head and walked out. Whitney closed the door with gentle restraint; otherwise, she'd have slammed it.

She was being ridiculous—just because Josh was too honorable to accept a bribe didn't mean he loved her. The exhilaration that threatened to overwhelm her was only confusing her, especially since she'd jumped off the porch swing when he tried to have a serious conversation with her. He hadn't even called her last night, as he normally did. No word today, either.

And now he'd been practically assaulted by her family. She wouldn't blame him for backing off.

That night, Whitney lay in bed and stared up at the dark ceiling with dry eyes. She ran scenarios in her head, where she went to work in Manhattan and tried to have some kind of long-distance relationship with Josh. She had the money to fly to see him anytime she wanted, but how often would she be able to get away? She still didn't know how she felt about him, and perhaps that signaled a death knell for it all.

Or should she just open her Valentine store and return to San Francisco, letting her family deal with the problems Chasz had caused? He wasn't the face of the company; maybe it would weather the storm of one bad employee.

Or should she stay in Valentine?

The whisper of such an idea gave her the chills, of both fear and exhilaration. She had no guarantees that anything more would happen with Josh. What if she stayed, then found out he'd expected her to leave, that she was just a late-summer fling? The town was so small, and they'd see each other all the time, and there could be awkwardness—

So? When had a broken relationship with a man ever made her question where she lived, who her friends were?

But here, her friends were *his* friends, his family. A breakup in Valentine wouldn't be as anonymous as one in San Francisco.

She had no idea what she was going to do, for the first time in her life. Even when she'd found out she couldn't be a part of Winslow Enterprises, she'd had a plan. And when that hadn't worked, she'd gotten her parents' attention with Whitney Wild. After the thrill of that had petered out, she'd charged with excitement and determination into building Leather and Lace.

And now? She was clueless, and it made her feel small and insignificant and alone.

And Josh didn't call.

The next day, the girls called Whitney up and invited her to lunch, so she was able to coolly tell her family she had plans. She couldn't go on ignoring them, she knew, but for now it made her feel better. It still appalled her that they thought they could *bribe* Josh to break up with her.

After a Mexican lunch at Rancheros, Brooke, Emily, Monica, and Whitney retreated to Sugar and Spice for dessert, because frankly, no one else made them as well as Emily. And Whitney told her that, too, making her blush. Emily waved to Steph, who had a half day off from school and was working the counter.

"Is she always here, Em?" Whitney asked softly.

"She keeps *asking* for more hours," Emily insisted, her voice lowered as she spoke to her friends. "She's up to twenty hours a week, and I think that's all a high-school senior busy with classes and a boyfriend—"

"And barrel racing," Brooke interrupted.

"—and looking at colleges, should do," Emily continued. "I enjoy her here, of course, but—"

"You're whispering!" Steph called, as a customer left the shop, her voice amused. Wiping her hands on a towel, she came around the counter and approached their table, blond ponytail bobbing. "So what are you whispering about?"

Emily hesitated.

"You," Brooke said. "Em's worried you're working too much, when you should be enjoying your senior year."

"But I'm enjoying *this,*" Steph said to her sister. "In fact, I've been thinking about an idea, and now's as good a time as any to bring it up. What would you say about actually teaching me to bake? You know, your secrets and everything."

Emily stared up at her, mouth parted in surprise. "But that's even more work for you."

"But I like it. I like experimenting with how things taste, and I like how happy people are when they eat our food. And if you teach me, I can take your place while you go on your honeymoon. Maybe around Christmastime, when I have off from school. It's all about me, you know," she added, smiling.

Whitney saw Emily's eyes fill just before she rose to hug her sister.

"I think your learning to bake would be wonderful," Emily said huskily. Then she broke the hug and held Steph's upper arms. "But you can change your mind if you don't like it."

Steph rolled her eyes. "I've already been working here a while. I think I'd know that. Who knows, maybe we could work here together forever." She grinned.

Then the front door opened, setting the bell jingling, and Steph turned to greet their customer, an older lady, before heading behind the counter.

And Emily stared after her, mouth agape.

"You'll catch flies in there," Monica said, bumping shoulders with her.

Emily swallowed. "I just . . . we had such troubles last year, and now . . . this." She cleared her throat and gave an embarrassed smile. "Sorry. When you had as little family interaction as I did growing up, this all still seems unreal."

Whitney felt a pang of sympathy and sadness. She knew just how Emily felt. But Emily had come here and found her real family, loving and supportive. Whitney's real family had followed her to Valentine just to use her now that they were desperate—and offend Josh, too. And he was so offended, maybe he'd dropped her altogether.

She didn't want to think about that just now, and instead, turned back to Brooke. "Did I mention you look nicely dressed up today?"

Brooke looked down at her navy pants, striped white and blue top, and summer sweater. "Thanks. Not my normal clothes, it's true. But I spent the morning making the rounds of businesses that might like to rent my indoor arena. You know, to help it pay for itself. And I mentioned the riding school, too, of course."

"So you weren't trying to entice Adam to propose?" Monica teased.

Brooke sighed. "He's busy coordinating the final renovations on a house meant for the returning-vet program. Good thing we work together, or I'd never see him." She reached into her blouse and pulled slowly on a necklace. "But we did camp up near the herd last night . . . and this was the result."

On the end of the chain dangled an engagement ring with an oval diamond winking in the sunlight.

Everyone screamed and gasped, leaving Brooke grinning.

"Congratulations!" Whitney said. "Come on, we need details. Did you have any idea it was coming?"

"How could she not?" Monica said. "The whole town knew she wanted a ring, and Adam's no fool."

Brooke laughed. "But it was still a surprise. We were roasting marshmallows—yeah, I know, a kid thing, but Adam likes them. He had the marshmallows, and he took my stick, and when he handed it back, rather than a marshmallow, the ring was dangling from it! I think I screamed and scared off every cow for miles."

They all took turns hugging her. As Whitney listened to the friends' suggestions and plans, she realized that when she left Valentine, all of these special moments would go on without her. Josh hadn't called last night or this morning, as if she wasn't even worth the fight, now that he knew she had even more reason to leave town. She told herself she didn't know what he was thinking, that maybe he was trying to find a way to break the news about what her family had done.

Brooke had donned her ring, and the other women were oohing and aahing over it. The stab of envy Whitney felt took her by surprise. She knew things hadn't been easy for Brooke and Adam, and this engagement was the culmination of a love story that took work.

So why did Whitney feel envious about a future marriage, when she herself could have the business world she'd long wanted? Hadn't that always been more important than a relationship with a man?

But that had been before Josh. And now this feeling of envy. Was she actually falling in love with him? Had he responded to her brother the way he had—because Josh might be falling in love with her, too? Dammit, but whatever happened, she could not just keep ignoring what her family had done. She had to talk to Josh.

Chapter Twenty-Four

At the ranch, Whitney couldn't find Josh anywhere in the barn or the main house, so she decided to wait for him in his loft. She sent him a text saying she was there but not to hurry. The afternoon crept by slowly, and as the dinner hour approached, she began to look through his cabinets and fridge. She didn't have a repertoire of menus off the top of her head and was too nervous to spend time searching online. When he texted that he was on his way, she sautéed some vegetables and prepared a couple of omelets, keeping them covered over a low temperature.

She heard a sound and turned to find him in the doorway, tall and broad-shouldered, and her heart-beat picked up automatically.

Josh.

She felt tears sting her eyes and wondered what that could be about, then gave him a smile that was far too tentative.

He smiled back. "Hi."

"Hi. Hope you don't mind that I barged in like this."

He sniffed the air. "Not at all. Smells good."

It was a bad sign that she was desperate for a touch, desperate to be reassured by his embrace.

"Let me go take a quick shower so I don't gross you out," was all he said.

"You do smell like manure."

He grinned. "Gee, thanks."

She practically paced while he was gone, wishing he would have asked her to join him in the shower, wishing she would have suggested it herself. No, they had important things to discuss before sex took everything over.

When he came out of the bathroom, he was wearing a pair of shorts and a t-shirt, as if she hadn't seen him with less. As if they were strangers.

Oh, God, her family had ruined everything.

She should feed him first, but instead blurted out, "My mother informed me that my brother told you everything, then—and then tried to bribe you."

Josh's smile faded a bit, and he sighed. "Yeah, it made me pretty mad."

Whitney winced. "I know I should have told you what they offered me—"

"That's not what made me mad," he interrupted.

"You're not angry I didn't tell you? You're way too understanding."

His smile was sad. "I understand what you've been going through."

"Look, I don't need your pity."

"Pity? Why would I feel that?"

She spent a moment pouring coffee into mugs, making his just the way he liked it. And even the fact that she knew his coffee preferences bothered her. She handed it over without meeting his gaze, then looked out the window across the endless, wind-blown pastures, empty until winter. "Don't you see? They didn't even make much of an attempt to talk *me* into helping them. I'm starting to think they came here just to get rid of you, as if without a man I would just crumble and fall into their desperate plot."

"Then they don't know you very well."

"No, they don't," she said, suddenly fierce. "Except—except—it's about the family, isn't it? The family business."

"I can't believe it won't survive your brother's scandal. He's not the head of the company."

"No, but he was going to be. And I don't know how shaky the board is. And me? I've spent my life dreaming of being there, with my family, and now they've finally offered, and it's only out of desperation. And that sucks. How am I supposed to know what's best for *me* when it's all about them?"

Josh sipped his coffee and said nothing. She almost wished he had some magical answer.

"Is there anything I can do to help?" he finally asked.

She sighed. "Can you ignore Chasz's stupidity? Even my parents, or whoever was involved. I know they offended you, and I can't say they didn't mean it, because frankly, they might not care."

He gave a grim smile. "I got that." Then he focused his serious hazel eyes on her. "But I don't care about them, only you."

"Do you, Josh?" she asked, searching his gaze. "Because I'm worried you've been using my family problems as an excuse to remove yourself from my life. You've been . . . distant these last few days, and I can't help wondering if I'm worth all this trouble to you. Am I that easy to give up?"

"Easy to give up?" he said, striding purposefully until he was right in front of her. "This has been the hardest couple days of my life, knowing they wanted you back and were offering the one thing you'd wanted your whole life. How could I compete with that? And the fact that you didn't tell me of their offer seemed to confirm that our relationship was just temporary."

"That's not why I didn't say anything!" she countered. "I thought I needed to make a decision first."

"You can't have been worried you'd hurt me," he said. "I'm not a little boy but a man who needs to know what he's up against."

"Up against?" she cried. "This isn't a competition—it's my life!"

"It's my life, too, and my decisions are just as important. I love you, Whitney, but I'm not going to be the one who held you back from your destiny, or whatever you think it is."

She blinked at him, aghast, "You love me? And this is how you tell me, as if it's unimportant, just a side topic?"

"I don't know that it *is* important to you," he said softly. "You might want things in life that I can't give."

"I don't know what I want," she said hoarsely, and found herself wiping away tears.

Josh took a step closer, whispering, "Whitney."

She held up a hand. "No, that's okay, I don't need your comfort. At least I know where you stand. You love me, but I'm not worth fighting for."

His eyes widened, then narrowed. "That's not fair. I'm trying to do what I think is right."

"And I have to do the same. I—I have to think. Go ahead and eat the omelet before it gets cold. I'll call you later."

She grabbed her purse and headed for the door. "Whitney—"

But she didn't stop, only ran down the steps and out into the sunshine. Surely it should have been raining, to match her mood. Josh loved her—why didn't she feel like celebrating?

Josh told himself he was being practical as he took a seat at his dining table with a plate of eggs in front of him. But he couldn't eat, and only sat there, hands gripping the edge of the table. Thoughts chased themselves around inside his head, and some of them were less than flattering.

He'd made a mess of everything—especially the ridiculous way he'd told her he loved her. Nope, no hearts and romance for him, just "I love you, but go ahead and leave me." He slapped himself on the forehead with the palm of his hand.

So many things could get worse now.

Would she settle for him and Valentine, since her family didn't want her free and clear in Winslow Enterprises?

Or would she return to Manhattan with them and take up the reins of power she'd always wanted, regardless of the circumstances?

He couldn't imagine any decision she might make that would leave her happy and free of doubts. He cared about what she wanted, and didn't want anything except her love. But she had to be the one to decide that, just like Nate said.

But it seemed Whitney didn't agree with that philosophy. If he wooed her, tried to persuade her to love him, she might resent him someday for forcing her hand. Backing off was one of the hardest decisions he'd ever had to make, and she'd acted like it was a crime.

And seeing her distraught face, realizing her fears that she wasn't worth fighting for, had made him want to beg for her love, beg her to stay.

But if he did that, she might give up her own dreams. And if he followed her, he'd be giving up on his own. There seemed to be no easy answer for the two of them.

Whitney was trying to read a magazine in bed that night when her phone rang. She saw Josh's ID and felt something inside of her ease.

"Hi," she said.

"Hey, Whitney."

She closed her eyes on hearing his voice, and thought again, *He loves me.*

"Are you still there?" he asked.

"Sorry, yes, I am. It's good to hear from you."

"I didn't know whether I should call, like I was pressuring you or anything, when I'm not. I don't need answers from you, Whitney, not until you're ready to give them. Or we could talk, you know, about the future. I just wanted you to know that I *do* love you, and what you choose to do won't change that. And I never meant for you to feel that I was backing away because you weren't important to me. If anything, you've become more important than anyone else in my life."

"Oh, Josh," she whispered, knowing how much he loved his family, and that putting her ahead of them really meant something.

Then she heard a knock on the door.

"Whitney?" It was her brother's voice.

"Chasz is here," she told Josh after clearing her throat. "I should let him stand in the hall, but he'd keep knocking and disturb the other guests."

"Go ahead. I'll talk to you tomorrow. Sleep tight."

And then he was gone, and she found herself staring with aching eyes at the phone as she set it down.

Chasz knocked again, and she pulled on a pair of yoga pants and a t-shirt. When she opened the door, she saw that his clothes were disheveled, his hair mussed, his eyes haggard.

"Can we talk?" he asked.

She stood in his way, and said coldly, "You said everything you had to say to Josh."

He winced. "I know Mom told you. I haven't been able to stop thinking about what I said, what I did. Please, can we talk?"

For the first time, she didn't see confidence and superiority in his expression, but the sad, weary look of a lost man. He was her brother, so she let him in. He slumped into a chair, and she sat on the bed.

They said nothing for endless minutes, until at last she spoke with exasperation. "Well, Chasz?"

"I talked to Courtney." He cleared his throat, and, still without looking at her, continued. "I've lost her."

"You didn't already realize that?"

He shrugged. "I guess . . . I guess I thought she'd forgive me. But this is too much humiliation, she said, too much proof that I can't possibly love her. But I do love her, Whitney," he said, meeting her eyes imploringly.

"But actions matter, and yours haven't shown that."

"I know. I acted so impulsively, like I could do anything I wanted. Mr. Invincible," he said bitterly. "I've lost her, I've ruined my life. And respect? I never thought that mattered, but now I've lost it all, even my own self-respect. And today—today I sank to a new low. When I left Josh, it was as if I was suddenly hit by everything I've done. I felt . . . dirty. Did he tell you I threatened him with rumors of a sex tape?"

She jumped to her feet, no longer able to keep her distance as she stood above him, vibrating with fury. "You did what?"

"I didn't think Mom would tell you that. I've done a lot these past weeks, feeling desperate, including trying to force you to do what I wanted. But threaten a guy with a sex-tape rumor? I disgusted even myself. The look in his eyes—" He broke off, his expression twisted with anguish. "For the first time it really hit home how much respect and reputation matter. And I've lost all of that."

Whitney forced herself to back away. "I know that those things matter. If you're really serious about changing, you can earn them again. It might take years, but you can make up for the past, perhaps be back at Winslow Enterprises. But I won't be there." The words were a surprise and a relief all at once. "My reputation matters, too, and I spent a lot of time and energy building up Leather and Lace, planning out my future, and watching it happen. And I did it on my own. It's just too important for me to give up."

Chasz studied her face a long moment, his expression bleak. "I told Mom and Dad you weren't going to do it, but they didn't believe me."

"I'm sure they thought I'd be thrilled by their offer." She eyed him. "You're not going to try to convince me?"

"No. I can see there's no point. And I don't blame you. You started fresh and succeeded."

"There's nothing saying you can't do that either."

He shrugged. "Guess I have to take one day at a time."

She saw him to the door, then leaned back against it in thought. Her business success had become more than proving to her family that she could succeed— she'd proven it to herself. And now she had to stop living her life in reaction to her family. If they couldn't understand that, well, it wasn't as if they'd been in her life all that much anyway.

But after seeing Josh and his family, she wanted that for herself. But not if it meant giving up on all she'd worked for.

Whitney hadn't even showered the next morning when there was an insistent knocking at her door. She left her computer, and with a sigh, opened the door to reveal her parents. Big surprise.

"Good morning, darling," Vanessa said, giving a tentative smile.

Her father just walked in, glancing around the old-fashioned room before turning to face her, hands on his hips. "Chasz told us your decision."

"I figured he would." Whitney shut the door. "Would you like to have breakfast with me in the dining room? Debbie allows extra guests."

"We already ate," Charles said. "Are you avoiding the subject?"

"No, just trying to be polite." She sighed and faced him. "Dad, I'm sorry I couldn't help you out. Besides being a member of the family and showing some con-tinuity, what could I have done to help? Other em-ployees are surely more knowledgeable."

"We've always had family in the business," he said sternly.

"I know. And when things die down, maybe Chasz will be able to step forward again. Your PR people can surely soften this someday. And people forget."

To Whitney's surprise, her mom was watching her with a twinkle in her eye, almost as if she . . . approved. That was revolutionary.

"I'm very disappointed, Whitney," he said.

She took his hand. "I know you are, Dad, but it's Chasz you should be most disappointed with. Don't let his mistakes affect our relationship."

Her dad let go of her hand and turned toward the window, as if he needed to marshal himself. Whitney knew how important the company was to him, but she truly hoped he would realize that family should mean more.

"So what will you do now?" Vanessa asked with obvious curiosity.

"Open my third store," Whitney said. "Then keep growing."

"What about Josh?"

Whitney hesitated, and even her father glanced over his shoulder to study her. "I . . . don't know. He told me he loves me." She blurted that last part out, surprised at herself.

Vanessa smiled. "I'd always hoped you'd find a good man."

Whitney blinked at her in surprise. Maybe her mother was eager to move on, to have a better relationship.

Vanessa continued, "Of course, he's not used to . . . our lifestyle."

"You mean he's not rich?" Whitney countered wryly.

"You must admit, you two were raised very differently. Sometimes that can be a problem."

"Maybe, but I don't think Josh cares all that much about money. He cares about people and family and being happy."

Charles faced her, frowning. "So caring about money means you can't care about family?"

"I didn't mean to imply that, Dad. It's just . . . I've never known anyone like him, so confident in himself but in a relaxed sort of way. His entire family works together in everything from crazy weather to life-or-death situations. It makes a person different, I guess."

"Sounds like you love him, too," Vanessa said quietly.

"I think I do." Her voice wobbled, and her eyes misted. "And I need to figure out a way to make it work."

"Maybe you should figure it out with Josh."

Whitney and her mom shared a smile. "I think you're right." Then she turned to her dad. "But you're my family, and you're important, too. I know you'll make everything work out with the Chasz situation, Dad. You always do."

"It'll just be harder without you," he said gruffly.

"I think I'll take that as a compliment."

Whitney had to work all day at Leather and Lace, getting her new employees together for the first time. She and Josh texted, and when she said she'd like to see him, he said she could find him at Tony's Tavern that night, for the Robbers' Roost poker game.

Poker? At a time like this?

But she had to remember that Josh didn't stress over things like she did. He'd said his piece—that he loved her!—and was waiting for her to make the next move. So, she was a little perturbed he wasn't holed up in his workshop in melancholy seclusion . . . and she wasn't about to ask him to cancel his game with his friends. But he might have offered . . .

All right, she was being ridiculous now.

When she arrived at Tony's after eight, she found the whole gang gathered—all the girls, all the guys, looking absolutely innocent while avoiding her gaze, playing pool or cards, or scanning the songs on the jukebox.

Josh immediately stood up and came over to her, and in that moment, she only saw him. He paused, as if judging her mood, but she hugged his waist, and when she felt his arms fold about her, a peace came over her that she'd never felt before.

"I've missed you," she whispered.

He kissed the top of her head, then cupped her face to kiss her mouth.

"Get a room!" someone yelled.

Josh straightened, grinning, and she looked at him wonderingly. He was such a contented, happy guy, with the same stresses and problems other people had, but his ability to deal with it all just amazed her.

"Josh, I wanted to let you know that my brother came by and told me what he'd said to you—told me everything," she added sternly, "even the stuff you didn't tell me."

Josh shrugged. "It didn't matter. I knew he was bluffing."

"It was ugly, and he realized it. He was falling apart when he came to me, upset with his behavior and what he'd done to his life. I just wanted you to know how he felt."

He took both her hands in his. "I already know. He called me to apologize."

"He did?" She felt a piece of her heart lighten. "I'm glad. He's not all bad. Things have changed him, but . . . I hope he can become better."

"I hope so, too."

She glanced at the poker game and considered trying to find a private place to talk, but where in Valentine would that be? People find out everything.

"Josh, I told my parents I wasn't accepting the company job."

He searched her face as his own grew more serious. "I would say 'Are you sure?' but I know you thought everything through."

"I did, for many days now. I'm sorry if I've been distracted, but . . . I didn't want to be their fallback, you know? I've spent these last six years making my own decisions, growing my own company—and I like it. It's not full of worldwide prestige, but it's mine. And I don't have to prove myself anymore, prove I'm not just a party girl or an heiress or even the CEO of my own little company. I'm happy with me, and I know what I want now."

He squeezed her hands a little tighter. "And what's that?"

"I want you," she whispered, stepping closer to him, not caring who was watching. "I love you, too."

"Whitney," he breathed, then leaned down to kiss her, drawing her into his arms until her toes barely skimmed the floor.

Somewhere in the background were whistles and catcalls, but it seemed so very far away.

He straightened and cocked his head as he looked down at her. "I've got to warn you in advance. I'm probably going to embarrass you."

"Embarrass me?" How could he think she cared *what* he did for a living, as long as he was happy?

"I've kind of agreed to help out the Preservation Fund committee, to do that calendar with the guys."

She almost snorted her laugh.

Then Will Sweet, who'd obviously been eavesdropping, stood up and began to do a striptease, sliding his shirt up his chest. Monica and Emily were laughing at him, but Brooke was looking at Josh and Whitney, tears shining in her eyes, her smile trembling. On seeing his sister, Josh paused and seemed to duck his head, then he simply pushed Will back into his seat.

Josh took Whitney's arm and pulled her closer to the wall. "Look, I don't want you to ever think you have to give up anything for me. If we end up together, I'll live half the year wherever you need to be."

"If we end up together?" she echoed, feeling her own eyes begin to fill. "I love you, Josh, and I don't take that lightly. We're together."

His grin widened. "Good. That's good. I've already talked to Matt Sweet about doing the leather stitching for me, so that'll free up even more time. I'll make any kind of compromise I can. I want this to work, Whitney. I need you."

His voice dropped into a husky tone that made her shiver.

"Josh, you don't have to live half the year away from here. Valentine Valley—hell, the Silver Creek Ranch—is who you are. And the fact that you'd spend so much time away really moves me to tears. But I can base my company here. I'll have to travel at least once or twice a month, but lots of people travel and make it work. And besides, I've been working way too hard and micromanaging my employees. I need to concentrate on the bigger picture."

"You'd stay here?" Josh said, as if he were amazed.

"I would. For you, I'd go anywhere, do anything. I want to start a new life, Josh. And I want to share it all with you."

To her shock, he dropped to one knee and solemnly asked, "Then would you marry me, Whitney?"

She gaped down at him as the room hushed.

"I don't want to wait," he continued. "I want to be a family, to have kids—and I want you all to myself."

"Until you have kids," Monica added wryly.

No one else said a word, waiting, and Whitney felt tears of happiness begin to leak down her cheeks. "Yes, oh yes, I'll marry you, Josh."

He grinned. "Good, because I came prepared."

Without standing, he fumbled in his jeans' pocket and pulled out a tiny circle made of the most delicate leather.

"It's not a traditional ring," he said sheepishly, "but I've been making it just for you."

She gasped and let him put it on her finger, staring in amazement at the delicate etched roses along a vine. "Josh, this is the most beautiful ring I've ever owned."

She threw her arms around his neck, almost knocking him sideways, but he stood up and twirled her around to lots of cheering. And then their friends descended on them—no longer just his friends and family, but hers, too. She'd found her home.

Epilogue

The Grand Opening of Leather and Lace took place in the second week of October, in plenty of time for the holidays and the ski season. To Whitney's surprise, her mom came, and Vanessa insisted that her dad would have come, too, but Chasz had an appointment to face the board. The two men actually sent a huge vase of flowers, which Monica personally delivered, knowing how thrilled Whitney would be.

And she *was* thrilled. She had everything she wanted, a new store with old-fashioned touches to fit in perfectly with the picturesque mountain town of Valentine Valley.

She had the final celebrity appearance of the famous Josh Thalberg, who insisted he was retiring from public life after the Opening.

And then there was Brooke, who was still teasing her baby brother for copying her and getting engaged only days later than she had.

Whitney pulled Josh away from his sister and through the crowd of people admiring the beautiful, romantic lingerie lying across antique hatboxes and pooling amidst old costume jewelry.

"Thanks for the rescue," Josh said.

She kept her arm around his waist. "You won't be thanking me for long. Guess what my mom just told me? They've bought a condo in Aspen to spend part of each year here."

"And you think I wouldn't like that my soon-to-be wife can see her family on a regular basis?"

"Your parents might not like sharing grandparent privileges all the time."

"We have a while before we worry about that . . ." His voice trailed off, and he stared at her. "Don't we?"

She shrugged and gave him a tentative smile. "Apparently we don't have as much time as I thought. I'm not quite sure how it happened but—"

Josh let out a whoop and swung her around, shouting, "I'm gonna be a dad! Hey, you better make me a husband first."

Can't get enough of Valentine Valley?

Good news, there is so much more to come!
When the wedding of the century comes to town,
flower shop owner, Monica Shaw,
finds herself falling for a Secret Service agent.

Keep reading for a look at

A Promise at Bluebell Hill

coming in March 2014 . . .

Chapter One

In the workroom of Monica's Flowers and Gifts, Monica Shaw stood at a large table, critically studying the flower arrangement for a wedding the next day. It was May in Valentine Valley, Colorado, the start of wedding season, one of her busiest times of the year. She loved every moment of it, from helping a nervous man find the perfect flowers to ask his girl to marry him, to making the bride feel like she was the centerpiece of the altar, framed in beautiful flowers: roses, tulips and dahlias, with a spray of white delphiniums. And she was good at what she did, as more and more of her customers confided that they'd been referred by their satisfied friends. The walls of the workroom were covered in photos from her successful events and reminded her of happy occasions and a job well done.

The bell at the front door jingled, and she glanced through the window that separated the workroom from the showroom. The door swung closed behind a tall man dressed in khakis, a dark blue polo shirt, and a windbreaker. He looked good—broad, muscled shoulders tapering to narrow hips. He had a square-jawed Captain-America face, beneath a military cut of deep auburn hair, and carried himself with a regality that seemed out of place in a flower shop—heck, in the whole town.

Dark sunglasses still hid his eyes as his head briefly turned from side to side. She knew the girly stuff he saw in her showroom: flowers, terrariums, plants in baskets along one side, and on the other, homemade crafts she took in on consignment, like quilted baby blankets, knitted layettes, ceramic vases, and leather frames. Behind the front counter were coolers full of flower arrangements anyone off the street could buy. Surely he was there for roses—he looked like a rose sort of lady's man, no spontaneously picked wildflowers for him.

He finally took off the sunglasses, revealing the deepest blue eyes Monica had ever seen, piercing and intelligent, cool and impassive, above a nose with a slight crook in it, as if he'd broken it once and hadn't bothered having it fixed. With those eyes he took in her work, her life, and didn't even twitch a lip in a smile. Monica immediately didn't want to like him, just from that lack of expression—but she was far too fascinated already.

Through the window, Monica watched Karista, her freckle-faced teenage sales associate, drop the tissue she'd shredded just looking at the stranger, to approach the counter and speak to him. The words were too muffled for Monica to hear, but when the man turned away, it was obvious he meant to browse. He glanced at Sugar and Spice's daily pastry laid out on the little wrought-iron table, today a raspberry torte, but moved on. How could he resist that? Not many people did.

Perhaps he was a Josh Thalberg groupie, trying to score leather-carved goods before they were all gone. Josh's fame had started in her store, but now he was creating expensive shoulder bags for an Aspen boutique and exclusive necklaces for his wife's lingerie store, Leather and Lace. He didn't have as much time for the checkbook covers, key chains, and frames he'd done for her in the past. People were starting to express their disappointment that she didn't have a larger selection, and she was surprised how much his popularity was playing with her head—as if her flower arrangements weren't enough to lure customers anymore.

The stranger did pause to look at Josh's work, intricate and unusual, standing out next to the crocheted baby bonnets. Then he gave Karista a nod, slid his sunglasses back on his face, and headed outside.

Monica hurried through the swinging door and said, "Who was that?" just as Karista exclaimed, "Did you see him?"

They laughed together.

"He can't be from around here," Karista said, light brown ponytail bobbing as she shook her head. "But he doesn't exactly look like a tourist either."

"And he was just browsing?"

"That's all he said. Real deep voice, too. Called me 'miss,' all formal."

Monica came around the counter and moved through her shop until she reached the big plate glass windows that bracketed the front door. She leaned across her flower displays and could just see the stranger studying the sign above the shop connected to her own, SUGAR AND SPICE, before going inside the bakery.

"Do you see him?" Karista asked as she reached her side.

"He just went into Em's place."

Emily Thalberg was one of Monica's best friends. She'd arrived in Valentine Valley a couple years before to sell a building she'd inherited, but ended up finding a passion for pastry and marrying a local cowboy, instead.

"And now he's left Em's empty-handed—guess he was browsing there, too—and is heading into Wine Country. Weird."

"He could just be sight-seeing. You never know what tourists want to see," Karista added, with a teenager's faint disdain.

Monica grinned. "He doesn't look like a tourist." Then her stomach growled. "Hey, Karista, I'm going to take my lunch outside and sit in the sun."

"You just want to spy on him," the girl teased.

"And maybe I do. I'll let you know while you slave over those bows that need to be made."

Karista gave a cute, fake pout and followed her behind the counter. Monica took her salad out from the flower cooler, grabbed a fork, napkin and her water bottle, and headed outside to sit on the bench in front of her big window. It was one of those crisp mountain days, brilliant blue sky encompassing the nearby Elk Mountains like an umbrella. Some of the hardier summer perennials were already filling planters along Main Street. Freestanding display signs stood on the sidewalk outside several businesses, advertising the day's specials. Her block was filled with two-story clapboard buildings painted blue and yellow and red like a field of flowers. At the end of the street, closest to the mountains, the stone tower of town hall rose up, the highest point in Valentine. The Hotel Colorado took up the whole block directly opposite her, three stories of stone, with arched columns along the first floor like the vaulted ceilings she'd seen in photos of castles.

Was the stranger noticing the prettiness of this little town? Or did he have something else in mind? He didn't seem like a browsing tourist. Sure enough, as she worked her way through the salad, she saw him appear out of another couple stores along the north side, then cross the street and go from store to store along the south, too, making his way slowly back toward her. Occasionally he answered a phone call or text. She didn't hide her curiosity, and she noticed him look at her. When he came out of another store, he glanced again, and this time she gave a little wave. What the hell. Maybe he'd come talk to her, and she'd figure out what was going on without having to chase him down. He didn't wave back.

She noticed the oddest thing about him, how he looked at every person he passed, even glancing down at their hands, both men and women. He seemed so . . . alert, not caught up in his "browsing," not like a tourist out for a sightseeing stroll. And if he was killing time before some kind of event, well, he'd chosen an odd way. Most guys would find a bar and watch a game. In fact, he'd already gone into the Halftime Sports Bar and come back out again.

He reached the hotel and put a hand on the big glass door to go inside—and then turned and looked at her again. She stiffened, waiting, then felt a sharp sizzle as he headed back across the street and straight toward her. Why was she letting this guy get to her? He was staying at the hotel, obviously just passing through, and man, did he look full of himself. And they hadn't even exchanged a word!

That was about to change.

He stepped onto the sidewalk and stopped in front of her. A couple strolling hand-in-hand shot him a look as they had to veer around him. They went inside her shop.

"Excuse me," he said, in the deepest, most delicious voice she'd heard in a long time, "but is there a reason you're watching me?"

Shielding her eyes with one hand, Monica gave him a sunny smile. "Is there a reason you're going from shop to shop, staying nowhere long, like someone casing each place?"

From behind the sunglasses, he lifted an eyebrow. "I'm new to town—you're bothered that I'm checking out places I might like to shop or eat?"

She thought she detected the faintest trace of amusement in his voice, as if he were trying to suppress it.

"Or you might want to buy flowers? Or jewelry?" she asked sweetly.

"I'm here a few weeks for business. Have to fill my time somehow," he added lightly. He glanced from her lunch spread to the flower shop sign. "So you work here?"

"I'm the owner."

He nodded as if in understanding. "No wonder you feel like you can interrogate customers."

She laughed. "Only ones who are trying to appear mysterious." She put out a hand. "I'm Monica Shaw. I don't suppose you want to sit down on this bench so I don't pull something in my neck trying to get a good look at you."

"Travis Beaumont."

His handshake was firm and warm. He sat down beside her, his back as straight as a character from one of her favorite historical romances—the duke who deigned to visit a commoner. But he didn't seem to be arrogant, just . . . alert, as his gaze scanned the street before resting with interest on her face again.

"Nice name, Travis Beaumont."

"Thank you. Not that I had anything to do with it."

"Your parents gave it to you, and you didn't make it up here on the spot?"

He cocked his head, his voice pleasant as he said, "If I didn't want you to know my name, I wouldn't have told you."

"Right, like the mysterious business trip." She held up a bag of almonds. "Want some?"

"No, thank you."

She got the feeling that he was waiting to see what she'd come up with next. Maybe he was flattered by her curiosity. "Have you ever been to Valentine Valley before?"

"No. I've been to Denver, but that was it. Have you lived here your whole life?"

"Yep. A small town girl, that's me. Except for college, of course."

"Where did you attend?"

"Think you know me from somewhere?"

"No, because I'm pretty sure I'd remember you."

"Flatterer." She took another bite of her salad, chewed, and swallowed before answering. "I have a business degree from Colorado State, and took courses in floral design. So I've answered your question, and now maybe you'll answer another of mine. Where are you from?"

"Right now, Washington, D.C."

"But that's not where you're originally from, of course."

He linked his hands together, forearms resting on his thighs. "I'm from a small town in Montana that you would never have heard of. My turn to ask. Do you own the shop with anyone else?"

Now *that* was a curious question. "Nope, I'm the sole owner."

He shrugged his shoulders. "Sorry if I'm out of line. You just seem young."

For some reason, she got the feeling that wasn't the whole explanation.

"I was going to ask the concierge a question," he continued, "but maybe you can help me. Do you know a place off the beaten path where my men can relax this evening?"

His men. Spoken like a soldier. Travis Beaumont seemed nothing like the laid-back guys she knew. But that was most of his appeal. And his handsome face, of course.

"Tony's Tavern. It's on Nellie Street, by Highway 82. Dark bar, pool table, darts. Maybe I'll see you there."

He stood up. "Thanks for the information. Nice meeting you." After nodding, he headed back across the street and disappeared inside the hotel.

Monica slowly gathered her lunch and took it inside. The strolling couple were just taking a bag from Karista, and they smiled as they passed Monica and went outside.

The door had barely closed when Karista said, "I could hardly concentrate on them—what was that hot guy saying to you?"

"Not much, but it was fun anyway."

Now she'd have to decide if she actually meant to search out Travis Beaumont at Tony's. There was something far too intriguing about him.

Secret Service Special Agent Travis Beaumont stood at the window of the third floor hotel room that he'd begun to transform into a command center. He stared thoughtfully at Monica's Flowers and Gifts down below, with its backdrop of mountains, some still dusted with snow at the peaks. Behind him a number of agents set up conference tables, radios, printers, and computers, which would eventually connect all of the agents on the ground with headquarters and the White House. President Alanna Torres would be visiting Valentine Valley within two weeks, attending her son's wedding—not that more than a handful of people in town knew those details yet. Travis had been entrusted with his first assignment as lead agent with the advance team. And he wasn't about to blow it because of a cute, flirtatious woman with the most incredible deep brown eyes.

He told himself to stop, that he was sounding hung up on her. But there was no denying she was gorgeous, with a head full of black curls like a starburst, light brown flawless skin, and high cheekbones that gave her an exotic look. Her slim cropped pants had hugged her hips, while her short-sleeve top had shown off toned arms. It had taken everything in him not to stare at her, to pretend indifference. It had been awhile since he felt this attracted to someone. After his divorce two years ago, he'd shied away from dating altogether, then occasionally had a meal out, mostly with women his buddies had set him up with. Nothing had clicked.

But all he'd had to do was look at Monica Shaw's wry grin to feel his pulse rev up. And that was bad news.

Walking the streets of Valentine Valley had almost reminded him of his own hometown, where as a boy, he could race the streets, playing cop or soldier, and someone would always be looking out for him, prepared to tell his mom if he was up to no good—or prepared to keep him safe. But this small town was now part of his job, and he would have to know it inside out, meeting with the police and fire chiefs, even the medical personnel at the closest hospital. And if he didn't have an exact presidential itinerary yet? Well, that was nothing new. Sometimes the president's junior staffers were clueless.

But at least there were parts of his job that were easy. His site agent had already scheduled a meeting with the Sweetheart Inn, where the wedding would take place. His transportation agent would be meeting with the local cops to get a feel for every street in town. He'd soon have 3-D models of Main Street from the Forensic Services Division, so they could find every vulnerability to guard the presidential motorcade. To that end, he'd spent his first afternoon looking at the street from on the ground, checking out the stores, the amount of customers, the sightseers. He also needed a place for an observation post, with a great sight line to the front entrance of the hotel, since the president would be staying there.

His team would be doing background checks on all the owners, of course, but the flower shop had an ideal location, right across the street, and a second floor. He saw the curtains of an apartment, not a business. The countersniper team would have a tactical advantage from such a location.

It didn't hurt that the owner was easy on the eyes, and that she'd sort of flirted with him. That usually didn't happen. He knew he gave off a serious, no-nonsense vibe, and most women were looking for fun. Not that he'd ever get involved with someone while on the job—it was difficult enough to deal with an ex-wife who was also an agent and the constant travel. He didn't have time for anything else. It was serious, crucial work, protecting the president, especially the first female president. The usual average of ten threats a day against a president were fifty percent higher for President Torres. All of them were taken seriously. He was focused on his job, and nothing would stand in his way.

But part of his job was making sure his team relaxed when they needed to, letting off steam during their brief hours away so they could be more alert on the job. Even though he didn't take advantage of the fun—besides a good beer and maybe a game of pool—he was one of them. He wanted to lead by example, and he wanted their respect.

And if they saw Monica flirting with him—well, it couldn't hurt him, as far as his men were concerned. And meanwhile, he'd be sizing her up, deciding if she'd be the perfect host for a countersniper team. He found himself hoping she'd show up at Tony's Tavern.

Keep reading for a look at where it all began
in

A Town Called Valentine

and

True Love at Silver Creek Ranch

and

A Wedding in Valentine

Available Now!

An Excerpt from

A Town Called Valentine

The car gave one last shudder as Emily Murphy came to a stop in a parking space just beneath the blinking sign of Tony's Tavern. She turned off the ignition and leaned back against the headrest as the rain drummed on the roof, and the evening's darkness settled around her. The car will be all right, she told herself firmly. Taking a deep breath, she willed her shoulders to relax after a long, stressful day driving up into the Colorado Rockies. Though the trip had been full of stunning mountain vistas still topped by snow in May, she had never let her focus waver from her mission.

She glanced up at the flashing neon sign, and her stomach growled. The tavern was near the highway and wasn't the most welcoming place. There were only two pickups and a motorcycle beside her car on this wet night.

Her stomach gurgled again, and with a sigh, she tugged up the hood of her raincoat, grabbed her purse, and stepped out into the rain. Gingerly jumping over puddles, she made it beneath the overhang above the door and went inside. A blast of heat and the smell of beer hit her face. The tavern was sparsely furnished, with a half dozen tables and a long bar on the right side of the room. Between neon signs advertising beer, mounted animal heads peered down at the half dozen customers. A man and a woman sat at one table, watching a baseball game on the flat screen TV—at least there was one other woman in the place. Another couple men hunched at the bar, glancing from beneath their cowboy hats at her before turning away. No surprise there.

When she hesitated, the bartender, a man in his thirties, with shaggy dark hair and pleasant features, gave her a nod. "Sit anywhere you'd like."

Smiling gratefully, she slipped off her raincoat, hung it on one of the many hooks near the door, and sat down. She discovered her table was opposite the only man at a table by himself. He was directly in her line of vision, making it hard to notice anything else. He was tall, by the length of his denim-clad legs. Beneath the shadowing brim of his cowboy hat, she could see an angular face and the faint lines at the corner of his eyes of a man who spent much of his day squinting in the sun. She thought he might be older than her thirty years but not by much.

When he tipped his hat back and met her eyes, Emily gave a start, realizing she'd been caught staring. It had been so long since she'd looked at any man but her ex-husband. Her face got hot, and she quickly pulled the slightly sticky menu out from its place between a napkin dispenser and a condiment basket.

A shadow loomed over her, and for a moment, she thought she'd given the cowboy some kind of signal. Maybe her presence alone in a bar late at night was enough.

But it was only the bartender, who gave her a tired smile. "Can I get you something to drink?"

She almost said a Diet Coke, but the weariness of the day overtook her, and she found herself ordering a beer. She studied the menu while he was gone, remembered her lack of funds, and asked for a burger when he returned. Some protein, some carbs, and with lettuce and tomato, it made a pretty well-rounded meal. She had to laugh at herself.

"I didn't know the menu was that funny," said a deep voice.

Not the bartender. Emily glanced up and met the solitary cowboy's gaze. Even from one table over, she could see the gleam of his green eyes. His big hand lifted a bottle of beer to his lips, yet he never stopped watching her.

Was a cowboy trying to pick her up in a mountain bar? She blinked at him and tried to contain her smile. "No, I was smiling at something else," she said, trying to sound polite but cool.

To her surprise, the cowboy simply nodded, took another swig of his beer, and glanced back at the TV. She did the same, drinking absentmindedly and trying to pretend she liked baseball. Her ex-husband had been a fan of the San Francisco Giants, so she'd gone to an occasional game when one of the partners couldn't attend.

By the time her hamburger arrived, she'd finished her beer. The cowboy was watching her again, and she recklessly ordered another. Why not? Though she hadn't eaten much today, the burger would certainly offset the alcohol. Hungrily, she dug in. The two men at the bar started to play darts, and she watched them for a while. The cowboy did, too, but he watched her more.

She studied him back. "Don't cowboys have to get up early? You're out awful late." What was she doing? Talking to a stranger in a tavern?

But she was away from home, and everything she'd thought about herself had gone up in flames this past year. Her belly had warmed with food and the pleasant buzz of her second beer. Emily Murphy would never talk to a man in a bar—but Greg had made sure she didn't feel like Emily Murphy anymore. Changing back to her maiden name would be a formality.

And then the cowboy gave her a slow smile, and she saw the dimples that creased the leanness of his cheeks and the amusement hovering in those grass green eyes. "Yes, ma'am, it's well past my bedtime."

She bit her lip, ready to finish her burger and scurry back to her car, like the old, properly married Emily would have done. But she wasn't that person anymore. A person was made up of what she wanted, and everything Emily had thought she wanted had fallen apart. She was becoming a new woman, an independent woman, who didn't need a husband, or a mother, to make a success of her life.

But tonight, she was also just a single woman in a bar. And who was that hurting if she was? She could smile at a man, even flirt a bit. She wasn't exactly dressed for the part, in her black sweater and jeans, but the cowboy didn't seem to mind looking at her. She felt a flush of reaction that surprised her. How long had it been since she'd felt desirable instead of just empty inside? Too long.

"You'll hear this a lot if you stick around," the cowboy continued, "but you're a stranger around here."

"Yes, I am," she said, taking the last swig of her beer. Her second beer, she thought. "I've just driven from San Francisco."

"Been here before?" he asked.

She grinned as she glanced at the mounted hunting trophies on the walls. "Not right here. But Valentine Valley? Yes, but it's been a long, long time. Since my childhood in fact. So no one will know me."

"Don't worry," he said dryly. "Everyone will make it their business to fix that."

She eased back in her chair, tilting her head as she eyed him. "You don't like that?"

He shrugged. "It's all I've ever known." Leaning his forearms on the table, he said, "Someone waiting for you tonight?"

"No." A little shiver of pleasure stirred deep in her stomach. She wouldn't let herself enjoy this too much. She was a free woman, flirting in a bar to pass the time after an exhausting day. It didn't mean anything. The bartender brought over another beer, and she didn't protest. "None of my family lives here anymore."

For a moment, the cowboy looked as if he would question that, but instead, he glanced at the bartender. "Tony, since the dartboard's taken, mind if we use the back room?"

Emily gaped at him.

The cowboy grinned as if he could read her mind. "Pool table. Do you play?"

She giggled. Oh, she'd really had too much to drink. But it was dark and raining, and she had no family here, and no one who cared what she did. She got to her feet and grabbed her beer. "Not since college. And I was never good. But if you need a reason to stay up past your bedtime . . ."

His laugh was a pleasurable, deep rumble. As she passed his table, he stood up, and for the first time she got a good look at the size of him, the width of his shoulders thanks to whatever work he did, the flannel shirt open over a dark t-shirt, those snug jeans following long legs down to well-used cowboy boots. *Damn.* He could really work a pair of jeans. And who would have thought she'd find cowboy boots hot? She'd always been drawn to a tailored suit and the subtle hint of a well-paid profession.

The back room was deserted on this stormy night. Low central lights hung over the table, brightly illuminating the playing surface but leaving the corners of the room in the shadows. Emily set her beer down on a nearby table, and the cowboy did the same.

He chose a cue stick. As she was pulling her hair back in a quick ponytail, he turned and came to a stop, watching her. His hungry gaze traveled down her body, and though she realized her posture emphasized her breasts, she didn't stop until her hair was out of her face. It had been so long since a man looked at her with admiration and desire and need. Surely she'd be flustered—if it wasn't for the beer.

She took the cue stick from him and smiled, saying, "Thanks," knowing he'd chosen for himself.

He laughed and put several quarters in the table to release the balls. She watched him, drinking her beer and having a handful of mixed nuts from a basket on the table. Normally, she never would have eaten from food that could have been sampled by anyone. Tonight, it didn't matter. She was a new woman.

"Do you have a name, cowboy?"

He'd been leaning over the table to rack the balls,

but he straightened and looked at her from beneath the brim of his hat. "Nate."

No last names. She felt a thrill of danger. "Emily."

"Pretty."

Though she normally would have blushed, this new, adventurous Emily smiled. "Thank you. But then I had no say in it."

"I wasn't talking about your name." His voice was a low drawl, his eyes narrowed and glittering.

Had it gotten warmer in here? she wondered, unable to stop looking at him. Though there were several windows, they were streaked with rain, and it would be foolish to open them. Her sweater felt like it clung to her damply.

"So, Nate," she said brightly, "are you going to take me for all my money?"

"I'm a high roller," he said. "I might bet all of a dollar."

She snorted, then covered her mouth.

"Or I might bet a kiss."

She stared at him, still smiling, playing his game and not thinking. She was so tired of thinking. "Is that the prize if I win or what I owe if I lose?"

He chuckled. "Depends, I guess. Am I worth it?"

She couldn't seem to take a deep enough breath. "I don't know. Guess we'll have to play and find out."

They didn't speak during the game, only watched each other play. Emily had to be honest with herself—she was watching him move. She liked the way his jeans tightened over his butt, how she could glimpse the muscles in his arms when he stretched out over the table. He took his hat off, and the waves in his black hair glinted under the light. The tension between them sizzled, and she wouldn't have been surprised to hear a hiss. They walked about the table, about each other, as if in a choreographed dance of evasion and teasing. This was flirtation as a high art, and he was far better at it than she'd ever been.

But the beer was helping. When it was her turn to lean over the table to line up a shot, she knew he was watching her hips, knew what, as a man, he was thinking. And although she would *never* have sex with a stranger, the thought that he desired her gave her a heady, powerful feeling. This new Emily, in the next stage of her life, could be lusty.

But not with a stranger, she reminded herself.

And then she lost the game, as she knew she would. She still had so many balls on the table as he sank his last one and slowly straightened to look at her.

"I'll take that kiss," he said, coming around the table.

Oh God. She was breathless already, looking up and up into those narrowed green eyes. He stopped right in front of her, her breasts almost touching his chest. She could feel the heat of him, the tension, the tug of danger, but it wasn't exactly him she was afraid of. She was drunk enough that she was afraid what she might do if she tasted him.

But she was also drunk enough to try it. As she stepped forward, their bodies brushed. His inhalation was sexy in itself, letting her know that she could affect him. She waited for him to lean down over her, arched her neck—and then he put his hands on her waist. She gasped as he lifted her off her feet and set her on the edge of the pool table. With wide eyes, feeling breathless, she watched him, unaware that she kept her legs pressed together until he leaned against them.

He smiled, she smiled, and then she parted her knees, holding her breath as he stepped between them. Their faces were almost level.

He leaned in and very lightly touched his lips to hers. "Breathe," he whispered, softly laughing.

She did with a sudden inhalation. What was she supposed to do with her hands? She was beginning to feel nervous and foolish and that she was making a mistake. And then he put his hands on the outside of her thighs and slowly slid them up, past the roundness of her hips to the dip in her waist.

"So delicate," he murmured huskily, and kissed her again.

Part of her had expected a drunken kiss of triumph, but he took his time, his slightly parted lips taking hers with soft, little strokes. Soon she couldn't keep herself from touching him, sliding her hands up his arms, feeling each ripple of muscle with an answering ripple of desire deep in her belly. Her thighs tightened around his hips, she slid her hands into his hair, then, as one, they deepened the kiss. He tasted of beer, and it was an aphrodisiac on this lost, lonely night. The rasp of his tongue along hers made her moan, and he pulled her tighter against him. She was lost in the heat of him, the feel of his warm, hard body in her arms. He tugged the band from her hair, and it spilled around her shoulders. She had no idea how long they kissed, only reveled in feeling absolutely wonderful. It had been so long.

He leaned over her, and she fell back, body arched beneath him, moaning again as he began to trail kisses down her jaw, then her neck. His big hands cupped her shoulders as he held her in place, her own hands clasped his head to her as if she would never let him go.

Deep inside, a whisper grew louder, that this was wrong. Another languid voice said no, they both wanted this, just a little while longer . . .

His mouth lightly touched the center V of her sweater; his hands cupped her ribs, his thumbs riding the outer curves of her breasts. The anticipation was unbearable; she wanted to writhe even as his hand slid up and over her breast as if feeling its weight. His thumb flicked across her nipple, and she jerked with pleasure. His hips were hard against hers, her legs spread to encompass him . . .

On a pool table, where anyone could walk into the back room and see them. The thrill of danger and excitement receded as guilt and worry rose up like hot bubbling water.

She was leading him on; he probably thought he could take her home and—

Torn between passion and mortification, she stiffened. "No," she whispered. Then louder, "No, please stop."

His hand froze, his head lifted until their eyes met.

She bit her lip, knowing she looked pathetic and remorseful and guilty. "I can't do this. Our bet was only for a kiss."

As he let his breath out, he straightened, pulling her up with him. He stayed between her thighs, watching her mouth. "Are you sure?" he whispered.

When she nodded, he stepped back as she jumped off the table. She stood there a moment, feeling shaky and foolish.

"I should go," she said, turning away and heading back to the bar.

At her table, she couldn't bear to wait for her bill, knowing that the bartender and the two dart players might have heard her moan. Her face was hot, her hands trembled, and she prayed that the TV had been loud enough. She threw down far more money than was probably necessary, but she just couldn't face the bartender. Grabbing her raincoat off the hook, she ran out into the rain, jumped into her car, and sat there, feeling so stupid. She'd never done anything like that in her life. That man—Nate, she remembered—must think her the worst tease.

After a minute's fumbling in the depths of her purse, she found her keys and slid them into the ignition. The car tried to turn over several times, but nothing happened. Emily closed her eyes and silently prayed. *Please, not now.*

She turned the ignition again, and although the engine strained once or twice, it wouldn't start. She stared out the rain-streaked windshield at the glowing sign for Tony's Tavern. She couldn't go back in there. Her brain was fuzzy from too much alcohol as she tried to remember what she'd driven past when she left the highway. A motel perhaps? She'd been so worried about her car and the pouring rain and her growling stomach. How far could she walk at midnight in a strange town in a storm?

With a groan, she closed her eyes, feeling moisture from the rain trickle down her neck.

An Excerpt from

True Love at Silver Creek Ranch

Her chestnut quarter horse, Sugar, was the first to notice something wrong, startling Brooke Thalberg from her troubled thoughts. The November wind high in the Colorado Rockies, just outside Valentine Valley, was unseasonably brutal, whipping snow off the peaks of the Elk Mountains like lumbering giants exhaling icy puffs of breath. Sugar raised her head, sniffing that wind, ears twitching, leaving Brooke unsettled, uneasy, as she rode the pastures of the Silver Creek Ranch. She was checking the fence line so that the cattle didn't find their way through and wander toward someone else's land.

It was usually peaceful work, but today she was looking down the long road of her future and feeling that something was . . . wrong. And she hated to feel that way because she'd been blessed with so much.

Sugar lifted her head and shook her mane, neighing, her body tensing. Whatever she sensed wasn't going away. Brooke lifted her own head—

And smelled smoke.

A shot of fear made her vault upright in the stirrups. She scanned her family's land, focusing on the house first, framed between clusters of evergreens and aspens. But its two-story log walls seemed as sturdy as always, a faint haze of smoke rising from the stone chimney. The newer barn and sheds nearest the house seemed fine, and gradually she widened her search until she saw the old horse barn, farthest from the house—smoke billowing through the open double doors.

She kicked Sugar into a gallop, leaning forward over the horse's twitching ears, the breath frozen in her throat. *Oh, God, the horses.* Frantically, she saw that several trotted nervously around the corral as if they, too, knew something was wrong. She tried to count them, but it was as if her brain had seized with the terror of what she was seeing.

Sugar's hooves thundered beneath her, faster than even in her barrel-racing days, the ground a blur. The smoke pouring out of the open door grew darker and more menacing, twisting Brooke's fear ever higher.

At last she reached the barn and threw herself off Sugar's back, stumbling momentarily in the dirt before she found her balance. The smoke made her lungs spasm in a cough, but even that didn't make her second-guess what she had to do. She pulled her neck scarf up over the lower half of her face and ran inside, keeping to a crouch. Immediately, the world became darker as the smoke swirled around her. Her shallow breathing was hot and stifled beneath the scarf. If she let herself panic, she could become disoriented, lost, so she kept a firm grip on her emotions. She'd yet to see flames, but she could hear several horses, their neighs more like screams that tore at her heart.

"I'm coming!" she cried, flailing toward the stalls.

She ran into something hard and was only saved from falling to the ground by hands that clasped the front of her coat.

A man pulled her toward him, a stranger, tall and broad-shouldered, his face beneath his cowboy hat obscured by a scarf just like hers was. She could only see a glimpse of his narrowed, glittering eyes, focused intently on her. Who was he? Had he set the fire? she wondered with outrage.

"Are you all right?" He shouted to be heard above the growing roar of the fire and the frightened cries of the horses. "How many horses are there?"

For a moment, her mouth moved, and nothing came out. She saw the tack-room door hanging ajar, its interior full of fire that crackled and writhed. The sight momentarily stunned and mesmerized her, then she suddenly snapped into a sharp awareness. She couldn't worry about who this man was or what he was doing there. He'd offered to help, and that was all that mattered. Mentally, she counted the horses she'd seen out in the corral. "Should be two inside—no three!"

"I'll take that side"—he pointed through the smoke toward the west side of the barn—"and you start here."

She nodded and turned her back, beginning to fling open each stall door. At the fourth door, she was met by hooves pawing through the air. She cried out, diving sideways as they slammed into the wall right beside her. Before Dusty could rear again, she grabbed a blanket hung near the door, flung it over his head, and grabbed ahold of his halter. For a moment he fought her, but she wouldn't give up.

"Please, Dusty, be a good boy. Come on!"

At last he seemed to dance toward her, and she felt a momentary triumph. She started to run, leading him toward the double doors open to the corral. As they reached fresh air, she pulled the blanket off Dusty's head and he charged to the far end, where the other horses huddled nervously.

Brooke turned around to head back into the barn, only to see the stranger leading two terrified horses outside. *Thank God,* she prayed silently. But could she have counted wrong? How could she take the chance? She tried to race past him back into the barn, but he caught her arm and wouldn't let go.

"You said three horses!" he shouted from beneath the scarf.

A groan seemed to emanate from the barn timbers, turning both their heads. Smoke wafted out in great streams to the sky, but the fire still seemed contained in the tack room.

"I can't be sure until I check each stall!" She tried to yank her elbow away, but his grip was strong. A blast of heat wafted out, engulfing her, making her sweat even more beneath her layers of winter clothing. She felt almost light-headed.

He loomed over her, and now she could see the sandy waves of hair plastered above his ears, and his narrowed eyes, brown as the sides of the barn but so intent on her.

"I checked all six on the west side. I didn't hear anything more coming from the east after you'd gone."

"I can't take that chance. I only got through four stalls on my side." She stared at the herd of horses clustered uneasily at the far end of the corral. Nate's horse, Apollo—was he there? She'd never forgive herself if anything happened to him. And then she saw the dappled gray gelding, and relief shuddered down her spine.

The man didn't answer her, and she turned to see him disappear into the barn, the smoke swirling out and around him as if to draw him deep inside. A stab of fear shocked her—why was he risking himself for her? Her eyes stung as she reached the entrance, but he was there again, stumbling into her, the upper half of his face dirtied by the soot, his eyes streaming.

"It's empty!" he called.

She could have staggered with relief that her beloved horses were all right—that this brave man hadn't been injured.

But relief was only momentary as she began to think about the structure itself, built by her family well over a hundred years before. She hugged herself against the sadness.

As if reading her mind, he said, "You can't do anything now. And I hear sirens."

The fire engine from Valentine Valley roared down the dirt road that wound its way through the ranch. The horses were going to be even more frightened, so she ran to the end of the corral and opened the gate so they could escape into the next pasture.

When she returned to the stranger's side, they were pushed out of the way by the trained professionals. Most were volunteers, like Sally Gillroy from the mayor's office, who liked to gossip, and Hal Abrams, the owner of the hardware store where her dad and Nate met fellow ranchers for coffee. She recognized all these men and women, but it was strange to see their grim faces rather than easygoing smiles.

"Are you all right?" Hal demanded, his glasses reflecting the flames that had begun to shoot out both doors.

Brooke nodded, still hugging herself, feeling the presence of the stranger at her back. She almost took comfort from it, and that was strange.

"Horses all saved?"

She nodded again, and was surprised to feel a wave of pride and even excitement. Knowing she'd risked herself made her feel more alive and aware than she'd felt in a long time. Everything in life could be so transitory, and she'd just been accepting things that happened to her rather than making choices. She couldn't live that way anymore. She had to find something that made her feel this alive, that gave her more purpose and focus.

And it scared the hell out of her.

"You're in the way," Hal said. "Go on up to the house and clean up. We'll wet down any nearby buildings to keep them safe. But the barn is a goner." He turned his shrewd eyes on the stranger. "Is that blood?"

Brooke spun around and saw that the stranger had lowered his scarf. In another situation, she might have been amused at the dark upper half of his face and the white lower half, but she saw blood oozing from a cut across his cheek.

"I'm fine." The stranger used his gloved hand to swipe at his cheek and made everything worse.

"Come on," Brooke said wearily, refusing to glance one last time at her family's barn although she could hear the crackle and roar of the fire. "The bunkhouse is close. We'll wash up there and see to your face."

And she could look into his eyes and see if he was

the sort who set fires for fun. He didn't seem it, for he didn't look back at the fire either, only trudged behind her.

The bunkhouse was an old log cabin, another of the original buildings from the nineteenth-century silver-boom days, when cattle from the Silver Creek Ranch had fed thousands of miners coming down from their claims to spend their riches in Valentine Valley. Brooke's father had updated the interior of the cabin to house the occasional temporary workers they needed during branding or haying season. There were a couple sets of bunk beds along the walls, an old couch before the stone hearth, a battered table and chairs, kitchen cabinets and basic appliances at the far end of the open room, and two doors that led into a single bedroom and bathroom.

The walls were filled with unframed photos of the various hands they'd employed to work the ranch over the years. Some of those photos, tacked up haphazardly and curling at the edges, were old black-and-whites going almost as far back as photography did.

Brooke shivered with a chill even as she removed her coat. The heat was only high enough to keep the pipes from freezing, and she went to raise the thermostat. When she turned around, the stranger had removed his hat and was shrugging out of his Carhartt jacket, revealing matted-down hair and a soot-stained face. He was wearing a long-sleeve red flannel shirt and jeans over cowboy boots.

To keep from staring at him, she pointed to the second door. "Go on and wash up in the bathroom. I'll find a first-aid kit."

He silently nodded and moved past her, limping slightly, shutting the door behind him. He might be hurt worse than he was saying, she thought with a wince. As she opened cabinet doors, she realized the kit was probably in the bathroom. Sighing even as she rolled up her sleeves, she let the water run in the kitchen sink until it was hot, then soaped up her black hands and started on her face. If her hair hadn't been in a long braid down her back, she'd have dunked her whole head under. She'd have to wait for a shower. Grabbing paper towels, she patted her skin dry.

A few minutes later, the stranger came out of the bathroom, his hair sticking up in short, damp curls, the first-aid kit in his hand. His face was clean now, and she could see that the two-inch cut was still bleeding.

"You probably need stitches," she said, even as the first inkling of recognition began to tease her. "You don't want a scar."

He met her gaze and held it, and she saw the faintest spark of amusement, as if he knew something she didn't.

"Don't worry about it, Brooke."

She hadn't told him her name. "So I do know you."

"It's been a long time," he said, eyeing her as openly as she was doing to him.

He was taller than her, well muscled beneath the flannel shirt that he'd pushed up to his elbows.

And then his name suddenly echoed like a shot in her mind. "Adam Desantis," she breathed. "It's been over ten years since you went off to join the Marines."

He gave a short nod.

No wonder he looked to be in such great physical shape. Feeling awkward, she forced her gaze back to his face. He'd been good-looking in high school—

and knew it—but now his face was rugged and masculine, a man grown.

She got flashes of memory then—Adam as the cool wide receiver all the high-school girls wanted, with his posse of arrogant sidekicks. He'd been able to rule the school, doing whatever he wanted—because his parents hadn't cared, she reminded herself. And then she had another memory of the sixth-grade science fair, where all the parents had helped their kids with experiments, except for his. His display had been crude and unfinished, and his mother had drunkenly told him so in front of every kid within hearing range. Whenever Brooke thought badly of his antics in high school, *that* was the memory that crept back up, making her feel ill with pity and sorrow.

"Your grandma talks about you all the time," she finally said. Mrs. Palmer spoke of him with glowing pride as he rose through the ranks to staff sergeant, a rarity at his age.

"Hope she doesn't bore everybody," he answered, showing sincerity rather than just tossing off something he didn't mean. "I hear she lives with your grandma. The Widows' Boardinghouse?"

"The name was their idea. They're kind of famous now, but those are stories for another day. Come here and let me look at your cheek." He moved toward her slowly, as if she were a horse needing to be calmed, which amused her.

"I can take care of it," he said.

"Sit down."

"I said—"

"Sit down!" She pulled out a kitchen chair and pointed. "I can't reach your face. I'm tall, but not that tall."

"Yes, ma'am," he answered gruffly.

She pressed her lips together to keep from smiling.

He eased into the chair just a touch slowly, but somehow she knew he didn't want any more questions about his health. Adam Desantis, she told herself again, shaking her head. He wasn't a stranger—and he wouldn't have started the fire, regardless of the trouble he'd once gotten into. She told herself to relax, but her body still tensed with an awareness that surprised her. She was just curious about him, that was all. She cleared her throat and tried to speak lightly. "I imagine you're used to taking orders."

"Not for the last six months. I left after my enlistment was up."

Tearing open an antiseptic towelette, she leaned toward him, feeling almost nervous. Nervous? she thought in surprise. She worked what most would call a man's job and dealt with men all day. What was her problem? She got a whiff of smoke from his clothes, but his face was scrubbed clean of it. She tilted his head, her fingers touching his whisker-rough square chin, marked with a deep cleft in the center. His eyes studied her, and she was so close she could see golden flecks deep inside the brown. She stared into them, and he stared back, and in that moment, she felt a rush of heat and embarrassment all rolled together. Hoping he hadn't noticed, she began to dab at his wound, feeling him tense with the sting of the antiseptic.

Damn it all, what was wrong with her? She hadn't been attracted to him in high school—he'd been an idiot, as far as she was concerned. She'd been focused on her family ranch and barrel racing and was not the kind of girl who would lavish all her attention on a boy, as he seemed to require. Brooke always felt that she had her own life to live and didn't need a boyfriend as some kind of status symbol.

But ten years later, Adam returned as an ex-Marine who saved her horses, a man with a square-cut face, faint lines fanning out from his eyes as if he'd squinted under desert suns, and she was turning into a schoolgirl all over again.

Adam stared into Brooke Thalberg's face as she bent over him, not bothering to hide his powerful curiosity. He remembered her, of course—who wouldn't? She was as tall as many guys and probably as strong, too, from all the hard work on her family ranch.

A brave woman, he admitted, remembering her fearlessness running into the fire, her concern for the horses more than herself. Now her hazel eyes stared at his face intently, their mix of browns and greens vivid and changeable. She turned away to search the med kit, and his gaze lingered on her slim back, covered in a checked Western shirt that was tucked into her belt. Her long braid tumbled down her back, almost to the sway of her jeans-clad hips. It's not like he hadn't seen a woman before. And this woman had been a pest through his childhood, too smart for her own good—seeing into his troubled life the things he'd tried to keep hidden—too confident in her own talent. She had a family who believed in her, and that gave a kid a special kind of confidence. He hadn't had that sort of family, so he recognized it when he saw it.

He wondered if she'd changed at all—he certainly had. After discovering his own confidence, he'd built a place and a name for himself in the Marines. His overconfidence had destroyed that, leaving him in a fog of uncertainty that had been hovering around him for half a year now.

Kind of like being in a barn fire, he guessed, feeling your way around, wondering if you were ever going to get out again. He still didn't know.

After using butterfly bandages to keep the wound closed, Brooke taped a small square of gauze to his face, then straightened, hands on her hips, to judge her handiwork. "You might need stitches if you want to avoid a scar."

He shrugged. "Got enough of those. One more won't hurt."

He rose slowly to his feet, feeling the stiffness in his leg that never quite went away. The docs had got most of the shrapnel out, but not quite all of it. The exertion of the fire had irritated the old wound, but that would ease with time. He was used to it by now, and the reminder that he was alive was more than he deserved, when there were so many men beneath the ground.

After closing the kit, Brooke turned back to face him, tilting her head to look up. They stared at each other a moment, too close, almost too intimate alone there. Drops of water still sparkled in her dark lashes, and her skin was fresh-scrubbed and free of makeup. She looked prettier than he remembered, a woman instead of the skinny girl.

Adam was surprised at the sensations her nearness inspired in him, this awareness of her as a woman, when back in high school she'd barely registered as that to him. He'd dated party girls and cheerleaders—including her best friend, Monica Shaw—not cowgirls. Now she held herself so tall and easily, with a confidence born of hard work and years of testing her body to the limits.

She cleared her throat, and her gaze dropped from his eyes to his mouth, then his shirtfront. "You have a limp," she said. "Did one of the horses kick you?"

"Had the limp on and off for a while. Nothing new."

She nodded, then stepped past him to return the med kit to the bathroom. When she came back out, she was wearing a fixed, polite smile, which, to his surprise, amused him. Not much amused him anymore.

"I'm glad you're not hurt bad," she said. "You did me—us—a big favor, and I can't thank you enough for helping rescue the horses. How'd you see the fire?"

"I was at the boardinghouse and saw the smoke out the window." If the trees hadn't been winter-bare, he might not have seen it at all, which made him think uneasily of Brooke, battling the fire alone. "Where are your brothers? They might have come in handy if I hadn't seen the fire. I assume they still work on the ranch?"

She nodded. "They're at the hospital with my dad, visiting my mom. Did you remember she has MS?"

He shook his head. "I never knew."

"She never talked about it much, so I'm not surprised. Most of the time, she only needs a cane, but she's battling a flare-up that's weakened her legs. The guys took their turn at the hospital today, while I rode fence. Guess I found more than I bargained for." She eyed him with speculation. "So you're back to visit your grandma."

She put her hands in her back pockets and rocked once on her heels, as if she didn't know what to do with herself. That stretched her shirt across her breasts, and he had to force himself to keep his gaze on her face.

"Grandma's letters were off," he admitted. "She seemed almost scattered."

Brooke focused on him with a frown. "Scattered? *Your* grandma?"

"My instincts were right. I got here, and she was a lot more frail, and she's using a cane now."

"A cane? That's new. And I see her often, so maybe I just didn't notice she'd slowly been . . ." She trailed off.

"Declining?" He almost grumbled the words. Grandma Palmer was in her seventies, but some part of him thought she never changed. She'd been the one woman who could briefly get him away from his parents to sleep on sheets that didn't smell of smoke, to eat meals that didn't come from a drive-thru. He was never hungry at Grandma Palmer's, whether for food or for love. There weren't holidays or birthdays unless Grandma had them. All he'd been to his teenage parents was an unwanted kid, the result of a broken condom, and they blamed him for making so little of their lives. He saw that now, but at the time? He'd been relieved to enlist in the Marines and start his life over.

Now he and Grandma Palmer only had each other. His parents had died after falling asleep in bed with cigarettes a few years back, and he hadn't experienced anywhere near the grief he now felt in worrying about her. He might have only seen her once or twice a year, but he'd written faithfully, and so had she. The packages she'd sent had been filled with his favorite books and food, enough to share with his buddies. He felt a spasm of pain at the memories. Some of those buddies were dead now. Good memories mingled with the bad, and he could still see Paul Ivanick cheerfully holding back Adam's care package until he promised to share Grandma Palmer's cookies.

Paul was dead now.

When Adam was discharged, it took everything in him not to run to his grandma like a little boy. But no one could make things right, not for him, or for the men who had died. The men, his Marine brothers, who were dead because of him. He didn't want to imagine what his grandma would think about him if she knew the truth.

"Those old women still seem strong," Brooke insisted. "Mrs. Ludlow may use a walker, and your grandma now a cane, but they have enough . . . well, gumption, to use their word, for ten women."

He shrugged. "All I know is what I see."

And then they stood there, two strangers who'd grown up in the same small town but never really knew each other.

"So what have you been up to?" Brooke asked, rocking on her heels again.

He crossed his arms over his chest. "Nothing much."

In a small town like Valentine Valley, everyone thought they deserved to know their neighbor's business. Brooke wouldn't think any different—hell, he remembered how she used to butt into his in high school, when they weren't even friends. She'd been curious about his studies, a do-gooder who thought she could change the world.

She hadn't seen the world and its cruelties, hadn't left the safety of this town, or her family, as far as he knew. *He'd* seen the world—too much of it. There was nothing he could tell her—nothing he wanted to remember.

"Oo-kay then," she said, drawing out the word.

He wondered if she felt as aware of the simmering tension between them and as uneasy as he did. He wouldn't let himself feel like this, uncertain whether he even deserved a normal life.

"What am I thinking?" she suddenly burst out, digging her hand into her pocket and coming out with a cell phone. "I haven't even called my dad."

She turned her back and stared out the window, where the firemen were hosing down the smoldering ruins of her family barn. For just a moment, Adam remembered coming to the Silver Creek Ranch as a kid when his dad would do the occasional odd jobs for the Thalbergs. He'd seen the close, teasing relationships between Brooke and her brothers, the way their parents guided and nurtured them with love. Their life had seemed so different, so foreign to him.

And now Brooke would never be able to understand the life he'd been leading. So he turned and quietly walked out the door.

An Excerpt from

A Wedding in Valentine

Heather Armstrong gasped as the plane dropped down between the Colorado mountains, which were painted a myriad of greens below the tree line, barren and brown at the top, awaiting the next winter's snow. The ground seemed to rush up, and only when they touched down at the small Aspen airport did she let her exhilaration at her first mountain landing subside back into wedding excitement. She was about to be a bridesmaid in the June wedding of an old friend, Emily Murphy.

As she waited for a call from Emily, she wandered the small airport. It bustled with people dressed casually for the outdoors, many carrying cases for fishing equipment, a pastime this valley was known for in the summer. She'd always preferred being a people watcher, a person in the background rather than commanding attention to herself. It was one of the reasons she'd never enjoyed being in charge of a restaurant's kitchen, and had opened her own catering business. But now her people-watching skills made her halt in her tracks as she caught a glimpse of a familiar face.

A man wearing a cowboy hat slouched in a chair near the main doors, as if he, too, was waiting for someone. With his head bent over a book, she couldn't quite see his face. A feeling of unease shivered up her spine and made her so wary that she backed up to where she was partially hidden around the corner. Peeking out again, she studied his pale blond hair beneath the hat, the checked Western shirt that snugly outlined his broad chest, the long legs encased in faded jeans above worn cowboy boots.

The bang of dropped luggage drew his attention, and he looked up. Heather recognized him instantly, and with a gasp, she retreated behind the safety of the wall. His name was Chris, and that was all she'd known when they'd been snowbound together in the Denver airport seven months ago. Late night drinks at the bar and mutual attraction—make that lust—shared with Chris had turned her into a person she'd never been before, a daring flirt who'd ended up in bed with a cowboy. They'd spent two wild days together, exploring and laughing and connecting on an intimate level that had surprised her with its depth, considering they'd been strangers and all. Though she'd left him her number, assuming they'd see each other again, he'd never called. She'd felt like an idiot, a slut, and whatever other bad names she'd called herself over the following months.

Gradually she'd accepted the "adventure" as a risk she'd obviously wanted to take, and had learned from. She wasn't cut out for one-night stands. She felt too much, expected too much. A man pursuing such a brief affair wanted only that and nothing else.

Today had been the first day airports hadn't made

her think about him, she thought bitterly. Tough luck
for her.

To find some peace, she'd chalked the experience
up to a valuable lesson. Other women had done
stupid things in college, but not her. She'd been too
focused on her business degree, and then culinary
school, the future her goal, little lured by frat parties
and wild drinking. She'd had a boyfriend or two, of
course, serious engineering or business students, and
that same pattern had continued throughout most of
her twenties. Never time for an intense relationship—
until Andrew, four years before. She'd thought everything so perfect, so wonderful, and hadn't even
seen that he was pulling away from her, that their sex
life was full of desperation more than real passion.
Everything on the surface had been too good to be
true. The breakup with him was probably what had
launched her desperation that snowy night in Denver.

But Chris's face had haunted her a long time, lean
and sculpted, his blue eyes almost startling in their
intensity. She hadn't been with another man since
him, had been ready to change her life, find a new
place to start over, all to forget her past and find
more peaceful surroundings.

Heather had always thought *she'd* be the first
one to give up the hectic, stressful pace of the city,
not Emily. She'd gone to San Francisco for culinary
school, and to make a name for herself, eventually establishing her own catering business. She came from
a small town herself, but her own mountain town in
California would never be able to support a fulltime
catering business. Emily had assured her that Valentine Valley could. And who could resist a name like
Valentine?

But was seeing Chris some kind of cosmic sign that a move here wasn't for her? She didn't believe in that sort of stuff, but still found herself praying that he was just passing through Aspen . . .

And then Emily Murphy walked through the outer doors, strawberry-blond hair bobbing in a ponytail, a bright yellow sundress matching the brilliance of her smile framed in her heart-shaped face. And why shouldn't she smile? She was the bride, about to marry her very own cowboy, Nate Thalberg. Heather felt tender affection relax her own worried expression, and she scolded herself for her panicky thoughts. She would find a way to avoid Chris and a possible scene. She wouldn't do anything to disrupt Emily's weekend.

But to her dismay, Chris rose to his feet and enfolded Emily in a big hug. *They knew each other?* Heather thought with disbelief. From her cowardly hiding place, she could hear their conversation.

"I thought you wanted me to pick up your friend?" Chris said.

Emily shrugged. "I know, but I got some things done and I just couldn't wait. You don't mind your big sister dropping in, do you?"

Big sister? Heather focused on those words in shock. She'd known Emily had found her biological father and stepmother in Valentine Valley, and more than once she'd mentioned her new siblings, but mostly Stephanie, the teenager who hadn't been exactly happy to meet Emily.

And then Heather covered her mouth as realization dawned. She'd confessed her fling to Emily, having needed to confide in someone—what would Emily say if she found out her own brother was the mystery man?

Not that Heather had given her any details like where or when. That had seemed too private even to share with a best friend. Heather didn't know if she could live down the embarrassment, nor could she stand the thought of destroying their friendship if Emily took it badly—and on her wedding weekend, too!

Emily gave Chris a curious tilt of the head. "So how did you plan to recognize Heather?"

"Well, you said she was a redhead. How could I miss?" He grinned when Emily put her hands on her hips skeptically. "Naw, really, I brought a sign with her name on it. It's folded in my book somewhere."

"You and your books," she teased. "She might have walked right past you."

"I was being careful."

Their conversation faded as Heather stiffened her shoulders with resolve. Her plans for a relaxing weekend were shot out the window, and there was nothing to do but grit her teeth and bear it for Emily's sake—and her own. She hoped it wouldn't be difficult to convince Chris to keep their affair a secret. Surely he cared about his sister's feelings. She prayed he'd keep his thoughts to himself until they had a chance to talk in private.

And as for how he'd treated Heather herself? She wasn't going to show this thoughtless cowboy that he'd hurt her by not calling. She'd make it perfectly clear that she was a worldly woman of the big city, who understood how unimportant a fling was.

If only she *was* that sort of woman . . . if only the thought of Emily being upset about their relationship didn't unnerve her. She'd never do anything to risk losing her friendship—but now it looked like she'd already risked everything.

She couldn't hide forever, she thought, taking a deep, cleansing breath to steady her nerves. Adjusting the large purse on her shoulder, she started to walk, pulling her suitcase behind. She felt like the entire airport was staring; instead it was just Chris who noticed her first. She couldn't read his expression, but experienced the magnetism of his blue eyes as if she were back in biology class, a butterfly pinned to a display board on the teacher's wall.

Did he recognize her? Did his heartbeat speed up like hers did—like hers *had* the first time she'd seen him in the Denver baggage area, trying to persuade a shuttle to drive through a rising snowstorm from the nearest hotel? His voice had been commanding but polite, and he'd at last won the operator over with easygoing cowboy charm, though she'd seen the tension in his fisted hands. The discrepancy had fascinated her, and she'd found her gaze constantly returning to him, as she waited in line to use the same hotel phone. And then he'd smiled at her, and she was lost. Now, months later, he was looking at her again, inspiring a mass of conflicting emotions: anger, hurt, and the undercurrent of desire that still flamed just as strong.

Emily must have realized Chris was looking past her shoulder, and she turned, her smile widening when she saw Heather. With a squeal, Emily opened her arms wide for a hug. After letting go of her suitcase, Heather enjoyed the temporary respite of being enfolded in Emily's warmth and caring.

"I'm so glad you're here!" Emily said, taking a step back, but still squeezing Heather's upper arms.

"Me, too," Heather answered, her attention firmly focused on her friend rather than the looming man behind Emily. "I can't believe you're getting married!"

"And in two days! I feel like there's so much to do, but that's just panic, I think. Nate says I need to calm down and enjoy the festivities, and of course, he's right." Emily laughed at herself. "Oh, and you may be wondering about this handsome guy behind me. I asked him to come get you, but then I was able to get away, too, so here we both are. Heather Armstrong this is my brother, Chris Sweet."

And then Heather was forced to meet his eyes again, and she didn't know how she kept up her polite smile. She was just as captivated as the first time, but if she was waiting for—dreading—an answering smolder of awareness, she got nothing, only a friendly smile in return. She swallowed hard, not knowing whether to be confused or grateful that he didn't spill out the truth. *Oh, I've met Heather before. Let me tell you the whole story . . .*

"Nice to meet you, Heather," Chris said, in that deep cowboy drawl that had once made her melt right on her bar stool when they'd decided to get a drink to pass the long snowbound evening.

She broke eye contact and chirped, "You, too!" She smiled at Emily, trying to smother her nervousness. She wasn't the kind of woman used to hiding secrets—which is why she'd confessed the fling. She wished she could link arms with Emily and march out of there, leaving Chris in the dust, but she wouldn't be so impolite. "Thanks for offering to pick me up."

"No problem," he said, giving his hat a polite tug.

Emily gave her brother a quick hug. "I'll let you head back to the ranch. Are you coming to the party tonight?"

"Of course."

Emily had sent a schedule ahead, so Heather knew exactly what they were talking about—a co-ed bachelor/bachelorette party. She'd probably see Chris Sweet at every single event over the weekend. She could have groaned. With her luck, they'd be paired up walking down the aisle!

"I'll leave you two girls to chat," Chris said. "See you later."

Had that been directed right at her? Heather wondered. But she put it aside, feeling slightly relieved as he walked away. If only she could have ignored the way his jeans clung to his hips—hadn't that gotten her in trouble with him the first time?

The half-hour drive through the Roaring Fork valley was beautiful, the mountains tall sentinels on either side of the highway, their peaks jutting unevenly above the tree line. The women's conversation flowed fast, and Heather was relieved to simply catch up in person rather than over the phone. When they were driving down Main Street in Valentine Valley, she let Emily's enthusiasm for her new hometown sweep over her. Beneath a vivid blue sky dotted with cotton-ball clouds, everything was so picturesque, like an old-fashioned postcard. One- and two-story clapboard or brick stores were interspersed with more majestic stone buildings like the Hotel Colorado and the Royal Theater. Emily slowed down to point toward her bakery, Sugar and Spice, with plate glass windows on either side of the door overflowing with mouthwatering displays of her creative genius, cakes and pastries and tarts. Everywhere planters spilled over with summer flowers, and U.S. flags heralded the coming Fourth of July holiday. People strolled arm in arm down the sidewalks, window-shopping or already carrying loaded bags.

"Do you see all those couples in love?" Emily said happily. "We're known for romance around here—and romance needs food. You really should move here, Heather. You've made no secret that you don't like living in the city. And we don't have a full-time caterer."

"So you've said," Heather began, looking over her shoulder at the hotel they'd just passed. "But that place looks like it would have a wonderful restaurant."

"It does, Main Street Steakhouse—and they get their beef from our ranch," she added proudly, before insisting, "But they're very busy—too busy for a lot of catering."

"Our ranch" was the Silver Creek Ranch, which Emily had told her had been in her fiancé's family for well over a hundred years. They'd raised cattle for generations, working together as a family. Even the groom's sister, Brooke, rode alongside her two brothers and shared in every chore.

They turned the corner where Main Street ended at the imposing town hall, with its clock tower jutting into the sky. And then Heather inhaled at the sight of a beautiful, sprawling Victorian mansion, nestled in the foothills of the nearby mountain range. Turrets rose up through three stories of the beautiful old home, and sunburst trim spanned between every porch rail.

"So this is the Sweetheart Inn," Heather breathed, reluctant to leave the car. "It's as beautiful as you said—with another great restaurant that caters, I bet. And your grandmother owns it?"

Emily nodded as she pulled the keys from the ignition and tossed them in her purse. "My dad mostly works their ranch, but several of my family help out around here. And the restaurant would be relieved to reduce its catering load. They turn away too many customers as it is."

Heather gave a reluctant smile. "You've done your research."

"You bet I have," Emily shot back, opening her car door.

As Heather walked around to the trunk she couldn't help wondering if Chris would be hanging around the inn. She wasn't going to ask about him, of course. If Emily suspected even a hint of interest, she would be trying to fix them up. *Now* that *would be a laugh*, she thought, seeing some humor in the situation for the first time.

Emily paused with her hand on the closed trunk and spoke in a sober voice. "You know, the Sweets could have rejected me. I was the child of a teenage romance, and my mom had lied to Joe Sweet for years about my true parentage. She never did confess before she died, not even to me."

Heather gently touched Emily's arm. "You don't need to relive this again. Memories can be so painful."

"I know you've heard it all before, but when you meet all of my family, I wanted you to remember how special they are. Dad was gentle and understanding about the crazy news, and so glad to know me. My brothers were open to a relationship, even happy they had another sister to tease—though I was their 'big' sister. I know I complained a lot to you about Steph disliking me, but she's really come around, and things are so much better."

Heather pulled her suitcase out of the trunk. So Chris was a nice guy when life threw the family a curve ball. That didn't change the fact that he'd picked her up in a bar—and that she'd let him, *encouraged* him, even. Emily wouldn't want to know such things about the brother she was just getting to know.

Heather forced a determined smile. "You sound so happy."

Emily bit her lip, as if to withhold a quiver. "I have everything I've ever wanted—and a wonderful man to share my life with. I can't wait for you to meet him tonight!"

Emily slammed the trunk and they began to walk up the path toward the wide front porch.

"I'm sure his pictures don't even do him justice. You sound like the perfect bride," Heather added, feeling a mild pang of envy. She cleared her throat. "You're lucky all your wedding guests can stay right where the reception is."

Emily gave her sidelong grin. "A change of topic from all the mushy stuff. I get it. Most of the guests live right here in town, but I'm sure there'll be a few to keep you company—not that I plan on letting you have a moment to yourself. We have such a packed schedule! But I'll give you a couple hours to relax. Can I pick you up around seven for the party? Don't wear anything fancy—it's a jeans-and-cowboy-boots kind of crowd."

Heather smiled. "Who'd have guessed?"

Checking in was painless, and she was able to

meet Mrs. Sweet, Emily's very proper grandmother. Her room had an incredible view of the mountains, and for a while she busied herself unpacking. To her surprise, she ended up dozing with her e-reader in her lap, then had to rush to get dressed. She debated over what to wear—everything was too proper or too relaxed. But when she and Emily met up in the lobby, and both were wearing short jean skirts, they burst out laughing and slung their arms around each other. It was as if they'd never been apart.

After a short drive across the little town and closer to the highway, Heather saw that the party was at a dive of a place where the blinking neon sign read TONY'S TAVERN.

Emily laughed at Heather's skeptical look. "This is where Nate and I first met. It holds a special place in my heart, and the owner is a wonderful man, one of Nate's good friends. All the guys hang out here pretty regularly."

The tavern had more neon signs between mounted animal heads and flat screen TVs. As they walked past the bar running along their right, Emily grinned and acknowledged all the well-wishes from jean-clad guys and girls wearing t-shirts and ball caps or cowboy hats.

When they entered a back room furnished with a pool table amidst scattered tables and chairs, there was a burst of cheering that made Emily put a hand to her chest and blink rapidly. "Oh my!"

People rushed forward, and Heather found herself overwhelmed by faces and names. She told herself she'd focus on learning the bridal party's names as soon as she could. At last she met Emily's groom, Nate Thalberg, a tall cowboy with dark wavy hair, and green eyes that barely saw anything beyond Emily. His tender gaze gave Heather all the proof she needed to know that her friend was in good and loving hands.

The bridal couple was swept away in the crowd, and for a moment, she was alone. She eyed a table filled with appetizers, nachos, veggies, and cheese trays, but her stomach was too clenched to eat. Someone put a beer in her hand and she took a cautious sip, knowing she had to stay coldly sober that night. She stiffened as she saw Emily say something to her brother Chris, and then his gaze darted Heather's way.

Oh God.

Alone, he purposefully came toward her, and it was all too much, the worry and the anxiety that had been building up since the moment she'd seen him again. She held up both hands until he came to a stop, then whispered urgently, "Look, you don't need to keep an eye on me. We don't owe each other anything. Nothing's going to happen between us, so let's just pretend—"

"I'm sorry," he interrupted, his stare full of confusion, "but I don't understand what's going on. I've never met you before today at the airport, have I?"

Heather could only gape at him. She'd been nervous all afternoon over how this first meeting alone would go—and he didn't even *remember* her?

IMP 0811